Teldin snapped his wrist s silver death, scribing a thick line of red across his attacker's belly. Sweat stung his eyes, and the tendons in his forearm burned with fatigue. His eyes met those of his attacker. They were empty, devoid of any human feeling. Still, they were capable of reading Teldin's doubts in his own eyes. As if to confirm that, the big man smiled.

Teldin felt something slam with crushing force into his wrist. His arm was batted aside, and his sword flew from suddenly numbed fingers. He staggered backward. The pain of the impact was incredible. He stepped away from the big swordsman, clutching his injured arm to his belly. His back pressed against the port rail of the forecastle. There was nowhere to run.

Teldin's killer stepped forward, a smile splitting his face. Teldin looked into the man's eyes. They were empty, almost soulless. There would be no mercy here. The man drew back his blade, readying for the cut that would tear Teldin in two.

THE CLOAKMASTER CYCLE
● ● ●

One • Beyond the Moons
Two • Into the Void
Three • The Maelstrom's Eye
Four • The Radiant Dragon

BOOKS

INTO THE VOID

Nigel Findley

To AF: For always telling me that I could . . .

INTO THE VOID

Copyright ©1991 TSR, Inc.
All Rights Reserved.

All characters in this book are fictitious. Any resemblance to actual persons, living or dead, is purely coincidental.

This book is protected under the copyright laws of the United States of America. Any reproduction or other unauthorized use of the material or artwork contained herein is prohibited without the express written permission of TSR, Inc.

Random House and its affiliate companies have worldwide distribution rights in the book trade for English language products of TSR, Inc.

Distributed to the book and hobby trade in the United Kingdom by TSR Ltd.

Cover art by Kelly Freas.

FORGOTTEN REALMS is a registered trademark owned by TSR, Inc. SPELLJAMMER and the TSR logo are trademarks owned by TSR, Inc.

First Printing: September 1991
Printed in the United States of America
Library of Congress Catalog Card Number: 90-71505

9 8 7 6 5 4 3 2 1

ISBN: 1-56076-154-7

TSR, Inc.	TSR, Ltd.
P.O. Box 756	120 Church End, Cherry Hinton
Lake Geneva, WI 53147	Cambridge CB1 3LB
U.S.A.	United Kingdom

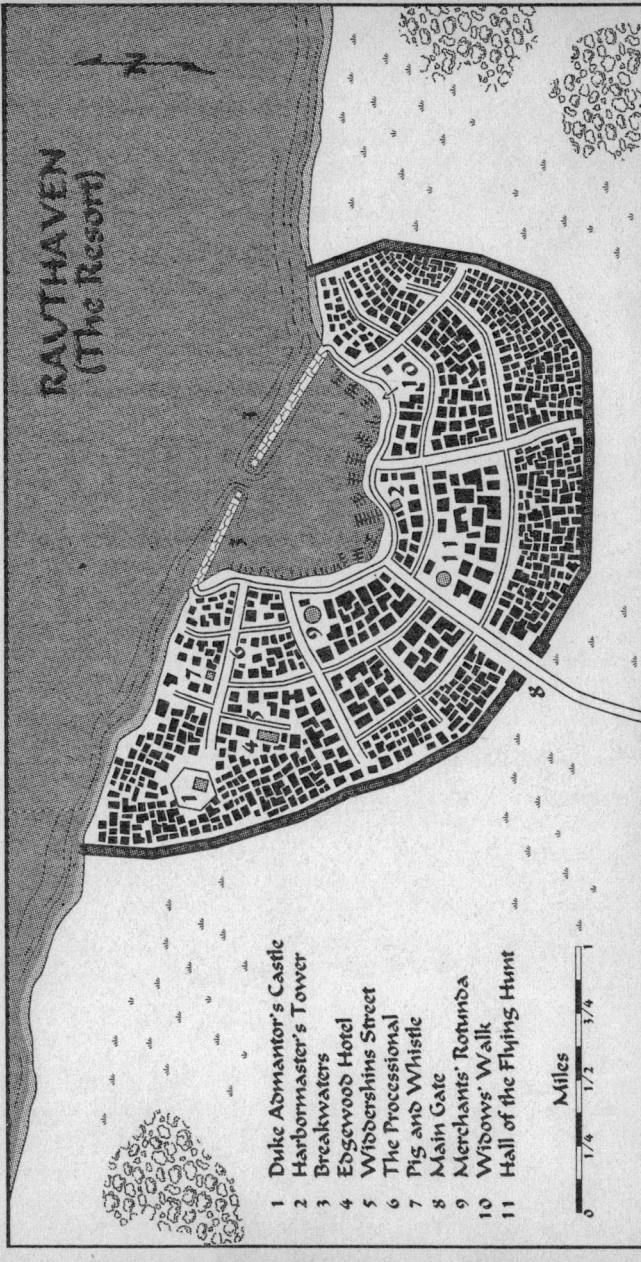

Chapter One

● ● ●

It was night, but a night such as Teldin Moore had never seen before. The sky was darker, a deep velvet blackness, and the stars brighter, more immediate, somehow closer. If he could just climb the gnomish ship's watchtower, Teldin found himself thinking, climb up to where the lookout crouched on his small platform . . . He might be able to touch a star, pluck it from the sky, and hold it like a gem, glittering coldly in his hand. He settled his slender, lanky frame more securely against the ship's starboard rail and leaned back farther to gaze directly upward. He brushed a lock of hair from his eyes.

Teldin was a man of thirty-two summers, a little under six feet tall with a light build. His features were finely chiseled—handsome, he'd been told many times, but in a comfortable way, attractive rather than beautiful. His smile was warm and winning, and women were attracted by the way it made his striking, cornflower-blue eyes sparkle. His sandy hair had a strong natural curl to it, making it difficult to control unless he kept it cropped fairly close to his head. Although slender-waisted, he had shoulders that were quite broad and slim arms that were surprisingly strong, though they didn't show large muscles.

The deck of the vessel shifted beneath his feet, *strangely*, not like the small river-going boats with which Teldin was familiar. It surged upward, like a thing alive, and Teldin tightened his grip on the rail. Steeling himself for the vertigo he feared—but which, surprisingly, had yet to come—he turned, looking over the rail, and down.

Below was land, not a river or an ocean, *land* that spread from horizon to horizon in the light of two of Krynn's three moons, looking like a tapestry of the most intricate detail. The gnomish vessel had been climbing steadily since it had pulled away from Mount Nevermind, and already Teldin was as far above the land below as the highest mountain peak. His home—the only environment he'd ever known, or ever dreamed of knowing—was two leagues and more beneath him and receding with each passing moment.

Sadness pierced him, a mourning for what he'd lost, what he was forsaking, perhaps forever. For a moment, he tried to pick out the familiar landmarks that had demarcated his life: the fields, the granaries, the market towns, the rivers, and the hills where tough, hardy sheep grazed, oblivious to the vessel that climbed into the sky above their heads—as oblivious as he had been, short weeks before. Part of him wanted to cling for as long as possible to the familiar, the safe.

But what he saw *wasn't* safe, he remembered with a pang. Death was below him, death that had come from the same sky that now beckoned him. He wanted to weep like a child for those he knew who had died: friends from his home; the tinker gnomes who had helped him when no one else would; and, most of all, Gomja—that sometimes-buffoonish, sometimes-noble creature who had sacrificed himself so that Teldin could live. At least the giff had met his end in the way he'd always desired, in battle after defeating overwhelming odds. As the barrel-chested creature had wished, his death had *meant* something, and in those last moments he'd known it. Would Teldin be able to say the same when his own time came? It was a thought that had never troubled him before. What did "dying well" matter to a farm boy?

That's all Teldin was and, until recently, all he'd really thought of being. His home had always been his land and, since his war years, he'd never wanted more. The world was large, as his grandfather had always told him, but he had little desire to see any more of it than the breadth of his family's farmlands. The thought that there were *other* worlds, other lands beyond the moons, had never occurred to him until the strange ship had crashed from the sky and shaken Teldin from his comfortable life.

The rigging overhead complained quietly as a gust of nightwind rocked the ship. To stave off its chill, he pulled tighter about him the cloak he'd been given by the grievously wounded stranger—that sky-traveler, that *spelljammer*. Hers had been the first death—a peaceful one, as such things go, as she'd faded quietly away despite everything Teldin had tried to do to prevent it, lying there in the mangled wreckage of her ship and Teldin's home. That death wasn't the last.

The spidership had come, a huge black shape sinking silently out of the nighttime sky. The *horrors*, too, had come. The smaller ones—half spider, half eel—and the larger, with their rending claws and clashing mandibles. Others had died, and their deaths had been far from peaceful.

With an effort of will, Teldin wrenched his gaze from the ground, and turned it back to the sky above. *That* was where his life was now—where it had to be—away from the land that had given him birth and sheltered him for thirty years. His life would be among the stars. He shivered, but not from the cold.

Perhaps seeking some kind of reassurance, he ran his hand over the coarse fabric of the cloak, no different in texture from any other traveling cloak, but somehow slightly colder than fabric had any right to be. It was a strange gift from one who knew she was dying, but an important one, if the traveler's rambling was to be believed. Teldin remembered for the hundredth—thousandth?—time the dying traveler's cryptic last words: "Take the cloak. Keep it from the neogi. Take it to the creators." The words still seemed as meaningless to him as when he'd first heard them. He shrugged, relegating the words to the back of his mind. His life up until now had been notably free of mysteries. He'd have to learn how to handle such things.

The vessel heeled slightly as the wind blew across its beam. A chill breeze caressed Teldin's face. He drew a deep breath in through his nose, hoping to catch for one final time the familiar scents of home—mown grass, blossoms, and the rich smell of good brown earth, but he was too high. The winds here were clean and crisp—sterile, one part of his brain told him, empty of life; fresh, another part countered, new and full of promise.

He looked down once more and gasped aloud with wonder. The view below had changed from a flat tapestry to something he could hardly have described, even to himself. The land curved away to the left and to the right in huge sweeping arcs. The table-flat land that his emotions had found so familiar had become a sphere. He knew from some schooling that the world was round, but to know it and to actually *see* it were two very different things. The sphere that was Krynn appeared to him in all its glory.

The sky above—and below?—was clear, but in the distance he could see moonlight-washed banks of clouds, spread out like a ghostly landscape of the dead. He could no longer make out any landmarks, but over there . . . that must be the great ocean. He searched his brain vainly for the name. A huge weather system, a spiral, was motionless when viewed from this height, but the shapes of the tortured clouds still seemed to imply violent action.

He turned to his right, to the aft of the vessel. There the distant limb of the planet seemed afire, burning gold. Then, in a silent concussion of light, the arc of the sun appeared above the edge of the world.

Teldin turned away, wiping streaming eyes. For the first time he noticed the small figure standing at the rail next to him. The figure's head, topped by a mass of gray braids, barely came up to his waist.

The gnome grinned up at him, teeth flashing white in the dark, wind-tanned face. "Impressive, wouldn't you say?" he asked. "Sunrise from space—one of the great gifts the universe gives to us. It's still a wonder to me, even after all these years."

Teldin wrestled with his memory, seeking the gnome's name, and was impressed with the small man's courtesy in speaking slowly. "Yes," he said wanly, "impressive." He sighed and admitted defeat. "You are . . . Wysdor?"

The gnome chuckled. "Captain Wysdor is my brother. You may call me Horvath. I am He-Who-Is-Fully-Responsible-For-And-Depended-On-With-Regard-To-Location-And-Distance . . ." With a visible effort, the little fellow stemmed the sudden and rapidly accelerating flow of words. He took a breath to settle himself. When he spoke again, it was in the same relatively slow cadence with which he'd first addressed Teldin. "You may call me the navigator, if the oversimplification doesn't worry you."

Teldin suppressed a grin. In his dealings with gnomes so far, it was their *lack* of simplification, the insistence on absolute precision at the expense of efficiency, that had worried him. "Then we haven't met?" he concluded.

Horvath shook his head. "No, Teldin Moore of Kalaman, we haven't." He grinned. "I can't explain it, you know. Gnomes are no more alike than . . . than star apples and pomegranates. You big folk only see the superficialities." He reached up to pat Teldin on the upper arm. "And that's why you're lucky to have us gnomes around, aren't you? To tell you what it is you're really looking at." The gnome's smile faded. "Tell me," he said after a moment. "I don't know all the details of what brought you to us, but stories spread on board ships. In fact, ships are the best places for stories. I heard you had some . . . troubles? Neogi, I hear tell, even before they attacked Mount Nevermind. Now, what I'm wondering is, why? No offense intended, of course—far be it from me to insult a man's homeland—but surely the neogi can find better places to come slave-hunting than *this* dust ball. Why were they interested in you?"

Teldin hesitated. He knew the answer to the gnome's question all too well, but should he tell Horvath? There might be some value in secrecy, after all.

He thought it through. The higher-ranking gnomes, specifically the three admirals aboard ship, knew what had brought him to Mount Nevermind, but Horvath seemed more experienced at space travel and probably would learn the truth from his own sources. Furthermore, Teldin realized he owed some kind of moral debt to these gnomes. He was certain that the neogi would come after him . . . which meant they'd be coming after the gnomes. What would be his ethical position if he withheld *anything* that could help the gnomes make it through alive?

"They're *not* interested in me," he answered, "not *as* me, if that makes any sense. They're after my cloak."

He saw understanding dawn in the gnome's eyes. "Ah, the

cloak," Horvath breathed. "I've heard about it, of course, the Cloak-That-Adapts-In-Size-And-Will-Not-Be-Sundered-From-Its-Wearer." He reached tentatively toward the cloak. "May I?"

Teldin paused a moment, then nodded. The diminutive figure took a corner of the cloak and rubbed the fabric between his fingers. He turned it over and looked at the delicately patterned silk lining. Holding the fabric in two hands, he tugged on it, testing the strength of the weave. Raising it to his bulbous nose, he sniffed at it audibly. It was only when he opened his mouth, apparently preparing to taste the fabric, that Teldin snatched it back from him.

If Horvath was disappointed over being unable to complete his investigation, he didn't show it. "Hmm," he snorted. "Neogi. They're crazier than an owl at noon, that's for sure, but they don't do *anything* that doesn't suit their purposes—whatever those purposes are. When they want something, they go after it, come doom or destruction. And they wanted that cloak, but I wonder why?"

That, of course, was the key question that had been gnawing at Teldin's peace of mind virtually since the outset. "I don't know," he said honestly.

The gnome shrugged. "Well," he said thoughtfully, "I suppose we could ask the neogi. . . ." He must have sensed Teldin's horror, because he quickly continued, "Presuming we ever see them again." He patted Teldin on the arm. "Don't worry about it now. Neogi aren't common in Krynnspace. I should know, because a few friends and I ran into—"

"Krynnspace?" Teldin interrupted.

The gnome casually changed the subject as he gestured around him, taking in the planet below and the stars above. "Krynnspace. All of this, everything inside this crystal sphere."

"Crystal . . . ?"

Horvath sighed. "Dirtkickers," he said resignedly. "What *do* they teach you in school?" He raised a bushy eyebrow ironically. "You *did* go to school, didn't you?"

For a moment, Teldin was taken aback, then he saw the gnome's barely concealed smile. He grinned in return. "Of course," he shot back. "The school of the land."

"Ah, that one," Horvath said with a chuckle. "I never graduated from that one, myself. No desire. The universe is a much bigger school. Of course, I haven't graduated from that one either, not yet, as if I ever will."

He smacked his lips and grinned up at Teldin. "It's time for a cup. Traveling always gives me a thirst and natural history always goes better over a draft of ale, wouldn't you say?"

Teldin followed the diminutive figure down a companionway that led below the ship's main deck. They navigated a narrow corridor—"Watch the overhead, it's low," warned Horvath, a trifle too late—and entered a small room laid out like a cozy tavern. There were two oaken tables surrounded by stools—all built to gnomish proportions, of course—and a low bar at the far end. A brass oil lamp swung on slender chains from the wooden beams overhead, and a small window—a porthole, Teldin supposed—gave a view of the outside. Teldin looked around him, bemused. Apart from the scale of the furniture and the view outside, the room could well have been the "snug," or back room, in any one of the taverns he had known at home.

Horvath must have noticed Teldin's expression, because he said with a smile, "Just because we travel doesn't mean we have to leave behind all the comforts of home." He walked around the bar and rapped on the end of a small barrel that was set into the wall. His grin broadened at the solid sound it made. "If there's one thing you dirtkickers do well, it's make ale." He retrieved two pewter mugs from a shelf overhead and manipulated the tap on the end of the barrel.

Returning around the bar, he thrust a mug into Teldin's hand and settled himself comfortably on a stool. "Take a seat. School is now in session."

Teldin hesitated, then sat on the end of the table next to the gnome. He took a draft of the nut-brown ale, savoring its richness. "Crystal spheres," he prompted.

"I know where I was," Horvath told him, a little aggrieved. "I'm just trying to say it simply without eliminating everything of importance."

The gnome took another swallow of his ale and gave a satisfied sigh. "You can think of crystal spheres like bubbles—or, better, like those glass floats fishermen use to support their nets. These spheres of wildspace float in the phlogiston, what we call the flow, or the Rainbow Ocean." He held up a hand to still Teldin's incipient question. "Give me a minute. I'll tell you about the flow in good time. So, the crystal spheres are like glass floats. Each one contains a world, often more than one world, and everything in its solar system. Take Krynnspace: It contains Krynn itself, its primary—you call it the sun, but then *everyone* calls their primary 'the sun'—and all the other planets, Sirion, Reorx, Chislev, and Zivilyn. Other spheres contain other solar systems. Greyspace, now *there's* a weird one: a flat world, cluster-worlds, and the sun revolving around the main planet, Oerth, rather than vice versa." Horvath shot a quick glance at Teldin. "You *do* know Krynn orbits your sun, don't you?"

Teldin snorted his derision. "What about the stars?" he asked.

"It varies from sphere to sphere. Here they're fixed to the inside of the crystal shell itself, huge, multifaceted gems—big as this ship, or bigger—and they glow like . . . well, like nothing you've ever seen. But they don't give off heat. In other places—"

Teldin cut him off. "So you can touch the stars?"

Horvath shook his head firmly. "No," he stated. "Or, to be more precise, you *can* touch them, but there's nothing left of you to remember the experience afterward. When I was second apprentice third assistant to the subordinate navigator, I heard a tale about the explorer Bethudniolanika—" The gnome closed his mouth with an audible snap and took a deep, calming breath. "Sorry."

Teldin waved off the apology and shook his head with amazement. "I can't believe it," he said as he took another draft from his mug. "I mean, I *do*, but . . . go on."

The gnome finished his ale with another long swallow. "Ah," he said, "education's thirsty work. Another?"

Teldin drank back the last of his ale and handed the mug to Horvath with a nod of thanks. The drink was already spreading its comforting warmth through his body. *Another couple of these, and I'll be taking all this for granted,* he thought.

"In other spheres, the stars are different," Horvath continued, as he drew two more mugfuls from the barrel. "Some places, they're like portholes in the crystal shell, letting in the light of the flow itself. In others, they're huge, glowing beetles that wander around the inside of the shell. They're a real sight, *that* I'll tell you. And in others . . . Well, I've heard this, but I've never seen it. They're great bowls of fire held aloft by huge statues of forgotten gods. At least, that's how the stories go."

"And you . . . you travel between these crystal spheres?"

"You mean gnomes? Certainly we do, though not very often," Horvath confirmed. "We trade, ferry passengers, but mostly just explore. That's what we were doing when . . ." The navigator cleared his throat softly as he recalled his previous flight from Krynn. Horvath briefly related how a group of gnomes had made it into space decades earlier, only to be attacked by neogi and sent racing back to their home sphere and world. Only he and a handful of veterans had survived the ensuing crash to tell the tale and oversee the *Unquenchable*'s manufacture.

"That's fantastic!" Teldin sensed his new friend's mixed emotions and changed the subject. "What exactly is the flow?"

"The flow? Well . . ." The gnome paused. "Whatever I said wouldn't be enough, and you wouldn't believe me anyway. You've got to *see* the flow to understand it. Just wait a few days."

A cold fist seemed to grasp Teldin's heart. "A few days?"

"Well, a week, maybe." Horvath paused and looked appraisingly at Teldin. When he spoke again, his voice was gentler. "Of *course* we're leaving this sphere. I thought you knew that."

Teldin closed his eyes. Yes, he'd known that the gnomish vessel was going *somewhere*, probably another planet, but he'd assumed it was somewhere else in Krynnspace. Then he recalled other gnomes aboard ship mentioning an excursion through the flow. He was leaving his world, which was bad enough, but to be told that he was leaving *everything* he thought of as his universe . . . For a moment he almost gave in to crushing despair, but the moment passed. With an effort, he brought himself back from the brink of discouragement and forced his eyes open. He realized that the gnome was still talking.

"Our course will take us to Devis, in a sphere called Pathspace," Horvath was saying, "then on to the Rock for a refit. He-Whose-Duties-Revolve-Around-Maintaining-And-Repairing . . ." He stopped short and started again. "Our shipmaster says we're about due, particularly after that scrap with the neogi spidership. You didn't think we'd hang around *here*, did you?"

"I didn't really think about it," Teldin replied, trying to keep his voice steady.

"Well, you should," Horvath said, not unkindly. "We're heading for the shell now. Good view on the way. We'll be passing close to Zivilyn. What a wild planet *that* is: twelve moons and more colors than you've got names for." The gnome set down his empty mug. "My advice to you is, don't worry about it. Enjoy the trip and learn everything you can. Once it gets in your blood, this is the only life that makes any sense. You'll never go back to being a dirtkicker again." He slapped his thighs and stood. "Well, I'm on watch shortly. Why don't you come up on deck with me? Just because I have the duty doesn't mean I can't talk."

Teldin followed the gnome up a different companionway and emerged on deck farther aft than he'd been before, just forward of the chaotic structure the gnomes called the sterncastle. He looked up and saw another gnome leaning over the sterncastle rail, looking down at them. Remembering Horvath's comment about humans only seeing the superficial, he tried with a critical eye to make out the differences between the two gnomes. But, if he discounted the minor differences in clothing, the two looked enough alike to be mirror images.

Horvath looked up at the other gnome and raised a hand in salute. "Greetings, Yourcaptainship, sir, CaptainWysdor, sir." Now that Horvath was speaking to another gnome, the words flooded forth so fast that, to Teldin's ears, they blurred inextricably together. "Wherewouldyoubewantingme?"

Captain Wysdor pointed forward and rattled off a speech even faster than Horvath's—so fast that Teldin could make no sense of it at all. Horvath obviously understood, however. He snapped another salute up at the captain and headed forward.

A little belatedly, Teldin followed. "What did he say?" the

former farmer asked.

Horvath looked puzzled for a moment, then grinned. "I'd forgotten I might need to translate," he said. "There's no watch this time. We took damage in the fight, and the captain needs to know how much. He told me to get Saliman and a couple of others and take the longboat to check us out from stem to stern. It shouldn't take too long." He took another couple of steps, then stopped again and turned back. "Would you like to come?"

Teldin looked down at Horvath. "Come?" He tried to keep his voice flat, to hide his sudden trepidation.

The gnome's smile told him he hadn't succeeded. "Certainly. You're Honorary Captain. You're entitled. And you've got a lot of questions, probably, about spelljammers, about the *Unquenchable*. Am I right? Well, the best way to learn is to look, as we gnomes say. Are you game? It'll be perfectly safe, I promise you."

Teldin hesitated, then a broad grin spread across his face. "If this is perfectly safe, it'll be the first safe thing I've done in weeks. I'm game."

"Good," Horvath said briskly. He turned away and called to a young gnome who was crossing the mizzen deck. "Migginseffivargonastro."

"Yo?"

"Get Salimanaduberostrafindal and, er, Danajustiantorala and join me at the longboat."

The young gnome nodded and trotted down a companionway leading belowdecks. "Come on," Horvath said as he led Teldin forward.

The longboat rested on blocks on the gnomish dreadnought's mizzen deck, hard against the port rail. Two large davits were bolted securely to the deck and the rail, and heavy block-and-tackle rigs were hooked to large eyes at the longboat's bow and stern. Teldin looked the longboat over with interest. Now *here* was a vessel he understood. About thirty feet long at the keel and tapered at bow and stern, it was a larger version of the small riverboats that Teldin knew from his childhood. Oarlocks were mounted on the gunwales, and two oars lay lengthwise across the thwarts that braced the hull. The only unusual feature was the enormous, broad-armed chair that was bolted securely in place in the longboat's stern. Made from heavy, dark wood and ornately carved, the chair looked more like a throne than something appropriate to a watergoing vessel, especially with the assorted bits of machinery that appeared to have been bolted to it at random.

Horvath noted where Teldin was looking. "Minor helm," he said as though that was sufficient answer, then he raised his voice. "Boat crew, get us ready to put out." A number of gnomes appeared from elsewhere on deck and checked the davits' rigging, then took up the slack on the lines. "In you get," Horvath told Teldin as he clambered over the gunwale. "Sit up in the bow if you like. It's a good view, and you'll be out of the way."

Obediently Teldin stepped over the gunwale—easy for someone of his size—and settled onto the forward thwart. As he did so, three other gnomes arrived and climbed aboard as well.

The youngest of the three—Miggi*something*, he remembered Horvath had called him—looked at Teldin curiously, then his face crinkled in a jaunty grin, and he winked broadly. "Welcome aboard the Ship of Fools," he said in a cheerful voice as he settled upon a thwart amidships. "You can call me Miggins."

The second gnome to board was a marked contrast to Miggins. He was short and squat, even shorter than Horvath, and his lined face made him look centuries older than Teldin's new friend. Instead of the off-white shirts and leather aprons favored by most of the crew, he wore an ankle-length robe of rich burgundy, its hems embellished with finely woven gold threads. Around his neck was a thin gold chain, bearing as a pendant a rough nugget of raw gold almost as large as the gnome's small fist. A thin circlet of gold was around his brow, holding his curly gray hair away from his face. Totally disinterested, he didn't spare Teldin a glance as he seated himself in the ornate throne and laid his hands palms-down on its broad arms.

The third gnome was different again. She was female, apparently about the same age as Horvath. She wore the standard apron, but the cut of her clothes was different to accommodate the swell of her full bosom. She shot a glare at

Teldin, and he realized he'd been staring impolitely. He looked aside quickly in embarrassment. The woman took her place on the same thwart as Miggins.

Horvath spoke up. "These are Dana, Miggins and Saliman," he said, indicating the individuals as he named them. Teldin was glad that Horvath had abbreviated the names. "Welcome our new shipmate, Teldin Moore," Horvath went on, "a mighty neogi-killer, I hear tell." The woman, Dana, shot him a quick glance that mixed surprise and disbelief, then looked away again. Horvath nudged Teldin with an elbow. "Watch out for Saliman," he said in a stage whisper, indicating with his thumb the elder gnome seated in the throne. "Give him a chance and he'll entrap you with his rhetoric. You'll be worshipping gnomish gods and wishing you *were* a gnome before he's through with you." He raised his voice to its normal pitch. "And you, Dana, I'll ask you to keep your lively good humor and ready wit to yourself, or you'll overwhelm our fine guest." Dana snorted and shot Teldin another disgusted look.

"Boat crew ready?" Horvath bellowed.

"Ready," responded one of the gnomes at the ropes.

"Then take us out."

The lines complained as the boat crew took up the slack and lifted the longboat clear of the deck. The davits pivoted with a groan as they swung the vessel over the rail.

"Lower away," Horvath ordered. "*Easy* this time."

The boat crew let out the lines, and the longboat descended slowly. When it reached where the waterline would be on a seagoing vessel, the ropes went slack. The longboat bobbed slightly as though it were floating on the ocean. Teldin looked over the gunwales at the blackness and distant stars below and tightened his grip on the thwart.

"Free the lines," Horvath called . . . and after a moment added, "Teldin, that means you."

Teldin glanced back over his shoulder, then looked at the bow rigging. The lines in the block-and-tackle were slack, but the large iron hook was still engaged with the eye on the bow. With a conscious effort he loosened his grip on the thwart and started to stand. The boat swayed alarmingly.

"Keep low!" Horvath shouted. "It's a long way down."

Needing no second urging, Teldin crouched in the bow and reached upward to release the hook. The lines swung free.

"Clear?"

"Clear," Teldin answered, as did Saliman from his position aft.

"Good. Now push us off."

Two gnomes wielding long poles with padded ends pushed on the longboat's hull. Slowly it moved away from the dreadnought. Even when the smaller vessel was too far away for the gnomes to keep pushing, it continued to drift slowly outward from the other ship.

"Oars out," Horvath said crisply. Dana and Miggins lifted the long oars, swung them outboard and mounted them firmly in the oarlocks. They held the oars as if ready for a stroke, but didn't pull on them. "Saliman, take us out . . . oh, a spear cast should do it. Oars parallel to the hull, please."

The older gnome nodded at Horvath's order. He closed his eyes and settled his hands more comfortably on the arms of his throne . . . and the longboat began to move. Slowly picking up speed, it drew farther away from the huge dreadnought. When they were about a hundred yards away, Teldin judged, Dana and Miggins changed the angle of the oars they held. The longboat maneuvered to a course parallel to that of the *Unquenchable*.

Teldin watched in fascination. He knew that the main motive power for a spelljamming vessel came from the "spelljamming helm." Somehow this device absorbed magical energy from any spellcaster who sat in it, and converted it into another form that drove the vessel. What purpose, then, did the longboat's oars serve . . . or for that matter, the almost-transparent sails used by the neogi deathspiders? After a few minutes of observation, of correlating the movements of the oars with the maneuvers of the longboat, he came to a conclusion. Although the helmsman had control over the vessel's motions, that control was only on a gross level. For finer maneuvering, the oars—and presumably the sails—were required. This conclusion still didn't answer everything, he knew—like, what did the oars push against?—but it did allow him to start to make sense of what he was seeing.

As the longboat maneuvered again, Teldin could see the

dreadnought in all its glory . . . if that was the right word. He'd seen it before in the lake at Mount Nevermind, but this perspective made it look even more impressive . . . and even more outrageous. Its broad-beamed hull was several hundred feet long, constructed of planking for the most part but patched and reinforced here and there with large plates of metal. A little aft of amidships were the huge paddle wheels, turning slowly as though to propel the vessel across a nonexistent river. Both forecastle and sterncastle loomed huge over the deck, massive constructions of wood and metal that would surely overturn any true seagoing vessel. Even to Teldin, who admitted he knew little to nothing of ship design, the structures looked fundamentally wrong. Chaotic they seemed, as though built piecemeal by multiple crews of artificers who weren't on speaking terms with each other.

Signs of battle were everywhere. The hull was marked and cracked here and there where it had been struck by catapult missiles, and splintered pieces of wood hung by fraying ropes from the rigging. To Teldin's unpracticed eye, the ship looked somewhat mauled but still "spaceworthy."

Horvath ordered course changes as he continued his inspection of the ship. As the longboat cruised on, Teldin felt his gaze drawn once more to the world they were leaving behind them.

Krynn was now a full sphere, half in sunlight, half in darkness. The day side had taken on a brilliant blue color, mottled over much of its surface with abstract patterns of white. The night side was dark, but not pitch black, and once he saw a flash of dim, cold radiance that could only have been the light of one of the moons reflecting off some body of water. It looked so beautiful and serene. How could this . . . this work of art, be a world where conflict had killed so many? he wondered.

Light caught Teldin's eye from an unexpected direction then. The brilliance of the sun reflected off a metal plate on the *Unquenchable*'s hull. Had the longboat changed course again?

No, it was the dreadnought itself that had maneuvered. As he watched, the massive vessel completed a turn. Its course was no longer parallel with that of the longboat, and the sidewheeler was picking up speed.

Teldin looked back. Horvath's eyes, too, were locked on the *Unquenchable*. "What's happening?" the human asked the gnome.

"Don't know," Horvath replied shortly, then snapped, "Saliman. Get us up to speed. Oars—" he gestured his confusion "—follow that dreadnought!"

The longboat surged and began to accelerate, but Teldin knew it would never catch the *Unquenchable* if the larger vessel maintained its present speed. Teldin shifted his position on the thwart, and his foot struck something that rolled on the planking with a metallic sound. He reached down into the scuppers and extracted a brass tube almost as long as his forearm. Although it was rare on Krynn, Teldin recognized the object immediately: a sailor's glass. He raised it to his eye and pointed the tube at the receding ship.

The dreadnought seemed to leap closer. Through the glass he could easily see the commotion on deck. Gnomes were running everywhere, swarming into the rigging.

"Ship ho!" The voice was Miggins's, booming from the midships thwart. The gnome was pointing generally forward and upward. "High on the port bow," he called, "ahead of the 'quenchable."

There was a cold prickling on Teldin's brow, and the flat, coppery taste of fear was in his mouth. He strained to make out the ship, bringing the glass around in the direction in which the gnome was pointing, but could see nothing against the blackness of space. You don't need to, his fear told him, you *know* what it looks like: a black spider, coming to kill you.

"Can you make it out?" Horvath asked.

"Is it neogi?" It took Teldin a moment to realize it was his own voice that had asked that.

In answer, the younger gnome reached forward and snatched the glass from Teldin's hands. "No, not neogi," Miggins replied after a dozen heartbeats, "not a deathspider. Wasp. No, *three* wasps."

Relief washed over Teldin like a wave. For the first time, he realized that his forearms were knotted from the death grip he had on the gunwale. With a conscious effort, he opened his hands and flexed them to restore the circulation in his fingers.

Once again he looked up into space in the direction that Miggins had indicated. He could see the ships—still too distant for him to pick out details, but recognizable as shapes totally different from the neogi spiderships he'd imagined. He sighed and smiled at Horvath.

"Any colors?" Horvath asked.

"None," Miggins answered, then immediately corrected himself. "Hoisting a flag now. Black field . . ." The young gnome's voice took on a harsher edge. " . . . red device. It's the neogi skull."

Teldin felt the sudden tension amid the rest of the crew. "What's happening?" he demanded. "You said they're not neogi."

"No, they're not neogi," Horvath confirmed flatly. "The neogi skull flag is universal. They're pirates."

Chapter Two

• • •

Teldin stared at the three ships closing rapidly with the dreadnought and spreading out into a line-abreast formation. In the harsh sunlight he could make out their angular, somehow brutal configuration. They seemed so small in contrast to the bulk of the dreadnought.

"Three wasps are serious trouble," Horvath said as if in answer to Teldin's thoughts. "They've got the maneuverability, and the *Unquenchable* isn't in any shape for a fight, not now."

"But it's sailing right to them!" Teldin yelled.

"Sure she is." It was Dana who snapped back the answer. "In a stern chase, at that range, we'd lose. They'd rake us, and we couldn't return fire until they chose to approach."

"Maybe they haven't the stomach for a foe that *wants* to close," Miggins added.

"What do we do?" asked Teldin.

"Nothing," Horvath told him. "They can't retrieve a boat in a battle. We stay back." The gnome grinned, but to Teldin it looked forced. "It won't be long. We've got enough air to hold out until this is over. Even now, the *Unquenchable* can give a good accounting of herself. Right?"

"Right," Miggins answered heartily, a little too heartily, Teldin thought.

"I wish I were aboard," Dana mumbled.

Teldin had never seen a space battle from this perspective,

and being *in* one wasn't the same thing at all. At first it seemed like a stately dance. From his vantage, the four ships seemed to be moving virtually at a crawl, maneuvering to get the advantage on their foe. The approaching wasps initially held to their line-abreast formation while the *Unquenchable* brought its bow to bear on the center pirate vessel. The dreadnought's stern was now pointing directly at the longboat. The line of wasps began to lengthen noticeably as the ships loosened up their formation.

It looked like the illustrations of naval skirmishes that Teldin had seen in his grandfather's books, but then everything changed and he realized for the first time exactly how complex a space battle could be. Suddenly, the two flanking wasps tipped their noses down and dived sharply. The line became a triangle, and suddenly another dimension had been added to the tactical picture.

"Classic tactics," Horvath muttered.

"What?"

Horvath shot an exasperated look at Teldin . . . then relented. "You can't know," he said tiredly. "Look you. It's the classic move for three ships engaging one. Form a triangle. If the enemy commits to attacking one ship, the other two maneuver to parallel the enemy, or 'cross its T' and rake it from astern. Whichever ship the *Unquenchable* goes after, the others have clean shots at her. And if the attackers have superior maneuverability and speed—which they do—all the *Unquenchable* can do is go after one ship. Unless . . ."

"Unless?"

The gnome grinned wolfishly. "Unless Wysdor remembers those dusty books we read a century or so back."

"But what can they do, anyway? They don't have any weapons left," Teldin exclaimed.

"They *didn't*," Horvath corrected him. "But we *do* have some members of the Weapons Guild aboard, and I doubt that even my brother could keep them from making some modifications over the last few hours. Now watch."

The dreadnought held its course, as though to drive straight through the center of the expanding triangle of wasp ships. Then the gnomish vessel's complex rigging shifted, and the bow started to come up until the stubby bowsprit was pointing directly at the wasp forming the triangle's apex. Teldin could almost feel the strain in the massive ship as it settled on its new course.

"I thought you said they *shouldn't* commit to one ship," Teldin said accusingly.

"Just watch," Horvath told him, "and learn something."

The dreadnought kept its bow pointing directly at the apex wasp. For the first time, Teldin started to sense the immense speed of closure as the ships hurtled head-on at each other. He reached back and took the glass from where it lay, forgotten, on Miggins's lap, and focused it on the pirate vessel.

The angular ship seemed to jump closer as Teldin focused through the clumsy device. It really *did* look like a wasp. The body was wide where the two sets of wings were mounted, but then tapered to a sharp point at the tail. The head—maybe the bridge, or maybe a fire platform—was cantilevered forward and down, giving the whole vessel a slightly hunchbacked, and decidedly evil, appearance. Six legs sprouted from the lower hull near the wing roots—probably landing gear of some kind, or maybe part of the ship's rigging, Teldin presumed. The whole ship, apart from its pale and slightly iridescent wings, was painted night black, making it difficult to focus on against the backdrop of space.

As he watched, two of the four wings shifted their angle and the vessel began to maneuver. Teldin tracked the glass over to the dreadnought, but the two vessels were too far apart to fit in the device's narrow field of view. He lowered the tube from his eye, understanding why Miggins had given up on the device: the naked eye was the only way to get a sense of the overall battle.

"The wasp's changing course," Miggins shouted.

"Aye," Horvath growled. "Getting edgy, as well it might." Teldin nodded. It must be more than slightly unnerving to have the huge bulk of a gnomish dreadnought bearing down on you.

The wasp changed course again—slight corrections only, but obviously to get it out of the *Unquenchable*'s path. Captain Wysdor was shifting his course, too, keeping his bow pointed directly at his foe. Collision course was maintained. A projectile hurtled from the small ballista in the bow of the wasp, to slam and shatter harmlessly against a metal hull plate.

With an effort, Teldin tore his gaze away from the apparently imminent collision. The other two wasps were changing course, too, just as Horvath had predicted. Their bows were coming up and turning inward, as they maneuvered to close with the dreadnought. Finally Teldin saw the wisdom of the pirates' tactics: even if the *Unquenchable* destroyed its single target, the other two ships would be maneuvering into position below and behind it, masked by the dreadnought's own hull from any weapons it might be carrying. Presumably the gnomish ship could roll, but by then the wasps could already have landed several damaging shots. And, according to Horvath, the dreadnought was in no condition to sustain prolonged fire from two fully armed wasps.

"Look!" Miggins yelled.

The closing ships were almost on top of each other. Again the wasp fired a ballista bolt—a clean miss this time. The gunner must have been distracted, Teldin mused, grinning wryly. Wonder why. The pirate captain tried a last-ditch move—a hard turn to port—but the *Unquenchable* matched the maneuver perfectly. There was no chance that the wasp could avoid a collision. . . .

Then the dreadnought's bow dropped into a steep dive beneath the still-climbing wasp. The gnomish ship's heavy mast smashed into the pirate ship's underside, tearing away two of its legs. At the same instant, a barrage leaped upward from the sterncastle, but a barrage such as Teldin had never seen before. Catapult stones and ballista bolts were one thing, but this fusillade seemed to consist of virtually anything that wasn't bolted down: a table and several stools, replacement lengths of spar, lanterns and flasks of oil, boxes and crates of supplies, even a barrel of ale. Teldin couldn't even begin to imagine what contraption the Weapons Guildsmen had fabricated to loft all those projectiles.

Whatever it was, it was certainly effective. The volley rocketed straight into the underside of the wasp. High-velocity foodstuffs tore through fragile wings; furniture smashed into the wooden hull. Something struck the root of the port wings and burst into flame.

The gnomes in the longboat roared their approval. "Good shooting!" bellowed Horvath in a voice three times his size. "And they're away. Look."

Sure enough, the dreadnought was accelerating again along its new course—down and away from the scene of battle. The two wasps that had been climbing to engage the gnomes were now well behind their target and heading the wrong way. They immediately began to come about, but even to Teldin's untrained eye it was obvious they'd be at a grave disadvantage by the time they completed their turn. It would be a stern chase, but this time the range would be much greater. He added his voice to the cheers of the gnomes. . . .

Then he stopped as a thought struck him. "What about us?" he asked.

"Aye," Horvath replied in the sudden silence. "That *is* a question. Oars, I think we—"

"Wasp ho!" Miggins's cry cut him off.

In the excitement of the *Unquenchable*'s escape, they'd forgotten the third wasp. Seriously damaged—virtually crippled—with sullen red fire licking from a hole in the hull, the vessel was still under power. Its last maneuver to avoid the collision had changed its heading. Maybe a sharp reversal of course was beyond the capabilities of the damaged ship, or maybe its captain and crew had decided they'd had their fill of battle. Whatever the reason, the wasp wasn't even trying to take up the pursuit of the dreadnought. Instead it moved slowly toward the longboat. Teldin could see movement on the wasp's foredeck.

"Oars," Horvath snapped, "take us about and down." Dana responded instantly, but Miggins sat transfixed. "*Oars!*" Horvath roared.

Miggins jumped guiltily and grabbed his oar, mirroring the angle at which Dana held hers. The longboat turned sharply, and the nose dropped. Teldin clutched at the thwart, expecting some kind of falling sensation. There wasn't one. To his sense of balance, the longboat seemed as steady as ever. It was everything else—the stars, the distant dreadnought, and the closing wasp—that seemed to wheel around him as though he were the center of the universe. Intuitively, it seemed, he grasped what that meant.

Or *was* it intuitively? Teldin had come to suspect that the cloak he wore was somehow supplying him with information. Was this another example of the process?

No matter what the source of the revelation, it made sense. Apparently, every spelljamming vessel, no matter how small, had its own field of gravity. "Up" and "down" had no significance, except when related to the vessel itself. As he'd seen when the longboat was lowered from the dreadnought, "down" didn't extend forever, or the boat would have plummeted to the surface of Krynn, hundreds of leagues below. There had to be some kind of "gravity plane" near what would be the waterline on an ocean-going vessel. It seemed logical that "down" might be the direction toward that gravity plane. But didn't that mean you should be able to walk on the underside of the *Unquenchable*'s hull?

"Give us a quarter roll to port," Horvath ordered, breaking into Teldin's deliberations. The oarsmen obeyed instantly. Once again the universe moved about Teldin, and the wasp disappeared below the longboat's hull. "Shielding us from bow shots," Horvath explained grimly. "We can't do much about anything heavier but get out of here fast. Saliman, if you please?" The gnomish priest furrowed his brow in concentration but gave no other sign of having heard.

With a splintering crash, the boat jolted as if struck by a titan's fist. Teldin sprawled in the scuppers, striking his head solidly against a thwart as he did so. His stomach was wrenched with nausea and he struggled to keep from vomiting. With a supreme effort he fought back the black veil that seemed to dim his vision.

The gnomes had fared better than he had, he saw . . . except for Saliman. The impact had tumbled the priest from his throne, and now he lay huddled in the scuppers, bleeding from a nasty gash on his brow. Horvath crouched beside him, his ear by the older gnome's mouth to listen for breathing. Teldin looked over the gunwale. The ship was surrounded by flotsam: splinters of wood, and a ballista bolt as large as a giant's spear shaft.

After a moment Horvath looked up from Saliman. "He's alive, but not for long if we hang about here." He reached beneath the carved throne and pulled out a leather case about two feet long and half that wide. "Teldin, can you see?"

"Yes."

"Then take this." The gnome threw the case forward to Teldin. "When you see somebody at the ballista, take 'em down, all right?"

Teldin opened the case. Inside was a light crossbow, its walnut stock lovingly polished and its metal limbs buffed. A smaller compartment held a dozen thick quarrels. He looked back at Horvath. "But I can't . . ."

The gnome sighed. "Look you," he said quietly. "You've *got* to. I need these two at the oars, and I've got to take the helm. Do you understand? Anyway—" he grinned again, but the expression looked forced, a grim mockery of the gnome's usual good-humor "—you're the neogi-killer, isn't that right? Why not add a couple of pirates to your bag?" Horvath settled himself in the throne and placed his palms on the wide arms. He took a deep breath and closed his eyes. "All right," he said, deadly calm, now, "here we go. I wish I'd taken my mother's advice and stayed in the priesthood."

The longboat surged once, then settled down to steady movement again. "Oars," Horvath ordered quietly, "hard a'port . . . *now!*"

Teldin jumped at the intensity in that last word. The gnomes on the oars responded as strongly, but more purposefully. The bow of the longboat came around fast, almost fast enough to unseat Teldin from his thwart. Out of the corner of his eye, he saw something flash silently by to the right of the tiny vessel, and he turned quickly to follow its flight.

It was another ballista bolt, visible for only an instant before it vanished into the depths of space. Without Horvath's sudden maneuver, the bolt probably would have hit its target. How did the gnome know, Teldin asked himself, with the wasp masked by the hull . . . and with his eyes closed?

Horvath's quiet words cut through his thoughts. "*That's* why you've got to do it, why you've got to take out their gunner," the gnome said. "I can't dodge them forever. Just tell me when you're ready."

Teldin tried to swallow the sharp taste that was in his mouth and picked up the crossbow . . . tentatively, as though it might do him some damage. He turned it over in his hands. In the war he'd seen crossbows and crossbowmen—albeit at a distance—and knew how lethally accurate the weapons could be in the right hands.

Personally, he knew precious little about using a crossbow. He'd never fired one, never cocked one, never even touched one. He pulled the woven wire bowstring back a couple of finger-breadths—much harder to do than he'd expected—and released it. The metal limbs of the bow sang. Taking a tighter grip on the bowstring, he began to draw it back. The bow's limbs bent, but not enough. The tendons in his forearm burned with the strain and the bowstring cut cruelly into the flesh of his fingers. With a muttered curse, he braced the weapon's butt against his belly and pulled on the bowstring with both hands. The bow bent farther, but still the string was almost a hand's span short of the metal tang that would hold it at full draw. The bowstring slipped from his sweaty fingers, and the bow limbs straightened with a dull *thwung*. Disgusted with himself—and not a little humiliated—he flexed his aching fingers. Setting the weapon down across his lap, he turned back to face the gnomes.

As he'd expected, Dana was glowering at him. Her expression communicated sheer contempt. A fire of anger flared within him. "All right," he growled, holding the weapon out toward her. "How?"

It was Miggins who answered. "It's a gnomish design, a very cunning one. The lever is on the bottom, under the stock. Move it forward to cock the bow."

Teldin turned the weapon over. A metal lever as long as his forearm ran along the underside of the crossbow. Its pivot point was within the wooden stock, directly under where the bowstring rested when the bow wasn't cocked. The other end of the lever was underneath the butt of the weapon. A recess in the wood gave enough space—just!—for Teldin's fingers to wrap around the lever.

"Put the nose of the weapon on the ground," the young gnome continued. "Grab the butt with one hand, the lever with the other, and pull."

Teldin did as he was instructed. As he moved the lever, he saw a hooked metal finger rise out of a groove in the wood, directly beneath the bowstring. Presumably, the finger was the other end of the lever. The hook caught the bowstring and started to draw it back. It was still an effort, but now Teldin had leverage—and the fact that he could use both his arms and the strong muscles of his back—to help him. With a metallic *snick*, the bowstring caught on the tang and held fast. Teldin returned the lever to its original position and hefted the cocked weapon.

"Now the quarrel." It was Miggins again. Apparently Dana didn't even consider him worth talking to.

"I know that much," he said dryly.

The quarrel was short and brutal, with only the smallest amount of fletching, but with a wickedly sharp head like crossed razors. He seated the missile in the groove ahead of the bowstring. "Now?"

"Left hand under the stock, right hand down by the trigger," Miggins directed. "Now put it against your shoulder."

"Which shoulder?"

The young gnome's control started to slip. "Whichever feels most natural, for the gods' sake," he snapped. "Just *do* it."

"Ready?" That was Horvath.

Teldin shrank the cloak so it was little more than a band of fabric around the back of his neck, then he took a deep breath, held it for half a dozen heartbeats, and let it out in a hissing sigh. "Relaxation ritual," he heard his grandfather's voice say in his mind. "Practice so you can do it anywhere, anytime." He wondered what his grandfather would think if he knew his teachings were being taken out of this world? "Ready," he answered Horvath flatly.

Horvath nodded, his eyes still closed. "Oars, quarter roll to starboard."

Miggins and Dana shifted their oars, as Teldin twisted on the thwart to face astern. The smooth wood of the crossbow was cool in his hands, its weight somehow reassuring. Once more the universe did its disconcerting pirouette around the longboat, and the wasp ship rose above the gunwale like an evil, angular moon. The pirate ship was close now, no more than a good dagger cast from the longboat, virtually point-blank range for the ballista mounted in the pirate vessel's bow.

Somebody was readying that weapon now, cranking fast on a windlass, winching back the thick bowstring. The wasp was close enough for Teldin to make out the pirate's loose-fitting white shirt, even the red bandanna holding his hair clear of his face. Teldin lifted the crossbow and jammed the curved butt into his left shoulder. He was almost certain this was wrong—he was "crossing his weapon" or something—but that was what seemed most natural.

"Sight along the quarrel," Miggins called to him. "Steady, and pull the trigger."

Teldin closed his right eye. He tried to line up the uppermost feather on the quarrel with the pirate crewman, but he couldn't hold the weapon steady. He tightened his grip on the wooden stock, but still his hands trembled. Once more he took a deep breath, stretching his chest to its fullest extent, . . . held, . . . then exhaled, blowing out with the air his tension and fear.

He sighted again. This time the weapon was steady as a rock and the quarrel's fletching bisected his target. He hesitated, wondering at the sudden sense of calm he felt. Tension was gone; he was like the weapon he held: solid, cold, dedicated totally to its purpose. *He* was a weapon. For a fleeting moment he felt as though this crystal clarity, this focus, might be somehow external to him, something enforced upon him from the outside, then he discarded the thought as meaningless. He was as he was.

The pirate had winched the ballista's bowstring fully back and was wrestling the heavy bolt into place. Teldin took another breath, let out half of it, and fired.

The crossbow jerked against his shoulder, but he hardly noticed. His time sense seemed to have changed. He could easily follow the quarrel's flight as it flashed across the intervening distance and buried itself in the base of the pirate's throat. The gunner's mouth opened in a death scream, but Teldin thankfully couldn't hear it. In a final convulsion, the pirate lurched backward, a flailing arm striking the ballista's firing lever.

The huge bow's limbs slammed forward, but there was no bolt in place, nothing for the bowstring to push against, nowhere for all that energy to go. When the bowstring reached the limits of its normal travel, momentum kept the limbs rocketing forward. Teldin watched in amazement as the ballista literally tore itself apart. He lowered the crossbow from his shoulder. The intense focus of just a moment ago had vanished, and he had to squeeze the weapon painfully tight to control the shaking of his hands.

"Dry-fired," Dana muttered. Then, reluctantly, she added to Teldin, "Well shot."

Teldin nodded. He felt no pride in his performance, even though he had to admit it was an amazing shot. There must be gods who watch out for novices like me, he thought. Next time he'd be lucky if he didn't shoot himself.

"We're not clear yet," Horvath said quietly. "They've still got the speed on us, and they've probably got other weapons aboard. Teldin, I'll take us up, over the top of them. I want you to pick off the captain. Can you do that?"

No! he wanted to shout, I can't. Don't depend on me. I'll kill you all. But, "I'll try," was all he answered.

"Good," Horvath acknowledged. "It should be no harder than the last shot. Fine shooting, by the way. You impress me, dirtkicker." Before Teldin could respond, the gnome shouted his orders. "Oars, loop us back, and another quarter roll to starboard. *Now*."

Dana and Miggins shifted their oars drastically, and the longboat maneuvered in response. This time, Teldin could feel the turn, an uncomfortable disorientation originating in his inner ears. The rapid wheeling of the stars didn't help, nor did the fact that the wasp was now above the longboat . . . and that Teldin was looking *down* onto its deck. He took another cleansing breath and concentrated on readying the crossbow for another shot.

"There he is," Dana yelled, "on the port rail. Get him!"

Teldin saw the man she meant, a tall figure with shoulder-length black hair. As the wasp swept by overhead, he snapped the crossbow to his shoulder. That same cool stillness came over his mind again as he brought the weapon to bear. For an instant, his gaze locked with that of the pirate captain. The man had eyes the gray of a winter sea. Teldin pulled the trigger.

The quarrel flew true . . . but at the last moment the captain flung himself backward. Razor-sharp steel grazed the man's cheek, then the missile buried itself deep in the wasp's port rail. In his peripheral vision, Teldin saw a flash of swift movement. . . .

And Miggins cried out. The longboat lurched and rolled, taking the wasp out of sight beneath the hull.

Miggins sprawled against the gunwale, clutching at his right shoulder, while his oar waved wildly. Crimson spread across his jerkin from where the shaft of an arrow protruded from his flesh. The longboat lurched again.

Reacting instinctively, Teldin dropped the crossbow and scrambled over the thwarts toward the oarsman. Miggins was trying to sit up, but seemed unable to find the strength. Teldin reached out to help him, but stopped. How badly was the boy injured? Would moving him make it worse?

The young gnome looked up at him with pain-glazed eyes. "It hurts, Teldin," he said dully. He tried once more to sit up, moving his oar as he did so. Again the longboat lurched, pitching Teldin against the gunwale.

"Take his oar," Dana shouted.

Once more, Teldin felt anger spark within him. "He's wounded," he roared at her.

"He'll be dead if you don't do it," assured Horvath, "and so will we." The calm tone of the older gnome's voice was unchanged.

A sharp rebuttal sprang to Teldin's lips, but then the anger within him died. The gnomes were right. As carefully as he could, he moved Miggins from the thwart—the youth was almost as light as a child in his arms—and took his place. He grasped the oar and felt it slippery with Miggins' sweat. "What do I do?" he asked.

"Unless I tell you otherwise, watch what Dana does," Horvath said, "and do just the opposite. She moves her oar up, you move yours down. She moves hers forward . . ."

"I move mine astern. I understand. I'll try."

"That's all we can ask. Dana, half roll. If we want to avoid the wasp, we've got to see it."

The woman snorted. Maybe she didn't agree with Horvath, Teldin thought, or maybe she just enjoyed snorting. Either way, she lowered her oar. Teldin raised his, trying to match the angle exactly. The stars swung, and the pirate ship came back into sight. It was astern again, but its heading matched that of the longboat, and it was much closer, a massive, asymmetrical shape with its missing legs and damaged wings looming in Teldin's field of vision. A cold fist seemed to squeeze his heart as he realized how fast the ship was closing. "Ramming!" he cried. To his own ears, his voice sounded like a croak, as though somebody were choking him.

"I know," Horvath replied. "We have to wait for the right moment. Teldin, when I say, bring your oar astern. *Hard*, do you understand me?"

"I understand." Where was that calmness he'd felt only a minute ago, Teldin wondered. There was certainly no sign of it now.

"Ready . . ." Horvath's voice sounded detached, disinterested. "And . . . now."

Teldin threw his weight on the oar. Beside him on the thwart, Dana did the same. The longboat turned sharply just in time. Silently—and the huge shape's movement was all the more terrifying for that—the wasp soared by to port, so close that Teldin felt he could almost touch one of its tattered wings.

As the vessel passed, his sense of balance swung and pitched the way the stars had done only moments before. His stomach lurched with vertigo, and he clung to his oar to counteract a sudden, terrifying sensation of falling. It was over in a moment as the universe seemed to right itself, almost fast enough that Teldin could believe he'd imagined the whole thing, but Horvath was shaking his head in discomfort; he'd obviously felt something too.

"Gravity effect," the gnome muttered. "We passed through their gravity field. That was close. Now, center oars."

Teldin responded instantly but kept his eye on the wasp. There was movement on the deck, but nobody was pointing a weapon at them. In fact, the pirate crew didn't seem to be watching the longboat at all. . . .

"Ship ho!" Dana screamed hoarsely. Her head was tipped back, eyes on something directly overhead. Teldin followed her gaze. There was another shape against the stars, another ship, this one with lines as smooth and streamlined as the wasp's were angular. Its hull was long and slender, tapering at the stern to a sharp point set with a vertical spanker sail. Its bow was rounded, reinforced by a metal ram. Metal lobes extended from the hull just aft of the ram, each with a circular port at its end, which reminded Teldin uncomfortably of an eye. Just aft of the lobes, vertical structures were visible on the hull, looking very much like the gill slits of some impossibly huge shark.

The new ship was several hundred yards away, too distant for Teldin to make out any details of its crew, though he could see movement on deck. The vessel's blunt bow was pointed directly at the pirate wasp, and it was under speed.

The wasp's crew had obviously spotted the approaching vessel as well. The pirate ship's torn wings shifted, and its bow began to bear off. Without warning, fire blossomed on the wasp's deck, a silent concussion of orange flame. The vessel shuddered but continued to turn away from its new enemy. As the wasp began to accelerate, Teldin saw that the fire was spreading, devouring the wing roots.

"The ship's dead," Dana hooted. In a transport of excitement, she clasped Teldin's shoulder as she would a comrade's. "They'll never control that fire," she cheered.

Teldin was silent, his eyes on the new ship, drawing ever nearer. "The enemy of my enemy is my friend," his grandfather had always told him, but was that true? Had it ever been true?

Dana fell silent and withdrew her hand from his shoulder. After a moment she asked quietly, "What do we do, Horvath?"

"We can't outrun that hammership," he said calmly. "I say we remember our wounded." He lifted his hands from the arms of the throne and clenched them into fists as though to relieve tension in his forearms. He brushed a light beading of sweat off his brow and looked at the approaching vessel—for the first time with his natural eyes, rather than the arcane senses provided by the minor helm. "Oars in, if you please," he requested. "And prepare to greet our rescuers."

Teldin watched as Dana quickly unseated the oarlock and brought her oar inboard, then tried to copy her actions. It wasn't nearly as easy as it looked. The oar's length made it clumsy, and he was hindered both by inexperience and his worry about jostling Miggins. By the time he had his oar safely shipped, the approaching vessel—the "hammership" as Horvath called it—was within a spear cast of the longboat and drawing smoothly closer. For the first time he could see the ship's crew: human, as far as he could tell. As if that was any kind of guarantee; the pirate wasp had been manned by humans, too. . . . At least they weren't neogi.

The long, blunt hull of the hammership drew alongside the longboat and eased to a stop with less than fifty feet separating the two vessels. For an instant Teldin's vision swam with vertigo, then the universe settled down once more.

Half a dozen of the hammership's crew were lining the near rail. They weren't wearing armor, and their weapons were limited to belt daggers or clasp-knives, but they had the same unmistakable air about them that Teldin remembered from the veterans he'd met in the war. There was nothing about their actions, or even their justifiable scrutiny of the longboat, that could be considered hostile. Still he recognized an unmistakable sense of readiness—whether to deal violence or receive it, he wasn't sure.

Something snaked across the intervening distance. Instinctively Teldin grabbed it—a rope.

"Cleat it off," a voice ordered from the hammership. Teldin had no trouble picking out the man who'd spoken. Holding on to the other end of the rope, he was easily a head taller than anyone else at the rail. His shoulders were broad and his chest deep and muscular. His hair—curly and close-cropped to his head—was pale enough at this distance to appear gray, but his face seemed to be that of a man not much older than Teldin himself. There was something about the man that spoke of command. "Well, cleat it off." The powerful voice boomed across space again.

Horvath gently took the rope from Teldin's hand, passed a bight around the midships thwart, and tied it off. "Tell him to bring it in," he told Teldin quietly. "Humans are more comfortable dealing with humans."

Teldin nodded. He cupped his hands around his mouth and yelled, "Bring us in."

The big man stepped back as three other crew members

took the rope and threw their weight against it. Teldin nodded to himself. The pale-haired man had the aura of command. Was he the captain?

The longboat moved closer and bumped against the hammership's hull. The smaller vessel floated at the same point on the hammership as it might were both ships floating in water. Teldin nodded to himself; this seemed to confirm his deductions about a "gravity plane." The larger vessel's rail was a good four feet higher than the longboat's gunwale—no difficulty for Teldin, but a significant obstacle for the gnomes.

The barrel-chested man must have recognized the same difficulty. He swung his legs over the hammership's rail and dropped lightly into the longboat. His face split in a lopsided grin as he asked Teldin, "Give you a hand with the crew?"

There was a flurry of movement beside Teldin. He glanced over toward Dana . . . and saw the gnome training a cocked and armed crossbow on the large man. When did she bring that out? he asked himself. When I was shipping the oar?

"Dana . . ." Horvath began.

"*No*," Dana cut him off, "we have to know." She settled her finger more firmly on the trigger and aimed the weapon at the center of the man's chest. "What do you want?"

The man's asymmetrical grin didn't falter. When he spoke, it was directly to Teldin. "Spirited, isn't she?" The big man's eyes didn't shift, but his hand lashed out with the speed of a striking snake. He batted the crossbow aside—the bolt thudded harmlessly into the hammership's hull as Dana pulled the trigger much too late—then gave the weapon a twist and wrenched it almost contemptuously from the woman's grasp. He glanced casually at the weapon in his hand—"Gnomish design, right?" he speculated—and handed it to Teldin. "Do they do this often?" he asked.

It was Horvath who answered. "There will be no more trouble," he said quietly. He gestured at the motionless Saliman and Miggins. "We have wounded."

The man nodded, but his grin remained. "That's right," he said, feigning wonder. "Almost half your crew injured. Grievous losses for taking out a wasp ship." He nudged Teldin with a rock-hard elbow. "Remind me to take gnomes more seriously in the future."

Two more of the hammership's crew clambered down into the longboat, easily passing the injured gnomes up to their fellows above. In response to a surprisingly cordial gesture of invitation from the large man, Horvath climbed onto the gunwale and extended his arms up, to be hoisted aboard the larger vessel. Dana hesitated for a moment to glare at the man who'd so easily disarmed her, then did the same. The others from the hammership swung themselves back aboard their ship, leaving Teldin alone with the big man.

For the first time, Teldin had time to really look the fellow over. He was a large man, at least a hand's breadth over six feet tall, with shoulders to match. Lines seamed his face around his eyes, making it difficult for Teldin to judge his age, and a scar, bone-white against weather-tanned skin, angled up from his right eyebrow into his curly blond hair. The large man extended a big-knuckled hand toward Teldin. "I'm Aelfred Silverhorn, of Toril." His voice was deep but not harsh, with a trace of an unfamiliar accent. "And you are?"

Teldin grasped the large warrior's wrist. "Teldin Moore of Krynn."

Aelfred's grip was firm. "Well met, Teldin Moore," he said. "Now, what do we do with the boat?"

"Bring it aboard?"

Aelfred shook his head. "No space."

Teldin frowned. At the speed the *Unquenchable* had taken off, it didn't seem likely it would be back soon . . . if it even survived. "Cut it loose, then."

"As you say." Aelfred put a boot onto the gunwale, reached up for the hammership's rail . . . then stepped down again. "After you," he said with a half-bow.

Teldin hesitated, not quite sure how to take the larger man's politeness. He shrugged. If I'm supposed to be captain, I'll be captain, he told himself. He stepped onto the longboat's gunwale, grabbed the rail above him, and swung himself over onto the hammership's deck. Saliman and Miggins were nowhere to be seen—presumably they'd been taken belowdecks and were being tended to—but Dana and Horvath were beside him. The two gnomes stood with their backs to the rail, looking with some trepidation at their new hosts. Most of the crewmen had returned to their tasks, but several still stood around, watching the gnomes with interest.

Aelfred, too, swung over the rail, tossing the rope to another crewman. Teldin tried to ignore the fact that their only possible escape from the hammership was now drifting away into the darkness of space, and he asked, "What's the name of your ship?"

The big man chuckled deep in his throat. "*My* ship? Oh, I'm not the captain. Lort—" he called to another crewman "—why don't you bring the captain on deck? Our guest would like to meet him."

Lort, a whip-thin boy of perhaps twenty summers but already showing the hard edge of a mercenary, grinned and vanished down a companionway.

"We spotted a gnomish dreadnought making high speed, with two wasps hard after it," Aelfred continued to Teldin. "It was too far away for us to get into the action. Your ship?"

Teldin was silent for a moment. The caution he'd learned over the last few weeks began to reassert itself. "In a manner of speaking," he temporized.

Aelfred didn't question him on it. The large man was watching the companionway where Lort had disappeared belowdecks. "You're interested in the captain?" he asked, a strange tone to his voice. "Teldin, meet my commanding officer."

A figure emerged from the companionway. It was almost as tall as Aelfred, but there the similarity ended. The captain's skin, mottled and purple, glistened, and the short tentacles that made up its lower face moved sinuously. Large white eyes with no visible pupils regarded Teldin icily. The figure was clad in a silken, midnight-purple robe, clasped high at the neck and long enough to brush the deck. A brooch of amethyst set in burnished silver was at the creature's throat.

Aelfred laid a calloused hand on Teldin's shoulder. "Welcome aboard," he said flatly.

Chapter Three

• • •

Teldin took an involuntary step backward and felt the ship's rail press against his spine. Nowhere to run, his fear told him. He was flanked to left and right by members of the hammership's crew. Nothing was actively hostile in their manner, but there was certainly nothing welcoming either. The harsh sunlight of space glinted off knives and daggers and illuminated hard and scar-etched faces.

Ahead of him, the captain—the monster—drew closer. *You're dead. Dead, dead* . . . The words hammered in the back of Teldin's brain. Images from childhood stories and horror tales flashed through his mind. He saw his own death, his head held immobile while writhing tentacles peeled away his skull like the shell of a hard-boiled egg. He felt his legs tense of their own volition, ready to heave him backward over the gunwale. Better the long, dizzying fall into nothingness than that ultimate obscenity. . . .

You have nothing to fear.

The voice was quiet, but as clear as the tone of a flute, completely unaccented. Teldin looked around wildly for the one who'd spoken. No one had moved: neither Dana nor Horvath, nor the crew of the monster's vessel. His gaze snapped back to the tentacled creature.

It raised a three-fingered hand, and Teldin flinched. The rail slammed into the small of his back, and for a moment his balance wavered. The firm hand of a crewman grasped his shoulder then, not painfully or threateningly, merely to steady him.

The clear voice sounded again, *I repeat, you have nothing to fear.* This time the voice was accompanied by an almost subliminal tingle within Teldin's skull, a momentary feeling of coolness a finger's breadth behind his left eyebrow. He stared at the monster. Although there was no change in its expression—if a thing with tentacles instead of a face could be said to have an expression—its gaze no longer looked threatening or even intense, merely curious.

What is your name? This time Teldin was sure of what he'd only just begun to suspect. The "voice" was sounding directly in his mind.

With a supreme effort, he forced control on his body, slowing and deepening his breathing, releasing the tension in his chest. "Teldin," he whispered. "Teldin Moore."

Teldin Moore, the mental voice repeated. *I welcome you aboard the good ship* Probe, *Teldin.* Tentacles moved in an intricate and graceful pattern—a gesture of greeting? *My name is* "Estriss."

It took Teldin a moment—and the startled reaction of the two gnomes beside him—to realize that the creature had spoken the last word aloud. Its voice was sharp and thin, a hissing sound more like the warning cry of a lizard or snake than the speech of a warm-blooded creature. But, of course, it's probably *not* warm-blooded, he thought with a shudder. "Estriss," he repeated.

Correct. The cool words formed inside his head once more. *Translated into your language, the name means 'Thought Taker.'*

"Thought . . . Taker?"

That is how my own people know me. Teldin felt a touch of something that could be humor—albeit cold and detached—in the monster's statement. *It is not as bad as it sounds. I am a philosopher, a student of the universe. I learn from others, borrow from their wisdom and learning. Thus 'Thought Taker,' Estriss. Do you understand?*

Teldin nodded dumbly. His trip-hammer heartbeat was slowing back to some semblance of normality, and, as before, Teldin was dully surprised at how fast his body seemed to be able to recover from shock so great that he should be curled into a gibbering, fetal ball. Was his resilience, he was coming to wonder, something to do with the cloak that was now just a strip of fabric around his neck. "What . . . what *are* you?" It took a conscious effort to force the question from his lips.

The name we use for ourselves has no cognate—no equivalent—in your symbology, the monster explained silently. *To some we are known as illithids. To others, mind flayers. You have not heard of us?* There was no expression in the creature's eyes, but Teldin somehow sensed what could be mild disappointment as he shook his head. *No matter,* the "illithid" continued. *What was your destination?*

Teldin glanced over at Horvath, but the gnome made no reaction. Apparently he hadn't "heard" Estriss's question.

"I don't know," Teldin answered honestly . . . then wondered why he'd bothered to speak aloud. Surely the illithid could read his thoughts without the clumsy intermediary of speech. He concentrated, willing Estriss to respond. But after a few seconds of no reaction, he said out loud, "You can't read my mind?"

Only when you speak. Forming the words focuses your thoughts enough for me to sense them. I have no need to hear the words, nor do I have to understand the language. But the action of speech must be there, and the communication must be intended for me. Have no fear. Your secrets are safe should you wish to keep them. The illithid gestured around it with a strangely articulated hand. *The* Probe's *destination is Toril, in Realmspace. You and your comrades*—here the gnomes looked up, startled, as though only now hearing Estriss's words—*are welcome to work off your passage as members of my crew. I would be glad to number you among them, particularly since your ship seems to have deserted you. Or, if you wish, you can be returned to Krynn. . . .*

"No!" Teldin was surprised by the force of his own voice.

Estriss was taken aback, too, if the sudden tilt to the creature's head was any indication.

Teldin cursed himself silently. He was a fugitive, and fugitives shouldn't draw attention to their plight. The gnomes had taken him aboard knowing he was being pursued—and look what happened to so many of them, his guilt interjected—but this mind flayer might decide that a fugitive represented too great a risk and return him to Krynn against his will . . . or simply kill him.

The illithid just nodded its head—a surprisingly human gesture. *So be it, then,* the cool voice rang in Teldin's brain. *My first mate will assign your quarters and duties.*

Aelfred Silverhorn stepped forward. "All right, you lot," he said, not unkindly. "Follow me and we'll get you squared away."

"Wait," Teldin interrupted. "The others . . ."

"The wounded are already below," the first mate answered. He patted Teldin's shoulder in a comradely manner. "Don't worry. We'll take good care of your, uh, men."

Dana snorted but, to Teldin's relief, made no comment. Horvath gave him a friendly wink as they followed Aelfred's broad figure. Teldin stopped at the head of the companionway that would lead him belowdecks and glanced back at Estriss. The illithid was watching him . . . and a smaller figure was watching him, too. A tiny face, with green reptilian skin and stubs of horns on its brow, peered out from behind Estriss's robes. It must have been there all the time, Teldin realized, whatever it was.

Aelfred reappeared in the companionway. "Hoi," he called to Teldin. "You coming?"

"Sorry," Teldin mumbled, and he turned to follow the first mate.

Aelfred glanced past Teldin at the illithid and shrugged. "You're the captain," he said in answer to an unspoken order, then disappeared below.

Estriss's "voice" sounded in Teldin's mind again. *You wonder about the kobold?*

The mind flayer reached down and laid a red-purple hand on the small creature's head. It gazed up trustingly at its master and stepped out from behind the shelter of the illithid's robe. Teldin looked at the kobold with interest. It stood about three feet tall, with a squat, barrel-shaped body and short but powerful legs. Dressed in a coarsely woven jerkin—from under which protruded its vestigial tail—it resembled some twisted parody of a human child. Once more it turned its trusting eyes on Estriss, and it took a fold of the illithid's robe in its short-fingered hand.

I charmed it, Estriss explained.

"Why?"

The illithid gestured with its tentacles in what might be its equivalent of a shrug. *It is my food*, it replied. *When I hunger, I will eat its brain.*

The kobold calmly squatted down on the deck, still holding on to the robe as a child might cling to its parent's clothing for comfort. Teldin stared at the kobold, then the illithid.

Kobolds are enemies of my kind as well as yours, Estriss's mental voice told him calmly.

"But . . ."

Estriss's words took on a sharper edge. *Better that I should eat your brain?* The mind flayer looked down at the kobold and stroked its scaled head once more. The small creature responded with a short, unintelligible phrase—its voice reminded Teldin of a small dog yapping—and scurried away, to vanish belowdecks. Teldin watched it disappear, his thoughts an uncomfortable mixture of emotions.

Come. The illithid had turned away and was walking toward the afterdeck of the hammership, obviously expecting Teldin to do likewise.

Teldin followed slowly. The illithid climbed the ladder to the raised sterncastle, Teldin at its heels. The creature settled itself against the aft rail and gazed out past the spanker sail. Teldin, too, leaned on the rail, a wary distance from the illithid. The planet of Krynn hung against the velvet blackness, like a large gibbous moon. The distance was too great for Teldin to pick out any details . . . and was growing greater with every heartbeat. Home was slipping inexorably away.

You are from Krynn. Teldin started when the liquid syllables formed in his brain.

"Yes," he replied.

Then how do you come to be aboard a gnomish sidewheeler—again there was that faint touch of detached humor—*particularly one so fickle?* The illithid turned and fixed him with its featureless white eyes. *I ask only out of curiosity. I intend no insult, but I think you have no familiarity with ships, or with wildspace. Is that so?*

Teldin hesitated, wondering exactly how much to tell the

creature.

You flee something, I feel.

It was Teldin's turn to stare at the illithid. *Can it read my mind?* he asked himself. It—*Estriss*—had said it couldn't, but how far could he trust such a monstrous being? "Yes," he said at last.

It must be something you fear greatly. Wildspace is rarely a safe haven . . . as you know from recent experience. The illithid shrugged its shoulders—a human gesture, but one that brought home to Teldin how . . . alien . . . its body structure was. Bones jutted under the robe in anomalous places, like a man who'd had both his collarbones—and maybe his neck— broken. He shuddered, an uncomfortable feeling in the pit of his stomach.

Well, the illithid continued, turning its gaze once more to the planet falling ever farther astern, *I trust you will tell me sometime, when you feel more comfortable in my presence.* The mental voice fell silent for a moment, then continued. *You fear me, is that not so? You see me as a monster?*

"Yes," Teldin answered truthfully. "You're so . . . different. We were told . . . When I was growing up . . ." He wasn't sure how to continue. "I was taught to fear things that were different," he finished lamely.

How typical of so many small minds, Estriss replied, a quiet, speculative quality to the illithid's "voice." *Generalizations are often dangerous. Some of my kind prey on humans, that is true, but then, so do some humans: pirates, bandits, marauders, those who attacked you, for example. Would it do to judge all humans based on the actions of a few? While some planet-bound illithids consider humans as cattle, I think you are not of the cattle. I think you know much. I think you have many stories. I would like*—the humor was back again—*I would like to take your thoughts. Not now, perhaps, but at some point in our voyage together. I would like to hear your stories. And you may take my thoughts in return. It seems to me that we might each have something to teach the other.* The illithid lapsed into mental silence.

Teldin cast a sidelong glance at the creature. Estriss, he mused. What *could* you teach me? To stay alive? But at what cost? Then he paused. The creature beside him was a brain-eater—it had admitted it—and showed neither pride nor shame in the admission. It was alien, yes . . . but was it a monster? Monsters don't discuss the philosophy of prejudice, nor offer to exchange tales. He'd have to think about this.

The illithid stirred again, its blank eyes still on the distant planet. *Why do you travel into wildspace?* it asked. *For a particular reason? Or just because wildspace is not Krynn?*

More than ever, Teldin was convinced that the mental tone of the last phrase was the creature's expression of humor. But it was still a question he didn't feel comfortable answering. Or was it the answer itself that made him uncomfortable? "Why are you heading to Realmspace?" he countered.

If the illithid cared about—or even noticed—Teldin's blunt attempt to change the subject, it gave no sign. Again it gave a broken-backed shrug. *I have business on Toril,* Estriss replied. *The city of Rauthaven, if you know of it. There is an auction of items . . .* The mental voice paused—almost shyly, it seemed to Teldin.

"Items . . . ?" he prompted, interested. What would a mind flayer be embarrassed about?

My life's work. Perhaps—if it interests you—we could discuss it . . . at a later date. . . .

Teldin looked at the creature beside him with renewed interest. Monsters don't want to discuss prejudice. They don't have a sense of humor . . . and they *certainly* don't get embarrassed talking about their life's work.

Well. Estriss's mental voice was brisk again. *I must discuss our course with the helmsman. We can continue our conversation later if you wish.*

Teldin nodded. "I'd enjoy that," he said . . . and he was telling the truth.

* * * * *

Belowdecks on the *Probe* was quite different from on the *Unquenchable*. The overheads were higher—Teldin wasn't putting his skull at risk whenever he moved—but the companionways were much more cramped. Certainly there was nothing like the little "snug" where Horvath had drawn him a pint of ale. The companionways and ladders—and what few compartments had their doors open—were scrupulously clean and uncluttered and showed no signs of the spontaneous "modifications" that the gnomes seemed to make as a matter of course.

One of the hammership's crew—the thin youth Aelfred had called Lort—tried to brush past him, but Teldin stopped him with a hand on his shoulder. "Where are . . . where's my crew?" he asked, trying to inject into his voice the confidence that he had heard in Aelfred's.

The boy gestured over his shoulder with his thumb. "Guest cabin," he said.

Teldin frowned. That wasn't much help. "Well, where—" he started.

"Port side, by the mainmast," Lort cut in impatiently. The youth shook off Teldin's hand and hurried on.

Teldin sighed. He didn't seem to have made the impression on the boy that he'd hoped.

Once he was heading in the right direction, it wasn't difficult to find the gnomes. Even from a distance he could hear Dana's sharp voice railing about something or other, and all he had to do was follow the sound.

The "guest cabin" was small and cramped—maybe ten feet long by half that wide—and obviously intended to house only one guest. It was made even more claustrophobic by the fact that two hammocks had been slung from brackets on the walls. His four shipmates were there. Miggins and Saliman lay in the hammocks—both conscious and apparently out of danger, he was glad to see—while Horvath sat comfortably on a folded sail. Dana, fists on her hips, paced the width of the compartment.

"Now it would be much better all around if you were to just calm down, Danajustiantorala," Horvath was saying at breakneck speed. "You know very well there's nothing we can do at the moment, and . . ." He broke off as he saw Teldin enter. "Well, well," he said, jumping to his feet. "Don't just stand there in the doorway. Come in and join us."

Teldin grasped his friend's offered hand and squeezed it warmly. Even though he'd tentatively decided that he didn't have anything to fear among the hammership's crew, he felt much more comfortable in the presence of the gnomes. He reached out and patted Miggins on the shoulder. "How are you feeling?"

"Much better," the young gnome replied with a grin. "They gave me some kind of potion. Tasted like . . . well, like something pretty awful if you want to know the truth, but it did the job." He moved his wounded shoulder experimentally. "It's still stiff, but it doesn't hurt much anymore."

Teldin nodded. "And Saliman?"

The gnomish cleric lay motionless on his hammock, an unfocused gaze on the ceiling. "Saliman?" Horvath prompted.

"Head hurts," Saliman said, with a totally ungnomish abruptness that indicated just how much pain he must be in.

"He'll be all right," Horvath finished. "They've treated us well." Dana snorted, but Horvath paid no attention. "Do you know the ship's destination?"

Teldin seated himself on a stack of folded blankets. The gnomes—even Saliman—were looking at him, waiting for his answer. "The *Probe* is going to Realmspace," he told them. "Horvath, what about the *Unquenchable*?"

The gnome sighed. "We were talking about that," he said. "There were still two pirate ships left and no guarantee that the *Unquenchable* will even survive."

"It'll survive," Dana muttered fiercely under her breath.

Horvath fixed her with a hard, steady gaze, and the younger gnome seemed almost to wilt under it. "No, Dana," he said flatly, "now is the time for realism, not false bravado. I say there's no guarantee the *Unquenchable* will survive, and you know that to be true as well as I. Even if the ship wins through, what do we do? Can we get back aboard her?" The diminutive figure shoved his fists deep into his pockets. Teldin could feel the pain this was bringing him, but the gnome kept his voice steady. "We could wait on the longboat and hope the *Unquenchable* comes back to find us before the air runs out. Or we could search for the *Unquenchable*, or for her wreckage, but Krynnspace is big. And that's if our fellows even stay within this sphere.

"Or we could go back down to the surface—" he smiled grimly "—but I don't think Teldin would be alone in his opposition to that. What say you to that?" There was no answer. Horvath continued, "Or we can stay aboard the . . . the *Probe*, you called it? Aye, the *Probe*. And we can travel to Toril aboard a solid ship. Not to say that it couldn't do with a few improvements, of course," he added with a grin. "What say you?"

Teldin spoke up. "Estriss—he's the captain—says we'd be welcome as crew members."

"Estriss," Dana snorted. "You're getting very chummy with that brain-eating monster, aren't you, now?"

Horvath turned to Teldin, pointedly ignoring Dana's comment. "That big fellow, Aelfred something. Now, he made us the same offer. I know, I'm like the rest of you—" he fixed each of the other gnomes with his gaze "—I'm wanting to get back aboard the *Unquenchable* with my own kind. But I don't see any way we can do that. Teldin, do you trust these big folk?"

Teldin was silent a moment. He remembered his brief conversation with Aelfred Silverhorn aboard the gnomish longboat. He'd felt some kind of kinship there, a strength tempered by a sense of balance. "Yes," he said.

"And the captain, the mind flayer? Do you trust *it*?"

The pause was longer this time. Teldin felt the responsibility, a tightness across his shoulders and the back of his neck. If he was wrong, he could be dooming the four gnomes as well as himself. But still, he knew what his answer would have to be. Monsters don't discuss philosophy.

"I trust Estriss," he answered.

Horvath nodded. "And I trust Teldin." He squared his shoulders. "I will sail to Realmspace with the *Probe*. How say you all? Saliman?"

"Aye."

"I'll stay," volunteered Miggins.

"Dana?" Horvath fixed her with his sharp gaze.

The woman dropped her eyes. "That mate," she grumbled, "he wants us to take up duties."

Teldin's patience had worn thin from Dana's surly manner. "What's wrong with that?" he snapped. "By the gods, they saved us, remember that. The wasp ship wasn't their fight. If, in return, we have to work like any other member of the crew, that's the least we can do." He saw the surprise in Dana's eyes and turned away.

Horvath laid a calming hand on his shoulder. "I'm with Teldin," he said quietly. "What he says only makes sense. Am I right?" Saliman and Miggins nodded. "Danajustiantorala, am I right?"

Dana didn't meet his gaze. "Aye," she grumbled.

"Very well, then." Horvath clapped his hands and rubbed them together. "Teldin, maybe you wish to tell the captain that his new crew members are ready to take up their duties—when you see fit, of course."

Teldin climbed to his feet. Something had changed in his relationship with the gnomes. He'd started to feel it in the last minutes aboard the longboat, but now it was even more pronounced. There was a change in Horvath's tone when the gnome talked to him, a change to the look in Miggins's eyes. Teldin hadn't sought this development, but it was definitely there. "I'll talk to Aelfred," he said.

"Teldin."

He turned. It was Saliman who'd spoken, the first time he'd actually addressed Teldin. "Yes, Saliman?"

"I . . ." The cleric hesitated. "Teldin, I need a quiet time each day for my devotions," he said quietly. "Could you, maybe, ask if . . . Well, could my duties be . . . ?"

"I'll talk to Aelfred." With that, Teldin felt the mantle of leadership for the small group—subtly but nonetheless surely—transferred to his own shoulders.

* * * * *

Aelfred Silverhorn was on the hammership's sterncastle, seated comfortably on the box that contained the shot for the *Probe*'s aft catapult. The larger man watched as Teldin climbed the starboard ladder, and he greeted him with a lopsided smile. "And how is your, er, your crew?" he asked with a touch of irony.

"Well," Teldin replied. He settled himself against the stern rail. "I'd like to thank you," he went on. "The two wounded men, you treated them kindly."

Aelfred waved the thanks away with a scarred hand. "What would you have us do?" he asked. "Ignore them? And have the young one bleed himself white all over the deck? We're not enemies—" a chuckle rumbled deep in his throat "—though that's not what the woman thinks. You might want to keep an eye on that one." He shifted his weight, and the wooden box creaked. "Tell me," he said, "you're from Krynn? Born there?"

"Krynn's always been my home," Teldin answered. Was this burly warrior going to ask the same uncomfortable questions as the illithid? he wondered.

"I've never been there," Aelfred mused. "Not that I haven't wanted to. We heard about the wars, you know. News of war always spreads fast. I even thought of taking passage there, see if I could get a commission, command a small unit. But . . ." He grinned. "The people of Krynn seem to have settled their own problems without my help. I thought when we came to this shell that I might at least have a chance to do some sightseeing, but the captain had his own plans, and we never came closer than one of the moons of Zivilyn. Apart from just recently, of course."

Teldin leaned forward with interest. "Why was Estriss interested in Zivilyn?" he asked.

The first mate shrugged his broad shoulders. "Research," he replied. "You two have been, um, talking, right? Didn't he tell you what he's up to?"

"Not really."

Aelfred grinned. "Surprising. He's always bending my ear about it . . . so to speak."

"Then . . . ?"

"Estriss is a historian," Aelfred said. "He's always knocking about the universe, looking for clues to some lost race. He calls them the Juna." The large man shrugged again. "The only schooling I got was at my own hands, so I don't really understand much of what he's talking about, but he's all fired up about it."

"Is that why we're going to Realmspace?"

"That's it. He thinks he's going to find some artifacts that can prove one of his pet theories. Truth be told, I think his ideas are all starshine and fertilizer, but then I don't really care one way or the other. I'm glad to be going home, even if it's just for a few days. It's been a long time."

"How long?"

"Almost a year, this trip," Aelfred replied. "Not to say we haven't made planetfall in all that time. We've put down on more worlds than I care to count. I can tell you some stories—" He stopped himself and grinned. "Now it's going to be me that bends your ear. Tell me," he said again, "were you in the wars?"

"Yes," Teldin answered . . . then added, "Well, in name, mainly. I was a mule skinner, nothing glamorous."

Aelfred snorted in disgust. "There's nothing glamorous about war. It's just a job."

"You're a mercenary, then?"

"That I am." There was no pride in the big warrior's voice; the phrase was just a flat statement of fact. "I've picked up my scars in—what?—half a dozen wars now, in half a dozen lands."

Teldin remembered the mercenaries he'd met on Krynn— most of them big-boned men like this one, full of swaggering pride and an endless supply of stories. "It must be an interesting life."

"Interesting?" the large warrior scoffed. "Like hell it's an interesting life. It's crushingly boring. Hard, tedious . . . Weeks of boredom interspersed with hours of abject terror. You get hardened to the whole thing, but the fear never goes away. To the Nine Hells with the fools who think it's glorious." He grinned wryly. "Not the fabulous tales you expect? I'll tell you, Teldin Moore. The mercenaries who survive are the ones who treat it like a business. Let the other men be the glory hounds and die for their countries. Good mercenaries don't learn from their mistakes. They learn from *other people's* mistakes. Tell me." He fixed Teldin with his cool blue eyes. "You fought a pirate ship and you won, and you'll have to tell me about that sometime. Was that glorious, or were you just scared?"

There was no need to answer. Teldin just smiled thinly and nodded.

Aelfred thumped Teldin on the shoulder with a fist the size of a small ham. "That's what it's like being a mercenary," he said flatly. "Just as glorious to be a mule skinner. In other words, not at all."

Teldin seated himself more comfortably on the rail. Despite his natural caution, he found himself liking this burly warrior.

There was something disarming about his easy familiarity and the honest warmth in his booming voice. "How did you come to be here?" he asked.

His new friend smiled. "Let's just say I was between engagements," he said. "I had a . . . call it a difference of opinion with my commanding officer over some back wages I was owed. He decided he wasn't going to pay me what I was owed and thought he'd terminate my commission with a broadsword." Aelfred grimaced. "Drunken bastard. I lost my best dagger when I didn't have time to pull it out of his neck."

Aelfred was warming to his tale. "So there I was in Westgate, with no money, no job to get money, and my one-time commander's criminal colleagues baying at my heels. I heard there was a ship of some strange design in the harbor and it was taking on crew, and I figured I could adapt easily enough to shipboard life. As they say, all bills are paid when you cast off from the dock. Of course," he mused with a smile, "it came as something of a shock when I met my captain . . . and when I learned the sailing we would be doing wasn't on the Inner Sea after all. I've been with the *Probe* for three years now, and I like it.

"I understand your story isn't too much different." Aelfred's voice was casual, but his ice-blue gaze was steady. When Teldin hesitated, he went on, "I believe that a man's background is his own to give out or not, as he sees fit. But your wounded crewman babbled while we were patching him up. Something about you being pursued, and you shipping out with the gnomes to get away. Is that the case?"

Teldin was silent for a moment. He trusted Aelfred, he decided, but there were still things he was uncomfortable talking about. Maybe when he'd sorted things out a little better in his own mind he could talk more freely. "Something like that," he answered.

Aelfred nodded, apparently unconcerned by Teldin's reticence. "If you're going to get yourself lost, there's no place like a ship in wildspace," he said, "as long as you can get yourself into the routine." He gave Teldin a sidelong glance. "Any bets as to whether that spitfire of yours—what's her name, Dana?—is going to get into the swing of things?"

Teldin grinned. "No bets, but I'll do what I can to make sure she tries."

Aelfred pounded Teldin's shoulder again good-humoredly. "Good." He paused. "I didn't know just what kind of duty to give your gnomes," he admitted after a moment. "They don't know the *Probe*, and I wanted to keep them away from anything they might try to, er, *improve*." Teldin smiled; it was obvious Aelfred shared his distrust of gnomish "improvements." "When the little one's better, I'll get him standing some watches, with your agreement. And the spitfire, I'll have her work with Bubbo, tuning the heavy weapons. If she figures out a way to aim a catapult at me, she deserves the results."

"I think she'll like that," Teldin said with a grin. "What about Horvath?"

Aelfred frowned. "He volunteered to help out in the galley," he said somewhat doubtfully. "Says he's a good cook. The problem is, I don't know much about gnomish food. Is he likely to serve us fricasseed rat or anything like that?"

Teldin thought back to the food he'd been served aboard the *Unquenchable*. The meals had mainly been vegetable stews or thick soups. The spices had been unfamiliar, but not at all unpleasant. "I don't think you have to worry," he said.

The ex-mercenary wasn't totally convinced. "We'll try it," he allowed, "but if he tries to 'improve' one of Dargo's recipes and ends up as the main course, on his own head be it. Now, about your cleric . . ."

"He asked me to find out if he could have some time every day for his devotions or whatever," Teldin put in.

"I'd thought about that," Aelfred told him. "I thought maybe I'd have him stand by to spell our helmsmen. Who knows, maybe he can even learn to steer by the stars and help out our navigator." The big man feigned a shudder. "You know the old saying, 'Better a hole in the hull than a gnome at the map table,' but I think Sylvie can keep him in line."

"And for me . . . ?"

Aelfred smiled broadly. "You can stand forward watches with me. When that Dana of yours wasn't railing at me, she was telling me how good you are with a crossbow." He leaned forward to poke an iron elbow into Teldin's ribs. "I think you've impressed the lady, Teldin my lad."

Teldin laughed out loud. "In your dreams," he responded.

* * * * *

Routine aboard the good ship *Probe* was very different from that aboard the *Unquenchable*, Teldin found quickly. For one thing, there *was* a routine. For a ship in space, there's no such thing as night and day, but diurnal creatures such as humans operate best on a regular cycle of about twenty-four hours. Thus the ship's day was divided into three watches, each eight hours long. At any time of day or night the major crew positions were manned. There were always lookouts standing watch on forecastle and sterncastle, gunners always lounged about near their weapons turrets, and there were always at least two officers in the chart room within the hammership's bow. The crew included three helmsmen, so that one was always awake and sitting in the major helm positioned in the lower bridge. The forty-five crew members—fifty including Teldin and the gnomes—stood one watch in three so that all had sixteen hours for sleep and relaxation out of every twenty-four. The sole exceptions appeared to be Aelfred and Estriss, who seemed always to be on the bridge or wandering about the ship, and the helmsman and head navigator, Sylvie.

Teldin had seen Sylvie at a distance but hadn't yet had a chance to speak with her—a condition that he promised himself he'd remedy at the earliest opportunity. She was a half-elf, as slender and supple-looking as a willow tree. Her face was finely chiseled, with pale skin that was silken-smooth. Teldin had never seen her actually smile, but she always seemed just on the verge of doing so, and she had a habit of brushing her flowing silver hair back from her slightly pointed ears that he found somehow enchanting. Every time he found some excuse to visit the chart room on the cargo deck she was there, poring over some chart or other, or discussing the ship's course with Aelfred or Estriss.

Meals were served at eight-hour intervals, and there was no distinction between dawnfry, highsunfeast or evenfeast. How could there be, when one-third of the crew had just risen, one was in the midst of a watch, and the third was getting ready to bunk down? Crew members who were on watch ate meals at their stations; those who were off duty ate in the two galleys. One of these was situated in the stern, directly below the sterncastle turret, the other in the lobe that extended from the port side of the main deck near the bow. Although it was traditionally reserved for the officers and senior crew members, Aelfred had reassured Teldin that he was welcome to eat here when he wasn't standing watch. Teldin was glad to accept the invitation. The officer's galley—or "mess," as it would have been called in the army—boasted a large, oval port of thick glass. This was one of the "eyes" that Teldin had noticed when he'd first seen the ship, and it gave a spectacular view of the star-studded void through which the ship sailed. Teldin quickly discovered there was something almost magical about sitting in a warm, lantern-lit room while gazing out into the cold vastness of space. Whenever he wasn't on duty or asleep, he'd often find himself drawn either to the galley or to the officers' saloon on the opposite side of the ship.

The only member of the *Probe*'s crew who never ate in either of the galleys was the captain himself. Estriss spent several hours each day in his private cabin, and what he did there was a matter of speculation among the crew. Some said he never slept, just spent his time poring over old scrolls and musty books that he kept in a chest beneath his small desk. Others claimed that he spent his time in dreamless sleep, empty white eyes open, while he hung a hand's span above his bunk. The one thing that was never a subject of discussion was the captain's eating habits . . . particularly after the kobold was no longer seen around the ship.

In the forward galley, while enjoying two relaxing meals each day—which, to his surprise were unsurpassedly delicious—Teldin had the chance to meet and talk with other members of the crew. Although none was as outgoing toward him as Aelfred had been, he'd found two who were willing to pass time in conversation. One was Sweor Tobregdan, a mercenary warrior who'd joined the ship in much the same way as Aelfred—as an alternative to having his head part company with his neck—and was now second mate and directly below Aelfred in the *Probe*'s chain of command.

The other was Vallus Leafbower. Vallus was a high elf who

hailed from the world of Oerth, in Greyspace, and a wizard of some power and repute. Although the elf seemed to prefer listening to speaking, Teldin had managed to extract the fact that he'd signed on aboard the *Probe* as helmsman simply because he was curious about the rest of the universe. "After five hundred years of exploring the world of Oerth," the white-haired elf had told him in his quiet voice, "I came to realize that another five hundred would be insufficient to learn all there was to know about my home. I looked up into the sky and knew there were other worlds out there. It was then that I decided it would please me more to know something of many worlds than everything of one."

Teldin's eight-hour shift of duty usually involved standing on the bow platform next to the forward catapult, the gnomish crossbow in his hands, scanning the skies for potential enemies. It would have been stultifyingly boring if it weren't for conversation with other members of the crew. There was never any enemy for him to look out for and nothing at which to shoot his crossbow—which was just as well, he thought, since his first two accurate shots probably were nothing more than luck.

So it was, on the fourth day since joining the *Probe*'s crew, that Teldin was standing at his duty station, leaning on the rail, and gazing at the planet Zivilyn as it was passing to starboard. It was Horvath who'd first mentioned this planet to Teldin, during his first days aboard the *Unquenchable*, and who'd described the gargantuan orb's wondrous beauty. At the time, Teldin had put the gnome's description down to an attempt to awe the "dirtkicker." Now he had to admit that Horvath hadn't done the world justice.

At this distance, Zivilyn filled almost half of Teldin's field of view, a massive globe streaked with all the colors of an insane painter's palette. Myriad bands, each its own hue, circled the planet. Some were broad stripes, others lines that looked as thin as a hair. The edges of the wider bands were rippled, turbulent, and some of the smaller striations seemed almost braided. Although no actual motion was visible—the ship was much too far away—the sensation of chaos, frenzied movement, and cataclysmic forces at work was almost overwhelming. In the upper hemisphere of the planet, near the right-hand limb, was a spiral that could only be a storm of some kind. Darker than the surrounding clouds, this vortex was made up of traces of many colors, blurred together like smeared paint. It was like the storm that Teldin had seen over Krynn as the gnomish dreadnought had climbed out of the atmosphere, and, in comparison to the diameter of the planet, looked hardly larger. Aelfred had told him, though, that the entire world of Krynn could vanish down the vortex of this storm without touching either side.

Zivilyn had twelve moons, he'd learned, perhaps even a thirteenth that had been sighted once but not yet had its position properly charted. Four of them were visible now, just as points of light that seemed brighter—and somehow nearer—than the stars. Each of those moons was a world in its own right, he'd been told, only slightly smaller than Krynn itself. *If Krynn is a world scaled for humans,* Teldin thought, *then Zivilyn is a world for the gods themselves.*

He set his crossbow down on the base of the bow catapult and crouched down to stretch the muscles in his thighs. One of his knees gave a disconcerting *pop*, and tendons complained at the unaccustomed effort. He swore quietly to himself. He'd always prided himself on his level of physical fitness. Working in the fields had strengthened the muscles, and his time in the army had proven what he'd always suspected: that a certain degree of conditioning could spell the difference between life and death. He'd never had to worry about actually exercising before; his daily life had provided all the exertion he'd really needed. But now there was precious little to do aboard ship but eat, sleep, and stand his watch. He'd noticed that several of the officers and crew were fighting a weight problem—in at least one case, a losing battle—and realized he might well face the same fate soon. How did Aelfred manage it? The burly warrior seemed no more active than Teldin, but his belly was hard and tight. And Sylvie, the navigator, appeared the least active of all, but there certainly didn't seem to be an ounce of fat anywhere on her body.

Teldin smiled and chuckled quietly to himself. Maybe he should just stroll down to the chart room and ask the striking half-elf how she kept herself so beautiful. After all, he justified, it would be in the ship's best interest if he learned how to keep himself at peak condition. . . .

A hoarse scream of agony from above him shattered his comfortable musings. Quickly slinging the crossbow's carrying strap over his shoulder, he clambered up the ladder that led from the forward bridge to the forecastle.

The forecastle was a scene of chaos. In addition to the skeleton crew of two sailors who always manned the turret's heavy ballista, Estriss, Aelfred, and Sylvie were present. One of the ballista crew, a woman named Preema, was down, clutching a torn shoulder and screaming in agony. The others crouched, weapons drawn, scanning the skies above them.

Where was the enemy? What had wounded Preema—had virtually torn her arm from her torso?

Out of the corner of his eye, Teldin saw a fast-moving shape hurtling toward him. Instinctively he threw himself to the deck, simultaneously snapping the crossbow up to his shoulder and pulling the trigger.

He felt a rush of air as the shape rocketed by above his sprawling body, and rough skin grazed his shoulder. As the shape retreated, he saw it properly for the first time. It was a night-black shark, he thought, but a shark rendered by a madman. It was more than three times longer than a man's height, and its powerful body was proportionately broad. Its fins and tail seemed no different from those of the small mud sharks he'd occasionally seen on fishmongers' barrows in the marketplaces of Krynn, but its head . . . From its gill slits forward, the creature seemed all teeth-filled mouth and single glaring eye.

The thing tore through the air, its body twisting in a grotesque mimicry of a swimming motion. Its speed was terrifying in a creature so large. It flashed away from the ship again, curving up and over the forecastle. Then, with an agility totally belying its mass, it turned end for end and drove back toward them in another high-speed pass. For an instant Teldin could see the fletching of his crossbow bolt, buried— apparently harmlessly—just behind the monster's gills, then he rolled aside into the shelter of the ballista turret.

The other gunner, the young man named Lort, crouched below the turret rail, his short sword clutched in a white-knuckled fist. As the monster rocketed past, he leaped to his feet and threw all his weight behind a thrust at the thing's head. But at the last instant, the creature twisted its body.

And Lort was gone. The youth's short sword clattered to the deck. The black space-shark soared away from the ship again, its great mouth making chewing motions. Blood streamed back along its flank, glistening in the harsh light of the distant sun. Teldin felt his gorge rise and tried to swallow the bitter taste of bile that filled his mouth. He rolled to the fallen sword and picked it up. The grip was slick with Lort's blood.

"Void scavver," Aelfred was saying. "Sylvie, can you . . . ?"

"I'll try," the woman answered. Amazingly, she climbed to her feet.

"No," Teldin croaked, but the woman paid him no mind.

The monster had turned again. Its mouth was empty; there was no sign of Lort, except for a red stain on its teeth. Again it steadied itself for a pass, this time from directly ahead of the vessel.

Sylvie faced the onrushing creature, her slender hands weaving a fluid pattern in the air before her. She hissed arcane syllables between her teeth and thrust her hands out toward the monster. Multicolored fire lashed out from her fingertips, striking the creature full in its hideous eye.

It shuddered, and for the first time it made a sound—a whistling shriek of pain—but still it came on. Sylvie was still standing, totally exposed, weaving her hands again as she struggled to put together another spell. There was no way she'd be able to get out of the way in time. Teldin looked at the creature's gaping maw and knew what he had to do.

As soon as the decision was made, he felt the cold, crystal clarity of thought that was becoming almost familiar. His time sense accelerated, and the monster seemed almost frozen in space. He had time to jump to his feet and take one, two steps across the forecastle and push the half-elf to the deck, then he turned to face the approaching scavver, clutching Lort's short sword before him in both hands, more a talisman than a weapon.

In his peripheral vision he could see Aelfred open his mouth to scream something—no doubt a warning—but it was too late for any warning. The scavver was almost upon him, filling almost all of his field of view. He knew he should feel terror, but somehow the emotion wouldn't come. His world was empty of anything that could interfere with thought or with volition.

The monster's mouth opened wider, preparing to snatch him the way it had snatched Lort, but at the last instant he flung himself to the deck. At the same time, as the huge mouth snapped shut on the empty air where his body had been a moment before, he thrust upward with the short sword. He felt the power in his arm muscles, felt the blade drive deep into firm flesh. Then the weapon was wrenched from his grasp. He felt a hard impact against his right hip, hard enough to tumble him over and over until he came to rest against Sylvie's prone body. Still seemingly in slow motion, the scavver arced over his head. Lort's short sword protruded from the underside of its throat, the weapon's cross-guard flush against the creature's skin. Green-black fluid pulsed from around the steel.

The scavver's inertia carried it forward, but it was obviously in serious trouble. It rolled to the right and started to drop. With a bubbling shriek it hurtled over the rear of the forecastle, barely missing the mainmast, and plummeted to the main deck below. With his still-accelerated time sense, Teldin was able to roll over and see the creature strike. So great was its speed that it skidded along the deck, leaving a trail of ichor, and slammed into the ladder that led up to the sterncastle.

A dozen crew members were on the main deck, armed with weapons ranging from swords to belaying pins from the rigging. At once they fell on the creature, slashing and bludgeoning it. Although it was mortally wounded, still the scavver thrashed and writhed, snapping wildly with its great mouth. The mindless ferocity of the creature was unbelievable. Even as the *Probe*'s crew dismembered it, it fought, smashing the ladder and tearing at its killers. The main deck was awash with blood, both green and red, when the scavver was finally still.

Teldin felt a calloused hand on his shoulder and suddenly his time sense returned to normal. The fear that had been absent as he faced the scavver washed over him like a wave, and his stomach knotted with nausea. Trembling, he rolled over to look up into the serious face of Aelfred Silverhorn.

"That was amazing," Aelfred told him quietly. "Stupid, suicidal, insane . . . but amazing." He squeezed Teldin's shoulder reassuringly, then the big warrior's face split in its familiar, lopsided grin. "Now about your sword technique—you handled that weapon like a shovel. If you're interested, I'll teach you a little something about the proper way to wield a sword—once you're put back together, that is. . . ."

"What do you . . . ?" Teldin started to ask, then he felt pressure on his right hip, the one that had been struck by the scavver. He looked down. Sylvie was pressing a folded cloth against the side of his hip. The cloth had originally been white, but now it was turning a rich, dark red. Pain struck him like a blow.

"Take him below," Aelfred ordered, and firm hands lifted him from the deck.

Chapter Four

● ● ●

Teldin kept his eyes closed and tried to ignore the gentle swinging of the hammock. His right hip throbbed, not with pain so much as with a nagging discomfort. Whenever he tried to move it into a more comfortable position, it started the hammock swinging again, which caused nausea to knot his stomach. He should really be grateful, he told himself. The healing potion had closed the wound on his hip. Nausea should be a minor price, one he should be glad to pay. *Tell that to my stomach!* In an effort to make himself more comfortable, he expanded the cloak to its full size and wrapped it around himself like a blanket.

A firm knock came on the door. "Yes?" he croaked.

He heard the door open and rolled over to look at his guest. The first thing he saw was Aelfred Silverhorn's crooked smile. "How are you feeling?" the first mate asked him.

Teldin ran a quick mental review of his body. His hip still throbbed in time with his heartbeat, but otherwise, "Pretty good, overall," he answered. "I suppose I'm ready to stop goldbricking." He sat up . . .

And the universe seemed to do a quick double flip around him. He sank back onto the hammock with a groan, closing his eyes in an attempt to quell the sudden resurgence of nausea that racked his body.

Aelfred put a restraining hand on his chest. "Not so fast, old son," he said quickly. "You lost a lot of blood and enough meat to make a small roast. Potion's are going to help, no doubt about that, but there's no way you're going to be doing handsprings for the next few days. You're to stay here and rest—that's a direct order from the captain, and from me too—until you're stronger. Got it?"

Teldin nodded wordlessly.

"Speaking of the captain," Aelfred went on, "he wants to talk to you, if you feel up to it. Probably wants to talk to you about what happened on the foredeck." His voice grew quieter, more serious. "I want to talk to you about the scavver, too. Like I told you, what you did was amazing. To be honest, and no offense meant, I didn't think you had it in you. You probably saved Sylvie's life—I don't think she could have gotten another spell off in time—and I know she wants to thank you for that when she gets off watch. The crew knows it was you who brought that thing down. Anyway—" his normal gruff manner returned "—the captain's waiting outside. Do you want me to send him in?"

"All right," Teldin replied. "Thanks, Aelfred."

The broad-shouldered warrior snorted as he went out the door.

Teldin tried to relax, but as soon as he closed his eyes, all he could picture was the tooth-filled mouth of the scavver rushing toward him. He was grateful for the distraction when he felt the cool mental touch of the illithid's "voice."

Teldin Moore, the words formed in his head. *Are you feeling strong enough for conversation?*

He opened his eyes again. Estriss stood in the doorway, his facial tentacles writhing in a way that made Teldin think the creature looked tense or worried. "I think so," he replied. "Come in." He looked around the cabin, but there was nothing he could offer the mind flayer as a seat.

Estriss didn't seem to notice. He walked over to Teldin's hammock and looked intently into his face. Teldin was uncomfortable under the scrutiny of the blank white eyes, but struggled to hide his reaction.

Something important happened earlier, Estriss said without preamble. *I wish to talk about it with you, if you will.* Teldin simply nodded. *Your reaction to the scavver,* the illithid went on, *there was more to it than the bravery that so impressed*

Aelfred Silverhorn. Is that not so? Will you tell me what you felt? What you thought?

Teldin hesitated. "I don't think I know what you mean."

The motion of the mind flayer's tentacles intensified, reminding Teldin more and more of a human wringing his hands with anxiety or anticipation. *Magic!* The word rang in Teldin's mind as though the creature had shouted it. *I sensed magic.* The illithid clutched his amethyst pendant in a three-fingered hand. *Or, rather, this did. You are not a spellcaster. I know this as a fact. The magic I sensed was not the directed, hidden magic of a normal enchanted item. It was* . . . Estriss hesitated, seemingly groping for the right words. *It was . . . almost autonomous, independent of your will, but not quite. Not the magic woven by sentience, and not the blind magic of a wizard's ring or wand . . . but something of both of them.* The creature leaned forward, intent, and a tenor almost of pleading entered his mental voice. *Tell me what you felt.*

"Well . . ." Teldin paused. There was something about the illithid's intensity that he found compelling. He needed to analyze for himself the strange sensations of those few moments, and maybe this was the best way to do it. "Well," he started again, "what I felt was *clarity*. Everything seemed to slow down around me, or maybe . . . maybe it was my thoughts that sped up. I . . . I . . ." It was his turn to struggle for words. He tried to force his mind back, to feel again what he'd experienced. "I felt like I'd, well, stepped outside myself, that everything was clear. I could think, I could concentrate, and I could *act* . . . and there was nothing that could interfere with what I wanted to do. It was . . . Well, it was like I was looking through a glass window, and the window had suddenly been wiped clean." He frowned, disturbed with his inability to communicate what he'd felt so absolutely. "That's not really it, but I don't think I have the words."

Was this the first time? Estriss asked. *Have you felt this before?*

"Yes," Teldin answered slowly. "Twice before."

Were the circumstances similar?

"Yes."

Tension? Danger? On both occasions?

"Yes," Teldin said positively. "When the wasp ship attacked

the longboat. I had a crossbow. The gnomes told me I had to shoot the ballista gunner, then the pirate captain."

And you did?

Teldin nodded. "I'd never shot a crossbow before, but it didn't seem to matter. I could concentrate. There were no distractions. I could . . . I could focus all my thoughts on what I had to do."

This focus—did it come from within you? There was a different tone to the illithid's words, a profound intensity, and Teldin knew they both realized this was the key question.

"No," he responded softly. "It felt . . . It came from outside."

The mind flayer's tentacles ceased their writhing but now quivered with tension. The creature's mental voice was silent for two score heartbeats, then it continued, gentler but still insistent. *Teldin,* Estriss asked, *do you possess any items of magic? Anything possessed of enchantment?*

Now it was Teldin who was silent. He knew with perfect clarity what the illithid was driving at, what it wanted to know. He knew he had the answer Estriss wanted . . . but was he willing to give it? Over the past weeks he'd thought more and more about his "gift" from the mortally wounded spelljammer, about the strange occurrences that happened around it. He knew that he needed to learn the cloak's significance.

But should he discuss it with Estriss? Could he trust the mind flayer with his secret? At home he'd never been one for secrets (except when it came to his father, of course, but that was different). He'd always found it much easier to be totally open with everyone. Sometimes people tried to take advantage of what they saw as his naivete, but much more frequently his honesty and forthrightness brought him the support he needed to follow the path he thought was right.

Of course, what importance could there be to the secrets of a farmer? Now he was playing a much deeper game, and the stakes were much higher—the neogi had taught him that. People had died because of the cloak. Would more die if he kept it a secret, or if he discussed it openly?

The illithid *knows,* though, he told himself, at least the general form of what I'm hiding. His questions showed that beyond any doubt. What sense did it make to continue to hide it? Maybe Estriss is the help I need to learn the answers I've got to have. He made his decision.

"I suspect," he answered at last, "it's the cloak."

Ahh. The word was a mental sigh. *I thought as much.* The mind flayer shook his head in puzzlement—another very human gesture. *Still, your cloak puzzles me,* Estriss admitted. *It is not enchanted in the sense that the word is normally used. It has no dweomer about it, no aura or quality of power to it. I have checked it to the limit of my abilities. But, when you faced the scavver, the sense of power was very intense. I have experienced nothing like this before. Will you tell me how you came to possess it?*

Teldin felt another twinge of doubt—should he tell the illithid everything?—but quickly suppressed it. Telling the story could do no further harm. "I . . . acquired it on Krynn," he began, "but it didn't come from there. Several weeks ago, a vessel—a spelljamming vessel—crashed near my farm. The owner of the cloak was badly wounded, dying. She gave me the cloak before she passed away, and she told me to take it to 'the creators.' " Teldin raised himself on one elbow to look into the illithid's eyes. "Who are 'the creators'?" he asked.

Estriss didn't answer directly. Instead, he asked, *What happened then?*

Teldin closed his eyes as a wave of sadness and pain washed over him. The fear and danger was too recent, all the deaths too immediate, for him to dwell on it. He wished he could just blot everything out of his mind.

Estriss must have sensed some of his emotions. *There is no need to tell me everything now,* he said gently. *There was pain and there was loss. You were pursued?*

"By neogi," Teldin confirmed. "They want the cloak."

The illithid nodded. *It is an artifact of some kind, and artifacts are usually notable for their power,* he said. *If the neogi are aware of the nature of the cloak, then they would want it. I refer to individual neogi, here. An individual neogi wants power, all it can acquire, and it cares not at all how it gets it.*

It was Teldin's turn to nod. That was the kind of behavior he'd come to associate with neogi. "The traveler told me to keep the cloak away from the neogi," he said.

Well that you do, Estriss agreed. *Until you learn more about it, you should keep it away from everyone.* Humor tinged the creature's mental voice. *Even from me.*

"Can you help me?" Teldin asked. "Who are 'the creators'?"

The mind flayer gave one of its broken-backed shrugs. *I have no knowledge of this*, he said after a moment, *only speculation, and that may well be groundless.*

"Tell me," Teldin prompted.

Estriss paused. Just as when they'd first spoken on the sterncastle, Teldin was convinced that the illithid was embarrassed. "Tell me," he urged again. "Please, I'm interested."

Estriss nodded his acquiescence. *I must tell you something of my life's work*, he began. *I told you that I am a scholar. I know you have spoken with my first mate, and I am certain he has told you a little more about my interests, even though I realize he considers my theories to be the utmost foolishness.* The words formed a statement, but the mental tone was questioning.

"The Juna," Teldin said.

The Juna, Estriss confirmed. *When I was younger, I became fascinated with the vast range of 'origin myths' that exist concerning the creation of the universe. Did you know*—he leaned forward, intently—*that virtually every sentient race has a legend or legends that tell of a reality, a universe where the constraints of space and time as we know them do not exist? And of the Great Powers that finally shaped the walls of time and space around that reality to form the worlds that we know today?* The illithid shrugged and waved off Teldin's imminent question with a purple-skinned hand. *That is merely poetic language*, he explained, *and the language varies from one version of the myth to another. But, I repeat, every sentient race has a similar myth, even yours and mine. Although*—and humor temporarily replaced intensity, as the creature gently stroked his facial tentacles—*the appearance of the Great Powers differs significantly between the two accounts.*

Teldin broke in, "What has that . . . ?"

. . . to do with the cloak? Estriss finished for him. *Nothing. Have patience. Each storyteller has his own way of telling a story. Will you allow me mine?*

"Sorry," Teldin responded, somewhat chastened. He settled himself more comfortably in his hammock. "Go on."

Initially, my interest was in the differences between the various origin myths, Estriss continued. *I thought . . . Well, in my youth and unsophistication, I thought that by correlating the differences in the accounts with the characteristics of the races involved, I might be able to cancel out the variations and expose the root of the matter: the true events that gave rise to the myths.* The mind flayer shrugged once more. *As I say, I was young.*

I never completed the task—unsurprising, since I now know it to be impossible—but I did discover something interesting. The most lucid and detailed version of the origin myth was to be found in the ancient epic poetry of the thri-kreen. Do you know of the race? Some call them mantis warriors.

"I've never heard of them," Teldin admitted.

They may not exist on Krynn, Estriss told him. *In any case, many millennia ago the People of the Celestial Mantis underwent a period of almost explosive expansion throughout the universe. The thri-kreen preceded your race—and mine—into the greater universe, perhaps by millions of years. They talk little of it now, even those who still dwell in the void. But they remember the glory. They remember it well.*

Teldin felt the mental equivalent of a sigh. *Those were the transcendent days of the People's race*, Estriss continued, *and their poetry reflects this. It was in this poetry that I sought the origin myths. And it was here that I found references to the Juna.*

Teldin found himself caught up by the sense of wonder in the illithid's mental voice. "Tell me about the Juna," he asked softly.

Estriss seemed not to have heard him. *My focus changed*, he continued. *The origin myth no longer had interest for me. My concentration was focused on the Juna.*

Now that I knew what to look for, I found references to them elsewhere. There is no need for me to describe the years I worked on the problem. Suffice it to say that I now know more about the Juna than, I believe, anyone else in the universe. The illithid paused a little uncomfortably. *I must admit that many scholars, perhaps most, share Aelfred Silverhorn's low opinion of my work.*

Teldin shook that off. "Tell me about them," he prompted.

The illithid went on, *The Juna were a mighty race. They were worshiped as gods on hundreds of worlds, by a myriad of peoples now extinct. I have seen representations of them carved on many ruins and painted on the walls of many caves. Their form is unmistakable, even when transformed through the eyes of misguided faith. And their symbol, the three-pointed star, finds its way into the symbology of many races.*

While your race and mine were barely taking our first steps away from our cosmic cradles, the Juna were already disappearing from this universe. Whether they died out, were destroyed, or moved on to another plane of existence, I know not.

Teldin shook his head in bewilderment. This was so far outside his ken as to be virtually incomprehensible. All his life, his world had been measured by acres and miles and seasons. To hear Estriss talk in terms of millions of years, hundred of worlds . . . Even though the words were familiar, he found himself unable to comprehend the reality those words were describing.

Apparently the illithid misinterpreted his reaction. *I understand your doubt,* he said, with a tinge of sadness. *Even those who have seen evidence mistrust my conclusions. I must have more tangible proof if I want my research to receive the credibility it deserves.*

Teldin remembered something that the illithid had told him earlier. "And that's why you're going to Realmspace?" he asked. "To get more proof?"

The mind flayer nodded eagerly. *A great collector of curiosities, of mysterious items and artifacts, has died,* Estriss explained, *and his collection is being auctioned off in the city of Rauthaven, on the island of Nimbral. For some time, I have known that his collection contained several items that might be connected with the Juna. But I also knew that he would never sell those items to me while he lived. Now, however . . . My only concern is that there may be others who recognize the significance of these items and bid the price out of my reach.*

"What kind of items?"

Several pieces of artwork, replied Estriss, *other items, and—so I believe—a twin to this.* The creature reached within his robe and drew out a long, curved knife. He handed the weapon to Teldin. *I carry it with me always*, the creature went on, somewhat diffidently, *for defense, but more importantly as a . . . as an amulet, if you will, against discouragement. Examine the weapon.*

Teldin hefted the knife in his hand. It was almost as long as his forearm, with the hilt taking up nearly half of that length. The blade was razor-sharp along the inside of the curve and sharpened perhaps a third of the way along the back. In the light of the room's single lantern, it shone dully like brushed steel. Teldin ran a finger along the flat of the blade . . . and stopped in surprise. He'd expected the blade to be cool to the touch. It wasn't, but neither was it warm. It seemed to have no temperature at all, as if it didn't register fully to the sense of touch. He looked up at Estriss questioningly.

The blade is not metal, the illithid explained, *nor is it forged in the normal sense. It is some form of crystalline material, and I believe the blade was grown into its current shape. It was once highly magical, but the enchantment has faded over the millennia.*

"How old is it?" Teldin's voice was hushed.

At least two million Krynn years.

Two million years . . . Teldin wrapped his hand around the hilt, preparatory to testing the balance. His fingers encountered strange ridges and channels, making it impossible to get a comfortable grip. Suddenly squeamish, he handed the knife back to the illithid. There was something unaccountably disturbing about holding a weapon that was obviously designed for manipulative organs only distantly related to human hands . . . "What did they look like?"

They had a trilateral symmetry, Estriss said, looking down at the blade he held in his hands. *Three legs, three arms . . . Like a xorn or a tirapheg, but unlike both.* The mind flayer's mental voice fell silent for a moment, as though he were contemplating the creatures he had just described. Then he shook his head, as if coming out of a doze, and returned the knife to its place within his robe.

There are other artifacts that I believe were created by the

Juna, Estriss said. *One more important than all the rest . . .* The mental voice trailed off.

"Go on."

Double eyelids hooded the illithid's white eyes, as though the creature were embarrassed to meet Teldin's puzzled gaze. *This is merely a theory,* he said hurriedly, *merely my own belief. I have no evidence, and others find the theory unbelievable. . . .*

"Tell me."

I believe the Juna created the Spelljammer.

A thrill, a tingle, shot through Teldin's body. He'd heard the word "spelljammer" before, of course, but never in this context, never as a proper name: "*the Spelljammer.*" There was something—maybe it was just the tone of the illithid's mental "voice"—that made it seem somehow wondrous. "What is the Spelljammer?" he asked.

Some call it a myth, replied Estriss, *but there have been enough independent reports to convince me that it exists. It is a huge ship, a tenth of a league long and almost twice that in width. It sails wildspace and the flow, and has been sighted in half a hundred crystal spheres. Its speed and maneuverability are unmatched, and it boasts armament sufficient to defeat an entire fleet. The body of legend that surrounds it is huge and growing larger every year.*

Some philosophers claim that the Spelljammer *was created by the gods, either as a test for the faithful or as a nemesis for the false. I believe it to have been built by mortal creatures, however. . . .*

"By the Juna?"

Estriss nodded. *So I believe. Few share my conviction, however, and there seems no way to prove or disprove my theory.*

Teldin shook his head. His initial atavistic reaction to the illithid's words had faded, and his normal levelheadedness was reasserting itself. "This is interesting . . ." he said.

But you wish to return to your original question? Estriss nodded. *There is a connection. I ask you to look at the cloak. Look at the pattern woven into the lining.*

Teldin ran his hand over the garment's silk-smooth inner surface. As always, it felt slightly cold to the touch. In the lantern's light it was almost impossible to judge the lining's color—was it green with a hint of gold, or brown with a subtle touch of yellow?—but Teldin knew from experience it was no better in clear sunlight. The cloak's color seemed to shift elusively depending on its surroundings. There was a subtle pattern worked into the finely woven cloth, a precise, geometrical motif.

The pattern includes the recurring symbol of a flower with three petals, Estriss continued. *Do you see it?*

Teldin looked closer at the cloth, changing its angle to the light. The pattern was composed of many fine lines, some no thicker than a slender, hair-thin thread of the woven material. The lines intersected, joined and branched in a network of almost dizzying complexity. There was nothing that his mind could resolve into a three-petaled flower.

Estriss responded to his dilemma. A four-jointed purple finger traced out a section of the pattern. *Here. Now do you see it?*

As the illithid traced the figure, it seemed to leap into visibility. It reminded Teldin of some of the cunning optical illusions he'd seen where the viewer could force the background and foreground of a drawing to reverse, changing its contents. "I see it now," he told the mind flayer. "But how could *you* see it?"

The mind flayer shrugged. *The vision of my race is highly attuned to geometrical patterns,* he explained. *Much more so than is yours.*

Teldin frowned. "Well, why is it important?"

I said that the three-pointed star is the symbol that represents the Juna, Estriss explained. *But so, too, is the three-petaled flower.*

"Then the Juna are 'the creators'!" Excitement surged within Teldin. Estriss had just given him the answer to the mystery. All he had to do now was find a representative of the Juna. . . .

The illithid's words checked his elation, however. *It is possible,* Estriss said doubtfully, *but there are three problems. First, she who gave you the cloak spoke as though 'the creators' still exist—otherwise how could you return the cloak to them? And the Juna have not been known in this universe for millennia. Second, if this cloak were created by the Juna, it would pre-*

sumably have to be millennia old. Certainly, a high enough level of enchantment can prevent the aging of an object, but it still must be considered.

Third, the three-petaled flower is a symbol also widely used by the arcane. I believe that they may have borrowed or adopted it from the Juna, but the effect is the same.

He wasn't going to give up without at least some struggle, Teldin decided. "Then how about the arcane?" he asked. "Could *they* be 'the creators'?" He paused. "And just who are the arcane anyway?"

Estriss was silent for a moment, and Teldin sensed the exercise of patience. *We may continue our discussion later,* the illithid told him finally. *You need rest to recuperate, and I must be on the bridge soon.*

"Why?"

We are about to leave this crystal sphere and enter the flow.

"I have to see this." Cautiously, steeling himself for a recurrence of the crippling nausea and dizziness he'd felt earlier, Teldin raised himself up onto both elbows. This time the world obediently held its place and didn't engage in any gymnastics around him. He swung himself down from the hammock and stood, swaying slightly. Aelfred was right, he thought, he wouldn't be doing any handsprings, but there was no need to remain bedridden as long as he took it easy and didn't push himself too hard. He took a step forward. . . .

And was thankful as the illithid's quick hand on his shoulder steadied him. "Thanks," he said a little self-consciously. "I'm as weak as a kitten."

Then perhaps . . .

"No," Teldin countered, somewhat more forcefully than he felt. "I'll make it."

* * * * *

The hammership's open forward bridge was more crowded than Teldin had ever seen it. Sylvie and Aelfred were there, of course; anything else would have been inconceivable. So were the second mate, Sweor Tobregdan, the elven helmsman, Vallus Leafbower, and two other crew members whose names Teldin didn't know.

As they'd climbed the companionway to the main deck, Teldin had been glad of Estriss's supporting hand. At first the pressure of four-jointed fingers was alien enough to make his skin crawl, but by the time he'd reached the bridge, he gave it no further thought. When they'd entered the bridge, Estriss had solicitously conducted him to an aft corner, where he could settle himself on a wooden seat that folded down from the bulkhead. The illithid had gestured away Teldin's thanks and joined Sylvie and Vallus at the secondary chart table. Both Aelfred and Sylvie had greeted him silently—he with a grin and a wink, she with a fleeting but warm smile—but had immediately started a low-voiced conversation with Estriss. The others had paid Teldin no attention; in fact, they'd seemed totally unaware of his arrival, with good reason. The view out of the bridge was . . . Teldin searched vainly for the right words. Awe-inspiring? Mind-bending? Terrifying? All were appropriate, but none was sufficient.

The *Probe* hung motionless in space. Ahead of the ship was a wall of impenetrable blackness, a plane of darkness that extended in all directions—up, down, port and starboard—seemingly to infinity. This must be how a fly views a mountainside, Teldin found himself thinking, though even this analogy simply didn't capture the magnitude of what he was experiencing.

On Krynn, Teldin had stood beneath the walls of huge buildings and at the foot of sheer mountainsides. In all of those cases, there had been the sense—totally false, but nonetheless disturbing—that the wall had sloped outward near the top, so that it was poised over him like a mighty weight ready to fall. This wasn't the case here. There was no sense that the black wall was anything but flat, no sense that it posed any threat of falling.

Yes, Teldin felt fear welling up inside him, but it was nothing so mundane as a fear of falling objects. It was the sheer scale that terrified, the very sense of infinity. There was no feeling of direct danger, either to him or to the ship as a whole. To acknowledge danger would, somehow, be to dignify oneself with too much significance, to fool oneself into believing that one's existence or nonexistence mattered one whit. It was that conceit that the black wall denied, and therein was its terror. In a universe in which such things could exist, how could anything as infinitesimal as Teldin Moore have any importance whatsoever?

"What is it?" he croaked.

It was Sylvie who turned away from the map table and answered him in her clear voice. "The crystal shell," she said. "The boundary of Krynnspace. We'll be there soon."

That didn't make sense. . . . "We're still moving?"

Sylvie chuckled, a sound that reminded Teldin of mountain streams. "At full speed," she told him. She came over to him and laid a seemingly weightless hand on his shoulder. "How far away do you think that is?" she asked him quietly.

Teldin paused in thought. There were no marks on that infinite plane, no features or details. It was totally unrelieved blackness, with nothing for his eyes to focus on. How can you focus on nothingness? At first he'd thought the wall was perhaps a bow shot away: one hundred paces, maybe two. But now? He realized his initial estimation had been a desperate attempt by his mind—and, if the truth be known, not a very successful one—to reduce what he was seeing to dimensions that he could comprehend. When he forced himself to be honest, he could no more estimate the distance to that wall than he could accurately gauge its size. "How far?" he asked, his voice almost a whisper.

"More than a thousand leagues," the half-elf replied. She glanced over her shoulder back toward the chart table. "They're ready to open the portal," she told him. "I'll talk to you later." She flashed him another of her instant smiles and returned to her duty station.

More than a thousand leagues . . .

At the map table, Vallus Leafbower glanced over at Estriss and replied to a silent question. "Yes, we're within range," the elf said. "Shall I proceed?" Teldin's brain didn't pick up the answer, but the elf nodded in agreement. He picked up a rolled parchment from the map table—Teldin had assumed it to be another navigation chart—and carefully unrolled it. His gray eyes darted over the scroll's contents, and he began to read.

"*Ilesté al tiveniel no aluviath béthude . . .*" The elf's voice was soft, and the syllables flowed fluidly off his tongue. Teldin felt the short hairs at the nape of his neck stir with his fear. He'd seen spellcasters weave their magic before; if Estriss was to be believed, the cloak was capable of something similar. But here, within sight of the infinite wall of blackness, the event seemed to take on much greater significance. He felt the sudden urge to cover his eyes, to withdraw. He was involved in things that were too great for him. What was he, anyway? A farm boy. And here this farm boy was, about to pass through the barrier that contained quite literally everything he'd ever known or experienced. It was only with the greatest effort that he kept his gaze steady on the blackness ahead of the ship.

" . . . menoa tiré aláo galatrivé." Vallus Leafbower fell silent. Directly ahead of the hammership, a new star burst into life: a point of fierce white light. A smile of satisfaction spread across the elf's face as he saw it. When he spoke, there was a slight tremor of exertion in his voice. "The portal is open."

Aelfred nodded to an unspoken order from Estriss. "Aye," he responded. "Flow stations. I'll spread the word." He gave Teldin another quick but reassuring grin. Then, stopping only long enough to extinguish the lantern that hung over the chart table, he left the bridge.

Teldin felt his eyes drawn back to the new star that had sprung to life in the firmament. It looked somehow different now from how it had been in its first moments of existence. For one thing, it seemed to twinkle slightly, to shimmer the way stars had always done when he'd looked at them from the ground. In contrast, all of the other stars were constant when viewed from space, totally unvarying in their hard light, like tiny crystals. There was now color, too; sometimes the new star seemed blue, sometimes red, changing its hue so rapidly that his eyes could hardly keep up with it.

Was it just his imagination, or was the star growing larger? At first it had been a point, totally dimensionless. Now he could swear that it had a disk. . . . Yes, there was no doubt at all. It *was* growing larger.

With a suddenness that was as shocking as a solid punch to the stomach, his perception of the universe instantly reordered itself. No longer was he looking at a star that was somehow, unaccountably, growing in size. He was looking at a hole in the blackness—a hole *through* it—leading to what lay beyond that infinite wall. The light he saw wasn't coming from an object. It was the light of whatever lay outside this crystal sphere, outside Krynnspace. The hole—the *portal*—wasn't growing. The *Probe* was hurtling toward it at inconceivable speed. . . .

Teldin couldn't control his reactions. He slapped both hands over his eyes and folded at the waist so his chest was against his knees. He heard a whimper of panic . . . and realized that the voice was his own.

He felt a hand on his back, and the cool touch of Estriss's voice in his mind. There were no words involved. It was the mental equivalent of a soothing murmur, the inarticulate sound of comfort parents make to their small children. Teldin drew strength from it. He sat up again, taking his hands away from his face. "I'm sorry," he mumbled. He couldn't meet the illithid's gaze, nor look up at the others standing around the map table. His humiliation was complete.

Words formed within his brain. *There is no reason to be sorry. Fear is natural when one is confronted by the unknown. The vast majority of those who travel the universe experience a reaction similar to yours at some time, . . . often the first time they see the boundary of a crystal sphere and realize its significance.* Humor tinged the mind flayer's words. *My own reaction was much the same as yours, perhaps more intense.* Estriss continued more seriously. *The shock typically strikes but once. After the first impact, the traveler is inured, at least partially.*

Come, a test. The illithid tightened his grip on Teldin's shoulder. *We are about to pass into the flow. Look on the portal and tell me your reaction.*

Somewhat hesitantly, Teldin raised his eyes. The view ahead of the ship was vastly different. The true nature of the portal was obvious now. It was perfectly circular, a great hole in the blackness. The margin of the portal—the circumference of the circle—glowed with a harsh and brilliant blue-white light that reminded Teldin of lightning storms over the mountains near his home. Under other circumstances, this glowing margin might have been bright enough to dazzle, but here it faded almost to insignificance—because the light of chaos itself seemed to flood through the portal!

Beyond the black plane of the crystal sphere was what looked like an ocean of multicolored fluids intermixing in turbulent, riotous confusion. Streaks and whorls of every color of the rainbow churned with hues for which Teldin had no names. All glowed with a radiance in which every object on the bridge cast shifting multihued shadows. Wisps and ribbons of color seemed about to leak through the portal, but appeared to evaporate at the last instant. This must be the flow. . . .

The ship's forward motion had slowed drastically. No longer did the portal seem to grow with such dramatic speed. Instead, the *Probe* seemed to be edging its way forward, cautiously, toward the unknown. For the first time, Teldin's brain could finally make sense of what he was seeing and grasp the scale involved. The portal was near now. He could tell that for sure; only a hundred paces or so remained. It wasn't as big as he'd initially guessed, only about twice the length of the *Probe*—a total of about five hundred feet—in diameter.

How do you feel? Estriss asked him.

Teldin didn't look at the illithid, didn't take his eyes off the view ahead. "Dazed," he replied quietly. "Amazed, but under control."

Good. The captain joined the others at the chart table. Even though the thought wasn't directed at him, Teldin "heard" the illithid's order: *Take us through.*

The *Probe* inched forward. The distance to the portal halved.

The chaotic colors of the flow seemed to bulge outward, away from the ship's bow, as though a bubble were forming in a liquid. As the ship advanced, so did the bubble. *It's like we're a ship in a bottle,* Teldin thought, remembering the intricate ship models he'd once seen an old man selling, impossibly constructed inside a narrow-necked glass bottle. If you immersed the bottle in paint, *this* is what the crew would see.

The *Probe*'s bow passed through the portal. For an instant, the black wall was invisible. A thin line of blue-white brilliance encircled the ship. Then the vessel was through.

Teldin's curiosity overcame the sense of weakness that still possessed him, and he forced himself to his feet. He edged his way past the officers at the chart table and descended the three shallow steps to the forward weapon deck. The crewman who was taking Teldin's watch duty was squatting on the deck, his back against the ballista's swivel mount, gazing around him with undisguised fascination. He heard Teldin's approaching steps and nodded a greeting before returning to his observations.

Teldin searched his memory for the man's name. After a moment, it came: Shandess. Older than most other members of the crew, he reminded Teldin of an ancient bit of chewed leather: very much the worse for wear, but still tough and resilient. "You've done this before?" Teldin asked him. He'd meant to speak in a normal voice—a way to prove to himself that he'd shaken off his earlier shock—but the words still came out in a whisper.

"The flow?" Shandess nodded. "Oh, aye, three score times, more maybe." He grinned, showing crooked and broken teeth. "It always gets you, don't it?" The old man pointed upward and astern, over the forecastle. "That's your home behind us, ye know."

Teldin turned. The black plane was visible again, but this time astern of the *Probe*. The sense of infinity was missing, simply because the flow itself wasn't perfectly transparent, and attenuated his vision over distance. Still, the sheer immensity of what he could see was quite impressive enough.

The stern of the vessel was just passing through the portal. From this perspective, it was easier to appreciate the shape and size of the air bubble that surrounded the ship. It looked like a smooth ovoid, about three times as long as the ship, and three times as wide as the *Probe*'s beam. As far as he could tell, the bubble's "walls" were totally insubstantial; the light of the flow didn't reflect or refract from anything. He knew that his initial image of the bubble as a glass bottle was wrong, but still it was very descriptive. As the ship moved forward, the intertwined rivulets of color parted for it, eddying slightly as they flowed backward along the bubble's periphery.

He looked astern once more. The portal was gone, closed. The black plane of the crystal sphere was unbroken and unmarked. Krynnspace—his entire life up to this point—was on the other side of that colossal barrier, and he was sundered from it, perhaps forever.

Chapter Five

• • •

The corridor was dark as Teldin made his way back toward the cabin he shared with the gnomes. Normally corridors and companionways were lit by small oil lamps mounted in brackets on the bulkheads, but now the brackets were empty. The only light came through open doors, and that was the shifting, colored light of the flow flooding in through portholes. Teldin wasn't sure if it was this dim but constantly changing illumination or his own weakness that made him sway almost drunkenly as he walked.

He could hear the conversation before he reached the cabin and found himself grinning. Although he couldn't distinguish the words, he recognized the tune. Dana's voice dominated, and from her tone he could tell she was voicing her displeasure about something aboard the *Probe*. Maybe it was the food again, or the way the ship's weapons master wouldn't let her adjust the action of the heavy ballista, or maybe it was something new. He had to give Dana credit: she had a gods-given ability to find something wrong with everything.

Rather surprisingly, the conversation cut off as he opened the door. The two hammocks were occupied by Miggins and Dana, while Horvath sat cross-legged on a cushion of folded canvas. Teldin stifled a sigh. The way his body felt right now, he needed a rest, and sacking out on the floor just wasn't comfortable, but what could he do?

Before he could lower himself to the deck, however, Dana

had swung herself out of her hammock . . . anticipating by an instant Miggins's attempt to do the same thing. The younger gnome shrugged and resettled himself comfortably.

Dana flopped down on a bundle of sails in the corner. "Take it," she said gruffly, indicating the hammock. Not once did she look up or meet his eyes.

Wordlessly, Teldin clambered into the hammock and relaxed with a sigh. He didn't know what to make of Dana's actions, but as a farmer he knew the inadvisability of looking a gift horse in the mouth. He glanced surreptitiously over to Miggins, hoping the boy would give him some clue, but the youth's smug smile didn't tell him anything—or, at least, anything he wanted to know, part of his mind admitted. He shook his head as if to clear it.

The chaotic light of the flow poured into the cabin, washing the bulkheads with ever-changing veneers of color. Under other circumstances, Teldin might have found it beautiful, even somewhat hypnotic. Now, however, it made him feel edgy and a little claustrophobic. Looking around, he saw that the cabin's single oil lamp wasn't burning—why should it be?—but at least it hadn't been removed like the ones in the corridor. "Can't we cover the portholes?" he said a little peevishly. "Here, I'll light the lamp." He reached for the steel and flint he always kept in his belt pouch. . . .

He didn't even see the gnome move, but suddenly Horvath's hand was like a steel band around his wrist. "*No!*" Horvath said sharply. "No fire."

Teldin looked at the other gnomes. They were all staring at him in horror. "All right," he said reasonably, "no fire, but why?"

Horvath still held his wrist, but the grip had loosened from its initial viselike tightness. "We're in the flow," he explained in a tone he'd reserve for a child or a congenital idiot. "We're in the phlogiston. Don't you know what that means?"

"Obviously not," Teldin replied. The gnome's manner irritated him somewhat, but he was sensible enough to realize that he'd been about to make some major mistake. "What's—" he stumbled over the word "—*flegisten?*"

"*Phlogiston*," Horvath repeated. He finally released his grip, leaving Teldin to rub his bruised wrist. "The flow is phlogiston."

"Which is . . . ?" Teldin prompted.

"Merely the most flammable substance in existence," Horvath said heavily, "flammable and explosive. Why do you think there isn't a light burning in the entire ship?"

Teldin didn't answer. Instead, he remembered Aelfred's actions on the bridge when the *Probe* had been preparing to move through the open portal. The first mate had said something about "flow stations" . . . then he'd extinguished the lantern over the chart table. At the time, Teldin hadn't attached any significance to it.

Horvath wasn't finished. "Do you know what would have happened if you'd struck a spark just now?"

Teldin felt a cold stirring in the pit of his stomach. "What?"

"You might well have blown your hand off," the gnome told him flatly. "At the very least, you'd have suffered a nasty burn, at the worst killed yourself, depending on how good your steel and flint are. That's why, when a ship's about to enter the flow, an officer always goes around to make sure everything's at 'flow stations'—no lights, nothing burning. Spacefarers are full of tales about ships being destroyed because the cook didn't know the ship was leaving wildspace and hadn't quenched his stove."

"I've got an idea for a flow-stove. . . ." Miggins piped up, but immediately fell silent again under Horvath's harsh glare.

Dana snorted. "That oversized lout of a first mate didn't believe we understood about flow stations."

Horvath's hard expression softened slightly. "Nobody told you that?"

"No," Teldin said, shaking his head vigorously. "I suppose they assumed I already knew it."

Horvath frowned. "Sloppy, that was," he said. "Never assume anything with dirtkickers." He patted Teldin's wrist reassuringly. "My apologies for my anger, Teldin. The fault was theirs—and, I suppose, ours—not yours."

Teldin shook his head. So close . . . "The phlogiston is really that flammable?" he asked.

"All that and more," Horvath assured him. "Why, my father was trying to invent a phlogiston bomb, a sealed flask of phlogiston with a fuse attached. Never managed it, may his soul rest in caverns of gold." The gnome placed a respectful hand on his chest.

With supreme effort, Teldin choked back a chuckle. He tried to keep his voice casual and amusement-free as he asked, "Did the bomb work too well?"

Horvath shot him a hard look, then his eyes twinkled and a grin split his face. "No, that's not the way of it. The bomb proved impossible simply because you can't bring phlogiston inside a crystal sphere, no matter what you do. No, my father died well, may the gods rest him, of old age with his family around him."

"I'm sorry," Teldin told him.

The gnome shrugged. "Why?" he asked, a little surprised. "My father's free of the troubles of the world. It's us that have to face them still. I only hope my end is as peaceful." He patted Teldin's wrist again. "Now, you came here to sleep, I warrant, and we're keeping you awake with our talk. We're on watch again soon, so we'll just leave you now." He winked knowingly. "Enjoy it while you can. I hear you'll be back on duty again tomorrow."

* * * * *

As the *Probe* cruised silently through the chaos of the flow, Teldin slept fitfully. His dreams were short, transitory things, but nonetheless disturbing. Night-black scavvers the size of the ship hurtled at him, or tore at the bodies of Aelfred Silverhorn, Sylvie, or the gnomes. Lort, the crewman devoured by the monster, stood before him, sheathed in his own blood, silently reproachful. Estriss, the mind flayer, stood on the forecastle, silhouetted against the brilliance of the phlogiston, trying to strike a light with Teldin's flint and steel.

In his hammock, Teldin writhed and moaned.

Finally, though, the images faded as he sank deeper and deeper into the well of sleep. Both his body and mind became still. . . .

* * * * *

Space. Velvet blackness and distant stars. Teldin felt as though he were hanging motionless in the darkness of the wildspace the Probe *had recently left. He had no body; there was nothing corporeal about him. There was no consciousness of physical existence, not even of thought in the normal sense. He was simply untrammeled perception. Experience impinged on his senses, and he recorded it but felt none of the normal process of analyzing that experience—nor any need for such. He was alone.*

Then no longer. With senses more acute than those any corporeal being could ever possess, he saw . . .

Something—a Presence—was moving against the blackness, eclipsing the stars. It was as black as the backdrop of space, without any discernible boundaries. The only way he could even be sure of its presence was the way in which stars winked out of existence as it moved before them, then reappeared after its passage. There was no way he could gauge the size of the Presence, out here with nothing to measure it against. As with the portal that had opened before the Probe, *it could be something small nearby, or of unimaginable size at great distance.*

For an unmeasurable time, sight was the only sense to which the Presence registered. There was no sound, no awareness of heat or cold. Then, as though his incorporeal body had somehow been granted another, more delicate sense, he felt something.

There was a sense of questing, as if a powerful intelligence were seeking something.

The capacity for thought returned, and with it came fear. Never had Teldin felt so exposed, so vulnerable. Was the Presence seeking him, *he wondered. How could he shield himself from so great a creature?*

As suddenly as it had come into being, the new sense was stripped from him. Only sight remained, then even that seemed to be wrenched away. The stars vanished from around him, and absolute darkness enfolded him. . . .

* * * * *

In his hammock aboard the *Probe*, Teldin flinched as his eyes sprang open. His body was cold, his clothes damp with sweat. His labored breathing rasped loudly through his dry throat. The terror from his dream remained, but the details of what he'd experienced instantly faded. Within a few pounding heartbeats, he could remember nothing. He'd been in space—he remembered that much—but what then? Nothing; he could recall nothing. . . .

He looked around him to find the cabin empty. The rainbow light of the flow still washed in through the porthole. How long had he been sleeping? He had no way of telling. It could have been hours, or only minutes. His mind wasn't rested, he knew that, but at least his body felt stronger than it had since the fight on the forecastle. He settled his head back down and closed his eyes. Maybe he could sleep a little more, clear the quickly fading tendrils of fear and confusion from his thoughts.

But it was no good, he decided almost immediately. Sleep had flown, and he knew enough about the way his body and mind worked to realize that it would be useless to pursue it.

A little cautiously he swung himself from his hammock, testing his balance. There was no trace of dizziness, he noted with relief. Whatever treatment the crew of the *Probe* had given him had certainly been effective. He left the cabin and made his way on deck.

By the time he was outside, even the remnants of fear left by the dream had gone. He remembered being afraid, but no amount of mental searching could bring back any recollection of what he'd been afraid *of*.

The main deck was empty, but he saw movement on the sterncastle. Probably just the catapult crew . . . but right now he felt the need for conversation with someone, anyone. He started to walk aft, but a booming call stopped him.

"Hoi, Teldin!"

He turned. Aelfred Silverhorn stood on the forecastle, silhouetted against the nightmarish sky of the flow.

"Just what the hell are we going to do about those gnomes of yours?" Aelfred bellowed down at him good-naturedly. "I caught that young one putting a lock on my cabin door, because he figured as first mate I deserved one." The warrior snorted. "Not *too* unreasonable an idea, but when he was trying it out, he locked himself in and had to take the door off its hinges to get back out."

Teldin stifled a chuckle. "So, how's the lock?" he asked innocently.

"I don't know," Aelfred shot back, "he didn't finish it. He got interested in 'improving' the door hinges he'd removed, and that's when I kicked him out of there. I had to get one of my own artificers to hang the bloody door again." He barked with laughter. "Now I know why you arranged for those pirates, just to get you away from the gnomes. Want to come up?"

Teldin grinned. "On my way." He went up the ladder to the forecastle fast, testing his level of fitness. He was gratified that he felt no reaction to the exertion.

Aelfred nodded approvingly, obviously understanding what Teldin had done. He slapped the smaller man heartily on the shoulder. "Feeling fit again?"

Teldin nodded with a smile. "Aye," he said, mimicking his large friend's boisterous manner. "Got any scavvers you need dealt with?"

"Scavvers, is it?" Aelfred laughed. "Well, maybe you can kill us two or three for dawnfry. If you're feeling frisky, there's something more important for you to do." His bantering manner faded. "What's your experience with the short sword?"

Teldin shrugged—a little warily, because he thought he knew where the burly warrior was leading. "Some, when I was in the army."

The mate snorted. "Everybody who's ever joined an army gets 'some' experience with the sword. Any training?"

"Some," Teldin repeated. "I learned some simple moves, mainly from bored soldiers who had nothing better to do than teach a novice some of their skills. Are you feeling bored, Aelfred?"

Aelfred chuckled dryly. "Bored enough," he answered. "Bored enough to teach you some *real* swordplay, something that'll maybe save your precious skin." He slapped at his left hip, and for the first time Teldin noticed that the big man had a short sword sheathed at his side. Aelfred noticed his glance. "Oh, aye, the deck crew's all armed now. Void scavvers don't often travel in schools, but it does happen." He turned and bellowed to one of the crewmen who was oiling the windlass that cranked back the heavy ballista. "Hoi, Gendi. Toss me your weapon." The man in the turret hesitated. "Come on, toss it here," Aelfred repeated. "You don't have to worry about scavvers with Teldin around."

The man smiled and drew his sword. He gripped it by the thick forte of the blade and with an easy underarm toss lofted it, hilt first, toward Aelfred. The polished steel reflected a riot of colors. With the utmost nonchalance, Aelfred reached up, and the hilt slapped into his hand. He reversed the weapon and held it out, grip toward Teldin.

"Take it," he instructed. "Well, take it." Teldin grasped the proffered weapon. "Now look at it. Closely. *Feel* it."

Teldin followed his friend's instruction. He adjusted his hand around the grip. It felt quite different from the sword—Lort's sword—he'd driven into the scavver. That weapon had possessed a smooth grip, wrapped in something that felt somehow both smooth and rough—perhaps sharkskin, which he'd heard was a common wrapping for sword hilts. This weapon's grip was metal, the same golden metal as the pommel and guard—probably bronze, he thought. It was ridged, worked into a complex pattern of scrolls and leaves. While he thought that it might become uncomfortable in protracted use, he had to admit that the ridges made for a sure grip and that the depressions would probably be good to prevent sweat or blood from making the hilt slippery. The cross-guard—or quillions, sprang the word from some deep recess of his memory—curved forward and branched. The inner branches came within a finger's span of the blade's edges, presumably to trap or break an opponent's blade and, so, disarm him. The blade itself was oiled steel, shiny and clean, with a razor-sharp edge along almost the full length. The blade thickened and became blunt only within a hand's span of the quillions. The thick portion of the blade—the forte—was etched with a delicate pattern similar to that on the grip. Toward the extreme point, the blade thickened slightly, but the point itself looked as sharp as a needle. He swung the weapon back and forth gently, using only his wrist. He guessed it weighed two or three pounds, with the balance point way back in the forte, near the grip. Finished with his examination, he looked expectantly up at Aelfred.

The warrior had drawn his own weapon, holding it lightly,

with a loose wrist. "Two things to remember about the short sword," Aelfred said. "First, it's a thrusting weapon, more precise than a broadsword. It doesn't have the heft to just hack away, like with a meat-axe, but if you put your weight behind the point, it'll go through most armor like it's soft cheese. Second, the point is mightier than the edge . . . but the short sword *does* have an edge. If you get an opening for a cut, *take* it, but keep it small, controlled. Like this." With the speed of a striking snake, Aelfred straightened his wrist from its partially bent position. Steel flashed like quicksilver in a short arc—a total distance less than the length of Teldin's forearm—and stopped as sharply as if it had struck a solid object. In even that short swing, the blade *whistled*. "See?" Aelfred asked. "Short, controlled. With a good edge, that's enough to split a man's skull. Try it."

Teldin gave the weapon a flip with his wrist, trying to imitate the big man's motion. The blade moved, but not nearly as fast, and it didn't stop sharply but continued its swing almost a hand's breadth beyond where Teldin wanted the swing to end. He felt his cheeks tingle a little in embarrassment. With his hours behind the plow and hewing wood on the farm, he figured his wrist should have been strong enough to do better.

Aelfred didn't notice his discomfiture—or if he did, the warrior chose to ignore it. "It's leverage," he explained. "That sword doesn't weigh much, but it's spread over two feet of blade. Does your wrist hurt?"

Teldin flexed the wrist experimentally. Yes, it did, he noted with surprise—and even more embarrassment. The tendons along the side of the wrist, the ones that continued down from his little finger, were slightly sore.

"There's not much the average person does that uses the same muscles swordplay does," Aelfred continued. "You want to know how to tell a swordsman? Look at my wrist." Transferring his sword to his left hand, he extended his right arm to Teldin.

Teldin looked. The tendons of the warrior's wrist were thick and ridged, even with his hand relaxed. Aelfred clenched his big fist, and the tendons stood out like ropes of steel. He turned his hand so Teldin could better see the side of his wrist. From the edge of his hand down into his forearm, the ligaments and muscles under the skin showed pronouncedly, as hard as rock.

"All it takes is lots of work," Aelfred grinned. "If you want, I'll show you some exercises later. For now, defend yourself."

Standing square to Aelfred, Teldin bent his knees slightly in what he thought might look something like a fighter's crouch. A little self-consciously, he lifted the sword and held it out directly in front of his chest.

So fast that he hardly saw the big man move, Aelfred shot his empty right arm forward and poked Teldin painfully in the center of the chest with a thick finger. Instinctively Teldin brought up his empty left hand to block the thrust, but much too late. Aelfred's arm flashed again, this time grabbing Teldin's left hand in an immobilizing grip. The warrior looked down at the hand he held in feigned amazement.

"What's this?" he asked scathingly. "Trying to stop a thrust with a bare hand? Are you so tired of that hand that you want it chopped off? Well, you're run through the heart, so it doesn't matter anyway." He let Teldin's hand go with the same revulsion he'd show for a dead fish.

Teldin's face burned with embarrassment. "I didn't want to hurt you," he muttered.

"I wouldn't have let you. Trust me on that."

"All right," Teldin said with a sigh. "What am I doing wrong?"

Aelfred laughed. "What *aren't* you doing wrong? First, your stance is too open. You're giving me your whole chest and belly to rip open if I want to. Turn like this." His hard hands took Teldin's shoulders and turned him until he was side-on. "There," he went on. "Smaller target area, right? Oh, aye, you'd fight more open if you had a dagger in your off hand, but one thing at a time, eh?" He grasped Teldin's right wrist and started to move the arm. "Relax," he growled. "Don't fight me. Bring your elbow down more. There." He stood back to examine his handiwork.

Teldin's elbow was lower, close against his right side. "Forearm parallel with the ground," Aelfred instructed. "Wrist straight and strong." The warrior's empty hand flashed again, dealing Teldin a stinging slap on the back of his left hand. "And get that left hand back. You're just asking to have it cut off. Tuck it under your belt if you have to."

Teldin nodded. With his forearm level and his wrist straight, the sword's blade angled upward and out, with the point on a level with his eyes. The position was very natural, he found, even comfortable. For the first time he started to feel like a swordsman . . . or at least a reasonable facsimile.

Aelfred stood back, appraising him. After a moment, the big man nodded his satisfaction. "Good," he growled. "Now the thrust. It's like this." With the sword back in his right hand, he lunged with a speed that belied his size. His sword point flicked out fast and hard as he took a short step forward. He recovered instantly, returning to the ready position so fast that it almost looked as though his arm had stretched. The fluid grace of the movement astounded Teldin.

"Watch the footwork this time," Aelfred instructed. "Watch the step forward." He repeated the motion. "The step extends your reach, but it also puts your weight behind the point. Got it?"

Teldin nodded.

"You try it, slowly. I'll talk you through it." He stood beside Teldin and took the smaller man's right wrist in his big hand. "Start with the wrist like this. Extend the arm, but keep the wrist straight." Teldin tried to relax, to let the seemingly inexorable force move his sword hand forward. "As it comes forward, you take a short step forward *now*. Got it? See how it makes you shift your weight so it's behind the blade?"

Teldin could feel the logic behind the moves. Even in slow motion, he felt the weight of his torso reinforcing the movement of his arm. "I've got it," he said.

Aelfred released him. "Have you, now?" he asked ironically. "Then I want you to kill the mainmast."

"What?"

"*Do it!*" Aelfred barked. "It's going to tear your face off and eat it for dawnfry. *Kill it!*"

Teldin heard a muffled chuckle from the crewman who'd lent him the sword but forced himself to ignore it. He stepped toward the mainmast until he was what he felt to be the right distance away and *lunged*.

It felt like he was doing everything right. The sword struck the thick mast . . . but not with the point. The blade had turned slightly out of true, and the flat of the blade glanced along the side of the mast. The impact—heavy, with his full weight behind it—bent his wrist back painfully, and the sword clattered to the deck.

"What happened?" Aelfred sneered. "Did the mast disarm you? *No.* Did you keep your wrist straight like I told you?"

"No," Teldin mumbled, cradling his sore wrist against his belly. "I bent it."

"Too bloody right, you bent it," Aelfred roared. "Pick up your sword and do it right. *Pick it up!*"

With a muttered curse, Teldin picked up the sword. He knew that Aelfred's feigned anger was a tactic used by military trainers everywhere, but that didn't mean it stung him any less. He dropped back into the ready position and poised on the balls of his feet. The weight of the sword hurt his wrist, but he tried to force the pain from his mind. He tried to concentrate, tried to slip into the state of focus he'd felt before, but it wouldn't come. Why not? he found himself wondering. If Estriss was right, and the concentration was some power of the cloak, why couldn't he summon it now? Was it something that happened only when he was in real danger? Or had it nothing to do with the cloak at all?

"What are you waiting for?" Aelfred asked, sarcasm dripping from his words. "Waiting for the mast to come up and impale itself? *Do it!*"

Teldin took a deep breath and lunged. At the last instant he remembered: *straight wrist*. His arm shot out, backed by the full weight of his body. At the moment of impact he expected a jolt of agony in his wrist, but it never came. Straight and firm, the joint took the impact with no pain or problem. With a solid *thunk* the sword drove deep into the mast.

The lunge had felt good, he realized. Everything worked, and it felt smooth, almost natural. He looked at the sword, buried in the mast at chest-height. A full hand's breadth of the blade had sunk into the seasoned ironwood. He let go of the sword—giving the handle a slight tug to the side as he did so, so that the weapon quivered and sang. He pulled himself to rigid attention and snapped Aelfred a perfect salute the way he'd learned in the army. "The mast is dead, *sir*," he barked.

He held the salute while Aelfred struggled vainly not to laugh. The warrior slapped him on the shoulder. "Good for you, lad," he chuckled. "Nice thrust. We'll do some more work on this later." He paused. "Tell you what, head on down to the officers' saloon. I'll join you as fast as I can. I feel the urge to buy you a drink." In perfect parade-ground style, he returned Teldin's salute and barked, "Dismissed," then he turned to the crewman who'd been watching everything with some amusement. "Well, Gendi? Aren't you going to come and get your sword?"

* * * * *

Teldin had come to appreciate the officers' saloon as a place to relax and to think. It was a comfortable room, much more so than any other cabin aboard the *Probe*. There was a single central table, large and circular, built out of a slice from the trunk of a great tree. The pale orange wood had been oiled and polished to bring out the complex grain structure, and Teldin found it beautiful. All his life he'd had an appreciation for the carpenter's art and enjoyed the feel of good wood and carving tools in his hands. At times he'd wished that his circumstances had been different, that he'd had time to devote to honing his skills. When—*if*—he ever returned home, he firmly intended to make himself a table like the one in the saloon.

The chairs that surrounded the table were covered in rich burgundy leather. The seats and backs were only slightly padded—probably with horsehair, he imagined—but their angle and form made them more comfortable than some of the deeply padded chairs he'd seen on his travels. There was a two-seat couch of the same construction against the forward bulkhead, and a small liquor cabinet—locked, with the only keys in the possession of the senior officers—in the corner just aft of the door.

The main feature of the officers' saloon, and the thing that attracted Teldin most of all, was the huge oval porthole mounted in the outboard bulkhead. This porthole filled the entire length of the bulkhead, more than the height of a man, and rose from the deck to the overhead. The crystal that filled it was quite different from the glass he'd seen in some windows on Krynn. While that glass had been rippled and uneven, distorting the view through it, this was smooth and uniform. It was thick, though; he could tell that from the fact that everything seen through it took on the faintest tinge of green. The crystal didn't feel like glass, either. A glass window would have been slightly chill to the touch. This, in contrast, seemed to have no temperature at all, and when he ran his hands over it, they left no streaks or fingerprints. The port was divided into panes: a central circle, like the pupil of an eye, surrounded by half a dozen curved segments.

During the voyage through wildspace before reaching the crystal shell, Teldin had found himself drawn to the saloon. He had often come here and drawn up one of the chairs in front of the port. Sometimes for hours he'd sat there, staring out on the blackness of space and the stars, given the faintest green tint by the crystal. There was beauty out there, he found. Not the beauty of the rugged mountains or rolling, golden-waved plains that he'd known on Krynn, but a pristine, crystal clear beauty that he found endlessly fascinating.

There was peace out there, too, peace for a troubled soul. There was danger in wildspace, he knew—the gnomes and Estriss had told him so, and he'd seen it for himself—but when he looked out on its perfection, that danger seemed less emotionally burdensome. Seated here, with the stars spread out before him like a mighty tapestry, he could think and he could remember without the pangs of fear and sorrow that so often almost overwhelmed him. Particularly when he was supposed to be sleeping.

Sometimes when he'd come here, there had been others in the room: officers sitting around in low-voiced discussion. All had been friendly enough, even when it was apparent that he didn't want to join their conversation, and they'd had the sensitivity not to disturb him when he drew up his chair and turned his back to them. Perhaps they felt the same wonder he did. In fact, he was sure that another—perhaps more than one—did much the same as he did. When he was done with his introspection, he'd always returned his chair to its original spot. Sometimes when he had entered the saloon, one of the chairs had already faced the port.

He was well familiar with the officers' saloon and approved of Aelfred's suggestion of it as a place to talk.

When he entered the saloon now, however, there was already a figure there. Estriss sat alone at the table, a goblet set before him. Teldin knew that the mind flayer didn't drink alcohol or even fruit juice, so he assumed the goblet contained either water or some illithid concoction. Teldin opened his mouth to greet the captain, but the creature beat him to it.

Welcome, Estriss said. *Come, join me.* He indicated a chair. *I saw your practice on the forecastle*, the creature continued as Teldin took the offered seat. *Aelfred Silverhorn is a good instructor, and you will gain much from his tutelage.*

"I need to," Teldin admitted.

The illithid's facial tentacles moved in a sinuous pattern that Teldin had tentatively identified as equivalent to a smile. *Perhaps.* Estriss raised his goblet into the midst of the tentacles, and Teldin heard a slurping sound. *I thought perhaps we might continue our earlier conversation*, the mind flayer continued. *You must have questions.*

Teldin hesitated. There *was* one thing he'd been wondering about. . . . Since he had come aboard the *Probe*, Teldin had referred to Estriss as "he," though he was never really sure of the creature's gender. "Are you male?" he blurted.

There was a booming laugh from the doorway. Both human and illithid turned.

Aelfred Silverhorn stood in the doorway, a broad grin on his face. "When I saw you were both here, I figured you were talking of weighty matters," he said, "and I walk in on this." He paused, then replied to a silent comment from Estriss, "Don't mind if I do. One for Teldin, too?" He sauntered over to the liquor cabinet and unlocked it. "Pray continue. Don't let me interrupt you."

From the burning in his cheeks, Teldin knew he was blushing furiously. Estriss seemed unaffected . . . but how could Teldin recognize embarrassment—or outrage—in a mind flayer? "No offense," he muttered.

None taken, Estriss replied immediately. *Curiosity is understandable. You wonder, quite naturally, about my sex. Simply put, I have none, not in the biological sense. Any individual of my race can bring forth young, and with no participation* from another individual. *I have often thought that this is the single factor that most sets my race apart from yours. Think how much of your culture derives from sexual origins, from the necessary interaction between males and females. My culture has none of this.* The illithid paused. *But I digress. In answer to your question, strictly, I am not male. Neither am I female. But, since I am not currently generating an offspring, and will not consider it in the foreseeable future, you may think of me as a male.*

"Except in one important point," Aelfred cut in as he set a pewter goblet down in front of Teldin. "Estriss won't try to steal your girl." He settled his bulk into a chair and lifted his booted feet up onto the table. He raised his own goblet. "Health, to both of you."

"Health." Teldin echoed the toast and took a tentative sip from the goblet. The sharp, somehow smoky taste and the tingling of his tongue identified the drink at once. It was a liquor called sagecoarse, distilled—so Aelfred had told him—from an extract of the plant bearing the same name. Neither drink nor plant was native to either Toril or Krynn. Apparently the burly first mate had discovered the liquor on some backwater world in another sphere, had developed a taste for it, and had ever since made sure he had a good supply available.

"It's an acquired taste," Aelfred had told him when he'd first poured him a sample, on Teldin's second day aboard the *Probe.* Teldin could easily accept that, but had wondered why anybody would bother. Now, however, after a few more opportunities to sample the liquor, Teldin found he didn't mind the flavor and rather enjoyed the sharp, tingling sensation it caused on his tongue. He'd never had any great penchant for hard liquor, though, and that attitude certainly wasn't going to be changed by sagecoarse. Whether or not it was unsophisticated—as Aelfred jokingly claimed—he still preferred a foaming tankard of good ale.

The mind flayer's silent words brought him back to the present. *Teldin wished to discuss the arcane,* Estriss said. *He has*—the illithid paused—*a curiosity about the other races of the universe, as he has just shown.* Estriss fixed Teldin with a white-eyed look.

The significance of neither the pause nor the look was lost

on Teldin. Estriss was clearly leaving it up to him whether or not he told Aelfred anything about the cloak. Teldin hesitated. He trusted Aelfred, but if he broached the subject now, he'd be bogged down in what, at the moment, were irrelevancies. He could always tell Aelfred later. "That's right," Teldin said smoothly, "I'm curious. Tell me about the arcane."

It was Aelfred who answered first. "Merchants," he grunted. "Traders. Gypsies of space. It doesn't matter who the customers are. If there's money in it, they'll deal."

Stripped of the negative emotion, Estriss continued, *the statements are accurate. The arcane are a race of humanoids— blue of skin and perhaps twice your height, but otherwise not that different in appearance from humans.*

"Maybe to an illithid," Aelfred snorted, but his quick smile robbed the words of any offense. "Wait till you see one, Teldin."

They are traders, Estriss continued patiently. *It is the arcane who are the suppliers of virtually all spacefaring technology used by my race, by yours, and by most other races in the universe. They build ships for the beholder nations, passage devices for the lizard men, planetary locators for the Elven Imperial Navy, and spelljamming helms for all and sundry.*

Teldin tried to keep his bewilderment from showing on his face. Estriss had casually tossed out names and concepts as though they were well known . . . which they probably were to people familiar with spacefaring. Teldin had heard legends about beholders and could—with a mental stretch—imagine the eye tyrants cruising the universe in ships of their own. But an Elven Imperial Navy? There was no way he could reconcile so grand a concept with the few soul-weary refugees from Silvanesti that he'd met. The rest—passage devices and all— were just so many meaningless words.

If he were to show his confusion, he knew Estriss would quite likely explain each concept in detail and never get around to the arcane. He kept his peace.

As Aelfred has stated, Estriss was continuing, *if their price is met, the arcane will deal with anyone . . . with one exception. They will not trade with the neogi.* He paused as if waiting for a response.

"Well, that's reassuring," Teldin offered weakly.

"Oh, aye," Aelfred said sarcastically. "The arcane won't trade with neogi, but they *will* trade with others, knowing full well that their customers are going to turn around and sell the goods to the neogi. I have no love for the arcane, I'll tell you that." He sighed, and his anger faded. "But it's true that we depend on them. Where do you think people like us buy the helms to run our ships? From the arcane. It's the only place you can get 'em. The blue ones are a necessary evil."

Teldin digested this for a moment, then asked, "Where's their home? Do they have their own planet?" He looked meaningfully at Estriss.

We presume they must have, the mind flayer answered, *or that they once did have, but its location—or perhaps its fate— is known only to the arcane. . . .*

"And they're not telling," Aelfred finished. "Oh, various groups have tried to find out. Some want to know just because they're curious, others because they think the knowledge will give them power. Maybe they think they can blackmail the arcane or something like that. Others, I'm sure, want to find it so they can conquer it, and then they'll own all the arcane's technology or magic or whatever it is that lets them create spelljamming helms. I like that one," he scoffed. "As if a race with that much power is going to let anyone just waltz in and take over."

"So the arcane are powerful at magic?" Teldin speculated.

Aelfred shrugged. "I guess they'd have to be. Spelljamming helms aren't technological, not the way you're probably thinking. If the arcane can create them—which, I suppose, isn't a sure thing—that means they're capable of enchanting powerful artifacts."

Teldin found himself fingering the hem of the cloak. He took his hand away quickly. "The arcane's world," he went on. "Nobody's found it?"

"Not even a clue," Aelfred said positively. "Nobody even knows what crystal shell it's in, or even if it exists anymore. There are legends, of course. Just about every group that's ever had dealings with the arcane has some kind of folk tale about them."

"Tell me some," Teldin said.

"Well . . ." The warrior thought for a moment. "There's

one that the arcane's world isn't in a crystal sphere at all, and that they've hidden it off somewhere in the flow. Impossible, of course. Then there's the one I like. According to a thri-kreen legend, the arcane traded their home world to some elder god for the *Spelljammer*—you've heard of the *Spelljammer*?" Teldin nodded, controlling his impulse to look at Estriss. "Well, the legend goes on that the arcane couldn't control the *Spelljammer* and that they somehow caused their world to fall into its sun, destroying it. That's why they're interstellar vagabonds."

"Do you believe that?" Teldin asked.

Aelfred looked a little scornful. "Of course I don't. It's just a good story."

Teldin allowed himself a sidelong glance at Estriss. "So where would you go if you want to meet an arcane?" he asked casually.

"Anywhere," Aelfred replied offhandedly. "You're as likely—or as *un*likely—to find a space-gypsy in any port city on any world in any crystal sphere as . . . Or, at least, any world that knows about spelljamming," he amended.

"How about on Toril?" Teldin suggested.

It was Estriss who answered him. *There are probably many arcane on Toril. I have met one in Calimport and another in Waterdeep. I hear rumors that they run an open trading post at a place called the Dock in the Wu Pi Te Shao Mountains, but I doubt this is true.* He paused. *Since they almost invariably work through human intermediaries, and reveal their presence only when it suits them to do so, there may be arcane in many cities of Toril.*

Teldin digested that for a moment. "What about . . . where is it we're going?"

Rauthaven, the illithid responded, then paused. *I have heard from travelers that at least two arcane dwell on the Beacon Rocks, northeast of the city, in the Great Sea. I am almost certain that there will be an arcane in Rauthaven, if only temporarily.*

"Why?" Teldin wondered.

Because of the auction I wish to attend. It seems likely that the arcane will be interested in many of the same artifacts as I am, and that they will send at least one representative to view them . . . and perhaps bid to acquire them.

"They're interested in the Juna, too?" Teldin asked in surprise. Before Estriss could answer, he went on, puzzled, "But I thought you said the arcane inherited their powers from the Juna in the first place. If that's true, why would they be interested in old stuff that a collector's had for years?"

Estriss was silent for a moment. His facial tentacles writhed, seemingly about to tie themselves in knots . . . and Teldin realized he now knew what illithid embarrassment looked like. *That is my theory, about the origin of the arcane's knowledge,* Estriss admitted finally, *but the arcane I have spoken with deny it, though such a secretive race would probably deny it even if it were true. In fact . . .* The illithid's mental voice slowed down, as if he were unwilling to go on. *In fact, the arcane I have spoken with claim to consider all my theories about the Juna as so much foundationless speculation. There was no such race as the Juna, they claim.* He raised a three-fingered hand as if to forestall Teldin's next question. *Certainly, I believe that if there is an arcane in attendance at the auction, it will lend some credence to my beliefs.*

Teldin shook his head. He was convinced there was a logical flaw in the illithid's argument somewhere, but he didn't feel the urge to pursue it. Estriss was entitled to his own beliefs—even to his own monomania, because that's what his research was starting to sound like—and while Teldin found the theories interesting on a casual level, the main issue came down to finding an arcane.

That, Teldin was sure, was very important. Despite the illithid's apparent belief to the contrary, Teldin was more and more of the opinion that the arcane were the "creators" he'd been sent to find. The only way he could think of to confirm this was to talk to an arcane—a situation that would represent its own risks and problems, of course. If Estriss was right, there would be an arcane in Rauthaven . . . and it might be better if he let the mind flayer think that's what Teldin expected. If not, it shouldn't be too difficult to get passage to the Beacon Rocks. After all, after a voyage from one world to another, how difficult could it be to get to some islands? And if the tales of arcane on the Beacon Rocks proved false, then Aelfred should be able to tell him how to get to Calimport or Waterdeep.

His reflections were interrupted by the loud clanging of a bell, apparently from on deck. He heard running footsteps in the corridor.

Aelfred catapulted out of his chair and flung open the saloon door. "What?" he bellowed.

A crewman who'd been running by—it was the old man, Shandess, Teldin saw—stopped to answer. "Ship ahoy, sir, approaching fast."

"What ship?" Aelfred demanded.

"Lookout says deathspider, sir."

Aelfred nodded. "Battle stations," he ordered. As Shandess ran on, Aelfred turned to Estriss. "Captain?"

Illithid and human left the saloon together. Teldin sat alone in the wash of flow-light, a cold fist of fear tightening on his heart.

Chapter Six

• • •

Much of the fear remained—of course!—but after a dozen or so heartbeats Teldin was able to shake off the worst of the mind-numbing terror that kept him frozen in his seat. He forced himself to his feet. Where would Estriss and Aelfred be during battle stations? The bridge, of course.

The forward bridge was almost as crowded as it had been during the passage into the phlogiston. The captain and first mate were there, as he'd expected, as were Sylvie and Sweor Tobregdan. Vallus Leafbower was conspicuously absent, but his place was filled by two others, whom Teldin had met but had barely spoken to: Liono Marlot and Bubbo.

The latter two made an almost absurd contrast; even in his present state, Teldin could appreciate that. Liono Marlot, the ship's "tactician," was a quick-tongued man, slender in build, and short. The top of his gray head came up to Teldin's chin . . . and up to Bubbo's armpit. Bubbo—if the man had a second name, Teldin had never heard it used—was the *Probe*'s weapons master, and his body matched the scale of the ship's heavy weapons, which were his responsibility and chief interest. He was a black-bearded mountain of a man with a good layer of fat sheathing powerful muscles. Friendly in a gruff sort of way, Bubbo would never use two words when one would do and seemed to prefer using none at all. Despite these differences, or perhaps because of them, Liono and Bubbo were fast friends and inveterate drinking companions in the saloon when both were off duty. Their normal camaraderie was absent now, and they shared the same air of tense expectation as the rest of the bridge crew.

Everyone's gaze was fixed firmly forward, presumably toward the approaching neogi vessel. Teldin scanned the bizarre sky of the flow. It was hard to make out anything against that background, through the intervening ribbons and sheets of color.

Finally he picked it out. At this range it was just a black dot, but Teldin's mind and memory filled in the details: a grossly swollen black body and the eight angular legs that gave the deathspider its name. Teldin fought the desperate urge to turn aside, to cover his eyes . . . to hide, but there was no safety in that. He struggled to force down the terrible memories that threatened to paralyse him. "Fear is the great killer," his grandfather had once told him. "Conquer that, and the battle is halfway yours." How would the old man deal with this, he wondered, a foe he'd never known existed, in an environment he could never have imagined? Very well, more than likely, Teldin admitted with grim humor. In any case, the thought of the old man's calm wisdom seemed to lend him strength. He forced the fear from his mind and observed.

"When did we drop to tactical speed?" Aelfred asked.

"I had the alert bell rung as soon as the ship was sighted," Sweor Tobregdan answered.

Aelfred looked upward at the overhead. "What heading the deathspider?" he bellowed.

After a moment, the answer echoed down from above—presumably from the spotter on the forecastle, or maybe relayed down from the high lookout in the crow's nest atop the mast. "Still directly toward us."

The first mate glanced over at Estriss and nodded in answer to a silent order. "Hard a-port," he boomed.

It was impossible to sense the ship's maneuver from watching the flow itself, but the black spot that was the deathspider shifted slowly to the right until it vanished behind the bulkhead.

"We should fight this from the forecastle," Aelfred said grimly.

"It's a fight, then?" This from Sylvie.

Aelfred raised an eyebrow skeptically. "With neogi? Of course it's a fight." He looked around the bridge. "Sylvie, stay below. Sweor, head aft. If we have visitors, I want you in command." Without a further word, he strode to one of the ladders that led up to the forecastle and started to climb. The others—Estriss, Bubbo and Liono—followed him, while Sweor left through the aft door.

Teldin hesitated. What about him? He wasn't an officer, not strictly speaking, but Aelfred, Estriss, and the others certainly seemed to accept him as more than just another crewman. He had no battle station duties—at least, nobody had told him what they were. Probably the best thing he could do would be to stay belowdecks and keep out of everyone's way, but he wanted to see what was happening. He didn't think he could stand knowing there was a neogi ship out there, apparently closing for the attack, but not being able to see how the battle was going. He didn't want to depend on what little information might trickle down to him. That was a sure recipe for madness.

Besides, Aelfred hadn't specifically told him to stay on the bridge, or to go anywhere else, for that matter. Teldin looked over at Sylvie, who was still standing by the map table. The lovely half-elf seemed to sense his scrutiny, and his thoughts. "I don't think they'll mind if you go up," she said with a quick smile. "Just stay out of the way."

Teldin returned her smile. "Sometimes I think that's what I'm best at." He scrambled up the portside ladder.

The forecastle turret was fully manned—Dana was among the four-person crew, Teldin noticed—and the heavy ballista had been pivoted around to point roughly astern. The large weapon had been cranked back, and a huge bolt placed in position, ready for a shot as soon as the enemy drew into range.

Estriss, Aelfred, Bubbo, and Liono were at the aft rail of the forecastle, near the mainmast. The first mate had a spyglass to his eye. Teldin moved aft, just close enough so he could hear their conversation, but not close enough to get in anyone's way. He squatted down, his back against the sloped metal wall of the turret. He looked out into the flow in the direction that Aelfred's glass and the ballista were pointing. It didn't take him long to spot the neogi vessel. It was still too far away to show as anything other than a black dot . . . but wasn't that dot looking bigger?

"She's still closing," Aelfred was saying. "She's fast, faster than the *Probe*." He lowered the spyglass and glanced over at Estriss. "No," he responded to a silent question from the illithid. "Vila's on the Helm. Thorn just got off duty, so he can't do anything." A pause—obviously another question. Aelfred frowned and shook his head. "No," he replied definitely. "We'd be faster if Vallus took the helm, but not much. Probably not enough to make a difference. Plus we'd lose ground during the changeover." He bared his teeth in an expression that mixed smile with snarl. "And finally, I want Vallus's spells. They're the only equalizer we've got."

Even through his fear, Teldin was able to notice—and be fascinated by—the dynamics of power that occurred between Estriss and Aelfred. The illithid was captain of the *Probe*, and everyone including Aelfred treated the creature with deference and respect, . . . but it seemed as though the captaincy might be in name only. Certainly, Aelfred seemed to have taken over the reins of command at the moment, and Estriss appeared unconcerned and uninclined to challenge his authority. *Why is that?* Teldin wondered. Because the crew would rather follow a human master? No, that didn't make sense. When Estriss issued orders, all the crew obeyed them willingly.

Wasn't it more likely that Estriss knew his own limitations and was acting within them? After all, by his own admission, the illithid was a scholar. What would a scholar be expected to know about ship-to-ship combat, particularly in this alien environment? Aelfred, on the other hand, was a mercenary, a warrior by trade and inclination. He'd be much more likely to respond correctly in a combat situation, more likely to give the correct orders, and to give them in a manner in which they'd be instantly obeyed.

He returned his attention to the group by the mainmast. Aelfred was speaking again. "All right, we have no doubts. The deathspider can outrun us. So what do we do about it? Turn and engage?" He looked one by one at the other officers.

Liono, the *Probe*'s tactician, answered. "No," he said resolutely. "We run, as fast and as long as we can."

Why? The illithid's question formed in Teldin's brain. In discussions like this, Estriss must broadcast his thoughts to everyone nearby, he concluded. *Why run?* Estriss asked again. *They will catch us eventually. You have said so.*

"That's so," Liono agreed, "but think. Most of a deathspider's weaponry aims aft. If this is a standard configuration, all they've got that fires forward are two ballistae. Aft, they've got two ballistae *plus* a heavy catapult and a heavy jettison."

"Lot of firepower," Bubbo rumbled.

Liono nodded. "The only way to keep us out of its arc of fire is to stay ahead of the deathspider," he said, "and the only way to guarantee that . . ."

"—is run," Aelfred finished.

"Right," Liono confirmed. "When they draw closer, we can fire on them."

"And they on us," Aelfred reminded the tactician. "Bubbo, can we hurt them?"

The huge man looked doubtful. "Some," he grumbled through his beard. "Maybe not enough. Big ship. With the forward catapult, we'll hurt 'em more."

Teldin understood what the huge weapons master was getting at. In a chase, the forward heavy catapult was masked by the rest of the hull and couldn't fire on an enemy approaching from astern. If the *Probe* had its bow to the enemy, on the other hand, all three heavy weapons could be brought to bear.

Aelfred was silent. He didn't look happy with what he'd heard. Finally he squared his shoulders and announced, "We're going to turn and close, hit 'em with everything we've got on the way in, and try to disable their grappling rams in case that's what they've got in mind. I want to get in close enough for Vallus to do what he can." He gripped Liono's shoulder. "Your points were well taken, old friend," he told the small tactician. "We'll do our damnedest to stay out of their rear arc, but we've got to hit 'em hard. Who knows? Maybe they haven't got the stomach for a foe that *wants* to fight."

Echoes of Horvath and the *Unquenchable*, Teldin thought uncomfortably.

Liono didn't seem convinced either. "Neogi?"

Aelfred slapped him on the back. "There's a first time for

everything." Now that the decision had been made, the big first mate—acting captain?—was in much better spirits. He raised his voice and yelled, "Weapons forward! Prepare to come about!"

From the main deck, crewmen clambered into the rigging, while others pulled on ropes to trim the ship's small sails. The hammership turned. As before, there was no sensation of movement, but the black dot of the neogi vessel swung through the sky until it was almost directly ahead of the *Probe*. With the vessels now speeding toward each other, the deathspider seemed to jump closer. Within a dozen heartbeats Teldin could make out the spindly "legs" that made up the vessel's grappling ram.

Aelfred was speaking quietly to Estriss, giving bearings and small course adjustments. Presumably the illithid was mentally relaying these to the helmsman two decks below and to the crew still in the rigging. The neogi ship shifted, then finally settled down off the port bow.

The forward turret rumbled as the ballista crew turned their weapon around. The same was happening with the aft turret's heavy catapult. For the first time, Teldin saw that the old man, Shandess, was part of the five-man catapult crew. Corded muscles stood out in his thin arms as he threw his weight against the massive weapon.

"Bubbo," Aelfred barked, "the weapons are yours. Fire as soon as we're in range. Aim for the head. If you can damage the helm, we've won."

Bubbo scowled. "I think gnomes messed with the ballista," he grumbled.

"Too late to worry about that now," Aelfred pointed out. Then he grinned. "Maybe they've improved things."

The big man didn't look reassured, but he nodded. He squinted into the flow-light, estimating the distance to the enemy. "Soon," he growled.

"Estriss," Aelfred went on, "get Vallus up here."

"Already done." Teldin turned at the soft but carrying voice. Vallus Leafbower stepped off the ladder that led to the main deck and joined the others on the forecastle.

"What can you do to *that*?" Aelfred stabbed a finger toward the deathspider.

The elf thought silently for a moment, then answered slowly, "I have several spells that should help the issue. The fact that we're in the flow limits me considerably, you understand."

"I understand. How close do we have to be?"

Vallus appraised the distance, a frown creasing his brow. "Closer than this," he replied.

Aelfred chuckled mirthlessly. "Oh, we'll get closer," he told the elf mage. "You're on your own, Vallus. You know better than me how to handle the magic side of it. Do whatever you can to give them trouble. If you can take out their helmsman, do it."

The elf nodded. "I'll do what I can." The first mate turned away to study the approaching enemy.

The deathspider was nearer, and Teldin was able to make out more details. Multiple round ports were set into the vessel's head. They glowed a sullen red, like inhuman eyes filled with hatred and blood-lust. Rigging was strung between the upper two pairs of legs: diaphanous sails that could almost be made of cobwebs, linked by silvery ropes. The ship's bulging abdomen seemed to have taken on a dull red tinge. Perhaps it was just the flow-light reflecting off it, or maybe it was light from within transmitted through the deathspider's crystalline hull. The overall effect was horrific, threatening. Even if Teldin hadn't known what he did about the neogi, there was no way he could picture any race using such a ship as anything but rapacious and evil.

To Teldin, it seemed that the rate of approach had slowed somewhat. Perhaps Aelfred was right and the horrors aboard the spidership were hesitant about dealing with a vessel that turned to the attack rather than fled. Or, more likely, the creatures were just being cautious. Why rush into something when there was little or nothing to be gained through speed?

It was difficult to judge the range accurately, both because of the shifting background and because the head-on attitude of the deathspider gave precious little detail from which to judge distance. Nevertheless, Teldin guessed the enemy was now less than ten thousand paces distant.

Bubbo had borrowed Aelfred's spyglass and had it trained on the approaching vessel. Now he lowered it and roared,

"Catapults away!"

Teldin turned to watch the aft catapult. Shandess pulled the lever that fired the heavy weapon. The catapult's arm pivoted forward and up, slowly at first but picking up speed at a frightening rate. Then the arm reached the full extent of its travel and slammed into the forward stop with an echoing boom. The massive stone that had been loaded into the cup at the end of the arm shot clear. Teldin heard it whistle overhead, barely clearing the rigging, as it hurtled slightly to port, directly at the deathspider. Almost simultaneously, he heard the forward catapult fire. He tried to follow the flight of the two stones, but quickly lost them against the turbulence of the phlogiston.

Bubbo had the spyglass back to his eye. "Two clean hits," he announced after a few moments, satisfaction apparent in his voice. "One to the head." Teldin tried to imagine the impact of one of those massive catapult stones, the splintered timber and shattered crystal. How could anything weather such a blow? The deathspider seemed unaffected, though—at least, any damage was totally invisible from this distance—and continued on its course.

The aft catapult crew was at work reloading the massive weapon. Four burly crewmen were heaving on two mighty windlasses, winching the catapult arm back toward its cocked position, while Shandess stood ready to lock it into place. It was slow work, and Teldin could sense their intensity.

He turned forward. The ballista crew in the forecastle turret was tense, ready. The weapon was cocked, ready to fire, and the head gunner was squinting along the length of the huge bolt, checking the accuracy of his aim. There was something different about the ballista's appearance, Teldin noted for the first time. It seemed more complex, somehow. He couldn't immediately identify what the changes were, but they made the heavy weapon look even more dangerous than ever.

After a moment, he saw what he knew to be the source of those changes. Dana was crouched by the firing lanyard, apparently making some quick adjustments to the mechanism. As if sensing Teldin's gaze on her, the gnome turned, and their eyes met. If the eyes are truly windows to the soul, then it seemed as though imminent danger had opened the shutters.

Teldin felt Dana's emotions hit him like a physical shock. Fear and determination were there, of course, but these were in the background. At the forefront were feelings directed at Teldin: respect and affection . . . and something more than affection. Shaken, Teldin gave the small woman a reassuring smile, then turned away. Now wasn't the time to deal with this new complexity. Later, maybe. If there *was* a later.

"Range?" Aelfred snapped.

"A thousand paces," Bubbo rumbled. "Closing."

The first mate nodded. "Now it gets interesting."

There was no warning, nothing to prepare Teldin for what happened next. Suddenly, shockingly, something tore through the rigging above his head. Canvas ripped, and a secondary boom shattered, raining wood splinters onto the deck. Instinctively, Teldin ducked below the rail, shielding his head with his arms. He heard something else *whoosh* harmlessly overhead.

"I take it we're in ballista range," Aelfred said dryly.

"Ballista away!" Bubbo ordered.

The head gunner checked the aim a final time, then nodded to Dana. The gnome pulled the lanyard. With a force that Teldin could feel through the deck, the huge bow fired and the bolt, with its massive metal head, hissed toward the enemy ship. Before the bow limbs had stopped quivering, the crew had leaped to the windlass and were winching the bowstring back for another shot.

"Hit!" Bubbo called. "*Good* hit!" He stared at Dana with undisguised surprise.

Both catapults fired again, within a few heartbeats of each other. This time Teldin had better success tracking the shots. One massive stone flew wide, passing harmlessly below the deathspider's head. The second, though, flew straight and true, smashing into the hideous ship at the base of one of the legs. The leg tilted drunkenly, but didn't come away from the hull.

"Clear the rigging," Aelfred cried. "Lookout down."

The crewmen who'd been aloft in the ratlines scrambled down to the relative safety of the deck, while the lookout came down the mast from the crow's nest scarcely slower than he would have had he fallen freely. Precise maneuvering didn't count for much now, Teldin assumed, and there was little use in putting a man at risk at high lookout when anyone with the poorest eyesight could see the enemy perfectly well from the deck.

The two ships were closing fast now. The distance between them halved, then halved again. The deathspider loomed large and hideous, its red-lit bow ports like eyes glaring at the *Probe*, its spindly legs seeming to reach out to grasp the hammership. One ship, or maybe both, had changed course, and the spidership was now directly ahead of the *Probe*.

"Too close for catapults," Bubbo grumbled. "Release the crews?"

Aelfred nodded. "Catapult crews to damage control stations," he yelled.

Words formed in Teldin's mind. *Are we to ram head-on?* Estriss asked.

"No," Aelfred answered, "I've got something else in mind, but let 'em think we are."

The *Probe*'s ballista fired again, at virtually point-blank range. Teldin watched the heavy missile slam straight into the bow of the deathspider. A circular port shattered, spraying debris into space. A strident cheer went up from the ballista crew. . . .

And quickly turned to screams of horror and agony. A missile from the deathspider slammed into the *Probe*'s forward turret, shattering the ballista and flinging the weapon's crew around like rag dolls. Without hesitation, Teldin hurled himself up the ladder and vaulted over the turret's rim.

The scene in the turret was total confusion. Wreckage was everywhere. When the enemy bolt had struck the hammership's ballista, the considerable energy contained in the partially bent limbs of the big bow had been released and had to go somewhere. In this case, it had torn the heavy weapon apart, throwing fragments everywhere. Two of the turret crew were still up and moving—Dana among them, Teldin was happy to see—but even they were bleeding from multiple small wounds and seemed somewhat stunned. The other two, however . . . Teldin saw at once there was nothing he—or anyone else—could do for them. One was crumpled against the turret wall, his back bent the wrong way; the other apparently had been struck directly by the neogi's shot, and the enormous missile had torn him in two. Teldin averted his eyes from what was left of the unfortunate man and struggled to control his rising gorge.

"Report!" Aelfred bellowed.

Teldin leaned over the turret rail, glad to turn his back on the carnage. "Two dead," he said, trying to keep his voice level and matter-of-fact, "two injured. The ballista's wrecked."

Aelfred's face had a grim cast, and his eyes were as cold and hard as flint. "If there's anything to salvage, do it," he ordered, "then get below and under cover. This is going to be bloody."

"No!" The vehemence of his own response came as a surprise to Teldin, and to Aelfred as well, judging by his expression. "No," Teldin repeated more reasonably. "You need every able-bodied man you can get."

Aelfred's face clouded over, and he blistered the air with a soldier's oath. Then, suddenly, his frown faded, replaced by an unwilling smile. "Your call," he told Teldin. "Make sure you're armed . . . and watch your back."

Teldin smiled. He didn't need that last bit of advice. His skin was very precious to him, and he'd do everything he could to make sure it remained reasonably intact. But . . . armed? He looked around the turret quickly. For the first time, he noticed—or *let* himself notice—the identity of the crewman who lay broken against the turret wall. It was Gendi, the one who'd lent Teldin his short sword for his practice session with Aelfred. The sword was still in its sheath on Gendi's belt, and it was certain that Gendi wouldn't be wanting it anymore. Carefully avoiding the messy reminders of the other crewman's fate, Teldin crossed the turret. He hesitated a moment—there was something about taking from the dead that gave him pause—then he drew the sword from Gengi's scabbard. He clutched the weapon in his fist tightly, to stop the disturbing tremor he noticed in his hand, and ran his left palm along the flat of the blade. The metal was cool and smooth, and somehow it seemed to shore up his flagging courage. He had nowhere to put the weapon and considered for a moment removing Gendi's sword belt. That would be too much, he decided, and it would mean moving the body. Even though Gendi was past feeling anything, Teldin couldn't bring himself to shift the broken-backed corpse.

Dana was watching him dumbly, her eyes still glazed with shock and pain. He raised the sword and held it before him, forcing a fierce grin onto his face. As he'd hoped, the gnomish woman responded. Her eyes cleared, and she drew the long dagger she had at her own hip. She smiled back at him. Once more she looked like the tough little warrior that he'd always considered her to be.

The *Probe* was almost upon the deathspider. It looked as though Aelfred was going to drive the hammership's blunt ram full into the head of the spidership. "Prepare to ram!" Aelfred's roar echoed throughout the ship. Everywhere, crewmen grabbed whatever purchase came to hand: gunwale rails, rigging, or fixed pieces of equipment. Teldin shrank the cloak to its smallest dimension, wrapped his left arm around the turret rail, and held on for dear life.

Above and below the *Probe*, the deathspider's huge legs swung inward like huge levers, preparing to grapple the hammership. To Teldin there seemed no possible way of avoiding their embrace, or the impending collision.

With only instants to spare, Aelfred bellowed, "Down a-port, *hard!*"

The blunt bow of the hammership dropped, and the ship swung rapidly to the left.

Impact! Even with his grip on the rail, the shock almost flung Teldin across the turret, and his left shoulder felt like his arm was being torn from the socket. He fought to keep his feet. Belowdecks he heard crashing as inadequately secured equipment, and perhaps even people, smashed into bulkheads and decks.

With a rush of fierce excitement, Teldin understood Aelfred's plan. The last-moment maneuver had changed the *Probe*'s course. Instead of driving full into the deathspider's bridge, the hammership's ram had instead smashed into the lower left-hand leg of the neogi vessel's grappling ram, near its root. It was the same leg that had been damaged by one of the *Probe*'s early catapult shots. In its entirety, the impetus of both massive vessels had been concentrated on that single spot. No matter how strong the material that made up the grappling ram, a single leg could only be so thick, and its structure was already seriously damaged. The iron-ribbed crystal had fractured, and the entire leg had been torn away from the vessel.

The massive black bulk of the deathspider slipped by, directly above the deck of the hammership. With a splintering of wood, the top one-third of the mainmast—and the crow's nest, thankfully empty—was carried away. Teldin's eardrums popped with a change in air pressure, and his balance swam as giddily as it had when the pirate wasp passed near the gnomish longboat.

Teldin looked over the turret rail to the forecastle deck. Vallus Leafbower had somehow kept his feet and was weaving intricate patterns in the air before him with delicate fingers. Although the elf was speaking for himself alone, the fluid syllables of the spell he was constructing easily carried through the sounds of chaos. Teldin could feel the power the elf mage was wielding; the hair on the backs of his hands stirred, and the air on the forecastle had the biting odor of a thunderstorm.

The incantation reached its climax, and the elf thrust a rigid finger out toward the underside of the deathspider. A beam of harsh green light lashed out from his fingertip and struck the deathspider in the middle of the thin "neck" connecting the head with the abdomen. Where the beam struck, the crystal of the hull exploded into dust. The dull red light within the spidership shone out through a ragged-edged hole in the hull. The great black ship groaned, as though in torment.

"Down a-port!" Aelfred yelled again. There was no response; the *Probe*'s course didn't change. "Down a-port!" the first mate repeated. "What the hell's going on . . . ?"

The mind flayer's mental voice cut him off. *The helm is down. Vila is unconscious.*

Aelfred's answer was a warrior's curse.

Vallus faced the first mate calmly. "Shall I . . . ?"

"No!" Aelfred fought his anger under control again. "No," he repeated, more calmly. "We'll need you on deck before long." He thought for a moment, then smiled. "Get that gnome—Saliman, is that his name? Get him on the helm, then get back up here *fast*, got it?"

The elf nodded his understanding and ran for the ladder to

the main deck. Aelfred looked up at the deathspider, still passing by above his head. His expression was grim.

Well it should be, Teldin realized. Liono had counseled against getting into the spidership's rear arc, and that's just where they were going to end up. There was nothing they could do about it, until the gnomish cleric took the helm and got the hammership under control.

The deathspider was almost past. "Take cover!" Aelfred roared.

Teldin looked around him. There was little enough cover here in the turret. He felt a tug on his arm. It was Dana. "Down here," she urged, pointing to the ruins of the ballista. It wasn't much, but it was better than nothing. They crouched beneath the smashed weapon, taking what little shelter they could. Teldin glanced up.

The deathspider had passed. Through a gap in the underside of the abdomen he saw what looked like a series of small catapults. Figures moved around the weapons, silhouettes against the dim red light within the vessel. Most looked vaguely human, but some were misshapen figures out of nightmares. As one, the multiple catapults fired. Teldin forced his body backward, pressing himself as close to the ballista's swivel mount as possible.

Not a moment too soon. There was a hiss, like sudden, heavy rain or hail, but this hail wasn't frozen water. A momentary deluge of small projectiles lashed against the deck: pebbles, scraps of metal, iron spikes, even some things that looked like fragments of shattered bone.

The rain of missiles lasted for only an instant, then there was silence, then the screaming began, cries of agony from all over the vessel. Teldin looked over at Dana. She appeared unharmed, but the other ballista crewman had tried to hide against the forward wall of the turret and hadn't been so lucky. His gray jerkin was already turning the color of burgundy, as he clutched uncomprehendingly at two jagged rips in his chest. His mouth worked silently as he turned pleading eyes on Teldin. A trickle of blood appeared at the corner of his mouth.

There's nothing I can do. The words echoed inside Teldin's mind. I know nothing of medicine. There's nothing I can do for you. He wanted to shout it out loud, but his throat was tight with horror.

Dana squeezed his arm, almost painfully. "I'll see what I can do," she told him. "Others may need help elsewhere."

He took a deep breath, forcing himself back under control, and nodded. He climbed from the turret to the forecastle deck.

The group of officers hadn't fared badly, and injuries seemed minor. Aelfred had a deep cut on his brow and was forced to keep wiping blood from his eyes. Estriss oozed silvery-white plasma from half a dozen minor nicks, while Bubbo paid absolutely no attention to a gash in his right arm that would have incapacitated any other man.

Things were considerably worse elsewhere. Of the crew on the main deck, perhaps one quarter were down—either disabled or dead—and most of the rest were injured in one way or another.

Aelfred cursed viciously. "If they keep pounding us with that jettison, we're dead."

Liono shook his head. "I don't think that's their plan," he said quietly.

All heads turned to observe the deathspider. The huge vessel had slowed down and was maneuvering. Ponderously but unmistakably, it was coming about. The stern, with its deadly jetsam—and, presumably, other heavy weapons—was swinging away. The three remaining legs of the grappling ram opened slowly.

"They're coming back to grapple," Aelfred muttered. "Why? Until the helm's up again, we're helpless. They can pound us to space dust."

Liono shrugged. "Slave hunt?" he proposed. "Or maybe they think we'll get away if they don't take us now."

Vallus reappeared up the ladder from the main deck. As always, the elf looked totally unruffled.

"Is the gnome on the helm?" Aelfred asked him.

"He's on it, but it will take time for him to gain control of it." The elf smiled gently. "He claims it's different from—and inferior to—the gnomish helms he's used to."

"Damn. How long?"

Vallus shrugged. "Minutes."

"Too long," the warrior pronounced. The deathspider had completed its turn and was moving slowly back toward the *Probe*. The hammership was now broadside-on, presenting its starboard side to the neogi vessel. "Can we maneuver at all?" Nobody answered, and that was answer enough. "Stand by to repel boarders."

The first mate's quiet order was relayed throughout the ship. Crewmen who'd been on damage control duty below flooded out onto the decks. Everywhere around him Teldin saw men and women—those who could still move—readying their weapons, preparing to fight and perhaps die. For his own part, Teldin was surprised to feel very little fear. Oh, certainly his stomach churned sickly, and he felt pricks of cold sweat on his brow, but now that the doubt and the waiting was coming to an end, now that battle was certain, he felt none of the incapacitating terror he'd expected at facing neogi again. He'd do what he could; what more could be expected of any man?

Can we take them? Teldin felt the words in his mind, but he knew Estriss had directed the question at Aelfred.

The burly warrior shrugged. "It'll be close," he said. "Neogi ships are manned by slaves, and slaves never fight as well as a free crew. If it looks like the monsters are on the losing end, some of the slaves will probably turn on them. Even without that . . ." His practiced eyes flicked about, coolly evaluating the tactical situation. "When they grapple, they've got to come over the bow. That's narrow, less than thirty feet, which means they can't send too many at once. We can pack everyone along the starboard rail and kill 'em as they try to come aboard. If we're lucky . . ." He paused, then turned to Vallus. "Have you got anything left that can get us out of the ram?"

The mage nodded. "I have another disintegrate spell."

"When the gnome's got the helm up, use it," Aelfred told him. "Until then, do whatever you can do to make trouble for them. And keep an eye on their forward ballistae. If they've got someone with brains commanding the crews, they'll be trying to take out anyone throwing spells."

Vallus nodded again. "Leave it to me," he said calmly.

The deathspider loomed closer, the three remaining legs of

the grappling ram beginning to close. Teldin could see the weapons deck in the upper arc of the ship's abdomen. There was a milling crowd there, packed around the twin ballistae, at least fifty strong. The vast majority were human, but here and there massive, misshapen figures loomed above the pack. Teldin recognized them as umber hulks and knew just how dangerous they were. Some bowmen among the *Probe*'s crew were already firing arrows into the massed enemy, trying to thin out their numbers before the fighting began in earnest. Surprisingly, no missiles had yet struck the hammership.

Twenty yards. The deathspider's three remaining grappling legs already extended past the *Probe*—two above, one below. Crewmen were casting fearful glances at the thin but strong shafts that hung over their heads. To Teldin it looked as though the hammership were already in their grasp. There seemed no way that the vessel could escape, no matter what Vallus thought to the contrary.

Fifty yards. Teldin could see through the central port of the deathspider's head, into the red-lit interior of the great ship's bridge. Silhouettes moved against the light, repulsive shapes that brought back horrible memories from the past weeks. The vessel's neogi masters were watching the final moments of the hammership's capture. Fifteen yards.

With a grinding crash, the *Probe*'s hull struck against the lower of the three grappling legs. Even with the slow rate of approach, the impact was severe, and Teldin kept his feet only with difficulty. The upper two legs started to move, to lower. They moved slowly but inexorably. With a rending of wood, one crushed the starboard rail just aft of the cargo hatch. The second struck the *Probe* five feet aft of the stern turret. The aftmost fin on the starboard side crumpled as though it were made of paper and balsa wood. The movement of the legs stopped. They seemed unable to exert enough pressure to crush, or even seriously damage, the hammership's reinforced hull, but they served their purpose nonetheless. The *Probe* was immobilized.

Sylvie hurried up the ladder from the main deck to join the other officers on the forecastle. Aelfred shot her an angry look. "Your station's below," he snapped.

The slender woman shrugged. "I don't think navigation's

much of an issue at the moment," she said dryly. "I can be more use up here."

Aelfred hesitated for a moment, then nodded. "Go to it," he told them.

Sylvie flashed him one of her momentary smiles. "I intend to." She drew a tiny object from the pouch on her belt. To Teldin it looked like a flat crystal of glasslike material. She then pulled out what looked like a small piece of animal fur. Mumbling fluid syllables under her breath, she rubbed the two gently together. Again Teldin felt the power she wielded grow in the air around her. She hissed the final words of the incantation through clenched teeth. Unlike Vallus's spell, there was no pyrotechnic display. Instead, the spidership's central bow port burst asunder, sending shards of crystal flying in all directions. Teldin heard inhuman shrieks of pain and alarm from within the enemy ship's bridge, and he felt his lips draw back from his teeth in a feral grin. "Hurt them!" he heard his own voice scream.

As if the bursting port had been the signal, the attack began in earnest. Arrows and crossbow bolts rained down on the hammership's deck as the slave bowmen fired their first salvo. The majority of the *Probe*'s crew was under some kind of cover, however—crouched below the starboard gunwale, or concealed behind the ship's small longboat—and casualties were light. The hammership's crew returned fire, with much greater effect, into the massed attackers.

With a hissing roar, something hurtled by over Teldin's head. Ballista bolt, probably, directed at the knot of officers on the forecastle. Aelfred and the others separated, spreading themselves out and eliminating the close grouping of people that must be an attractive target for the deathspider's gunners.

A roar burst from the throats of the neogi vessel's crew members as they charged across the upper surface of the spidership's bridge. The umber hulks who had been among them were now behind them, urging them on, forcing them forward. The hammership's crew was still firing, and the arrows and bolts tore into the front ranks. Teldin saw a man stop, howling in pain, a longbow arrow protruding from his chest. The man threw his weapon down and tried to turn back, to escape the carnage. He tried to force his way through the pack of attackers, back toward the relative safety of the deathspider. For a moment the charge wavered, its momentum broken, then an umber hulk pressed forward and lashed out with an iron-hard claw. The wounded man shrieked again, louder, and his torn and twitching body plunged off the ship and into the darkness, spewing blood. Teldin turned away.

This object lesson wasn't lost on the other attackers. They rushed forward once more, with even more vigor.

Aelfred had been right in his analysis. The bridge section of the deathspider was narrow, which meant that not all the attackers could advance at once. They came forward in waves, full into the devastating fire of the hammership's crew. Men rushed forward, under the urging of the umber hulks . . . and they died. "We're holding them," Aelfred muttered.

But the situation couldn't last for long. Some of the umber hulks forced their way to the front of the attacking group, knocking humans aside like dolls, tumbling unfortunates over the side of the vessel into space. The *Probe*'s defenders kept firing, but their murderous barrage couldn't stop the armored monsters' advance. Arrows glanced harmlessly off the creatures' shells; bolts lodged in plates of natural armor, but didn't penetrate. The monstrosities continued their approach across the deathspider's bridge.

"Vallus!" Aelfred shouted.

The elf was already weaving the power of another spell. He extended one hand, fingers outspread, toward the attacking monsters. An arrow seemed to spring from the tips of his fingers, driving deep into the chest of the leading hulk. It bellowed its agony, tearing at its own flesh as if to pluck out the arrow, then collapsed to the deck.

Sylvie had joined the fray as well. In response to her incantation, a dozen or more rubbery, black tentacles burst from the spidership's hull and wrapped themselves around the legs and torsos of the advancing hulks. Some of the creatures quickly tore the tentacles away; others weren't so lucky. Teldin watched in mixed awe and horror as several of the tentacles tightened around their victims, immobilizing them, and started to crush their hard carapaces. One umber hulk lurched back, one arm virtually torn away, and fell into the darkness. Another collapsed where it stood, its head a shattered ruin.

Mighty though it was, the magical assault wasn't enough to stop the attack. Half a dozen hulks still survived, though most of those were wounded to one degree or another. As the mages paused to prepare new spells, the attackers lumbered forward. With rattling barks of triumph, the creatures reached the hammership's rail and swung their massive bodies over. Still being forced along by the remaining hulks, the human slaves followed the gruesome shock troops. The second phase of the defense of the *Probe* had begun.

The main deck was a pandemonium of brawling figures. Packs of *Probe* crewmen harried individual umber hulks, striking at the monsters' backs and flanks, desperately struggling to stay out of reach of the creatures' rending claws. Others fought in knots, or one on one, against the human and demihuman attackers from the deathspider. The air was filled with screams of rage and agony and grunts of exertion, punctuated by the umber hulks' barking cries. Above all was the clash and skirl of steel on steel.

Sweor Tobregdan, Aelfred's second mate, bellowed orders from the sterncastle, trying to direct the defense. If there was any plan to the fight, however, Teldin couldn't see it. People fought where they had to, or where an opportunity presented itself. This wasn't organized warfare, with its lines of offense and defense, coordinated sorties, and countercharges. This was more like a barroom brawl: no order, no central command, and no quarter asked or given.

The second mate must have seen the futility of yelling orders that nobody could hear, because he leaped down the ladder to the main deck and threw himself into the fray. Almost instantly, four of the deathspider's human crewmen sprang at him, and he went down under them.

"*Sweor!*" Aelfred yelled. He made to leap into the midst of the fray and somehow cut his way to where his friend needed him, but Bubbo's hand landed heavily on his shoulder. For a moment, the big warrior fought—vainly—to escape the grip of the even bigger weapons master. Then reason quieted Aelfred's anger. He nodded his thanks to Bubbo.

Sweor needed no help, as it turned out. An instant later, he reappeared, his clothing and blade drenched with blood—not his own—leaving his erstwhile adversaries motionless on the deck.

Another spell split the air. A fan of seven shimmering multicolored rays lashed from Vallus's outstretched hands and struck two umber hulks on the deck below. One fell instantly lifeless, a huge, smoking rent torn in the armor of its chest. The other screamed its agony, flailing about wildly with an arm now blackened and twisted and missing perhaps half of its length. The *Probe* crewmen who faced the beast seized the opportunity. Two lunged in on its other flank and buried their swords hilt-deep in the creature's abdomen. The hulk lashed out with its good arm, striking one of its attackers with back-breaking force, but a crewman on the other side crouched low and swung his axe at the monster's ankle. It connected and, with another ear-splitting shriek, the creature crashed to the deck. Its assailants were on it at once.

Teldin didn't see the creature's death. A clash of steel on steel from close by drew his attention. Some of the attackers were trying to reach the forecastle, he saw at once. Two were trying to climb the starboard ladder from the main deck. Liono was holding them off, and they hadn't yet reached the forecastle deck itself, but their swordwork was good enough— even on the ladder—that the aged tactician was unable to kill them. Other attackers were swarming up the port ladder, and Bubbo was lumbering over to deal with them. Teldin hefted Gendi's short sword and felt the tension of fear in the tendons of his forearm.

With no warning, a spear hissed past Teldin's ear and drove, quivering, into the side of the forward turret. Another slammed into Liono's ribs, transfixing his thin body. The tactician fell silently. Teldin looked around wildly for the new attackers.

The assault was coming from a totally new direction. Some of the deathspider's crew had managed to clamber over onto the lobe that extended from the starboard side of the *Probe*'s hull—in fact, onto the metalwork that formed the roof of the officer's saloon. Teldin estimated maybe a dozen men, being herded forward by another umber hulk.

"Starboard side forward!" Teldin bellowed at the top of his lungs. He pointed toward the new danger.

It was Sylvie who reacted first. She spun and again hissed syllables of power. A chunk of metal-braced wood from the shattered ballista lifted from the deck and was hurled with inhuman force into the new group of attackers. Several fell, screaming, but the others had reached the forecastle and were now in the partial shelter of the forward turret. Aelfred and Sylvie hurried forward to engage them. Teldin moved to follow his friends.

At the last instant, his peripheral vision spotted motion. Instinctively he ducked . . . and another spear whistled over his head, to glance off the turret side and disappear over the rail.

With Liono gone, his two opponents, followed by a handful of others, had reached the forecastle deck unopposed. Teldin saw one leap toward Estriss, sword swinging to cleave the mind flayer's head in two. He tried to yell a warning to his friend—friend? *yes!*—but sickeningly knew it was too late.

Estriss made no move to defend himself. The creature just turned featureless, white eyes on its murderer.

And suddenly the attacker arched backward, as though he'd been struck full in the face by a tremendous blow. The attacker screamed, clutching his head with both hands. His sword clattered to the deck.

With a sinuous speed that Teldin had never seen from the illithid before, Estriss lunged forward and flung himself atop the writhing man. Red-tinged hands pried the man's own hands away from his head. Estriss bent low, and his facial tentacles lashed out to cup the human's skull. The neogi slave screamed again. . . .

Nausea and horror washed over Teldin, and he turned away.

He was just in time. Two attackers were moving his way, weapons at the ready. Teldin tightened his grip on his sword and dropped into the defensive stance that Aelfred had shown him. He backed away cautiously. His two opponents advanced, no less tentatively, and separated as though to flank him. Both were scrawny men, he noticed, actually emaciated. Their eyes looked wild, almost insane. One was about his own size, while the other was considerably taller, but neither could have weighed nearly as much as he did. The larger man was naked to the waist, and Teldin could easily see his ribs showing under his skin. On the man's upper left chest was some kind of discoloration. It took him a moment to understand that it was a tattoo of some kind, a marking totally alien in its symbology.

Disgust and pity warred with his fear. This had to be the mark identifying the slave's owner.

With a grunt of exertion, the larger man lunged forward, thrusting the point of his sword directly at Teldin's throat.

The almost familiar sense of focus closed over Teldin's mind like a reassuring blanket. Once again his time sense changed. His attacker's fast thrust became something that was so slow as to be almost lethargic. Teldin had plenty of time to gauge the man's attack and judge that the thrust could be deflected if he positioned his own weapon . . . *there*.

His sword came up fast. Steel rang on steel, and the attacker's blade deflected past Teldin's shoulder. The man's weight shift carried him on, and Teldin found himself staring into the man's surprised face. As a continuation of his own parry, Teldin drove his fist out. His knuckles, backed by the mass and momentum of his sword hilt, slammed into the man's jaw with stunning force. The big man's head snapped back on his neck, and his eyes glazed with pain.

The other attacker was moving, too, aiming a whistling cut at Teldin's side. Teldin had plenty of time to bring his own blade around to parry that attack, too. When their blades struck, Teldin was braced and ready, but still the impact jarred painfully up his arm. The small man was already dropping back to avoid Teldin's thrust.

The point is mightier than the edge. Aelfred's words rang in Teldin's head. *But the short sword does have an edge.* Quickly, before his small assailant could jump completely out of the way, Teldin snapped his wrist straight, the way Aelfred had done. His blade licked out like silver death, scribing a thick line of red across his attacker's belly. The smaller man staggered back, howling, arms clutching his abdomen as if to keep his entrails where they belonged.

The larger attacker had shaken off the effects of Teldin's blow and was moving in again. Teldin feinted once for the man's face, then tried to thrust into his belly when his opponent raised his guard. Although everything around him still seemed to be moving in slow motion, Teldin's own motions were starting to slow, too. His opponent had fallen for the feint but still managed to bring his blade back down in time to parry Teldin's lunge. The big man countered with a cut that would have torn Teldin's chest open if he hadn't danced back out of range.

Sweat stung Teldin's eyes, and the tendons in his forearm burned with fatigue. The cloak—if that was what was responsible for this—could focus his mind, he realized, but it could do little for his body. And he was no hardened and conditioned swordsman.

His eyes met those of his attacker. They were empty, devoid of any human feeling. Still, Teldin thought, inexplicably, they were capable of reading Teldin's doubts in his own eyes. As if to confirm that, the big man smiled.

Teldin knew no tactics, no skillful techniques with the short sword. With the knife he'd been taught various moves—the flick thrust, the wrist cut, even the throw—but to drop his sword and draw his knife would be suicide. The only thing that Aelfred had taught him was the lunge, and he used it.

His blade licked out like a striking serpent, straight for his opponent's heart. The big man was still slightly open after his wild cut, and his parry was late. There was no way he could get his blade back in time to deflect the thrust. Satisfaction, even exultation, dimly penetrated Teldin's almost unemotional concentration.

Then something slammed with crushing force into Teldin's wrist. His arm was batted aside, and his sword flew from suddenly numbed fingers. He staggered backward.

The man hadn't had enough time to parry the thrust properly, Teldin knew, but he *had* found just enough time to smash the pommel of his sword into Teldin's wrist.

The pain of the impact was incredible. His wrist must be broken, Teldin thought. He took another couple of steps away from the big swordsman, clutching his injured arm to his belly. His back pressed against the port rail of the forecastle. There was nowhere to run. Even now, with death imminent, he saw the ironic parallel between this moment and his first meeting with Estriss.

Maybe it was the pain that broke the effect, but Teldin's intense sense of focus evaporated. His time sense returned to normal, and the fear that had been somehow held in abeyance crashed through his body like a mighty wave. Teldin's killer stepped forward, a smile splitting his face. Teldin looked into the man's eyes. They were empty, almost soulless. There would be no mercy here. The man drew back his blade, readying for the cut that would tear Teldin in two.

Chapter Seven

• • •

He was looking death in the face, Teldin realized. Out of the corner of his eye he saw the figure of Estriss, racing to his aid, but he knew the illithid would arrive much too late. His killer's sword flashed downward. With an inarticulate cry, Teldin reached out toward the descending sword arm, a futile attempt to fend off destruction.

And power flared—behind him, around him, within him. The cloak around his neck crackled with power. His skin tingled with it; his bones burned with it. The feeling was like lying naked under the noontime sun, but infinitely magnified. He felt that the very bones of his body must be glowing with the blue-white radiance of lightning, their brilliance shining right through his skin. He flung his head back and he *howled*, as though the sound had been ripped out of him. He thrust his hand out—no longer to block his attacker's slash, now directly toward the big man's chest.

His howl turned to a scream of agony—or was it ecstacy? Tiny, burning lights burst from his outstretched fingers. Intense, three-pointed stars—dazzling, almost blinding—sizzled through the air, forming a curtain, a curved shield of light, between him and his adversary. Teldin could see the shock dawn in the swordsman's eyes, but it was much too late for the man to check his swing. The sword struck that hissing curtain.

There was a crack like thunder. The sword's blade stopped

as suddenly as if it had hit a stone wall. For an instant it was frozen there, glowing with the same actinic radiance as the curtain itself, then it exploded into tiny fragments. The swordsman reeled back, screaming in terror. His body was covered, head to toe, with tiny nicks from the splinters of his own sword. He stared with horror and disbelief at Teldin, then he turned and fled the foredeck.

As suddenly as it had sprung into being, the sizzling curtain of light vanished. Teldin lowered his arm. The sense of power was gone; no trace of it remained. In its place, coldness and weakness washed through him. His heart pounded, and he gasped with exertion and horror.

How? *How* could he have done that? He knew that the power came from outside of him, from the cloak—there was no doubt about that now. But *how*? How was it triggered, and why? What was its purpose?

He shook his head. Now was definitely not the time. With an ultimate effort, he forced his questions, his doubt, from the forefront of his mind. *Later*, he told himself, *if there is a later.*

The balance of the battle had swung in favor of the *Probe*'s crew, Teldin saw quickly. The majority of the attackers—human and monstrous—lay dead on the hammership's deck. Most of the remainder were actually trying to withdraw, back onto the deathspider from the killing ground that the *Probe*'s deck had become. There were pockets of resistance where the attackers were still holding out—mainly centered around the two surviving umber hulks—but in most other places aboard the hammership the battle had degenerated into mopping up.

There was still fighting on the *Probe*'s foredeck. Aelfred, now assisted by Bubbo and Estriss and two other crewmen, was driving a desperate group of attackers back. There was nowhere for them to go except out onto the upper surface of the officers' saloon. From there, they'd have to clamber back onto the deathspider's grappling leg and thence to the big ship's bridge, all the while being harried by the *Probe*'s best warriors. If they didn't make it, they'd fall into space. From his vantage point, Teldin could see a dozen bodies floating in space along the deathspider's gravity plane. They bobbed gently as though floating in water and were slowly moving outward from the ship. It was as though they were being drawn toward the margin of the air envelope that surrounded the ships. Presumably, when they reached the edge of that envelope—and the edge of the ship's gravitational effect—they'd drift in the phlogiston, free of any gravity.

Most of the remaining bodies were obviously and messily dead, but a few still moved and called feebly for help. Nobody aboard the deathspider paid them any attention, and the crew of the *Probe* was too busy to help them.

There was a cry from the foredeck. One of the attackers, with a sudden burst of fury, had broken through the cordon of hammership crewmen. The man was bleeding profusely from a dozen wounds, but he was still very much alive. His wild, empty eyes fixed on Teldin, and he rushed forward, swinging his notched broadsword.

Desperately, Teldin snatched up the short sword he'd dropped and brought the weapon up to block the mighty cut that would have taken his head off. The blades clashed, and Teldin cried out at the agony that shot through his wrist at the impact. He backpedaled quickly, keeping the sword out before him. Sweat blurred his vision, and the tendons of his forearm burned like fire. The light sword in his hand felt like a bar of lead. He sought within him, desperately, for the calm, the focus he'd felt earlier, but there was no response—either from the cloak or from within himself. Maybe the flare of power had drained all energy from the cloak, or perhaps in his exhausted state he was simply unable to call it forth.

If he'd *ever* been able to call it. Even at the best of times, the power he'd felt had never been anything he could really depend on.

He blocked another swing, deflecting his opponent's blade so that it clove the air above Teldin's head. While the man was open, Teldin tried to lunge, but his movements were slow and his enemy jumped back in plenty of time. It was all Teldin could do to get his own blade in position to parry the man's cat-quick riposte.

There was no hope that he was going to last, Teldin realized dully. The man he faced was a good swordsman, infinitely more skilled than Teldin, and the man seemed almost fresh, unaffected by the wounds that had turned his clothing burgundy. Teldin had just managed to block his preliminary attacks, but there was no way that would last. If nothing else, the man would be able to wear Teldin down until he couldn't hold his sword up anymore, then the broadsword would end his life.

He had to do something desperate. He backed away again to give himself a few precious moments. With his left hand he drew his belt knife and turned the weapon so he held it by the broad base of the blade. His enemy stepped forward again, readying for another cut.

Teldin yelled—a last-ditch attempt to distract the swordsman—and simultaneously flipped his knife out in an underarm throw. The blade flashed in the flow-light, and sank into the left side of the man's belly. He cried out with pain. Teldin lunged, but his enemy was better than that. Even distracted by the agony of the knife in his guts, he was easily able to bring his sword down and parry Teldin's thrust.

Teldin threw himself back again, barely evading his opponent's riposte. The swordsman stepped forward once more, and Teldin looked into his eyes. They were dull with pain, and with something more than pain. The man was dying; he knew it and Teldin knew it, but the swordsman also knew that he'd have more than enough time for one last kill before he collapsed. Teldin tried to yell, to scream for help, but his throat was too tight. The only sound he could make was a pitiful croak. The man raised his sword for a final strike.

Teldin heard a swish and a meaty *thunk*. The swordsman lurched forward, the broad head of a spear growing—magically, it seemed—out of his chest. Teldin looked for a moment into uncomprehending eyes, then the eyes closed and the man collapsed.

Teldin saw Aelfred across the forecastle. The big man was still following through after his spear cast. The spear, Teldin realized, was the one that had been buried in the forward turret wall. The warrior had torn it out and thrown it at the last instant. Aelfred smiled grimly, then drew his sword again and rejoined the fray on the foredeck.

Exhaustion and the aftereffects of terror hit Teldin like a blow. His belly cramped, and it was all he could do to stop himself from retching. His sword arm hung limply by his side. If another enemy came upon him like this, he realized, he wouldn't even be able to move while the other struck him dead.

But there were no other enemies on the forecastle. Vallus stood by the starboard rail, as unruffled as always. He gave Teldin a reassuring smile. Teldin crossed the deck to join him.

As he did, the *Probe* lurched slightly beneath his feet.

The helm is operating. Estriss's "voice" was crystal-clear in his mind.

"Vallus, do it!" Aelfred ordered.

The elf mage hadn't waited for the instruction. Once more his hands wove the threads of magic. His voice echoed across the deck. Again the blinding lance of green light shot from his fingertip, this time striking the root of the remaining grappling leg beneath the *Probe*. Black crystal exploded into dust, and the slender leg sheared off cleanly at its base. The hammership lurched again.

"Get us out of here!" Aelfred bellowed.

Slowly at first, but with ever-increasing speed, the *Probe* dropped away from the deathspider. With both lower legs gone, there was nothing to hold it from beneath, nothing to prevent its escape. As the hammership drew away, Vallus delivered one final stroke. Multicolored beams of light slashed through the void once more, this time striking directly *through* the spidership's bow port that had been shattered by an earlier spell.

"I take it the helm is on the bridge?" the elf said dryly.

Aelfred smiled broadly. "You take it right." He patted Vallus on the shoulder. "That should slow them down, maybe permanently. Good move."

The hammership accelerated away from the deathspider. It changed course rapidly, just once, to avoid the severed leg that was wheeling slowly through space, then it poured on the speed. The distance between the ships grew rapidly. As if to bear out Aelfred's words, the hideous ship remained stationary, presumably unable to pursue. It would only be minutes before the *Probe* could accelerate to its full spelljamming speed, then there would be little chance that the neogi could catch them.

Teldin watched the receding spidership. The space around it was littered with debris—fragments from the shattered leg, small chunks of hull, and the small shapes that were the dead and dying. He was glad when the distance was so great that he could no longer see those figures.

When the hammership pulled away from the deathspider, the situation on deck changed drastically. There were half a dozen human attackers and one umber hulk still alive. As soon as it was obvious that the *Probe* had escaped, most of the humans immediately threw down their weapons and surrendered, begging the hammership's crew for mercy. The others turned on the single remaining hulk, attacking it ferociously. With the full surviving complement of the *Probe* plus the erstwhile slaves attacking it, the monster didn't last long. Teldin heard its barking shrieks getting fainter and fainter, then the monster was silent.

Teldin looked around the ship. Casualties had been horrendous. Most of the dead were the unarmored and lightly armed slaves from the deathspider, but many of the *Probe*'s crew had fallen as well. Sweor Tobregdan lay on the main deck, coughing out his last breaths in bright blood. Teldin spotted Miggins crumpled against the port rail. The young gnome was still alive—barely—but he clutched the torn ruin of what had been his left arm. Liono, the spear still transfixing his chest, lay on the starboard side of the forecastle. The cloying smell of blood was thick in the air, and Teldin's ears were filled with the moans of the injured and dying. The *Probe* was like a charnel house.

Teldin slumped down against the forward turret and let the sword slip from his cramped hand. His stomach knotted with nausea. So many dead. He remembered the other battlefields he'd seen and recalled Aelfred's words: To the Nine Hells with the fools who think it's glorious. The big warrior was right. There was no glory in battle, just horror, pain, and death.

Dully he looked up to see Aelfred standing at the forecastle's aft rail, surveying the carnage below. The big man had bound a cloth around his brow to staunch the bleeding of his head wound. Small wounds showed almost everywhere on the warrior's body, but he seemed unaware of them. He shook his head and bent down to clean his blade on the shirt of someone who had no further use for it.

A junior officer—Julia, Teldin thought her name was—climbed the ladder from the main deck to the forecastle. Teldin had always thought she looked pert and attractive with her short-cropped red hair and petite figure. Now she was covered in blood, and she looked utterly exhausted.

Aelfred looked up as he heard her approach. "Report," he said quietly.

The woman's voice was dull, as though she were tired unto death. "Limited structural damage," she responded, "nothing serious. We're spaceworthy."

"Casualties?"

"Fourteen dead, to my knowledge. Four missing that I know about: Shandess, Morla, Zeb, and Kevan. Probably overboard and dead—" she paused "—maybe captured."

Aelfred shook his head. "Let's hope dead," he said flatly.

Teldin recognized one of the names. Shandess was the old man who'd spoken to him on the foredeck immediately after they'd passed into the flow. He looked back at the receding deathspider and remembered the tattoo on the shoulder of one of his attackers, the wild, soul-destroyed look in his eyes. He nodded to himself. *Let's hope dead.*

"Can we run the ship?" Aelfred continued.

Julia nodded. "Just. If we use the slaves to help, we should be all right. In no shape for another battle, but all right."

Estriss joined the two at the rail. There was blood on the tips of his facial tentacles: red blood, human blood. Teldin tried to blot the significance of that from his mind. *Do we trust them?* the illithid asked.

"We have to," Aelfred said flatly, then amended, "to some extent, at least. I've seen this before. They'll work for us—we saved them from the neogi, remember?—and they'll follow orders. It's the slave mentality." He swore viciously, then forced himself to be calm. "They'll follow orders," he repeated, "but that's all they'll be good for. Don't expect any initiative, any motivation. Sometimes they can come back, learn to think for themselves. Sometimes. It all depends on how long they were on the deathspider, what happened to them there."

Teldin looked away. His fear was draining from him, but horror and disgust still remained.

"Teldin."

He turned at the sound of his own name. An exhausted-looking Horvath was approaching across the forecastle. He was carrying something, a bundle not much smaller than the gnome himself. "Teldin," he said again.

Teldin struggled to his feet. He read in the gnome's expression, in the dullness of his voice, what the burden must be, but knowing and seeing were two different things. He didn't want to look at the bundle that the gnome had set gently down on the deck, but he had to. He stood beside his friend and looked down.

It was Dana, as he knew it had to be. Her face was peaceful, at rest, for the first time in his experience. Her eyes were closed, and her lips were curved in a faint smile. She could have been asleep, if it hadn't been for the great wound in her chest.

"She wanted to see you," Horvath said, his voice cracking with emotion. "She wanted me to take her to you, but she went before I could reach you."

Teldin's heart was cold in his chest, and tears that he couldn't let himself shed stung behind his eyes. If he let himself cry, he thought, he'd never be able to stop. Hers was another death, another innocent laid at his feet, this time quite literally. The responsibility was his. He and his burden had brought death to another friend. He knelt beside the still shape and laid a hand tenderly against her cheek.

The cold in his breast burst into fire. He threw back his head and howled his torment and fury at the colors of the flow. "Damn you!" he screamed. "*Damn you to the Abyss!*" If anyone had asked, he couldn't have told who he was cursing. The neogi, the dying stranger who'd laid this burden—this curse—on him . . . or maybe himself.

A soft hand was on his shoulder. He tried to shake it off, but the grip strengthened. He looked up into Sylvie's troubled eyes. "I'll take you below," the half-elf said gently.

His anger faded to a dull ache. He hung his head. "All right," he mumbled. Horvath and Sylvie helped him to his feet, and she led him away.

* * * * *

Prissith Nerro walked through the red-lit slave quarters of the deathspider. All around, the neogi could hear the sibilant speech of others of its kind, the rattling growls of umber hulks, the moans of the surviving slaves. Normally it would feel the fierce and burning pride that came with viewing its possessions: its slaves, its umber hulk lordservants, its lesser neogi kin-slaves, most of all the great ship itself, the *Void Reaper*. Now the pride was submerged under a tide of anger. Nerro hissed its rage and frustration. It wanted to lash out with its jaws, to tear the flesh of a human slave, to taste its victim's hot blood, but it knew that too many slaves had already died today, that it couldn't spare another even for the worthy purpose of settling its own troubled spirit.

Another neogi was in the hallway ahead of Nerro, sidling forward tentatively, its claws clicking on the crystal deck. The pattern of colored dye on the other neogi's fur identified it as second in command of the *Void Reaper*. Prissith Ulm, its name was. Prissith Nerro could smell its brood-brother's fear, and that, at least, was some consolation. The prize that Nerro sought was still out of its reach—perhaps farther than ever, after today's failure—but at least the overlord knew that it still commanded the fear and respect of its underlings.

"Prissith Nerro Master," the subordinate neogi hissed, bobbing its head in a gesture of respect. "The captive meat is prepared, as you commanded."

Nerro snarled its satisfaction. "Take me to it," it ordered.

The captive human was in one of the slave cells. He lay on a hard wooden pallet, his limbs bound to prevent escape or attack. His clothing had been ripped away, leaving him naked and defenseless. Nerro examined him with a stirring of interest. The man was old, obviously, older than any neogi slave would be allowed to become. His body was withered, his white skin wrinkled. Nerro found itself wondering how the prey's flesh would taste, whether age would improve or worsen the flavor, then it dismissed the thought. This food was probably too old to be palatable, except in an emergency. Once again, Nerro found itself wondering at the strange habits of these humans. Why would they leave one such as this to survive for so long? To eat the food that could be given to other, more deserving, creatures? To decay? It was sheer waste, and waste disgusted and angered Prissith Nerro.

The human was unconscious, Nerro noted. Possibly blood loss from the deep wound that marred the man's chest. Nerro brought its head closer to that wound and sniffed. Withered or not, the creature's blood still smelled appetizing.

"Prissith Nerro Master," Prissith Ulm said softly.

Nerro turned on it with a spit of anger. "What?" it demanded.

"We believe it is dying, Prissith Nerro Master."

Nerro considered for a moment. "If this is true," it hissed, "it is well you told me." There was much to do, to learn, and if the time remaining to do so was limited, it was best to know it. "Wake it," Prissith Nerro ordered.

* * * * *

All Shandess knew was pain. His body burned with it, his thoughts were filled with it. Darkness was all around him, and the darkness danced with pain.

He was vaguely aware of his body. He knew that he lay on his back upon a hard surface, and he knew that he wasn't cold. Most of all, though, he knew that his chest hurt with an agony that spoke unmistakably of approaching death.

Something grasped his jaw, forced his mouth open. He felt something cold and hard being driven cruelly between his teeth, then a liquid struck the back of his throat, a liquid that burned like all the cheap liquor he'd drunk on a dozen planets, all combined into one harsh draft. He coughed, and agony tore at his chest. This must be death, he thought.

Somehow, though, he didn't die. In fact, he felt a little control returning to his body and mind. After the initial burst of torment, the pain seemed to retreat to a manageable level. He forced his eyes open.

For a moment, his brain couldn't make sense of what he was seeing, then the meaning penetrated. He screwed his eyes shut again to block out the scene—to deny the reality of it, if he could. He would have screamed in horror, but he couldn't draw a deep enough breath.

He was in a small room or a cell, perhaps five feet wide and not much more than that long. Walls and ceiling were dull black, and the only illumination came from a small disk overhead that glowed with a dim, blood-red light. Two faces were above him, looking down at him. Not human faces. They were more like the heads of giant snakes—or perhaps the moray eels he'd seen on one of the worlds he'd visited. Their grinning mouths were filled with needlelike teeth, and their small eyes were red-tinged and staring.

Shandess knew he was dying, but he also knew, suddenly, that there were some things he feared more than death. Instinctively, he tried to fend off the hideous creatures with his hands but found his wrists—and his ankles, when he tried to move them—securely bound. He whimpered deep in his throat.

"Withered meat, eyes open." That voice could never have come from a human throat. It was the voice of a giant snake, if such a creature could have the power of speech. From the order of the words, Shandess could tell the monster was struggling with a foreign language. "Meat eyes open," the sibilant voice repeated, "or master eyelids from meat tear."

Shandess forced his eyes open once more. One of the monsters had backed away. It was the nearest one that had spoken.

"Good," the neogi said. "Meat master 'Prissith Nerro Master' call. Meat speak." Shandess couldn't force his throat to work. The monster lashed down with its head until its teeth were a mere hand's span from the old man's face. Its breath, reeking of corruption, washed over him, and its saliva dripped on his face. "Meat speak!"

Shandess forced the words out. His voice was a croak. "Prissith Nerro Master."

The neogi reared back. "Yes," it spat. "Master. Meat obey. If no—" the creature's mouth opened wider into an evil grin "—if no, master meat tear. Master meat rip. Master flesh from bone pull. But meat obey, master meat kill swiftly." The monster's voice became almost wheedling. "Now. Meat questions answer?"

"Yes," Shandess croaked. With blinding speed, the second neogi lashed out with a claw and opened a gash in the old man's arm. "Yes, Prissith Nerro Master!" Shandess shrieked.

"Good," Prissith Nerro breathed. "First. Ship where bound?"

Shandess hesitated. The *Probe*'s destination was no secret, but . . . The second neogi's claw ripped his flesh again. "Realmspace," he screamed.

Nerro nodded. Its wicked smile remained unchanged. "Meat aboard ship," it went on, "master must know about. Meat cloak has. Cloak—" the neogi hesitated "—*power* has, value has. Such power, meat commander must be, inconceivable else. Old meat master tell, of cloak, of meat aboard ship. Old meat master tell everything."

Shandess was confused. Fear, and the monster's garbled language, were making it hard for him to understand what the neogi wanted. Something about a commander . . . Aelfred Silverhorn was the highest-ranking human aboard the *Probe*. That had to be whom the monster was referring to—but to Shandess's knowledge, the first mate had no cloak . . . at least, nothing magical, nothing that could interest this neogi. "I know our leader," he said quickly, "we call him Mate." There was no reason to give this monstrosity Aelfred's name, he decided. "But as to the rest," he went on, "I don't know what you're talking about. He has no cloak."

"Meat lie!" the neogi spat. Then its smile widened, showing more of its needle teeth. "And glad I am. Meat no resist, I feared. Pleasure master denied, I feared."

"I'm not lying!" Shandess yelled. "I'm telling the truth!"

The neogi hardly seemed to be listening. "Pleasure I have now. Knowledge I have later," the creature hissed, almost to itself. "Pleasure." Slowly the monster brought its mouth down toward Shandess's throat. "Now, withered meat," it said quietly, "your taste I will know, after all."

Shandess fought vainly against the bonds. The creature's breath was on his face, then his chest, then his belly. . . . Horror overwhelmed him.

Shandess knew it would serve no purpose to scream, but he screamed anyway.

* * * * *

Teldin Moore sat alone in the *Probe*'s saloon, gazing out at the flow. Although it was nowhere nearly as beautiful as the star-specked sky of wildspace, today the view of the phlogiston served the same purpose. Gazing at the universe, Teldin could temporarily forget—or at least minimize the torment of—his responsibilities, his fears, and his memories. He felt drained, both emotionally and physically. When Sylvie had led him belowdecks, she'd started to take him to his cabin, but he'd had enough mental spark left to know that wouldn't be the right place. Dana was gone, Miggins was in the infirmary—expected to live, but probably missing an arm—and Horvath's presence would have been a reminder that it was all his, Teldin's, responsibility. He'd insisted on visiting the officers' saloon instead, and Sylvie had agreed without argument. As she'd left him, she'd touched his hand and given him a gentle smile. "There are those who can help you," she'd told him softly, then had left him alone, shutting the door behind her. He hadn't known just what to make of her cryptic words, but had recognized that he was hardly in the best condition to puzzle them out. There would always be later.

Teldin could hear the crew moving around the *Probe*'s decks: cleaning up the blood, repairing the damage, and throwing the bodies of the dead overboard. Elsewhere, he knew that the ship's healers were treating those who could be saved and easing the last hours of those who couldn't. Julia, promoted to second mate after the death of Sweor Tobregdan, was seeing to the erstwhile neogi slaves, teaching them what she could about ship routine and explaining their duties. Everybody had duties, the officers most of all, so it wasn't surprising that he was alone in the saloon.

Everyone has duties except me, Teldin thought. They don't know what to do with me. From the start, he'd been more—or perhaps less—than a full member of the hammership's crew. His friendship with Aelfred and the way the big warrior treated him set him apart from the others, and, over the days, that had only increased. The rest of the crew had seen him hobnob with the captain and the first mate, and this he felt was the reason for the respect in which the crew seemed to hold him. Even when he was standing watch, the crew always treated him more like an officer than as one of them. And now?

As Sylvie had led him down from the forecastle, he'd seen the crew's reaction. They'd watched him—all the while trying to pretend they *weren't* watching him—and had moved out of his way, as though they expected three-rayed stars to burst from his fingertips and form a hissing curtain about him. He'd heard somebody mutter, "Fighter-mage," but when he'd turned to see who had said it, no one would meet his glance.

He'd always seemed to come, somehow, to the forefront of any group he was a member of, Teldin had to admit. In general, he got on well with the vast majority of people. Not that they always liked him, or he them, of course, but there was something about his manner that made it possible to deal with virtually anyone. There was no conceit in this admission; it just happened to be the case. After a while, people came to him for advice, and they listened to his answers. Even when he intended to keep his opinion quiet on a particular subject, people would try to secure that opinion from him as though it were something of value. It seemed that the more he remained aloof, the more he tried to stay out of the focus of an issue, the more people would believe his silence was a kind of calm wisdom. Teldin had never been able to understand this. He knew from personal experience that he was no more wise than the majority of people; quite the opposite, perhaps. He found it amusing, albeit somewhat irritating, at times. His grandfather had been like that, too, Teldin remembered, but the old man had shrugged it off with a typical grandfatherly comment: Better to keep your peace and be thought a fool than to open your mouth and remove all doubt. Of course, the aphorism wasn't appropriate: nobody thought grandfather a fool, except for perhaps his son.

The respect—no, more like awe—that he'd seen on the faces of the *Probe*'s crew was something totally different. It wasn't him they respected, he was convinced, it was the power that he'd displayed on the forecastle. They thought of him as a wizard now, someone like Vallus or Sylvie, who could wield spells to protect them, to strike down enemies. They wouldn't understand or believe that he had no control of that power, no knowledge of its source, purpose, or significance. They'd come to depend on him—as he'd come to depend, at least in part, on the focusing power of the cloak—and then the power wouldn't be there, and they'd suffer or die. This realization chilled him. It was yet another burden to bear.

"Ahem." Someone coughed behind him.

He turned quickly to see Aelfred standing in the middle of the saloon, hands on his hips, his lopsided smile in place. The warrior had replaced the bandage around his head with a clean one, Teldin noticed, but Aelfred still looked dirty and tired. "How long have you been there?" he asked.

Aelfred shrugged. "Long enough for you to solve the problems of the universe, maybe." He pulled a chair up near Teldin and flopped down into it.

"How goes it above?"

For a moment, the big man seemed to sag. His exhaustion showed, making him look twenty years older. "Messy." He drew a scarred hand across his eyes. "We lost a lot of good people."

"I know."

Aelfred looked at him a moment, his eyes steady. "Yes," he said quietly, "I suppose you do, as much as any of us. Well." He slapped his palms against his muscular thighs, shaking off his fatigue like a dog shakes off water. "Estriss will be down in a while to speak to you, but, in the meantime . . ." The warrior leaned forward, his voice low and intense, his eyes boring holes into Teldin. "Just what in the name of all the demons of the pit went on up there? First you're fighting like an old hand, much better than you have any right to, and then . . ." He shook his big head in amazement. "And then you're throwing spells like Elminster himself. And *then* you can't even defend yourself against someone who's already half-dead." His voice took on a joking tone, but his eyes remained deadly serious. "Don't you think there's something you should tell me?"

"Yes," Teldin sighed heavily. "I would have told you earlier, but . . ." He paused. "Some of it's as much a surprise to me as it is to you."

And to me. Liquid words formed in Teldin's mind. He looked up to see Estriss standing in the doorway. *My day to be surprised*, he thought. *May I join you?* the illithid asked.

Both Aelfred and Teldin waved the mind flayer to a seat.

"I don't really know what to say," Teldin told his warrior friend. "I should have been honest with you from the start. I just . . ."

Aelfred gestured him to silence. "Water under the keel," he said flatly. "You didn't know if you could trust me, so you held your tongue. If you want to keep breathing in this universe, that's what you've got to do. In fact," he added thoughtfully, "you should still ask yourself that question: Do you trust me? Don't answer too fast. You can always say something later, but you can't *unsay* it." He sat back, watching Teldin calmly.

Teldin considered the big warrior's words for a moment, then nodded. "I'm going to tell you," he said firmly. "What happened today—"

The illithid's mental voice cut him off. *Background is often important*, Estriss said, *and in this case I feel it is key. Perhaps you should start from the beginning.*

Teldin nodded agreement. Quickly but thoroughly he repeated the tale of how he'd come to possess the cloak, of his encounters with the neogi, and how he'd escaped from Krynn with the gnomes. Throughout, Aelfred remained silent, taking it all in. Teldin watched the big man's intelligent eyes. He quickly recognized the flicker that indicated that he'd left something out or hadn't given enough detail, and made sure to remedy that immediately. As a result, there was no need for questions. "That takes us up to today," Teldin eventually concluded.

Aelfred rubbed his tired eyes. "Improbable, incredible, impossible," he grumbled. "If I hadn't seen what I saw today, I wouldn't believe a word of it."

The power is there, Estriss interjected, *and the tale has its own kind of consistency.*

"I know that," Aelfred countered, "and I don't disbelieve you, Teldin. It's just that . . ." He waved his hand in the air to indicate confusion. "I don't understand magic . . . and truth be told, I don't trust it or like it much, not deep down." He sighed. "You've got no idea who these . . . these *creators* are?"

"Estriss believes they might be the Juna," Teldin answered slowly.

Aelfred let out a bark of laughter. "Well, he would, now, wouldn't he? No offense meant, Estriss. It's just that you—or anybody, I'm no different—you're going to see everything through your own interests and preconceptions." He shot

Teldin a keen glance. "What do *you* think?"

Teldin hesitated a moment, then shrugged.

The first mate laughed again. "Playing it close to the chest, I see. Of course you don't know who the creators are. Of course you don't have any suspicions. And of course your interest in the arcane was just coincidental. Well, I freely admit I know nothing of such things." The big man's humor faded, and his face grew serious again. "This cloak has cost a lot," he pointed out quietly.

Teldin felt cold. The cost weighed heavily on him, probably always would. All the deaths—the gnomes in Mount Nevermind, the crewmen aboard the *Probe*—were his fault, and would haunt him for the rest of his life. He nodded miserably.

Aelfred's hand grasped his shoulder and squeezed reassuringly. Teldin looked up. The warrior's expression was still grim, but there was understanding in his eyes. "Don't get me wrong," the first mate told him. "It's cost *you*, too. I'm not blaming you. Nobody who knew the facts could. You had no choice through any of this." He spat a curse. "*Neogi*. May the gods damn them to the lowest pits of the Nine Hells. How did they find us anyway?"

It seems possible the neogi are able to somehow track the cloak, Estriss remarked.

"How?" Teldin demanded, very glad that the conversation was on another subject. "You said you could only sense magic from it when it actually did something."

Estriss gave a broken-backed shrug. *Through the use of my limited abilities, yes,* he admitted, *but that does not mean that others cannot sense it even in its dormant state. In fact, there are many legends that tell how various artifacts have other artifacts that are attuned to them.* The illithid paused. *There is also another possibility. Perhaps, when the cloak's power is used, the characteristics of that power can be detected and recognized from a distance. Did you first experience the powers of the cloak before or after the neogi pursuit began?*

Teldin searched back through his memory to the start of this whole affair: not long ago, in the grand scheme of things, but it seemed now like a lifetime. Memories had begun to fade. . . . When *had* he first realized there was something unique about the cloak? Surely it was soon after the ship crashed, but was that before or after the first spidership had arrived? "It was after," he said slowly, "I think."

"You're not sure," Aelfred said flatly, "and how could you be? How could you know just what the cloak was doing, and when? Hells, it could have been protecting you from bird droppings from the first moment you saw it, and you just thought the birds had lousy aim." The warrior grumbled into silence for a moment, then took off on another tangent. "Neogi aren't common in Krynnspace," he mused. "It's one of the few places you're reasonably safe from them, but what happens? We take you—and your cloak—aboard, and we get intercepted by a deathspider. Coincidence?"

Perhaps, Estriss replied. *It happens.*

"I know it happens," Aelfred rumbled, "but think. We know there were neogi in Krynnspace, the ones who were after Teldin. It's possible—vaguely—that we were just unlucky enough to run into them, but do you know what the odds are of passing another ship in the flow so close that you're dropped to tactical speed?"

It happens, Estriss said again. *Neogi, by nature, will attack any ship they encounter. That means nothing one way or the other.*

Aelfred growled in frustration. "I know, I know, but I can't help thinking. If the neogi can track the cloak somehow, that explains how they intercepted us. It makes me wonder, Teldin. Those pirates who attacked the gnomish dreadnought, *were* they pirates? *Just* pirates? Or were they after the dreadnought for a reason?"

You may as well ask why the Probe *happened along when it did*, Estriss put in mildly.

Aelfred had no answer for a moment, then he smiled ruefully. "Aye, I know," he said, "that way lies paranoia." He turned to Teldin. "We've been arguing past you as though you've got nothing to say, while you're the person who can probably say the most. Have you got anything to add, or ask, or anything?"

Teldin had to admit he'd welcomed the respite while the other two shot comments and theories back and forth. While they debated, he could pretend the whole thing was an intellectual exercise, the kind of discussion he'd sometimes overheard between his grandfather and the old man's friends: interesting in its own way, but with little relevance to the real world of crops and plantings. Now he was forced to accept how deadly serious the whole thing was.

The other two were looking at him steadily, expecting an answer. He sighed, bone-weary of the whole burden. Why him? he asked yet again. But the burden *was* his, and he had to bear it as best he could. It hadn't been laid on Dana, or Sweor, or Shandess, or any of the others who'd died aboard the *Probe*. It had been laid on him and him alone.

"If the neogi can somehow track the cloak," he said slowly, "if they can—and I think we have to assume they can—then I have to leave the ship."

Teldin wasn't sure what kind of response he expected from the other two. What he *didn't* expect was the reaction he got from Aelfred.

The first mate threw back his head and roared with laughter. "You'll find it a long walk back to Krynn, old son," the warrior said.

Teldin felt his cheeks coloring. "You can drop me on some other planet," he said sharply. "Anywhere will do."

Aelfred sobered immediately and laid a calming hand on Teldin's shoulder. "Sorry, friend," he said earnestly. "I shouldn't have laughed. What you said was *nobly* said, but none too practical. If the neogi *can* track the cloak, then they'll come and get you wherever you hide. If you're by yourself, they'll kill you and get the cloak." He grinned deprecatingly. "Truth be told, I'm just an old mercenary. I know little about magic, and that's just the way I like it, but I *do* know one thing." His voice hardened. "I've got good reason to hate the neogi, and just because they want something—whatever it is—well, that's quite enough reason to keep it away from them."

For me as well, Estriss put in. *It seems to me that the best way to keep the neogi's prize from them is to learn how to use it, to control its power.* The creature's featureless white eyes settled on Teldin. *But not now,* the illithid finished. *You are tired. Perhaps after sleep we can continue this.*

Teldin felt exhaustion wash over him like a wave. Despite his attempts to keep them open, his eyes began to hood.

"Use my cabin," Aelfred told him. "It's certain I'm not going to get the chance for a good while."

"Thanks," Teldin said weakly. He *was* tired. Maybe it was something the illithid had done—he remembered an attacker collapsing under the mind flayer's mental attack—or maybe it was something to do with the cloak. Or maybe it was something less mysterious: the stress, fear, and exertion of the day finally getting to him. In any case, he was only barely aware of Aelfred helping him across the hallway to the first mate's cabin, and sleep swallowed him the instant he lay on the bed.

Chapter Eight

● ● ●

Consciousness returned slowly. For an immeasurable time, Teldin luxuriated in a relaxed state of half-sleep, half-wakefulness. Thoughts that were almost dreams drifted through his mind. Real events of the past weeks combined with memories of his childhood. People and places mixed and matched in totally illogical combinations. Grandfather and Aelfred collaborated on teaching Teldin to use a short sword, while Estriss and Dana—now inexplicably wearing Teldin's cloak—stood on the forecastle, watching. Throughout, the only emotion he felt was mild puzzlement, not the deep pain that by rights should have accompanied some of the images.

As he drifted closer and closer to full consciousness, he found that he could manipulate some of the thoughts, some of the images. For the first time, he could review events at least somewhat objectively. Lying there, he went over the decisions he'd made, the points where he could have turned the course of events to a different path. There were, he realized, all too few of them. His actions had been more constrained than he'd perceived. At each branch point, he'd really had only one option that made complete sense, and—he saw now—if he'd strayed from the most logical path, the outcome would almost certainly have been worse than it was now. The vast majority of other paths ended with him dead, and with the cloak in the hands of the neogi.

So it was with a grim sense of relief—of exoneration, even of redemption—that he finally returned to full consciousness. The results of his actions still weighed heavily on him—and he knew they always would—but at least now he felt better prepared to bear the burden he'd been given.

He opened his eyes and squinted in the flow-light that poured in through the porthole. For a moment he didn't remember exactly where he was, then memory returned fully. He was in Aelfred's cabin.

He swung himself off the narrow bunk and looked around with interest. He'd expected the first mate's cabin to somehow match the big man's personality and background. There would be mementos mounted on the bulkheads, possibly an old, notched broadsword that he'd taken from a worthy foe or the pennant of a unit he'd fought with. There would be charts and books piled everywhere. It would be a comfortable refuge for a man who needed escape from his responsibilities.

If Teldin had ever considered himself an infallible judge of character, Aelfred's cabin would have destroyed that notion for good. The small cabin was spartan, almost bare. There were no trophies on the bulkheads, no books—in fact, nothing at all that gave it any sense of the owner's personality. A traveling chest—presumably containing Aelfred's personal effects—was at the foot of the narrow wooden bunk. A small desk was bolted to the bulkhead beside the door, and a padded bench was mounted below the porthole. The only thing that matched Teldin's expectations was the chart: there *was* a star chart on the desk, held in place by small metal clips.

In retrospect, Teldin realized that this was the kind of cabin he should have expected all along. How much time did Aelfred actually spend in his cabin? Virtually none, it seemed. The warrior was always on the bridge or wandering about the ship. To a man like that, a cabin would be a place to sleep, nothing more. Why would he bother to decorate it, or even give it the stamp of his own personality, when he'd have virtually no time to see it?

Teldin smiled to himself. Aelfred was still something of an enigma in some ways, but Teldin was slowly coming to understand the burly warrior better.

He stretched luxuriously. Well, he thought, it's time I was out and about. What time was it, anyway? That was something about shipboard life he'd never quite gotten used to. Whether the ship was in wildspace or in the flow, there was no way to tell what the time was just by looking. You had to depend on the ship's bell, and even then it wasn't obvious what watch it was.

He listened for a moment. The ship was fairly quiet, no loud noises on deck. That didn't mean much, of course. After the battle with the neogi, Aelfred would probably choose to run the ship with as few people on watch as possible and give the others a chance to sleep.

Where *was* Aelfred, anyway?

Teldin opened the cabin door. A crew member was passing but stopped when she saw Teldin standing in the doorway. She edged back a little, as if to give him plenty of room.

"What time is it?" he asked.

"Two bells, sir."

Teldin raised an eyebrow. "Sir," was it? The level of respect had grown even more than he'd thought. He had to admit it was pleasant, in a way, but it was based on a misinterpretation. Oh, well, he thought, there wasn't much he could do about it now.

Two bells. That meant he'd been asleep for about eight solid hours. He stretched again, enjoying the tension in his well-rested muscles. He gestured with his thumb forward toward the bridge. "Who has forenoon watch on the bridge?" he asked.

The woman looked at him strangely. "It's two bells in the *night* watch, sir," she told him.

Absently he thanked her, and she went about her business. Night watch meant he'd been asleep for about *twenty-four* hours. No wonder he felt so fully rested.

"Where's Aelfred Silverhorn?" he suddenly thought to call after the woman, but she'd already vanished down the companionway to the cargo deck. He shrugged. Odds were, the first mate was on the bridge. He started forward.

Then a noise from across the corridor—from the officers' saloon—stopped him. It was a snorting rumble of some kind. At first he couldn't identify it, then a broad grin spread across his face. Quietly he crossed to the saloon door and opened it.

He'd found Aelfred. The first mate was sprawled bonelessly

in a chair, booted feet on the table. His arms dangled limply on both sides of the chair, so his fingers brushed the deck. His mouth hung loosely open and gave vent to the rumbling snore Teldin had heard. Gently, Teldin shut the door again. Let the man sleep, he thought, he needs it.

Words formed in Teldin's mind. *So you rejoin the land of the wakeful.*

There's one problem with mental communication, Teldin thought: you can't tell what direction it's coming from. He looked all around for Estriss.

The illithid approached from the aft end of the corridor. *Do you feel better?* the creature continued.

"Much better," Teldin replied. "I feel like I've come back to life."

Estriss nodded. *You were drained. Not simply tired, but drained. I could sense the difference.*

"What does that mean?"

I believe it means that the cloak draws some of its energy from you, the illithid explained. *The vast majority of enchanted items do not work in that way. They draw all of the energy they need from elsewhere, and the will of the user is just a trigger, not a power source as well.*

Teldin shook his head. There was something emotionally disturbing about what Estriss was saying. "Is it meant to do that?" he asked.

I am certain it is not, Estriss told him. Suddenly, as though realizing for the first time where they were, the illithid glanced around. *Some things are best spoken of in private,* he said. *May we continue this in my cabin?*

* * * * *

If Aelfred's cabin was devoid of personality, the mind flayer's cabin was almost overfull. Nearly every square inch of the large cabin's bulkheads was covered with some form of artwork: paintings, tapestries, and art forms that Teldin had never seen before. For example, in pride of place on the aft wall was a large, circular ring of metal more than two feet in diameter. Crisscrossing the ring were fine wires of different colors of metal. Where the wires crossed near the middle of the ring, they twisted and knotted around each other, building up into an intricate interweaving of metal threads. The pattern seemed somehow right on the edge between chaos and order. When Teldin concentrated on the arrangement, the whole thing seemed totally random, but when he didn't concentrate, just let his mind drift and experience the design without analyzing it, he couldn't avoid the feeling that there *was* some organization, some higher order of pattern, to the wires . . . but one that was just beyond his mind's ability to perceive.

The paintings and tapestries were more familiar forms of art, but there was something unusual about them, too. In those that depicted scenery or figures, there seemed to be missing detail in certain places—surprising, since overall the works were incredibly intricate. Even the tapestries made up of abstract geometric patterns didn't look right. Otherwise regularly repeating geometric motifs seemed to be broken up here and there by featureless areas of dark red. For some reason, Teldin found those pieces mildly frustrating.

He turned to Estriss, who'd been watching his inspection with obvious interest. "Is this illithid art?" he asked.

It is. How do you find it?

Teldin paused. He suddenly felt a little edgy. How much did he know about Estriss, after all? In the creature's hours of privacy in his cabin, the mind flayer might have been creating these paintings, these tapestries. Teldin didn't want to offend his friend. "Very interesting," he said enthusiastically. "I like them."

Do they convey emotions to you? Estriss asked. He pointed to one tapestry, an intricate tessellation of five-pointed stars, broken here and there by large regions of featureless red. *This one, for example. What emotion does it portray to you?*

Teldin looked closer at the tapestry. The weaving was incredibly intricate, and it was fascinating the way the stars—each subtly different in shape—interlocked so perfectly, but . . . "No real emotion," he had to admit.

Estriss looked disappointed. *Truly? It is one of the most emotionally evocative works I have ever found.* Estriss fixed Teldin with his white eyes. *Are you sure? No sense of pride, of exultation?*

"None."

The illithid gave a whistling sigh. *There seem to be some things that simply cannot cross racial boundaries,* he mused. *Of course, much of it may be due to differences in our optical apparatuses.* He reached out a red-tinged finger and touched one of the featureless patches of deep red on the tapestry. *Do you see the continuation of the pattern here?*

Teldin looked closer, but the region remained undifferentiated red. "No," he said. "What do you mean?"

To my eyes, the illithid explained, *the pattern is as clear there as it is here.* He pointed to a region where the stars were strongly contrasting blues and greens.

"How is that possible?"

My eyes are adapted to see farther into the infrared than are humans', Estriss explained. *When I see a rainbow, I see two bands of color beyond red, colors that humans cannot see.*

Teldin felt a sense of wonder growing within him. "What do they look like, these colors?" he asked.

The illithid's tentacles writhed with amusement. *First describe to me what green looks like,* he suggested.

Teldin was taken aback. "What? Well, it looks . . ." His voice trailed off, and he had to smile. "It looks *green*," he finished. "All right, it was a dumb question."

Estriss gave one of his shattered-spine shrugs. *We drift far from the point,* he remarked. *We were speaking of the cloak.*

A little self-consciously, Teldin touched the garment, still a small band around the back of his neck. "You say it drains energy from me," he said. "How?"

There is no way for me to be sure, Estriss admitted. *Most enchanted items draw their energy directly from elsewhere— from the Positive or Negative Material Planes, for example— much as do spells.*

"I thought wizards were the power source for their own spells," Teldin put in.

Estriss shook his head. *Not possible,* he said flatly. *Do you know how much energy is involved in even the simplest of spells? If that power were drawn directly from the caster, it would leave him exhausted at the very least, but more likely a lifeless husk. No, the energy comes from elsewhere. Now with enchanted objects*—he moved smoothly back to his origi nal point—*the energy is focused by the item and directed so as to have an effect in the physical world. It is like*—he struggled for an analogy—*like when you carry a lantern. The energy of the lantern's light is produced and focused by the lantern itself, though it is you who directs that energy by moving the lantern. Do you understand?*

"I think so," Teldin said slowly. "The cloak is different?"

The cloak is different, Estriss confirmed. *When you used magic to defend yourself from your attacker, the power was channeled through you, through your body. It was as if the cloak poured power into your body, then you released that power in the manner and direction that you willed. Was that not how it felt?*

Teldin remembered the sensations: the flood of heat through his body, the feeling that he must be burning with light, the terror, the pain, and the ecstasy. . . . He nodded wordlessly.

In that way, the cloak is different from anything I have experience with, the illithid continued. *And there is more. The fact that you were drained after the experience tells me that some of your own energy was added to what was released. You contributed to the power—not much, or else you would now be dead, but to some degree.* The mind flayer's facial tentacles writhed, adding to the tone of intensity in his mental words. *Do you realize what that means?* he asked. *It means that you actively* participated *in using magic, but you are not a mage. I have never heard of anything like this before.*

Teldin shook his head again. This was getting deep, and he'd never really had the interest or the determination to worry about philosophy. It was also getting scary. "Is that the way it should work?" he asked.

I seriously doubt it, Estriss replied at once. *I think it is a result of you not knowing how to control the cloak's functions.*

"Is it dangerous?"

I believe it may well be, the illithid told him soberly. *Although it was impressive, and highly effective, the power you wielded on the forecastle was relatively minor, as such things go. There is no reason to believe that the display we witnessed is the most powerful capability the cloak possesses. It is possible you may accidentally trigger a facility that is more signifi-*

cant, that will pour more power through your body. It is also possible that your unintended . . . participation . . . in this energy flow might permanently damage you.

"Or kill me," Teldin added quietly.

Or kill you.

"What do I do? Never use the cloak? I don't know how I used it this time."

No, the illithid said sharply. *Deciding never to use the cloak is useless. The power was triggered accidentally this time. You did not consciously intend to wield it. It seems likely, perhaps inevitable, that you will again trigger it by accident.*

"But, then, what do I do?" Teldin asked desperately. "I can't take the cloak off, and if I *don't* take it off, eventually it's going to kill me, isn't that what you're saying?" He spat one of Aelfred's mercenary oaths. "The only question is, what will kill me first, the cloak or the neogi?"

There is another way, Estriss cut him off firmly. *I said that the draining effect is simply because you are unfamiliar with controlling the cloak. If you were to become familiar, however . . .*

Teldin was silent for several heartbeats, then, "How?" he asked forcefully. "It's never done anything when I've wanted it to, only when *it's* wanted." He shivered. For a moment, he could almost believe that the cloak on his back was some kind of intelligence—maybe a malign one, considering what had been happening to him lately—that was playing with him like a cat plays with a mouse . . . before killing it.

Estriss shook his head so violently that his facial tentacles flailed. *It is an easy trap to fall into, to ascribe intelligence to the cloak,* he said firmly, *but I urge you not to fall into it. The cloak has no sentience—none—but . . .* The creature's eyes hooded under double eyelids. *But you are right, in a way. The problem lies in triggering the cloak.*

"How do you normally trigger a magic item?"

It varies widely, the illithid said. *For some, it is a word that must be spoken aloud, or repeated mentally. For others, it is sufficient to visualize the desired outcome. For others still, it is simply an act of will, as when you move your arm.* The creature paused. *From my research on the Juna,* he continued at length, *it seems there are other ways. A word of command is,* after all, merely a number of symbols—in this case, spoken syllables—strung together in a sequence. There are other kinds of symbols as well. My research implies that some items may be triggered by visualizing a sequence of geometrical forms or relationships. Or even, perhaps, a sequence of emotions. Do you understand?

"Only vaguely," Teldin admitted, "but then I don't really understand how a word can trigger something either." He hesitated. "How does this matter?"

What did you feel, Teldin? Estriss asked intensely. *What did you feel, what did you think, when you fought the man on the forecastle? Try to recall.*

"I felt fear," Teldin replied instantly. "I thought . . . I thought I was going to die."

Be more precise.

"I don't know."

I saw your movements, as I tried to reach you. You reached out with your hand, toward your attacker. Why? What were you thinking? What, exactly?

Teldin tried to force his mind back to that moment, but it was difficult. The memory was blurred, indistinct. Yes, the illithid was right. He had reached out. Why? To save himself. To block the swing of that deadly sword. . . . "To *stop* him."

How?

"I don't know," Teldin said, "it was just a reflex. It wouldn't have worked."

But you did stop him, Estriss reminded him. *Perhaps it was your emotion the cloak responded to, your desire to stop the man, in any way possible. Perhaps it was that desire, that unintentional act of will . . . if that makes any sense.* The illithid thought for a moment. *What did you feel when the power was released?*

"Heat," Teldin responded, "and light. The cloak burst into light—"

There was no light that I saw, Estriss interrupted.

Teldin frowned. "That's what I felt, though, like the sun at my back, but much more so. The light and heat spread through my body."

You cried out.

"It hurt . . . but it didn't." Teldin paused, trying to make sense of the memory. "I don't know," he said eventually. "It hurt so much it felt good. Or it felt so good it hurt. I can't really remember which, and I can't be sure I even knew at the time."

Estriss nodded. *I wish you to try an experiment*, he said. *Try to recreate those feelings. I want you to imagine them. Imagine them so strongly that you can feel them again. And*—he pointed at the cabin door—*I want you to protect yourself from that door.*

Teldin gaped. "What?"

The cloak came to your defense once, the illithid said. *It saved your life. What good is a defense if you cannot use it at will? I believe you must learn to control the cloak's power, and there is only one way to learn. To experiment. To try. Try for me*, he urged. *The door is a creature that wishes to kill you, and you must protect yourself. Do it.*

Teldin smiled; the illithid's words were so reminiscent of Aelfred's sword lesson. Nevertheless, he had to admit to himself the idea was intriguing, attractive in a grim kind of way. He'd seen Vallus wield magic, to save his own life and the lives of his colleagues, and he'd assumed that such power would forever be beyond his grasp. But here was Estriss, telling him that he may be able to do something similar.

He couldn't ignore the illithid's words about the dangers of the cloak. If Estriss was right, if the only way to prevent the cloak from someday killing him was to become practiced in its use, then he had to try.

He nodded and closed his eyes. Relive the experience, he told himself. I'm back there, I have to do *something* or I'm dead. He remembered the sense of heat on his back, concentrated on it, tried to feel it once again. Heat and light flaring around his shoulders, pouring into his body, burning through his bones like lightning. The sense of overwhelming energy, licking through him, forcing its way out. Pain and pleasure, pleasure and pain. *Live* it, he told himself. He tried to recreate the sense of power welling up inside him, welling up so strongly it had to go *somewhere* or he'd explode. He shot a hand out toward the door. . . .

Nothing.

The intensity of the memory faded. He let it go—not without a twinge of sadness—let his concentration slip away. He opened his eyes. His chest burned from holding his breath, and when he wiped his forehead his fingers came away sweat-dampened. "I can't," he said dully.

Estriss nodded. *Emotion is a great part of it, I think,* he mused. *You feared for your life, you wished to do anything to stop your attacker, and the cloak responded to that.* The creature paused. *If we were to carry the experiment to its logical conclusion, I suppose I should try to attack you.* His tentacles gestured amusement. *But I fear the experiment might succeed too well.*

There is another possibility I would like you to try, the illithid went on, *if you are willing.*

Teldin took a deep breath to ease the tension in his chest and nodded. "Nothing too drastic," he suggested.

Less drastic than the last experiment, Estriss assured him.

"What is it?"

Let me tell you something more of my research into the Juna, Estriss suggested.

Teldin looked around for somewhere to sit. There was no mattress on the cabin's bunk, but at least it was flat, so he settled himself on the edge.

The legends and myths that deal with the Juna all seem to share one motif, the illithid went on. *In some it is central, in others merely touched on, but it does seem to be common.* He paused.

"Go on," Teldin prompted dutifully. "What is it?"

Shapeshifting, Estriss said. *The ability to change form, to take on different appearances. Initially I believed that this was symbolic, merely a representation of the ability to adapt to different situations, but as I delved further, I concluded that the stories were at least partially naturalistic. I believe that the Juna were experts at shapeshifting magic.* He hesitated. *Will you trust me in this conclusion, or should I explain my evidence?*

"I trust you," Teldin answered hastily.

Estriss nodded. *If the cloak was created by the Juna, as I suspect, then it may incorporate some form of shapeshifting enchantment. Will you try this for me?*

This is getting just too strange, Teldin found himself thinking, but he couldn't say that to the illithid. After all, with what he'd seen over the past couple of days, how could he refuse to consider something just because it sounded bizarre? "How do you mean?" he asked.

Simply put, I want you to try to assume the form of another. Aelfred Silverhorn, for example.

"How?"

The illithid's mental voice took on a calming, almost fatherly, tone. *I realize it sounds outlandish*, Estriss said. *Or perhaps 'outlandish' is not a strong enough word. Believe me when I say I would not even suggest this if there were not some evidence to support my ideas.* He paused. *I understand that you feel somewhat embarrassed by this, is that not so?*

Teldin had to nod. He didn't quite know why—after all, he and the illithid were the only people in the room—but he *did* feel embarrassed, even humiliated.

I find it difficult to understand human emotions, Estriss went on. *Would it lessen your embarrassment if I assured you that I am not doing this to put you in a position of dishonor?*

Teldin couldn't help but smile. The illithid seemed so earnest, so guileless. "Tell me what to do," he suggested.

I can only guess at this, so you must bear with me, Estriss said. *First, please close your eyes and build up, in your mind, a detailed picture of Aelfred Silverhorn.*

Teldin did as he was instructed. With his eyes closed, he pictured Aelfred's face hanging in space before him. Slowly he let it build in detail: curly blond hair, close-cropped to the head; bone-white scar above the right eyebrow; lines in his weather-tanned skin, framing steady eyes; lopsided grin.

Do you have it? Estriss asked.

Teldin answered without opening his eyes. "Yes."

Take the next step. Imagine your own face next to Aelfred's. Again, make it as detailed as you can.

Teldin was a little surprised at how much more difficult it was to build up a picture of himself. Surely he should be more familiar with his own face, the one he wore every day? But no, he realized after a moment, that wasn't necessarily the case. When did he see his own face? In the mirror when he shaved each day, and that was about it.

Again he let the picture build in detail: lean face, with finely chiseled cheekbones; tanned skin, even darker than Aelfred's; short hair of sun-bleached brown; network of crow's-feet bracketing bright, cornflower-blue eyes.

Now move your picture of Aelfred's face over that of yours, Estriss instructed. *Aelfred's face must totally cover yours. Where the two faces are superimposed, both faces still exist, but only Aelfred's is visible. Do you understand?*

In fear that speaking might somehow break his concentration, Teldin nodded wordlessly. In his mind's eye, Aelfred's face moved until it overlaid his own. At first he could see both sets of features in some kind of strange superimposition. Blue and gray eyes stared out of the same sockets; hair that was both brown and blond covered the head. Then, slowly, his own features began to fade from view.

Power! He felt it, a warm tingling in his shoulders, spreading through to his chest. It was a lot more subtle than what he'd felt on the foredeck. In fact, was it really there at all? Or was it just wishful thinking on his part? After what the illithid had told him, he *wanted* to be able to summon the power of the cloak. . . .

The mental pictures started to fade. With an effort of will, Teldin ignored his questions and the hint of power—if that was what it was—and pushed both from his mind. All that mattered at the moment were the faces he visualized.

In his mental picture, his own features finally vanished. Only Aelfred's remained.

He heard a sharp, hissing intake of breath from Estriss. Slowly he opened his eyes.

The mind flayer was looking at him intently. The illithid's facial tentacles were still. In fact, the creature was as motionless as a statue.

"Did it work?" Teldin asked.

Estriss was silent for a moment, then asked, *What do you feel?* His mental tone was emotionless, noncommittal.

The illithid's intense scrutiny was making Teldin uneasy. He shifted on the edge of the bunk. "I think I felt something," he said slowly, "but I'm not sure. It could have been my imagination."

How do you feel now? Estriss pressed. *Warm? Cold?*

Teldin paused. Now that the mind flayer mentioned it, he

did feel as if the temperature in the cabin had dropped a couple of degrees. Plus, he felt the thin, somehow edgy feeling he always associated with not enough sleep or not enough to eat. "Slightly cool," he replied at last. "Estriss, did it work?"

Estriss didn't answer immediately, and that was answer enough. Teldin raised a hand to his face, ran his fingers over his nose and cheek. . . .

And snatched his hand away with a stifled cry. It wasn't his face that he'd touched. The nose was broader, the cheekbones less pronounced. Even the texture of the skin was different. The sensations from his fingers were as if he'd reached out and touched someone else's face, yet the nerves of his face felt his exploring fingers as if nothing at all were amiss. The combination of the prosaic with the alien was shocking—terrifying at some deep level of his being. He sprang to his feet and looked around the cabin for something he could use for a mirror.

Estriss had anticipated his need. The illithid had removed a thin disk of finely polished silver metal from a drawer in the desk and now handed it to Teldin without a word.

Teldin held the mirror at chest level for a few heartbeats. He knew what he was going to see; there would be no surprise. How would it feel to see someone else's face in place of his? How would he react? He took a deep breath and raised the mirror.

The biggest shock was that there was no real shock. The face in the polished silver was Aelfred's, there was no doubt about that, but emotionally it had little real impact. It was as if Aelfred was standing beside him and Teldin was holding the mirror at such an angle that it reflected the other man's face. He raised his hand to his cheek again.

That's when the shock struck him, almost powerfully enough to make him drop the mirror. It was the juxtaposition of the familiar and the bizarre again. The muscles of his arm and hand told him that he was raising his hand to his own face. The mirror told him he was reaching for Aelfred's face. The reassuring falsehood that the face in the mirror somehow wasn't associated with his body was shattered. He clenched his jaw to stop himself from whimpering with atavistic dread. In the mirror, Aelfred's face mimicked the movement.

A touch on his shoulder made him jump. Estriss's hand

squeezed his shoulder reassuringly. With an effort, Teldin brought his jumbled emotions a little more under control. "I'm all right," he said quietly. Surprisingly, his voice sounded steady in his own ears. He examined the face in the mirror again, this time trying to be more critical and less emotional in his reactions.

There was something wrong with the image, he realized at once—apart from the total wrongness of his wearing the wrong face, of course. The individual features seemed correct, almost perfectly matching his memory of Aelfred, but there was something else, and it took him several moments to recognize it. The face was Aelfred's, but the neck and shoulders beneath it were Teldin's. Aelfred's head was large—in keeping with the rest of his body—and his neck was thick and muscular. In the mirror, the warrior's big head sat atop Teldin's relatively slender neck.

He felt his neck with his fingers. At least there was no discontinuity there; his neck felt the way it always had. *Can I change it?* he wondered. He closed his eyes and started to concentrate on rebuilding his mental image of Aelfred—the neck too, this time.

The illithid's grip on his shoulder tightened, breaking into his concentration. He opened his eyes again.

Estriss was distressed, that was obvious from the jerky movements of his facial tentacles. *No,* his mental voice said urgently. *Do nothing more, not for the moment. Let us move slowly. Tell me again, what do you feel?*

Teldin quickly gave himself a mental once-over. The sense of cold, of somehow being *stretched*—that was the only way he could describe it, even to himself—was still there. Maybe it was slightly more noticeable. He described the sensation to Estriss.

The mind flayer nodded thoughtfully. *You are sensing the drain,* he mused. *You are contributing energy to the process.* Estriss considered for a moment. *The shapechange appears to be stable,* he went on. *Tell me, are you concentrating on maintaining it?*

"I don't think so," replied Teldin.

Relax, Estriss instructed. *Let go. Let the change slip away.*

Obediently, Teldin took a deep breath, held it for a few

heartbeats, then released it slowly. He felt tension drain out of his neck and shoulders. He repeated the process again, this time concentrating on relaxing his mind as well as his body, then he raised the mirror. Aelfred's face still looked back at him, and he felt a twinge of fear. What if he couldn't reverse the change? What would he do? "Estriss . . . ?"

You are right, the illithid remarked, *you do not need to concentrate on the new shape to maintain it. It must require an act of will to return to your normal form. That is good.*

"But how do I do it?" Teldin snapped.

Try this, Estriss replied at once. *Visualize Aelfred's features melting away to reveal your own.*

Teldin shut his eyes. He took another calming breath to slow his pounding heart a little, then let the image of Aelfred develop once more in his mind. This time it was much easier, and he was amazed at how quickly the details established themselves. It must be the cloak that's doing this, he found himself thinking, I don't have that good a memory for details.

As Estriss had suggested, he imagined Aelfred's features melting away—becoming transparent and running away like water. Instantly his own, familiar features started to reappear in his mental image. The eyes became blue once more, the hair brown, the bone structure more slender. As his own face appeared, he realized that this felt quite different from when he'd had to first create a mental picture of himself. Then he'd been building up the features from nothing. Now it felt as though the features were already there, independent of his will, and he was merely revealing them. There was no sensation of power this time, not even the hint of it. Instead he felt the cold, stretched feeling fade and eventually vanish. He opened his eyes.

Fascinating. The illithid's voice was a mental whisper.

Teldin raised the mirror and found himself looking into his familiar bright blue eyes. He smiled with relief, and the smile in the mirror was his own.

How do you feel now? Estriss asked.

"Fine."

Are you not tired?

Teldin hesitated. "A little tired, I suppose," he said, "as though I'd walked a few miles." He hesitated. "What does it look like?" he asked suddenly. "The change . . ."

It looks . . . unusual, Estriss answered. *Your face appears to be concealed by a gray haze, similar to a smudge on a painting. When the haze vanishes, the change is complete.* It was the illithid's turn to hesitate. *I will admit,* he said slowly, *that I am glad for the haze. The sight of your features rearranging themselves—openly, without concealment—would, I think, be highly disturbing to me.* He shook himself, as if to drive away an uncomfortable thought or image. *Will you perform one more test for me?*

"What is it?"

Take on another face, Estriss urged, *someone other than Aelfred. I wish to see if you find it easier the second time. Just the face,* he added. *There is no need to risk overreaching yourself. First, however, do you object to having Aelfred Silverhorn witness this? I believe it is important that he knows—both because he is your friend, and because he should know anything that might have some significance to running the ship.*

Teldin hesitated. He agreed that Aelfred should know about this, but he knew that the big warrior felt uncomfortable about magic. Plus, "He's asleep," Teldin told the illithid.

Estriss shrugged. *I have called him. If he answers the call, he was not asleep. I repeat, do you object?*

"No."

There was a sharp rap on the door. The illithid's mental voice rang out, *Come in.*

It was Aelfred, of course. The big man looked bedraggled, Teldin noted immediately: short hair in disarray, face pale, and the skin below his eyes puffy. He might have slept, but it certainly hadn't been enough. "Yes?" he said, his voice still a sleep-roughened burr.

The warrior's quick eyes took in the scene—both Teldin and Estriss standing, tense, in the middle of the room—and his face lit up with interest. "Oh *ho*," he rumbled. "Having a deep little discussion, are we? Any more surprises for us, Teldin, old son?"

We wish you to witness something. Estriss's mental voice was calm, reassuring. *We think you should be aware of it.* The illithid turned to Teldin. *Do it as quickly as you can,* the creature instructed. *As part of the test.*

Teldin nodded and closed his eyes again.

He could tell immediately that it was going to be much easier this time. A detailed vision of his own face sprang to mind instantly—almost as though it had been there all along, just waiting for him to need it. Whose should be the other face? he wondered.

He wasn't even aware that he'd decided until the image appeared in his mind. He let the new face superimpose itself over his own. . . .

"By all the gods . . . !" Aelfred's voice was hushed, amazed—horrified?

Teldin opened his eyes. Another familiar face was staring back at him from the mirror—one with tight-curled brown hair and dark, flashing eyes. Teldin reached up with his hand and touched the cheek of Dana, the gnome. *I can't bring you back*, he thought, *but if I can learn enough about my burden that it won't claim any more innocent lives, as it claimed yours, at least that'll be something.* He turned Dana's eyes on Aelfred.

The burly warrior was staring in open stupefaction. He blinked his eyes hard, as if to clear them, then he shook his head. "I don't believe it," he said flatly. "I out and out don't believe it. Teldin, this is your doing?" He instantly answered his own question. "Of course it is—who else's?" He shook his head again, then his face suddenly split in its familiar asymmetrical grin. "By the gods," he roared, "I can think of some situations where I wish I could have done that."

Estriss kept his white eyes fixed on Teldin. *That was considerably faster than the first time*, he announced. *This change took perhaps ten seconds, the first almost a minute. How do you feel?*

"Well," Teldin started . . . and stopped. When he'd worn Aelfred's face, he hadn't consciously noticed the fact that his voice was unchanged. Now, though, his male voice was coming from Dana's female lips. Until that moment, the fascination—and the personal fear—of what he was doing had filled his mind. The initial shock had faded, however, and the consequences of what he was doing really began to penetrate.

This is *wrong*, he found himself thinking, very wrong. He shut his eyes and melted away Dana's features as quickly as he could. He checked the mirror. Yes, he was Teldin again. A little shakily, he sat down on the illithid's bare bunk.

Estriss was watching him fixedly. *What is wrong?* he asked. *Was there pain? Exhaustion?*

"No," Teldin mumbled. "No, none of that."

The cold you felt the first time, was it repeated? More intense, or less?

"What? Oh, less. Much less."

How do you feel now? Are you more tired than you were before?

"A little. Not much."

The illithid might have had another question, but Aelfred's deep voice cut him off. "What's wrong, Teldin?"

"*This* is," Teldin snapped. "This whole thing. Putting on somebody else's face."

Estriss's tentacles gestured incomprehension. *Why? Why is this wrong?*

"It *is*." Teldin hesitated, searching for the right words to communicate what he felt so clearly inside. "It's a lie," he tried. "I . . . I was brought up to value the truth, both in myself and in others. The truth. It's what I've always worked toward. It's . . ." Suddenly he recalled a phrase from a book his grandfather had given him years ago. " 'The truth is a light,' " he quoted, " 'a light that banisheth the shadows which beset us.' Do you understand what I'm saying? This—" his gesture included himself, the cloak, the mirror "—this is a lie."

There was silence for more than a dozen heartbeats, then Aelfred asked gently, "You probably wouldn't feel so strongly if you hadn't chosen Dana's face, would you, now?"

Good question, part of Teldin's mind responded. Would I? Probably not. He shrugged.

The experiments may have disturbed you, Estriss said firmly, *but they were important and valuable. Consider what we have learned. The cloak has powers related to shapeshifting, which are now under your control. The first time you used this power, you felt the drain quite strongly, but the second time you found it much easier and the drain was considerably less. Is that not so?*

Teldin had to agree.

Then you are starting to control the tendency to give up

your own energy, Estriss continued. *Correct? And finally . . .* He leaned forward urgently. *Finally, you have gained a great advantage over those who may be pursuing you. Do you not see that? They may be searching for a man of six feet with short brown hair. Would they spare a second glance at a woman of five feet with blond hair to her waist?*

Teldin nodded slowly. That was true, but . . . "What if they can track the cloak itself?" he asked.

If that is the case, there is nothing you can do, but are we certain that everyone whose hand is turned against you can detect the cloak itself? It seems to me much more likely that only some few have this ability, if any. Against the others, you now have a significant advantage.

"It's one I'm not comfortable with," Teldin muttered.

Perhaps that comes from lack of focus, Estriss replied. To his surprise, Teldin sensed more emotion in the illithid's mental voice than ever before. *I heard what you said about valuing what is true. For myself, I would extend that. I value what is right. How best can we, both of us, serve the right, Teldin Moore? By allowing this cloak of yours to fall into the hands of the neogi? Or by doing whatever is in our power to prevent that? I know what my answer must be.*

The illithid turned away suddenly and busied itself with returning the silver mirror to the desk drawer. It was almost as if Estriss felt embarrassed by his emotional outburst, Teldin realized with surprise.

Aelfred was watching him silently, understanding in the big man's eyes. Teldin bowed his head. "You're right," Teldin said quietly. "Thank you for reminding me of that."

Estriss shrugged off the thanks. *It is only logical,* he said. *What is also logical is that you should practice this ability of the cloak every day, perhaps several times each day. The drain you felt was less the second time, but it was still there.*

"I don't know what in all the hells you're talking about," Aelfred rumbled, "but just on principle I back the captain. Practice. It's important." He was silent for a moment, then went on, "One thing: I don't think it's a good idea to let the rest of the crew know about any of this. I think they've accepted you as some kind of warrior-mage—" he snorted with amusement at this "—so that won't worry them, but if they don't know if the person they're on watch with is who they think it is, or it's you practicing . . . It's going to do something to morale, if you get my drift."

"I understand."

Aelfred slapped Teldin comradely on the arm. "Well," he said, "if you don't have any more miracles to show me, I should get back on duty. We've got some of the new inductees on the rigging, and if I don't keep an eye on them, we're just as likely to end up back at Krynn as we are at Realmspace." He grimaced. "I know it's a touchy subject, but your diminutive friend, Horvath, has threatened to oversee repairs. Scary."

* * * * *

Despite Aelfred's misgivings, the remainder of the journey through the flow was notable for its lack of mishaps. The "new inductees," as Aelfred called them—actually the surviving members of the deathspider's boarding party—seemed to integrate with the rest of the *Probe*'s crew without any major difficulties. Over the first couple of days after the battle, Teldin could tell a "new inductee" a ship-length away. There was something about the way they walked and stood, as though they wished they could sink into the deck or the bulkhead and just fade from view—"trying to look invisible" was Aelfred's phrase for it. If anyone spoke to them—or even looked at them—they flinched, as though they expected to be beaten. Or worse, Teldin speculated, remembering his own experiences with neogi on Krynn.

Plus, they had a tendency to stand around, trying to look invisible, unless they had specific orders to do something. On the third day after the battle, Teldin saw a perfect example of this. One of the hammership's regular crewmen—a little man named Garay—was standing on the rail, cleaning the sheaves of a rigging block with a marlin spike. As he shifted position, the spike fell from his hand. It landed on the deck, barely a foot in front of a new inductee named Tregimesticus, who just stood there, looking at the spike near his feet.

"Well?" Garay called down from the rigging. "Aren't you going to pick the bloody thing up?"

Tregimesticus jumped as though he'd been whipped,

snatched the spike off the deck, and scampered up the rigging to place it right into Garay's hand.

When the man was gone, Garay climbed down and came over to where Teldin was standing. "Dead from the neck up," the crewman grumbled. "I'll be flogged if any of them come around to right thinking."

Surprisingly, though, some of them did start to come around. Perhaps they were the ones who hadn't been aboard the deathspider as long—nobody felt comfortable asking, of course—or perhaps they were just the ones who naturally had stronger wills. In any case, of the ten "new inductees," four seemed slowly to be returning to the land of the living. They started talking to the other crew members—even when they hadn't been spoken to first—and even began to strike up friendships. The other six, including Tregimesticus, didn't seem so lucky or so adaptable. They followed orders with a speed that made the regular crew of the *Probe* look like sluggards, but they never showed anything that could be mistaken for initiative, and they kept the habit of trying to look invisible.

In any case, the voyage progressed uneventfully. For Teldin, it was a pleasurable time. There was something comforting about the strict routine aboard the *Probe*. Aelfred returned him to normal watch-standing, which meant that eight hours out of every day was spent scanning the flow for possible danger. The rest of the time he was free to do as he liked. He still shared the cabin with the three surviving gnomes—Horvath, Miggins, and Saliman, but found that his watch-standing schedule was opposed to theirs; when they were on watch, he was asleep, and vice versa.

This didn't mean that they never met, of course. As soon as he had time after the battle, Teldin made a point of tracking down Miggins. He found the young gnome in the starboard side stateroom that had been converted into an infirmary for the many injured in the deathspider's attack. Teldin found it uncomfortable to enter the cabin—like many people who depended on health and strength for their livelihood, he found it deeply disturbing to be around those who were physically impaired—but he forced his qualms out of his mind and put on a smile.

Miggins was almost indecently glad to see him. Although he

hadn't seen it, he'd heard about Teldin's exploits on the forecastle. As always, the tales had grown with the telling, and Teldin found that he'd become a sort of personal hero to the youth. Teldin was a little troubled about this but decided this was neither the time nor the place to change Miggins's attitude.

Miggins was progressing well and was glad to tell Teldin all about it. His left arm was grievously wounded, and there was a significant chance that he'd never regain full use of it, but at least the healers' initial concern—that they'd have to amputate to save the gnome's life—had turned out to be baseless.

Conversation had inevitably turned to Dana. "I miss her," Miggins had admitted, "but, you know, I could never really think of her as a gnome. She was more like one of you big folk. She was never too interested in the way things work, and she liked action much more than she did talk."

Teldin had nodded, remembering her feisty manner and the way she'd tried to stand up to Aelfred in the longboat.

"Ah, well," Miggins had continued, "at least she died the way she always said she wanted to—in battle."

Another one who died a "good" death, Teldin had found himself thinking. *What would be a good death for me? Or does it really matter?*

The injured gnome tired easily, so he'd left soon thereafter. It had saddened him to talk about Dana, but in another way it had been somehow freeing, as if in talking about her—celebrating her existence—he'd come to terms with her passing.

In the days that followed, even though he didn't see the gnomes, he was reminded of their existence by shipboard gossip. Virtually everyone aboard had a favorite "gnome story," about how the small creatures would have "remodeled" the *Probe* if somebody hadn't caught them before the damage was done. Teldin's favorite was Miggins's suggestion that a hole be cut in the hull to allow the underside of the hammership to be used as a secondary weapons platform. Explanations that this would make the vessel as seaworthy as a brick when it put down on water didn't dissuade the young gnome. All he did was come back with a bewildering description of baffles and gaskets to solve the problem. Predictably, some of the less patient crew members threatened the small creature with death if he so much as mentioned the idea again.

When he wasn't sleeping, Teldin had taken to wandering the ship and talking with those crewmen he met. This had turned out to be a very good idea. Initially the crew had treated him with a respect that contained a healthy measure of fear. They'd stayed out of his way—after all, wasn't he a fighter-mage who could cut them in two or burn them down in their tracks?—and called him "sir." Teldin had decided that the best way to react to this was not to react at all. If he'd told them not to call him sir, he knew they'd have stopped, but that would just have reinforced the aura of authority that he'd inadvertently acquired. Instead, he'd chosen to talk with them exactly the same way he had when he'd first come aboard the *Probe*. Let them call him sir. He'd chat with them the way he always had and ask the same naive questions.

To his surprise, this tactic had worked, and quickly. At first, most of the crew had been a little reticent in answering him, but he'd just talked on freely, and he could almost feel the reserve melt away. The first time that a crewman had laughed at one of his questions and clapped him companionably on the shoulder, he'd taken it as a major victory. Within a couple of days, the crewmen of the *Probe* were treating him as one of them—in fact, more so than they ever had. The one exception was that they never asked him about what happened on the forecastle, or about any details of his apparent powers.

That was all to the good, he figured. Let them reach their own conclusions. It was highly unlikely that anyone would guess the cloak's significance. The fewer people who knew about that, the safer he felt.

The fact that his watches and those of the gnomes were staggered turned out to be a blessing. He knew, for example, that there were eight hours out of each day when he'd be alone in the cabin. At those times, he could shut the door, secure it with a small wooden wedge, and know he wouldn't be interrupted. Each day he took advantage of the privacy to practice the cloak's shapeshifting abilities.

Estriss was right, it turned out: Each time he used the power, it became easier. The chilled, strained feeling lessened steadily until it vanished altogether, and the residual fatigue also faded away. His control improved significantly as well. He could now change his face in two or three heartbeats, and without the total concentration the first few shifts had required.

His control now extended to more than his face. Carefully, he'd experimented with changing the appearance of his body as well. He was still cautious with this part of it. Never had he tried any major changes—like shrinking to the size of a gnome or expanding to the bulk of an umber hulk, for example—but he now regularly altered his build to match Aelfred's muscular physique or Vallus's willowy bone structure.

No matter how hard he tried, however, he couldn't affect the clothes he wore. When he took on Aelfred's physique, his jerkin almost burst at the seams; when he duplicated Vallus or Sylvie, his clothes hung on him like a tent. The only exception was the cloak itself: whatever form he took, it subtly enlarged or contracted to fit perfectly around whatever neck he happened to have at the time.

His voice was also a problem. At first he'd assumed that, when he took on Aelfred's body, the larger chest cavity would give him the same booming voice as the first mate. It didn't happen that way, however. If there was any change in his voice, it was of the utmost subtlety—and he couldn't be totally sure that even this wasn't wishful thinking. Whether he looked like Aelfred Silverhorn or Vallus Leafbower, he always sounded like Teldin Moore. The contrast was even more noticeable when he took on the form of Sylvie, the navigator, or Julia, the second mate. Although the throat and mouth were female, the voice was most definitely male. There was absolutely no way he could use the cloak's powers to impersonate another person if the "audience" had ever heard the real person speak.

That was just as well, he concluded. He still felt there was something inherently *wrong* with taking another's form, no matter what the motive. The knowledge that it was impossible to take another's complete identity was somehow reassuring.

Chapter Nine

● ● ●

So the rest of the voyage passed. Fifty-three days from Krynn they reached the crystal shell that contained Realmspace. So inured to the wonders of space did Teldin find himself that he didn't feel disappointed when he learned that they'd pass through the shell during his sleep period. When he went to bed for his fifty-third night aboard the *Probe*, the view through the cabin's porthole was the tempestuous colors of the flow. When he woke several hours later, the cabin was dark for the first time in weeks and there was blackness on the other side of the port. Teldin swung himself out of his hammock and went on deck.

The sky around the hammership at first looked identical to the familiar one that he'd seen all his life: velvet blackness studded with stars shining with a light that looked somehow brittle. After a few moments, though, the familiarity slipped away. The orientation of these stars was nothing like what he was used to. There seemed many more of them, clustered into totally alien groupings. The constellations that had been his friends from childhood were nowhere to be seen, and his mind was unable to impose any order on the stars that he saw. Over to the port side, just over the rail, was something that he'd never seen before: a smoky haze, glowing faintly. When he looked at it directly, it seemed to fade away, but when he looked at it with peripheral vision, he could make out a kind of structure to it.

That structure was familiar, he realized with a mild shock. It reminded him unmistakably of the weather pattern he'd seen over Krynn as the *Unquenchable* pulled away from the planet. There was the same circular core, with curving arms sweeping out from it. The only thing that was missing was the sense of motion that the storm had given him. Maybe it was the black, featureless background, or the motionless stars that surrounded it. In any case, the sensation that *this* pattern gave him was one of limitless distance. The *Probe*'s crew had told him that it was no more distant than the other stars, but that both the stars and this swirling shape were actually gates to another plane—the Plane of Radiance—set into the inner surface of the crystal sphere. No matter what he *knew*, he *felt* that this spiral pattern was unimaginably farther than the other points of light.

For the first time, Teldin noticed that there was someone else on the deck—someone who was watching him with an expression of mild amusement. It was Vallus Leafbower, the elven mage, one of the *Probe*'s helmsmen. Teldin shot him a quick smile but hesitated to walk over and join him. There were two reasons for his reluctance: One was that he was enjoying the sense of solitude, of being alone beneath the unfamiliar stars; the second was the same reason he'd been avoiding the elf since the battle: Vallus obviously was a mage of significant power. As such, he might be more inclined to question Teldin about his own displays of ability. While the other crew members had avoided the topic—at least partially out of fear, Teldin guessed—Vallus wasn't likely to do the same.

Teldin's reticence turned out to be irrelevant when the elf crossed the deck and joined him.

Vallus nodded a greeting. Even when he was making efforts to be friendly, Teldin had noted, there was a sense of aloofness about the elf, a feeling that he was somehow apart from everyone and watching from some unapproachable vantage of knowledge and wisdom. There was also a strong sense of exclusivity—that was the closest word that Teldin could come up with—a sense that the elf wasn't revealing everything he knew or thought.

Perhaps it was just a consequence of the fact that he'd lived ten years or more for each year that Teldin and the others had been alive. Whatever the reason, it had a chilling effect on any sense of friendship that Teldin might otherwise feel, and made it very difficult for him to trust the elf.

Vallus spoke first. "I noticed you weren't on deck when we entered this shell," he remarked. "Unfortunate. You missed something, something that you would have found fascinating." His eyes seemed to shine with intensity. "We saw the Wanderers," he concluded in a hushed voice.

There was something portentous about the word, something that struck some kind of chord in Teldin's soul. "What are the Wanderers?" he whispered.

"As we passed through the portal, we saw them," the elf answered, "a line of figures—a geometrically straight line, hundreds of thousands of figures long. Perhaps millions long. They were walking on the inner surface of the crystal shell. Walking, walking endlessly. They paid us no attention."

Teldin shook his head in wonderment. "Why?" he asked. "What are they?"

The elf shrugged. "No one truly knows," he replied. "There are legends, of course. Some say their marching, and their silent chanting, are what allow spontaneous portals to open in the shell of Realmspace. According to this legend, the Wanderers are the souls of individuals who died performing evil deeds of horrific proportions. How they came to their present condition, even the legends fail to say, but they all are reputed to bear the mark of Torm, God of Guardians, on their palms." Vallus shrugged again. "Whatever their origin, or their purpose, it was a wondrous sight." He smiled wryly. "Such things make me realize how much poorer my life would have been had I never left my home world."

Teldin was silent. There was something about the image of an endless line of figures, eternally trudging around the surface of the crystal sphere, that caught his imagination. Without warning, he found his thoughts turning to his father. *How small your world was,* he thought, *how impoverished you were by your refusal to look outward. And,* he added, *how bleak would my own have been if it hadn't been for the circumstances that drove me outward.* For a moment, he felt almost gratitude toward the stranger who'd given him the cloak. *You might have doomed me,* his thoughts ran, *but you also broad-*

ened my horizons in ways I could never have imagined. Even if I die soon, my life is richer for my experiences.

"I think that you enjoy the sky of wildspace as much as I do," the elf continued, unaware of Teldin's musings. "There seems something of purity about it, doesn't there? A sense of perfection, of changelessness. Do you know the constellations of Realmspace, by any chance?"

Teldin shook his head.

"No, I suppose not. That, over there—" he reached out with a slender hand and traced shapes among the stars "—is the Harp. That, the Sword and Dagger. And that is the new constellation, the Lady of Mystery."

Teldin glanced over at the elf. "How can a constellation be new?" he asked.

"Of course the pattern itself is as old as any," the elf explained with a half-smile. "The meaning has changed, that's all. Once it was two constellations, the Dragon of Dawn and the Firbolg, but after the Time of Troubles, many inhabitants of the Realms decided it would be best to devise a constellation to revere the new goddess, the Wounded Lady. Do you know the story?"

"No," Teldin admitted, "but maybe . . ."

"Maybe another time, yes." The elf turned and pointed forward. "Do you see that bright star, just over the forecastle?"

Teldin looked where Vallus indicated. "Yes."

"That's Realmspace's primary, called—predictably—'the sun.' And *that*—" he pointed to another dot of light, nowhere near as brilliant as the first but still brighter than the other stars "—is Chandos, one of the giants of the Realmspace system, some seven thousand leagues across. For comparison, your own world is perhaps one thousand leagues across, and Toril is about the same. Do you realize that Chandos is about nine *million* leagues from us? And yet its light is almost enough to rival the sun. How can we not feel insignificant in the face of scales such as this?" He shook his head in wonder.

Teldin shrugged his shoulders but said nothing. *The universe might be huge,* he found himself thinking, *but most of it seems to be eager to make sure my stay here isn't as long as I'd like.* "How long to Toril?" he asked eventually.

"Another thirty days, perhaps," the elf answered casually.

He must have seen Teldin's expression of astonishment, because he chuckled. "Yes, it surprises me, too, at times. We traveled from one crystal sphere to another in, what, thirty days or so? Then, once we're within our destination sphere, we have to spend another thirty days to reach the planet we're interested in. Somehow it seems all wrong, but you should understand: There are rivers that flow in the phlogiston, rivers that can greatly increase one's speed if one's navigator is good enough to find them. Sylvie is one of the best. Once within a shell, there are no rivers, and even the smallest sphere is immense. Again, when it comes to understanding the universe—as with so much else—perspective is all-important. Wouldn't you say?"

With that, Vallus strolled away, leaving Teldin to his own contemplations.

* * * * *

The *Probe* was eighteen days inbound from the crystal sphere when the derelict ship was spotted. The hammership had, two days before, made its closest approach to Chandos, and the huge blue-green world was shrinking astern.

Teldin was leaning on the sterncastle rail, gazing out past the ship's stern spanker sails. Even at this distance, the great water world was an impressive sight. It had none of the dramatic hues of Zivilyn in the Krynn system, none of the great clashing bands of color. Instead, it was a study in subtle gradients as blues shaded imperceptibly into greens. The planet displayed an unbelievable range of intensities, from royal blues so deep they were almost purple to greens so faint they could almost be gray. Teldin could pick out three unusually bright points of light that appeared very close to the planet. Although nobody he'd spoken to had mentioned moons, he presumed these brilliant specks of light were satellites in orbit around the great planet.

The emotions that Teldin associated with this massive world were quite different from those he'd felt while viewing Zivilyn, too. Zivilyn, the giant of Krynn's system, seemed to embody dynamic change, energy, and turmoil. Chandos, on the other hand, made him feel calm, at peace with himself and with the universe as a whole.

"Ship ahoy!" The call echoed from the crow's nest atop the hastily repaired mainmast.

"Bearing?" That was Aelfred's call from up forward. Teldin turned and saw the big first mate climbing the ladder to the forecastle deck. A brass spyglass was under his arm.

"High on the starboard bow," the lookout answered.

Teldin looked up to the recently repaired crow's nest. He could see the lookout in his jury-rigged perch, arm outstretched and pointing. Teldin tried to pick out the exact angle the man was indicating, but from this perspective it was difficult.

Aelfred seemed to have no such problem. He snapped the brass tube up to his eye and trained it forward, slightly above and to the right of the *Probe*'s bow. "Got it," he called after a few moments. "Mosquito, it looks like. No lights . . ." His voice took on a harder edge. "She's tumbling. *Crew on deck!*"

From below Teldin heard the clanging of the bell that called the crew to their stations. The deck pounded with running feet as crewmen burst out onto the deck. Men swung into the rigging, and weapons crews prepared their catapults.

"Teldin! Over here!" Aelfred stood beside the forward turret, beckoning with a raised arm. Teldin crossed the main deck—doing his best to stay out of the way of the crewmen who were still rushing to their stations—and joined his friend.

Aelfred was leaning against the turret, his gaze directed forward toward the other ship that Teldin had yet to see. The turret was still immobilized after the damaging ballista strike from the deathspider, but that hardly mattered. The heavy ballista it contained was ruined, and there wasn't the material aboard necessary to rebuild or replace it, though, according to shipboard gossip, Horvath had offered to rig up a "suitable substitute." Bubbo, the weapons master, had threatened to clap the gnome in irons if he even tried.

As Teldin approached, the first mate turned to face him. The warrior's expression was troubled. "Teldin," he said, "I want you to . . ." He moved his palm in front of his face, as though rearranging his features. "Understand?"

"Why?" Teldin's eyes strayed to the star field in the direction in which the other ship must lie. "Are they enemies?"

"I don't think so," Aelfred said reluctantly, "I think she might be a derelict, but . . ." He snorted in disgust. "I'm getting paranoid. Look." His voice became more persuasive. "Where's the harm? If the ship's empty, just reverse it. If there are people aboard the ship, you might be saving your life."

Teldin paused. The first mate was right, he thought, Aelfred *was* being paranoid, but he had to admit, it might be a necessary kind of paranoia. Teldin still didn't like shapeshifting on principle, but what good would it do if he stood on principle so firmly that the neogi ended up with the cloak? He sighed and nodded. "I agree," he said quietly.

He glanced around him. There was nobody else on the forecastle. With the ballista wrecked, there was no call for a weapon crew. All the other crew members he could see were busy preparing the *Probe* for the unknown.

He pulled the hood of the cloak up over his head and forward so that it shadowed his face. He closed his eyes and took a calming breath.

What face should he take? For the first time this was a relevant question. Up until now in his practice, he'd been assuming the face and form of others that he knew on board the hammership. Obviously, this wasn't a good idea; how would Garay—for example—react if he ran into his own twin?

Unbidden, the image of his father came into his mind. He paused. Why not? He let the image build in intensity, then started making minor changes. His father was too old. Remove some of the lines from around his eyes, then. His eyes were the same rich blue as Teldin's own. Too much of a similarity; change them to dark brown. Finally, remove the gray streaks from the black hair. He mentally examined the picture he'd built up and was satisfied. As to the body, change the frame a little, but not so much that his clothes didn't fit right. Broaden the shoulders slightly, make the chest a tad deeper, and that was it.

Teldin's daily practice had paid off. The whole process took no more than a couple of heartbeats. He opened his eyes again.

Aelfred shook his head and rumbled deep in his throat. "I'll never get used to that." Teldin reached up to remove the hood, but the first mate's hand stopped him. "No," Aelfred said, "keep it on. No reason to draw attention to the fact that somebody else is wearing Teldin's clothes." He paused in thought. "For the same reason, don't talk unless you have to, all right?"

Teldin nodded.

Aelfred's distinctive grin returned. "Good. You can stay here and watch if you want, but if things get nasty, either get belowdecks out of the way—" he slapped Teldin's shoulder "—or, if it strikes your fancy, feel free to fry as many of the bad guys as you like."

The *Probe* maneuvered cautiously closer to the unidentified ship. It wasn't long before Teldin could pick it out against the blackness of wildspace. At first it was just a small, faint dot reflecting the distant sun's light with changing intensity. Presumably it fluctuated because the ship was tumbling and the surface area it presented to reflect the sunlight was constantly changing. Slowly it started to show detail.

The ship was tiny, Teldin could tell at once, much smaller than the hammership, and while the hammership resembled a great fish or shark, the other vessel looked much more like an insect. Its hull was thin and elongated, tapering to a delicate, upswept point at the stern. It had slender legs, as did the pirate wasp ships that had attacked the *Unquenchable*: four extended below the hull, presumably as landing gear, while the aft two legs were bent up and back, extending above the body. Delicate wings of a thin, silklike material arced aft over the hull, and a long, thin spine extended forward from the bow. Overall, the term that Aelfred had used for the vessel was absolutely appropriate: mosquito.

The ship showed no lights that Teldin could see, and it certainly wasn't moving in any controlled way. In fact, it was tumbling slowly, end over end, making one rotation in about a minute. There was no movement on deck—if the small ship *had* a deck. For all Teldin could tell, the mosquito was either dead or deserted.

As it turned out, the tumbling motion of the ship proved the greatest obstacle to finding out more about it. The *Probe* couldn't draw too near without running the risk of getting struck by a leg or wing, or by the extended stern of the hull itself.

As the hammership cautiously approached, Estriss and Vallus joined Aelfred on the forecastle. Teldin, his cloak hood still pulled forward to partially hide his changed features, stood well back from the group, hoping that nobody would pay him any notice. Estriss glanced his way and gave him a slight nod, as if to confirm the wisdom of what he'd done. Vallus, however, studied him a little more intently. Teldin was afraid that the elf would say something to draw attention to him, but after a few seconds of scrutiny, Vallus contented himself with a raised eyebrow and an aloof smile and turned back to the others, behavior quite out of character for the elf.

Aelfred put the problem into words. "Normally we'd fire a grappling iron with a rope attached," he explained, "take up the slack, and slow the ship that way, but without a ballista that's out of the question." He turned to the elven mage. "Vallus, any ideas?"

The wizard thought for a moment. "How heavy is that ship?" he asked eventually.

"I'd guess around six tons," Aelfred answered. "Can you slow it down with magic?"

"No," Vallus said firmly, "it's much too heavy for that." He paused in thought again. "I could fly over to it with a rope, and tie it off to the hull."

Aelfred shook his head. "And if there's something aboard that's hostile? You'd be a sitting duck."

The elf greeted that with a somewhat condescending grin. "I assure you, I can take good care of myself."

"I'd rather you didn't have to," the first mate shot back. "Could you fly somebody else—me, for example—over there?"

"I could," the elf confirmed, "but the same objection applies, doesn't it? There is, however, another option." His voice became more businesslike. "Have the crew prepare the grappling iron and rope you mentioned earlier. You won't need the ballista after all."

Aelfred barked orders, and the crew hurried to obey. Down on the main deck, amidships, a long rope was tied to the eye of a grappling iron, and the rope coiled on the deck. Twenty-five crewmen stood ready to do whatever was necessary. Vallus climbed down to the main deck and joined them.

When all was in readiness, the elf looked up expectantly at Aelfred.

"Go," the first mate ordered. "Deck crew, stand ready."

The elf's long fingers wove intricate patterns in the air before him. From where he stood on the forecastle, Teldin couldn't hear the incantation the mage was murmuring under his breath.

On the deck, the grappling iron quivered like something alive, then silently lifted from the planking. Slowly, trailing the rope behind it like a tail, it floated toward the tumbling mosquito. The coiled rope paid out smoothly.

The iron neared the angular vessel. "Rope crew ready," Vallus instructed quietly.

One crewman laid out the remaining rope across the deck. The other crew members spat in their palms, took up the rope, and braced themselves.

Carefully, the mage adjusted the position of the grappling iron. As the mosquito's slender stern swung up and over, the iron flicked into position. Its sharp tines bit into the wood near the aftmost end. "Take up the slack," the elf instructed.

Twenty-five men groaned as one as the rope crew took the load. The mosquito's tumbling slowed noticeably, but the ship was still moving.

"Give me some slack." The crew did as Vallus instructed. Under the elf's mental control, the grappling iron repositioned itself, this time near the mosquito's bow. "Take up the slack," Vallus ordered again, and again the men groaned, again the small ship slowed.

"Once more." The grappling iron moved again to the stern. This time the elf didn't have to give the order. As soon as the iron was positioned, the crew took up the load, then they relaxed, stretching strained muscles and muttering congratulations to one another. The mosquito lay at rest beside the hammership.

Vallus rejoined the others on the forecastle. "I thought that would work," he said mildly.

"Good job," Aelfred told him. The first mate called down to the rope crew, "Bring her alongside. *Slowly.*"

Now that the mosquito wasn't moving, and because speed wasn't an issue, only a dozen men were needed on the rope.

The others picked up weapons and stood along the rail. Those with bows had arrows nocked and ready, but didn't draw.

Silently the mosquito inched nearer. Still nothing moved on board the small ship. Eventually the hammership rocked slightly as the two hulls met.

"Boarding party," Aelfred roared. "Two people. Julia and Garay."

The red-haired officer and the muscular crewman drew their swords and clambered over the rail. Cautiously they moved about the mosquito's tiny deck.

"Nobody on deck," Julia called back. "Maybe below, but the air's fouled. I don't hold out much hope."

"Check it out," Aelfred ordered, "but no heroics. I want you both back."

Julia flipped the first mate a quick salute. She and Garay moved from sight.

Almost immediately they reappeared. Julia was in the lead, Garay following, with a large bundle in his arms. With a twinge, Teldin recognized the shape of that bundle: another body. Julia swung quickly back over the rail aboard the *Probe*. Garay handed his burden up to another crewman and followed.

Aelfred and the other officers hurried down to the main deck. Teldin followed, a little hesitantly. As he drew closer, he knew he'd been right in his identification of the bundle. Lying on the deck, it was unmistakably a human body, wrapped in a heavy green traveling cloak. Aelfred knelt beside it, and slowly reached out a hand to pull the cloak back from the face.

The body sat up. With a slender hand, it pulled the cloak back from its face and shook out its long blonde hair. "Well," the body said in a rich contralto voice, smiling into Aelfred's astonished face, "if this is death, it's not as bad as I expected."

* * * * *

The officers' saloon was as full as Teldin had ever seen it. Aelfred, Sylvie, and Julia—as Aelfred's second-in-command after the death of Sweor Tobregdan—sat around the central table. Estriss was notably absent, but presumably the illithid had decided his presence might disrupt the proceedings.

Teldin was present, too, though he'd pulled a chair away from the table and sat in a back corner. Nobody had actually invited him, but neither had he been excluded from the meeting, and—as his grandfather had always told him—it's easier to get forgiveness than permission, so he'd tagged along with the others. At first he'd considered keeping the hood of his cloak in place, then had decided Sylvie and Julia would have more important things on their minds than his changed appearance. He'd been right; neither woman had given him so much as a second glance. Their attention was focused totally on the sole inhabitant of the mosquito ship.

His own attention was focused pretty much in the same place, Teldin had to admit. He also had to admit that it was warranted.

The newcomer sat at the table, her back to the large port that looked out to the star-studded blackness of wildspace. She'd removed the heavy cloak she'd been wrapped in, and Teldin thought that was a great improvement. She was tall—almost as tall as Teldin himself—and slender, but her movements seemed to imply there was considerable strength in her supple body. She wore a jerkin and tights of forest green, not too different from the clothes worn by most aboard the *Probe*, but her garb was well-tailored to show off the curves of her figure. On her feet were boots of soft mahogany-brown leather that came halfway up shapely calves. Her face was slender, but her features were more rounded than sharply chiseled, and her small nose was slightly upturned. When she smiled—which was often—the tanned skin around her green eyes crinkled in what Teldin thought of as "laugh-lines," and she became even more beautiful than when her face was at rest. When she spoke, her warm voice seemed to have an undercurrent of laughter.

She was speaking now, brushing shoulder-length curls of honey-blond hair back from her face. "My name is Rianna Wyvernsbane," she said, "and, first thing, I want to thank you all for saving me. I thought I was dead."

Aelfred gave a half-smile and shook his head as though to dismiss the thanks. "What happened to your ship?" he asked.

"I was inward bound from Garden," Rianna answered.

"For Toril?" Sylvie put in.

"For Dragon Rock, in the Tears of Selune. I live on Toril, but I keep my ship—the *Ghost*—on the Rock."

"Toril to Garden's a long flight in a mosquito," Sylvie remarked.

"Not really," Rianna replied with a throaty chuckle, "not if you don't mind your own company. I make my living as a message-runner. If you need a message delivered to any planet in Realmspace—fast, with no complications—I'm your girl."

"You were telling us what happened," Aelfred reminded her.

Rianna favored him with a smile. "That's right, I was." She sat back in her chair. She seemed completely relaxed, Teldin thought, totally unconcerned that she was aboard a strange ship surrounded by potential enemies. Was she so brave that the thought didn't bother her, or so stupid that the danger hadn't even occurred to her? Or was her apparent relaxation just a facade?

"I'd delivered my message to the party in question," Rianna went on, "and I was climbing away from Garden when I saw another vessel coming up ahead. A deathspider."

Aelfred cursed. "Neogi again."

Rianna shot him a curious look, but he waved her on with her story. "The *Ghost* isn't much to look at," she continued, "and she's not much in combat, but I've stripped her for maneuverability, and she's fast. . . ." She grinned wryly. "The long and the short of it is, I ran, down toward Garden again. If you know Garden at all, you know it's a cluster of large rocks in one atmosphere envelope. I ducked in among the rocks to lose the deathspider. It worked. *Just.*" She grimaced. "Those neogi are nothing if not persistent. They got a few shots away, and the poor old *Ghost* took a bad hit. . . ."

"I didn't notice any damage," Sylvie pointed out.

"Take a look at the starboard wing root," Rianna suggested, "you'll see it's held on by rope, a little wire, and a whole lot of good intentions. The keel is cracked, too, ready to give way, I think."

"Go on," Aelfred prompted.

"They followed me down," the woman continued, "right on my tail, until they had to break off or slam full into one of the rocks. I went on through. They had to reverse course, then take the long way around, so I had a good head start, good enough to get away."

"What were the neogi doing there?" The question slipped out before Teldin could stop it.

Rianna's green-eyed gaze settled on Teldin for the first time. I wish I'd made myself more handsome, he caught himself thinking. Now where did *that* thought come from?

"I don't know," she replied with a smile, "I didn't stop to ask them."

"And then?" Aelfred prompted.

"Then I headed for Toril. I pushed the *Ghost* as hard as I could, for as long as I could keep my mind clear. I was well away from Garden, and I couldn't see the neogi anymore. That's when my helm died. No warning. One moment I'm tearing along at full spelljamming speed, the next, I'm moving at a crawl with no control over the ship at all."

Teldin felt a current of sympathy around the table. He could understand why. Vallus Leafbower's comments about distance in wildspace were still with him. The idea of being stranded in that vastness was terrifying.

"Bad," Sylvie commiserated, echoing the feelings of everyone else in the saloon. "What was wrong with the helm?"

Rianna shook her head, and her blond tresses swung. "I'm not an arcane," she chuckled. "I can run a helm. I can't troubleshoot one. It was just *dead*."

"And then?" Aelfred prompted again.

"Then I drifted. What else could I do? I was too far from Garden for its gravity to affect me, but I did still have *some* speed—though not much—and I was heading toward the sun. I figured the best thing—the *only* thing—was to conserve the air I had. No work, no movement that I could avoid. Just hope that some ship would find me before I suffocated." She bathed everyone at the table with a warm smile. "I slept a lot, but I didn't enjoy the dreams."

"The air was foul aboard your ship," Julia noted. "How long were you adrift?"

"Twenty-three days."

The female officer looked at her uncertainly. "You had food and water for twenty-three days? On a mosquito?"

"Water, yes," Rianna replied. "I don't do cargo runs, so I

load the *Ghost*'s cargo space with as much water as I can. You never know, do you? But food, no. I've been on very thin rations, and for the last couple of days nothing at all. So maybe when we're finished here . . . ?" She patted her stomach.

"We're almost finished," Aelfred said briskly, "then you can get something to eat. Your destination is Toril?"

"Dragon Rock," Rianna corrected him, "if you're going near there . . ."

"Our destination is Toril," the first mate told her.

She shrugged. "Close enough."

"About your ship," Aelfred pressed on. "We can't take her aboard."

"Tow her?" Rianna suggested.

The first mate shook his head. "Not practical. If the keel *is* cracked, she'll break up. Plus, we can't land with a ship in tow."

Rianna digested this in silence, eyes lowered. "Ah, well," she sighed eventually, "I suppose I knew the *Ghost* and I had taken our last voyage together. Cut her loose if you have to."

Sylvie reacted to the woman's sadness. "We'll post a salvage claim on the hull," she said reassuringly. "That way maybe you'll recover something from her."

The newcomer nodded her thanks, then she turned back to Aelfred. "What port on Toril?" she asked.

"Rauthaven. Naturally, we'll give you passage to there."

"Nimbral?" She looked somber for a moment, then brightened. "Well, it could be worse. I should be able to get passage to Dragon Rock from Rauthaven, then maybe another ship, and I'm back in business." She smiled at Aelfred. "If we're through here, maybe we could do something about that meal . . . ?"

* * * * *

As the *Probe* drew closer to Toril, Teldin came to realize that Rianna Wyvernsbane's status aboard ship was almost as ambiguous as his, though for quite different reasons. Almost immediately after she'd eaten, Rianna had sought out Aelfred and insisted that he assign her duties in return for passage to Toril. She'd offered to take shifts on the hammership's helm—

after all, she *was* mage enough to run the *Ghost*—but the *Probe* already had enough helmsmen. Instead he assigned her to assist Sylvie with plotting the approach to Rauthaven.

The crew knew that Rianna was at least nominally an officer—by virtue of her assignment alone, though she couldn't officially give orders—but they couldn't help but respond to her on a nonprofessional level as well. She was, after all, strikingly beautiful, and it was apparent that she had no close friendship—or any other relationship—with anyone on board. That was just another factor that set her apart from most of the other women on board. There were no rules aboard the *Probe* that prohibited relationships or even casual liaisons between crew members—as long as they didn't interfere with the smooth running of the ship—and the hammership's female crew members were generally as glad to enjoy the benefits of this freedom as the males.

It was easy to learn just where Rianna was aboard the *Probe*, Teldin noted with amusement, just look for the largest group of off-duty male crew members. The size of her entourage seemed pretty constant, though its membership varied according to time of day.

Even when Rianna wasn't present, she was often the topic of conversation among the "temporarily unattached" men aboard. Discussions over who did or didn't "have a chance" with her were common, and some of these exchanges sometimes grew a little heated. One, in fact, almost came to blows, forcing Aelfred Silverhorn to exercise his considerable disciplinary powers. The two men involved found themselves standing back-to-back watches for three days.

Rianna did nothing to foster these controversies, but her naturally friendly nature did nothing to discourage them either. She was always ready to talk to anyone nearby, and male members of the crew frequently competed to see who could best elicit her warm and throaty laugh.

Teldin's own situation was different, too. Once it was established that Rianna would stay aboard until the *Probe* made landfall, he suggested to Aelfred that it might be best if he dropped the charade that he was becoming less and less comfortable maintaining. To his surprise, Aelfred disagreed vehemently. "It's not that I have any reason to distrust her," the first mate explained, "quite the opposite, in fact, but why take the risk? It's safer if you don't show your own face. I'm not ordering you, Teldin," he added, "just asking, as a friend, all right?" Teldin had accepted the big warrior's argument, but wasn't happy with it.

As the days passed, there was no way he could keep his new face hidden. At first, crew members had shown surprise over the "new man" aboard the *Probe*, but his own voice—which he was still incapable of disguising—quickly gave away his true identity. The crew's reaction to this had surprised him deeply. He'd expected that people would question him, but that simply never happened. Instead, the crew just shrugged and seemed to write it off as another magical eccentricity of the "fighter-mage" in their midst. He learned that Estriss, as captain, had quietly passed the word that no crew member was to tell Rianna about Teldin's true identity, on pain of losing one half of the culprit's pay for the voyage. Considering, cynically, that any crewman would give up that one-half share and more for a better chance at Rianna's favors, Teldin doubted that this edict would have any effect at all.

Teldin made no effort to speak to Rianna and, in fact, went out of his way to avoid meeting her. Even though he found her as attractive as did every other male member of the crew, he knew that talking to her would force him into a position of lying about his identity, and that was something he simply didn't want to be compelled to do.

So, for the first five days after her arrival on board, Teldin saw Rianna Wyvernsbane only at a distance.

There was no way that could continue, of course. On the sixth day after the *Probe* had encountered the Mosquito, Teldin found himself unable to sleep. As he usually did on occasions such as this, he went to the officers' saloon.

When he opened the door, he saw that Rianna was already there. Unaccountably, she was alone, somehow having managed to shake off her retinue of admirers. She was sprawled, boneless and relaxed, in one chair, with her long legs propped up on another, gazing out the port into the depths of space. He started to withdraw.

Rianna must have sensed his presence somehow, for she turned her green-eyed gaze on him and greeted him with a slow smile. "Well met," she said lazily. "Join me?" She patted another chair.

Teldin hesitated. There was no way he could leave now without being unforgivably rude. . . . Plus he had to admit that he found the tall blonde very attractive, and the chance to talk to her alone wasn't something to pass up lightly.

His hesitation was long enough for Rianna to notice. Her warm smile faded a little. "If you'd rather not . . ." she said quietly, a hint of disappointment in her voice.

Quickly he stepped into the room, closing the door behind him. "No," he answered, "I'd like to." He took the chair she had indicated. It was close to her, close enough for him to notice a subtle aroma. Some kind of musky perfume? None of the other women aboard wore scent. Or was it just her natural fragrance? He sat in the chair a little stiffly, then forced himself to relax. For the first time, he had the opportunity to study the woman from close up. At this range, it was possible to be a little more critical. Taken individually, her features weren't as perfect as they appeared from a distance. Her mouth, for example, was a little large for her face, filled with white teeth. When she smiled, her upper lip pulled back to display a line of pink gum. Her jawline was hard, giving her a "stubborn" chin.

But that was nit-picking. When he looked into Rianna's face, it was the totality that mattered, the way the individual features combined into a harmonious whole. He had to admit that Rianna Wyvernsbane was one of the most beautiful women he'd ever seen, let alone spoken to.

He'd never been good at judging women's ages—and that fact had gotten him into minor trouble on occasion. Rianna simply reinforced the fact. Initially he'd guessed that she was around twenty summers. Now he had to revise that estimate upward. The laugh-lines around her eyes were deeper and remained visible—if only as a network of spiderweb-thin traces—even when her face was in repose. The eyes themselves were clear and steady and seemed to contain wisdom out of keeping with someone as young as his original guess. If he were forced to estimate now, he'd have to say she was about his own age, maybe even a couple of years older.

If Rianna noticed his close appraisal, she gave no sign. "I

remember you were here when I first arrived," she said, "so you know who I am. . . ." She let the statement trail off.

"My name is Aldyn Brewer," Teldin told her, a name that Estriss had suggested he use. Its rhythm was much the same as his real name, as were the sounds of its individual syllables. The illithid had reasoned that Teldin would be better able to remember—and respond to—a name with a cadence similar to his own.

"Aldyn Brewer," Rianna repeated. The name sounded so much better rolling off her tongue, Teldin thought. "Did you come here looking for me, Aldyn Brewer?"

"No," Teldin answered honestly. "I often come here to relax."

"To be alone with the stars," Rianna amplified. "Yes. That's why I came here. I miss it, being on a big ship. That's what I liked about the *Ghost*. Alone with the stars for days, weeks at a time. Do you like your own company, Aldyn Brewer?" Her voice was slow, lazy, as though she were merely vocalizing her wandering thoughts.

"Sometimes," he replied, "but I enjoy conversation, too."

She chuckled throatily. "Well spoken. What kind of conversation would you enjoy now?"

He shrugged, returning her smile. "Any that you'd care to give me."

"Ah—" she laughed "—the give and take of witty repartee. All right, then. Where do you hail from, Aldyn Brewer?"

Teldin's stomach went cold. He had a false name, but no false story to go with it. He desperately searched his memory. "From Wayspace," he said, clutching at the name of a crystal shell that Aelfred had mentioned visiting. "From Waypoint," he said, naming what he thought he recalled being the major world in that sphere. When she nodded, he asked, with a sinking feeling, "Do you know it?"

She shook her head. "Know it, no," she answered. "Know *of* it, yes. I've heard the name, but I don't know much about it. Tell me about your life on Waypoint, Aldyn."

"It's not that interesting," Teldin mumbled uncomfortably.

Rianna wasn't going to be put off that easily. "Perhaps not to you," she pointed out, "but I like learning everything I can about other worlds: the *feel* of the world, what it's like to live there." She sat up straighter in her chair and tucked her booted feet beneath her. Hugging her knees, she smiled at him again. "What did you do on Waypoint, Aldyn Brewer?"

One part of Teldin's mind—the logical part—was telling him this was crazy, dangerous. He should make some excuse and get himself out of here right now. Another part admitted that this was the last thing he wanted to do. With Rianna sitting near him, and her fragrance in his nostrils, he certainly didn't want to leave. In any case, he found himself reasoning, he should be able to keep the topic of conversation away from anything sensitive. This would be good practice if he had to do it under other, more dangerous, circumstances.

Thus reassured, he relaxed back into his chair. "I was a farmer," he told her with a smile, "nothing interesting."

She shook her head, and her golden curls danced. "Don't undervalue yourself," she told him. "You left your world to seek adventure in space, didn't you? How many people actually do that? One in a hundred thousand? One in a million? *You* did. *I* find that interesting. Tell me about your farm. Was it yours?"

"My father's," Teldin answered, "but I ran it, ever since I came back from . . ." He paused. He'd almost said "back from the wars." He had to be more careful. " . . . from military training," he concluded quickly.

"Your land has an army?"

"I think all lands do," Teldin answered honestly.

She grinned. "Perhaps. What did you grow, Aldyn?"

"Some of everything," Teldin replied. He was beginning to enjoy this, despite—or maybe because of—the knowledge that he was taking a risk. "We were self-sufficient and grew enough to sell. We weren't rich—far from it—but we were comfortable. It was a good life, a pleasant life."

"But too dull, else you'd never have left to come into space, right?" She nodded as if answering her own question. "Were you married?"

"No. Never."

"Why not?" Rianna's grin grew mischievous. "Were you having too much fun breaking farm maids' hearts? Would marriage have put too great a limit on your freedom?"

Teldin shook his head firmly. "No," he answered again. "I

just never found the right woman. Maybe—" he had to smile at his own unaccustomed flight of rhetoric "—maybe that's why I left home, to seek her among the stars."

Rianna's eyes sparkled like emeralds. Her laugh seemed to thrill through Teldin's body. "Would you know her if you found her, Aldyn Brewer?" she asked.

"Who's to say I haven't, Rianna Wyvernsbane?" he joked.

The woman laughed again. "If all men of Waypoint are as silver-tongued as you, maybe the place is worth a visit, but you know, it's interesting. . . ." Her voice took on a musing tone, but her gaze was steady and appraising. "I always thought that Waypoint was a desert world, and all you could farm there was dust and lizards."

Teldin had felt like he was drifting through a warm, comfortable dream. Now reality struck him like a bucket of cold water. *Stupid*, he cursed himself. He'd let himself get blinded by Rianna's beauty and apparent friendliness, and she'd led him straight into a stupid contradiction. Damn it! She knew he was hiding something. What else did she know?

The woman's green eyes were still on him. Well, he thought, he could at least do *some* damage control. "That must be the southern hemisphere you're thinking of," he said as casually as he could manage. "Well, it's been a pleasure, Rianna. . . ." He started to climb to his feet, but Rianna reached out a hand and took his arm.

"No, don't," she said quietly. "Don't leave yet."

The woman's grip on his arm was surprisingly firm. Teldin could have broken it, but not without some effort. And, even now, he had to admit he didn't want to break it. He took his seat again.

"I could well be mistaken about Waypoint," Rianna told him. Her hand was still on his arm; he could feel its warmth. It was her gaze, now, that fixed him in place, rather than her grip. It held his own firmly, made it impossible for him to look away even if he'd wanted to.

"We should change the subject," she went on. "You've told me something about you, and it's my turn now. In my business, I deal with lots of people who have secrets. I think just about everyone has secrets. You know, I think your secrets are probably the most personal possessions you ever have, and no matter how rich you are, they're probably the most valuable. Do you see what I'm saying? I think you should treat a person's secrets with the same respect you'd treat any other valuable item they have. You can accept some item of value as a gift, but you don't take it. It's the same with secrets." She smiled. "There. I've just told you something that's important to me, one of the rules I live by. Like a gift, I hope you take it in the spirit in which it was given."

Although the woman's tone was light, almost joking, and her mouth was smiling, the glib expression didn't reach her green eyes. Her gaze still held Teldin's, and in it was an intensity that was almost uncomfortable. He couldn't look away—not that he was sure he wanted to. Those deep, emerald eyes seemed intent on passing a message that wasn't contained in her words. Or maybe it was, but deep below the surface. Teldin thought he understood that message, thought it was meant to reassure him, but he couldn't accept that message at face value, not right now.

Rianna seemed to sense his thoughts as clearly as if he'd spoken them aloud. She nodded as if in answer to a question or statement of his, then she let her eyes soften into the smile that was already playing about her lips. The intensity faded from her gaze.

"Well," she said—and her tone was as light as ever—"I hear Rauthaven is our port of call. I've been to the Resort several times. Maybe when we land I can show you around a little."

"I'd like that," Teldin told her, and again he was telling the truth.

Her smile grew warmer, if that were possible. "So would I."

Chapter Ten

• • •

From space, Toril was to all practical purposes indistinguishable from Krynn. Teldin was surprised and somewhat disappointed to find this out. Both worlds were simple blue spheres streaked with irregular patterns of white clouds. From Teldin's vantage on the forecastle, Toril appeared about as big as his clenched fist held at arm's length. There was no way he could see anything through the cloud cover, no way to pick out the shapes of the seas and the continents that would prove that he was actually seeing a new world. Currently, Teldin thought, if he were feeling particularly paranoid, he could easily convince himself that the planet he was looking at was Krynn, and that the whole voyage had been some kind of elaborate hoax. *Let's just sail out and back and confuse the dirtkicker.* Of course, he *didn't* believe that, but in some ways it was an attractive concept. It would mean that what those white clouds concealed was *home.*

Teldin shook his head. It would be good to get off the *Probe,* he thought. He needed to feel real ground under his feet, see a real sky overhead. Feel the wind, taste the rain, smell growing things. While he'd lived on the farm, he'd never been consciously aware of the close bond that he felt with the world around him. It was only this forced isolation he'd experienced aboard ship that had brought this fact to his notice. *Why do we have to lose something to realize we have it?* he wondered. He'd noted that trait in others but was surprised to find it in himself.

The symptoms of his isolation had started subtly—vivid dreams of home, of walking through familiar woods, of hiking the hills that bordered his farm—then he'd found that his mind would sometimes wander off down strange pathways, contemplating bizarre thoughts, the one about the trip to Toril being a hoax, for example. There was never any temptation to accept these weird conceptions as real, so he didn't fear for his sanity, but he did quickly come to realize that he wasn't by nature cut out for long voyages in the claustrophobic atmosphere of a ship—even one as large as the hammership. How could Rianna stand it? he wondered. Her ship was much smaller than this one. All in all, it would be much better if he could get onto solid ground, find an arcane, get the cloak off, and be done with it. Maybe he could go home to Krynn. Or— he glanced over at Rianna, who leaned on the forecastle rail next to him—perhaps he'd prefer to make a new life for himself on Toril. One never knew. . . .

"You look so serious." Rianna's warm contralto voice cut through his reflections. "A copper for your thoughts."

He smiled at her. "Save your money. I was just thinking how much Toril looks like . . . like my home. It's a strange world, an alien world. Shouldn't it look strange or alien?"

Rianna gave a throaty chuckle. "It's *not* strange or alien," she chided him, "it's my home." She sobered. "I do know what you mean, though. It's . . . disappointing that so many worlds look alike. Of course, there are some old spacedogs who claim they can tell how the continents are laid out by looking at how they disturb the clouds, and so claim that all worlds look different to them."

"I can't believe that."

She laughed again. "Neither can I, but I'm sure the stories are good for a few pints at dockside taverns."

They sank back into a comfortable silence. Over the last several days, Teldin and Rianna had spent more time together. It was nothing extreme and didn't even seem to be purposeful on either of their parts. It was just a matter of taking opportunities that came up—and, Teldin had to admit, being more conscious of such opportunities. Whenever the two of them met, at meals or while wandering the ship when neither had the watch, they'd take the opportunity for brief chats. These talks were just enjoyable ways of whiling away some time. They'd rarely touch on anything of much significance, preferring to keep the exchanges light. It was obvious to Teldin that Rianna enjoyed his company, and he knew that their impromptu discussions were generally the brightest parts of his day. It was impossible to deny that a warm friendship was developing between them.

Or, more correctly, between Rianna Wyvernsbane and Aldyn Brewer, Teldin thought somewhat bitterly. Since Rianna's crippled mosquito had first been spotted, he hadn't shown his real face, even when alone in his cabin. The *Probe*'s officers were very careful to refer to him only as "Aldyn," and the way things were working out, the hammership's crew had less and less reason to refer to him at all.

The growing relationship—if you could call it that—didn't go unnoticed. When it comes to such things, after all, even the largest ship is very small. The retinue of male crew members that had been following Rianna around the ship began to tail off in number. While she was still considered by far the most beautiful and alluring female aboard ship, it was generally accepted—at least according to the gossip that Teldin heard—that she'd made her choice as to the man with whom she wanted to spend her time. With anyone else, that might have led to some uncomfortable, jealousy-fueled confrontations. In Teldin's case, however, the crew seemed unwilling to provoke an incident with the warrior-mage who now wanted to be called Aldyn. Envy and jealousy did still appear, but in the harmless forms of generally shunning Teldin and not talking to him unless absolutely necessary—which, Teldin found, was just fine with him at the moment.

The *Probe*'s officers were a different case. Rianna seemed to have totally won them over—particularly Sylvie, it seemed. Teldin had frequently seen them in private *tete-a-tetes*. Now the half-elven woman was quite likely to shoot Teldin knowing—and somehow sly—glances whenever they met. Only Julia seemed to feel anything less than total friendship for the blond woman, and that, Teldin decided, was merely jealousy. While the red-haired officer was attractive in her own way, she definitely paled in comparison with Rianna.

Aelfred and Estriss seemed to view the whole thing with what could only be called paternal amusement—which Teldin found patronizing but was unable to complain about. The illithid had reminded him that it was still a good idea to maintain his new identity, no matter how he felt to the contrary. Aelfred's only comment had been that "Aldyn's" face looked great, but that he hoped the illusion was as good all over his body—this said with an expression of studious innocence.

Teldin wanted to argue about the whole thing. He enjoyed Rianna's company, and apparently vice versa, but that's all it was. Not even friendship, really, just close-acquaintanceship, if there were such a word. He well knew that it'd do more harm than good to argue the point. Oh, well, what did it matter? He was enjoying himself at the moment, and he might be nearing the end of his quest, if Estriss was right about the arcane.

Estriss. That was another interesting issue. Rianna had been aboard the *Probe* only a couple of days when she'd marched onto the bridge—so said Aelfred—and demanded to see the captain. She'd figured out that the captain was keeping himself hidden, she'd explained, and had concluded it was because he wasn't human or demihuman. Was he a lizard man? she'd asked. Or maybe an illithid?

Aelfred had been surprised, but admitted to Teldin that he'd also been quite impressed. He'd immediately arranged a meeting between Rianna and Estriss, wondering if the woman would handle matters as well when she met the "brain-sucking monster" face to face. If he'd been expecting any show of fear, he'd been disappointed. "She carried it off perfectly," the first mate had told Teldin, "greeted Estriss politely, then started asking if 'the honorable captain' ever had any need for a message-runner." The big man had chuckled deep in his throat. "I'm coming to like her a lot."

"Not too much, I hope," Teldin had replied.

* * * * *

Neither Teldin nor Rianna were on duty as the *Probe* spiralled slowly down toward the surface of Toril. There was nobody on the forecastle, so they'd taken it as their private viewpoint.

As they'd drawn closer to the planet, and—presumably—as the *Probe*'s navigator picked the course that would best take them to Rauthaven, the cloud cover had thinned beneath them. Now Teldin could look down through patchy white clouds. There was water below them, water of an almost breathtakingly pure blue. Here and there was a flash as sunlight reflected off waves—at least, that's what Rianna assured him the glints were. From this vantage point, Teldin found he had no way of judging their altitude, and hence no way of estimating the size of the body of water below them. It could just as easily be a small lake or a great ocean. He remarked on that to Rianna.

"It's the Great Sea," she told him. She pointed. "See that island? That's Nimbral, called the Sea-Haven. Rauthaven's near the southeast tip."

Teldin moved closer to her so he could sight down her arm. In fact, he could pick out the island she was referring to, but why pass up on an opportunity like this? he thought. Her shoulder was warm against his chest as he lowered his head to sight down along her arm. He took a quiet breath, enjoying the subtle smell of her.

She nudged him playfully. "See it?"

"Oh, *there*," he responded in feigned surprise. Her laugh told him she knew what he was doing, and—more importantly—that she, too, enjoyed their closeness. "So that's where we're going."

"That's it," she confirmed. "Of course, you won't see the city itself until we get much lower."

Even though she'd lowered her arm, Teldin felt no great desire to move away from her. She leaned in a little more against his chest. After a moment's hesitation, he slipped his arm around her waist and let his hand settle on the point of her hip. She made no movement to pull away or remove his arm. "Where were you born?" he asked, more to simply hear her voice again than from any need for the information.

She laughed softly. "Sorry, I can't point it out to you," she said teasingly, "we can't see it from here. It's called Waterdeep, on the Sword Coast, a long way away."

"But you've been to Rauthaven."

"I've been a lot of places. My father traveled a lot, and then I followed in the family tradition."

"What did he do, your father?"

She shrugged, and he felt strong muscles shift under her soft skin. "He was a merchant, I suppose you'd say," she replied. "But, like me, he dealt more in information than hard goods. There are always people willing to pay to have their messages delivered without having to trust to wizards."

"You're a wizard, too, aren't you?" Teldin remarked. "You've got to be to pilot a ship, don't you? Unless you're a priest . . ."

Rianna laughed out loud. "Oh, I'm no priest, Aldyn Brewer," she told him. "Yes, I'm a wizard, but not much of one, just enough to fly my ship. I learned it young. It didn't take me long to realize that the world's full of creatures that would like nothing more than a nice, harmless messenger for evenfeast. Magic's an equalizer, and I always like to have an equalizer." With the suddenness that Teldin had come to expect from her, she changed the subject. "You're *with* this ship but not *of* it, at least that's how I read it," she said. "How come you're going to Rauthaven?"

Teldin didn't hesitate. Since their first meeting in the officers' saloon, he'd taken the time to work up a good background story and the answers to the questions Rianna—or anyone else—was most likely to ask him. He didn't have to like it, and he didn't, but he recognized it was necessary—for now, part of his mind added. "I need to meet with an arcane," he told her smoothly. "Estriss tells me there's likely to be one around because of the auction. You know about the auction?"

"Yes, he told me. Why an arcane? What do you need with one of them?"

Again Teldin had an answer ready. "That's what I've been hired to do," he said. "My principal—the one who's paying me—needs me to pass a message on to one of the arcane, and that's what I'm going to do."

Rianna accepted that with a nod, and Teldin knew he'd guessed right in his prevarication. Someone whose livelihood lay in trading messages and information would consider the "mysterious employer" as a normal condition, and as a sacrosanct trust.

As the two had spoken, the *Probe* had slipped lower into the atmosphere. The world below had changed, unnoticed, from a section of a sphere to a flat plane that was for the first time truly below the vessel. As the viewpoint had changed, features had expanded and retreated, to be lost by distance and curvature. The southeastern tip of the island had expanded until it filled almost the entire view beneath the *Probe*. It continued to expand, too, bringing home to Teldin just how fast the ship was descending. The scattered clouds that had been just streaks overlaying the distant landscape were suddenly great islands of fleecy white, fantasy landscapes that could in tales become the homes of pegasi or dragons. The ship then plunged into one of the drifting islands, and everything was white. Teldin felt moisture on his face. Tendrils of mist whipped past him.

With breathtaking suddenness, the ship was out of the cloud and the view was clear again. They were much lower now, perhaps not much higher than the tallest mountain. The peninsula had vanished. There was just an indented coastline, roughly straight for as far as he could see in either direction.

There was no farmland, he noticed with some surprise. Did that mean that all the food necessary to support a city was shipped in from elsewhere? It wasn't that the region was barren; in fact, it seemed like it would make excellent farmland. Everywhere was lush and green, like the tended private parkland of a noble—except that this private park stretched from horizon to horizon. There were regions of uninterrupted greenery that could only be woods. At one point a thin line of green meandered through grasslands to reach the sea—a river lined with trees; it could be nothing else. The land was beautiful here, Teldin thought. There were much worse places for a man to settle down and make his living. Perhaps after this business with the cloak was finally concluded, he could buy himself some land here and be happy. Of course, where would he get the money? Ah, well, he told himself with a grin, burn those bridges when you come to them.

Rianna took his shoulder and pointed. The *Probe* had continued its spiral approach and was now on a different heading. While he'd initially been looking to sea, Teldin was now gazing inland. He was still unsure about the scale, but he guessed that the parkland extended five miles or so from the coast. Then, suddenly, the flat landscape changed. Rising out of the plain like walls were rugged, tree-covered hills. There was no hint of foothills. It looked almost as though the hills had just been placed randomly in the midst of arable land. Okay, let's set one down here, he could imagine one godlike workman saying to his fellow. The hills probably weren't that tall, he thought, but the contrast with the surrounding terrain made them look much higher. What would it be like to live at the foot of one of those? he found himself wondering. Claustrophobic? Or would you eventually get used to it and just not notice anymore?

He turned to Rianna. "Who delivered the mountains?" he asked jokingly.

She laughed in reply. "If they want to compete in my business, I'm getting out of it."

The ship continued its slow spiral, dropping lower and lower with each turn. Teldin found himself looking at the coastline again, but now he was close enough to the ground to see the narrow white-sand beaches that lined the ocean. From here it looked as though the parkland came within a hundred feet or less of the water, then there was a low cliff—it was difficult to tell how high, because of the foreshortening effect of the ship's altitude—dropping down to a narrow strand, then the ocean. From this angle it wasn't the pure blue he'd seen from higher up; it had taken on a deep, almost metallic green and had gentle wrinkles like the marks of hammer blows on the forged steel of a plow blade. He could make out here and there the white froth of waves breaking on the sand.

Rianna squeezed his shoulder again and pointed forward.

There was the city, Rauthaven, a walled port town built around the circumference of a small bay that made for a perfectly sheltered harbor. Breakwaters extended from both sides of the bay's mouth, closing the entry into the harbor down to a narrow passage. There were watchtowers at the extreme ends of the breakwaters, and Teldin imagined that in time of war chains could be drawn across the passage. The harbor itself looked packed with ships; vessels ranging from tiny fishing boats to coasters to ships-of-the-line swung at anchor, seemingly at random.

The city itself rose up the sides of the low hills that surrounded the bay. Once more altitude made it difficult to estimate sizes, but Teldin thought that the buildings were generally small and the streets wide and spacious. The larger of those streets radiated outward and uphill from the harbor like the spokes of a wagon wheel. Narrower streets followed generally concentric curves around the harbor. Around the city's walls, however, this sense of order broke down. The harbor was roughly circular, but the outlying regions of the city were much more irregular. For example, the city extended farther along the coast to the northwest, which put the harbor nearer the southeast end of the town. The buildings got larger as you headed northwest, until the largest of all were atop the low hill—with, no doubt, a spectacular view down into the harbor. Those would have to be the homes of the noble families, or whoever it was who governed the city, plus the richest of the merchants, Teldin thought.

In his travels, Teldin had seen a few cities, but nothing to rival Rauthaven in beauty. Krynn cities generally looked like jumbled assortments of buildings, some stone, some wood, tossed together with no kind of overall plan. Architectural styles warred and colors clashed. Here, even though they varied in size, all of the buildings seemed to share one architectural style, leading to a sense of harmony he'd never experienced before. The colors, too, were consistent. The vast majority of the buildings had white walls, with sloping roofs of what could only be red tile. As he watched, the sun came out from behind a cloud and the city practically glowed. He felt the breath catch in his throat. Again he found himself thinking, I could live here.

The *Probe* had changed course again and was now heading out to sea. This only made sense, Teldin reasoned: There was no space for the hammership to land within the harbor, and the natives might get a little nervous about a strange flying vessel heading straight for them.

Now *there* was an issue. He turned to Rianna. "Are they likely to shoot at us?" he asked.

Her reply was a chuckle. "Only if we do something untoward," she elaborated. "Believe it or not, Rauthaven gets a considerable share of Toril's spacefaring traffic. Mostly that's because the whole of Nimbral is much more open to magic, and to things that would be too strange for the rest of Toril. It's also got a lot to do with its sheltered harbor. Spelljamming ships are built for space, even those that can land on the water—like this one—and they don't do well in heavy seas. So when you put one down, you want to get it into a snug harbor, and right quick, too."

"How are we going to land?" Teldin asked. It was interesting. In all the conversations he'd had on spelljamming with Estriss, Aelfred, and the others, this was one topic they'd never touched on.

"It depends on the harbormaster," Rianna replied, not quite answering his question. "The lookouts will have spotted us by this time, and the harbormaster will be giving us our instructions on wind direction and speed, where we should drop anchor, that kind of thing."

"Give us orders? How?"

"By flags. And—" Rianna pointed over the rail to the harbor that was now below them "—there they are."

Teldin leaned over the rail, but not too far. While they had been in space with, presumably, uncounted millions of miles to fall, he'd felt no sense of vertigo, but now that they were only a thousand feet up, he felt an uncomfortable stirring in the pit of his stomach.

Rianna seemed to sense his discomfort and had the perfect cure for it. She leaned into him again so the sides of their bodies were pressed together from knee to shoulder. Teldin, not surprisingly, found he no longer noticed his vertigo. Rianna pointed again.

He sighted along her arm. At the innermost point of the harbor, directly opposite the passage through the breakwater, was another watchtowerlike structure—presumably the harbormaster's office or whatever served its function in Rauthaven. From this angle, he could easily see a tall flagpole atop the building. A string of small, brightly colored flags extended the entire length of the pole. All except the uppermost were similar to the signal flags he'd seen used in the army. In pride of place atop the string was a larger flag that bore a red device—from this height, it was impossible to make it out—on a field of green. No doubt this was the flag or ensign of the city itself.

Teldin tried to read the message in the flags, using the code he half-remembered from his military service, but got only gibberish. They must be using a different code. The only information he could glean from the message was that the wind was blowing from the west—and this solely from the direction the flags were fluttering. "What do they say?" he asked.

"Wind from the west, ten knots," Rianna told him. "We're told to identify ourselves." She looked back over her shoulder. "Look," she said, "we're answering."

Teldin turned, too. On the main deck, several crewmen were running a string of flags up the hammership's mainmast.

"They say we're the *Probe*," Rianna translated quickly, "registered out of the planet Parcelius."

Teldin looked again at the harbor below, fascinated by the efficiency of this silent conversation. As he watched, the harbormaster's flags were brought down and another string run up the staff. He looked to Rianna for the translation.

"We're approved to land outside the harbor," she told him, "and to anchor at . . . Well, they're coordinates. I'd have to have a harbor chart to know what they meant."

Teldin turned to watch the *Probe*'s reply. There was none; the crewmen on the main deck just took the flag string down. There *was* some movement on the sterncastle, though. Two crew members were mounting a short jackstay on the aft rail. When it was secure, they trailed another, larger flag from it. Teldin recognized it to be the same design as the lowermost flag in the *Probe*'s recent message. He tapped Rianna on the shoulder and pointed it out, his expression questioning.

"It's the Parcelius ensign," she told him. "Laws of the spaceways are like those of the sea. You always run up the ensign of your home world at the stern, or your home port if it has its own ensign. If you're being formal, you really should run up the flag of your destination at the bow or on the mainmast, but most people aren't too picky about that. If you do much traveling at all, your entire cargo capacity's going to be taken up with flags," she concluded with a chuckle.

The hammership turned slightly more to the northeast, out over the ocean now, and continued to descend. For the first time, Teldin could see whitecaps on the waves below. The ship was only a couple of hundred feet up, he guessed. Then the big vessel maneuvered again, pointing its bow into the westering sun. It decelerated gently and swept lower still.

Aelfred Silverhorn's head popped into view. He climbed the ladder from the bridge below and spared the two a broad smile before he took his place at the forward rail. "Raise port and starboard fins!" he bellowed.

On the main deck, crewmen threw their weight on lines that led out to the four triangular sails extending out and slightly down from the hammership's hull like the fins of a shark. As they pulled, the sails folded upward until they stood vertically against the gunwales.

"Dead slow," Aelfred called. "Prepare for landing."

The *Probe* slowed still more and dropped lower. They were now no more than fifty feet above the wave caps, Teldin saw. Forty feet, thirty . . . Aelfred had ordered "dead slow"—and, compared to the hammership's top speed, that's how fast they were going—but watching the waves whip by underneath, Teldin realized the *Probe* was still moving about as fast as a running man. The sensation of riding something as big as the hammership this fast, this low, was exhilarating . . . and terrifying. He could easily imagine the vessel slamming into the water hard enough to snap its keel, breaking it apart into quickly sinking fragments.

Ten feet, five . . . The first crest slapped against the bottom of the hull. "Brace for landing," Aelfred called back. He was grinning from ear to ear. Teldin took a solid grip on the rail and noticed that Rianna had already done so and was braced in a wide-legged stance.

The ship touched down with a roar of water pounding against the hull. The deck surged hard beneath Teldin's feet, almost breaking his grip on the rail. Curtains of spray, catching the light like countless diamonds, arched high on both sides of the vessel, then fell back with a hiss. A fine mist of chill water washed back over the forecastle. The *Probe* was down.

"Helm down," ordered the first mate.

The hammership slowed quickly. Looking aft, Teldin could see the broad white wake that the ship had left. He walked forward to join Aelfred and looked over the bow rail.

The hammership rode low in the water. The waterline appeared to be about level with the main deck itself, which gave the vessel very little freeboard, particularly in the bow itself. Teldin remembered Rianna's comment: spelljamming ships are built for space. Even with his minimal knowledge of things nautical, he recognized that the slightest storm would swamp the hammership and send it to the bottom.

Aelfred, still grinning, pounded him on the shoulder. "Exciting, eh?" he enthused. "I live for that."

Teldin nodded halfheartedly. "Fun," he said without conviction.

The motion of the ship had changed, Teldin noticed. To be precise, now the ship *had* motion. Except during the most drastic maneuvers, or when the ship struck something, the *Probe* in space had felt as solid and motionless as Krynn itself. Now, however, the big ship was rolling slightly with the waves, which were striking it abeam. This was another problem with spelljamming vessels when they were out of their true element, he realized. Their stability was dreadful.

Something else had changed, too. For the first time, he could feel a cool, salt breeze on his face. As the *Probe* had soared in for its landing, the air on deck had been totally still. Now that the ship was virtually at rest, a steady wind blew across its bow from out of the west. He mentioned it to Rianna.

"Of course," she answered. "When the helm goes down, so does the atmosphere envelope." His face must have shown his confusion, because she grinned. "Atmosphere envelope, that's the bubble of air the ship takes with it into space. When the helm's operating, the ship keeps a bubble of relatively still air around it even when it's in the atmosphere of a world . . . generally speaking, of course."

Teldin nodded intelligently, trying to pretend that he understood even half of what Rianna was saying. Suddenly, without warning, his stomach twisted uncomfortably. What? Oh, no . . . He couldn't be seasick, could he? He took a deep breath of the sharp sea air, stretching his lungs to the limit. The nausea lessened a little. He breathed again, trying to ignore the motion of the deck beneath his feet.

Aelfred must have recognized his plight, because the big warrior remarked, "It's worst when we're at rest. She's much more stable when we're underway." He turned aft and bellowed, "Sea sail up."

Crewmen swung into the rigging and started hauling up the large sail reserved for ocean maneuvering. The big ship heeled slightly as the west wind filled the canvas. Ropes complained as the rigging took the strain and the boom swung to expose the maximum sail area. Waves slapped against the hull.

"Hard a-port," Aelfred ordered. "Bring us in."

The *Probe* turned its blunt bow southward, toward the port of Rauthaven.

* * * * *

It was evening, and the sun had set perhaps half an hour before. The *Probe* swung gently at anchor—under the stars now, rather than among them—in the crowded inner harbor of Rauthaven's port. Lanterns burned at bow and stern and atop the tall mainmast. Around the ship was a swarm of other such lanterns. It was too dark to discern the shapes of the ships that bore them; all that could be seen were the points of yellow light. It was as though some god had taken a constellation from the sky and brought it down to earth, Teldin found himself thinking. He stood on the main deck, leaning on the port rail, gazing toward shore.

Rauthaven itself was another constellation of lights: braziers to keep the city watch warm through the chill nights; open windows of cozy homes and snug taverns, spilling their welcoming light into the streets; and here and there a moving spark that had to be a lantern mounted on a carriage. From this angle, down in the harbor surrounded by the hills of the city, Teldin could make out no definite horizon, no demarcation between city and sky. The scattered lights of the city seemed to blend imperceptibly with the scattered stars. If he ignored the motion of the ship, the night wind on his face, and the smell of the sea, Teldin could almost make himself believe that he were back in space.

In fact, part of him wished that were true. Where had that thought come from? he wondered. At first space had been a dangerous unknown, and his greatest desire had been to get back to the safe, planet-bound life that he knew. Now, however, part of his mind equated space with safety, while Rauthaven—and Toril as a whole—was the dangerous unknown. Why? After all, wasn't he now near the end of his quest? If he could find an arcane and discharge his obligation to the dead owner of the cloak, he'd be free to live his own life again, as he saw fit. Why wasn't he welcoming landfall on Toril as the penultimate step in freeing himself from his burden?

When he phrased the question that way, the answer was obvious. What if he found out that the arcane *weren't* the creators of the cloak and were as helpless as the gnomes of Mount Nevermind when it came to removing it? This entire trip would have been a wild-goose chase. Worse, where would he go from here? Instead of the end of his journey, Rauthaven could turn out to be just the first step in a much greater one. It just didn't bear thinking about.

That, he knew, was why he found himself wishing he were back in space. On the journey, he'd enjoyed the anticipation of solving the problem. Now that he was here, there was a very real possibility that he *didn't* have the solution. He found that he was deeply afraid of finding that out. Stupid, he thought, it's like hiding from a messenger because you're afraid he might be bearing bad news. Stupid, maybe, but the feeling was very real. He shook his head hard, trying to banish the thoughts, the doubts.

There was somebody approaching across the main deck. He strained his eyes through the darkness. He could barely make out the shape of a man about his own height but more lightly built. As the figure drew closer, Teldin could discern the face.

The man's features weren't familiar at all; Teldin didn't recognize him. How can that be? he asked himself. There are no strangers aboard ship. It could be one of the new crewmen the *Probe* had acquired from the neogi deathspider, he supposed, but he thought he'd met all of them. Who was this stranger? For the first time, he felt the stirring of fear. His hand dropped to the hilt of his short sword.

Stay your hand. The words formed directly in Teldin's brain. There was no mistaking that mental voice.

"Estriss?" Teldin gasped.

The figure before him smiled—or, at least, it was probably

intended to be a smile. The lips drew back from the teeth, but the expression looked clumsy, somehow artificial.

It is I, the mental voice confirmed. *You are not the only one with access to shapeshifting magic.*

"How?"

A hat of disguise, the illithid answered. *I purchased it long ago for times such as these.*

"What do you mean?"

Humor tinged the mind flayer's words. *Even in a city such as Rauthaven, those of my kind are not overly welcome. People react with fear, and fearful people are unlikely to give me the information I need. So the charade. To those of Rauthaven, I am Bale Estriss, collector of antiquities . . . and, sadly, a mute who can only communicate by writing notes.*

Teldin nodded in understanding. Clever, he thought. That way the illithid wouldn't have to use his telepathic abilities.

I found you to discuss plans, the mind flayer went on. *I must find out what I can about the upcoming auction. A boat will be coming to ferry me and some others in. Do you still wish to make contact with an arcane?*

"Definitely," Teldin replied.

Estriss nodded. *While I am abroad in the town, I promise to make what inquiries I can. As I told you before, there are no guarantees, but it seems to me very likely that there will be at least one arcane in Rauthaven.*

"Good." Teldin thought for a moment. "Maybe I should go into town myself."

I would advise you not to do so, the illithid replied quickly. *You do not know this city.*

Teldin was surprised to realize he felt a little miffed by the mind flayer's quick rejection. "Do you?" he shot back.

Estriss hesitated, and Teldin knew he'd guessed right. *Not well*, the illithid answered slowly, *but I do have experience in finding my way around unfamiliar worlds, while you do not.* The mind flayer's mental tone changed. *I apologize*, he said. *I have offended you, and that was not my intention. My only excuse is the proximity of the auction, which is so important to my work. Will you accept that my concern is for your safety?*

Teldin knew that what Estriss was saying only made sense: There was nothing Teldin himself could do, abroad in

Rauthaven, that the illithid couldn't do, perhaps better. He nodded.

The disguised Estriss laid a reassuring hand on Teldin's shoulder. *I am glad. I should be only an hour or two. Hopefully, when I return, I will have news.*

* * * * *

According to the ship's bells, Estriss was ashore for little more than two hours. To Teldin it seemed much longer. In an attempt to pass the time, he went below and chatted with Horvath and Miggins. The two gnomes had come up with a complex replacement for the *Probe*'s sea sail, one that they said would nearly double the ship's speed on the ocean. They'd mentioned it to Aelfred, they told Teldin, and the first mate had given them permission to rig a prototype . . . *if* they supplied all the materials themselves and *if* they made no permanent modifications to the hammership's rigging without Aelfred's express authorization. The gnomes were so excited that Teldin couldn't tell them his interpretation of the big warrior's behavior. Teldin was convinced Aelfred saw this as a way to keep the gnomes busy and out from underfoot.

After that, he'd spent a comfortable half-hour chatting with Rianna in the officer's saloon. The woman had easily sensed his tension but had shown the sensitivity not to question him about it. Instead, she'd kept the conversation superficial.

No matter how much he counseled himself to patience, Teldin was almost vibrating with tension when he saw the small, open tender that did ferry duty around the harbor approaching. With a quick explanation to Rianna about business matters, he hurried up on deck.

"Did you find out anything?" he asked as soon as Estriss was aboard.

I certainly did, the illithid replied. His mental voice was filled with excitement. *The auction takes place early the day after tomorrow, at the Merchants' Rotunda, a central meeting place. We were lucky to arrive in time. I have heard further descriptions of some of the items to be included, and they certainly sound like the artifacts I want. This is the perfect oppor-*

tunity I have waited for. The illithid's magically disguised face smiled clumsily at Teldin. *If you wish to attend with me, you would be most welcome.*

"Well, yes," he said slowly, "that's good, but about the arcane . . . ?"

The disguised illithid looked at him in puzzlement for a moment, then realization showed on his features. *Of course,* he said hastily, *my apologies, I forgot. Yes, there is known to be one arcane who will be attending the auction as well. His name is* "T'k'Pek." The illithid spoke the name aloud, exaggerating the clicking consonants. *I'm sure you can speak to it tomorrow at the auction.*

Teldin shook his head. "No," he said firmly, "I need to speak to the arcane in private, preferably *before* the auction."

Estriss hesitated. *I doubt that will be practical.*

"Estriss," Teldin said sharply, "this is important. Where's the arcane staying in town? I can arrange a visit." Teldin was somewhat surprised by his own decisiveness, and both Estriss's and Aelfred's reactions confirmed that it was a shock to them.

T'k'Pek is not staying in Rauthaven, Estriss answered. *I understand that he will remain on his ship, in orbit around Toril, until the time of the auction.*

"*Where* in orbit?"

The illithid shrugged. In his disguised form, the gesture looked a lot more natural. *No one has told me. I would expect that no one knows.*

Teldin turned to Aelfred. "Can we look for it?"

Aelfred glanced uncomfortably at Estriss. Teldin could tell what was going through his mind: Estriss is officially captain of the *Probe*, and the first mate must abide by the decisions of his superior. Strictly speaking, this couldn't be Aelfred's decision. "We could, I suppose," the burly warrior said slowly. "*Theoretically* we could, but finding it's another question again. Compared to a planet, a ship's a very tiny needle in a bloody big haystack. If you don't have any details on altitude or the orientation of the ship's path, it can take days."

Teldin found himself grinding his teeth in frustration. He was so close: too close to fail now. He turned to Estriss. "The *Probe* is your ship," he said, keeping his voice as unemotional as he could. "Would you allow this?"

It was the mind flayer's turn to pause uncomfortably. *There may be no need,* he said after a moment. *As is typical with the arcane, T'k'Pek conducts most business through a representative—a factor, if you will—in Rauthaven. This man is called Barrab. It should be possible to make contact with him. . . .* The mental voice trailed off uncertainly.

"Why didn't you tell me this earlier?" Teldin demanded.

It may be of no help. The words that formed in Teldin's mind held a tone of complete candidness. *If the arcane has seen fit to employ a representative, it will probably be because he does not want to deal directly with others. The factor's job, then, will be to prevent the kind of contact that you seek.*

"You may be right," Teldin admitted, "but I have to try."

Doing so would draw attention to you, Estriss pointed out. *It would expose you to risk, and risk the loss of*—he glanced around furtively, even though there were only the three of them on the forecastle—*of that which you must protect.*

"I have to try," Teldin repeated stubbornly.

Estriss was about to object, but Aelfred cut in with a snort. "The lad's right," he said firmly. "This is important, for several reasons. I know it's a risk, but look. I'll go along with him, maybe take another crewman." He smiled down at Teldin. "We'll keep you out of trouble. Where's this Barrab staying, 'Bale'?"

The illithid shrugged again, this time in resignation. *He stays at the Edgewood, on Widdershins Street.*

"Good." Aelfred turned back to Teldin. "We can go at once if you like. If the ship can't do without me for a few hours, we've got the wrong crew."

Gratitude toward the first mate—his friend—swelled within Teldin's breast, but he knew that thanks would just embarrass the big warrior. With an effort, he kept his emotions out of his voice. "At once would be . . . convenient," he said.

Chapter Eleven

• • •

Prissith Nerro's claws clicked on the deck as the neogi descended the ramp and entered the bridge of the *Void Reaper*. The monster raised its head and sniffed the air. There was still the tang of smoke, of burned flesh, normally not a distasteful smell, but the cause robbed it of its pleasure. The neogi captain looked around the bridge.

Most of the damage was repaired—the worst of it, at least. The forward port, the one shattered by that foul elf's magic, had been replaced, and the burn scars on the deck and bulkheads patched. Still, there's the smell of burning in the air? the creature wondered. Or does it linger only in my mind? Prissith Nerro snarled its anger. The bridge crew backed away, knowing the rashness of disturbing their captain when it was in this mood.

We do not have the prize yet, the neogi told itself, but at least we have valuable information. It smacked its lips as it remembered the tastes of the interrogation. The simple pleasures of tearing flesh made up for the horrendous difficulties the creature had with the human language. What was it about the tongue that made its grammar and syntax so alien to the neogi mind? The creature knew well that it was far from fluent in the grotesque language—the prisoner's reactions had frequently made that clear—and suspected that none of its race fared any better.

My plan is a good one, it reassured itself. If only it didn't have to depend on lesser races for its success. The creature spat in disgust.

There was a sound behind the captain. Prissith Nerro spun, teeth bared, ready to tear. It was Prissith Ulm. The captain felt grudging admiration for the fact that it's brood-brother hadn't even flinched. "What?" it snarled in its own tongue.

The subordinate neogi bobbed its head in respect. "Prissith Nerro Master," it hissed. "We have word from our asset on Toril."

At last, good news. "What?" the captain demanded.

Prissith Ulm bowed again. "The bearer of the cloak has arrived," it said respectfully, "as you said it would. That has been confirmed."

Prissith Nerro hissed with pleasure. "What more?"

"By now, the cloak bearer knows of the arcane and his representative, Barrab," the sub-captain continued. "Our asset is certain the creature will attempt to contact Barrab, and hence the arcane." It hesitated—questioning the captain was a risky business at the best of times, but it had to know. "Do we proceed as you outlined, Prissith Nerro Master?"

The captain spat with harsh neogi laughter. "Yes, brood-brother," it said. "We will let my plan progress a little further before we intervene."

* * * * *

Barrab was a large man, almost as tall and broad as Aelfred Silverhorn, and weighing about as much. While the big warrior was all muscle and bone, without an ounce of fat on his frame, however, Barrab was softly rounded everywhere. His black, rather stringy hair was shoulder-length, framing a round, pale face. His thick lips were always curved in a beatific smile. At first, Teldin had thought the expression made the man look like some kind of giant cherub, then he'd noticed that the smile didn't quite reach the man's small eyes, which were cold and hard. Teldin judged that he was in his early forties, though he had to admit to himself that there was at least a five-year margin of error in that estimate. Barrab sat back in his leather-backed chair and watched Teldin and Aelfred coolly as they stood before the table he was using as a desk.

There had been no problem in finding the Edgewood: it was well-known throughout Rauthaven as the best restaurant, wine room, and inn in the city. The Edgewood was located in what was known as the 'High Quarter'—the district just a little downhill from Duke Admantor's castle—and its architecture and decor immediately identified it as a haven for the upper class. Its entry off Widdershins Street and its halls were spotless, all floors covered by carpets of the finest workmanship, and the rooms—if Barrab's was any indication—as sumptuous as a king's palace.

They'd had no difficulty in getting in to see Barrab. Presumably, as the arcane's representative, he had to be available at all times to any business opportunity. All they'd had to do was ask the functionary in the Edgewood's lobby, and they'd been given directions to Barrab's room.

When they'd reached the door, Teldin had suggested that Aelfred and Julia, who was the second "bodyguard," wait outside, but the first mate had squelched that idea in short order. "Forget it," he'd told Teldin bluntly. "First, there's no telling if there's somebody who wants to put a knife into the back of 'Aldyn Brewer,' for whatever reason. Second, this is a business delegation. What kind of respect are you going to get if you don't have your 'personal assistant' with you, eh?"

Teldin had to admit that it was reassuring to accept the big warrior's arguments. Even though Aelfred was in "civvies," a green jerkin with a garish red sash at his waist, he still carried his short sword with him, and Teldin didn't doubt that he had a couple of throwing daggers concealed on his person. He and Aelfred had entered Barrab's "office," the first mate following his "employer" a respectful step to the left and behind. Julia had stayed in the hallway, exchanging steely glares with the dagger-armed bravo who stood sentry outside Barrab's room.

Barrab sat while they stood. He looked them up and down leisurely, the cherubic smile never faltering. He reached out and, with a delicacy that belied the size of his fingers, picked up a swollen green seed from a glass bowl on the table before him and popped it into his mouth. He sucked contemplatively while he continued his scrutiny. Finally he spoke. "You have business with me, yes?" Teldin was surprised by the man's voice. It was quiet, gentle—weak, Teldin thought, but that was probably a facade the representative used in business situations. The hard eyes were anything but weak.

Teldin had worked out his approach with Aelfred on the way over. Now he was glad of the preparation. He kept his voice steady, almost disinterested. "Not with you," he told the factor, "with your employer."

Barrab raised an eyebrow so thin that it seemed to have been plucked. "Indeed?" The word spoke amusement and a little disdain.

"Indeed," Teldin replied flatly. "I understand that you are T'k'Pek's representative in Rauthaven. Sometimes it's . . . *polite* . . . to follow conventional channels."

"Oh?" Barrab seemed a little surprised at this. "And you have access to *un*conventional channels?"

"If need be, but it would be inconvenient to be forced to use them."

Barrab's gaze grew even harder, if that were possible. "Indeed," he repeated coldly. "And just what is your business with T'k'Pek?"

Teldin had a quick answer for that one. "That is between your master and myself." He injected a hint of contempt into his voice.

The representative picked up on it, as Teldin had known he would. "I am empowered to review all business concerning T'k—concerning my master, and determine whether it's worth his time and attention."

"For rudimentary, day-to-day business, I would agree that you are ideally suited to review it for your master," Teldin shot back. "The business I have with T'k'Pek is not of that ilk. It can only be discussed between your master and myself." He was silent for a moment. Enough darts, he thought. Time for the carrot. . . . "It seems to me," he said, his tone more reasonable, "that, to be trusted, a representative must have the wisdom to recognize when unusual circumstances arrive, and the authority to pass them directly to his superior. Isn't that so?"

Barrab sat back, still smiling his beatific smile, and spread his soft hand. "I'm afraid you credit me with more authority than I actually have," he said, feigned sadness in his voice. "My instructions are strict on this." Casually he took another seed and put it into his mouth.

"That's your final word?"

"I'm afraid so, but if you'll tell me what your business is, I assure you . . ." He trailed off expectantly.

Time for the stick, Teldin thought. He shook his head in irritation. "Unfortunate," he mused. He started to turn away. "T'k'Pek has never been the type to take it kindly when an officious underling delays important information."

There was a sharp crack as Barrab's jaws crushed the seed in his mouth. With an effort that was apparent to Teldin, he kept his voice steady. "You know T'k'Pek?"

Teldin simply smiled. "I suppose I must pursue those unconventional channels," he said quietly, almost to himself. "That will take time." He turned for the door. "Aelfred," he snapped. Playing the role of the loyal henchman to the hilt, Aelfred turned on his heel and hurried to join his "master." Teldin grasped the doorknob, twisted it . . . then turned back to Barrab, a rather uncomfortable-looking Barrab, he judged. "I'll be aboard my vessel, the hammership *Probe*, if you wish to speak to me."

With that he left. Aelfred shut the door on Barrab's response. In the hallway, Julia fell into step with the others, both officers flanking Teldin. None turned back.

They kept their silence until they were well away from the Edgewood, then Aelfred roared the laughter he'd been biting back and pounded Teldin on the shoulder. "Smoothly done!" He guffawed. "Julia, you should have seen it. Remind me never to face this one across a hand of cards. He bluffs better than I do."

"Will it work?" Teldin wondered.

"I'd say the odds are good," Aelfred judged. "I read that Barrab as a minor underling with delusions of grandeur. If I'm right, he'll be scrabbling to cover his assets. Now it's just a matter of waiting."

Teldin nodded. "I can't wait too long."

* * * * *

Aelfred accompanied Teldin and Julia halfway back to the harbor, then left to go about his own business. "I've got to talk to someone about repairing the ship," he explained. The female officer seemed lost in her own thoughts, and she and Teldin finished the walk in silence.

As they reached the harbor, the small tender was just coming alongside the dock, packed with familiar faces. There was "Bale Estriss" and two officers from the *Probe*. Vallus Leafbower was accompanied by Horvath and Miggins. Teldin was most pleased to see Rianna smiling up at him from the vessel.

The tender's passengers disembarked. The ship's officers strode away immediately, with the avowed intention of arranging for the *Probe*'s repair and resupply, then finding a tavern. Estriss wandered off to pursue his investigations, and Vallus Leafbower faded into the night without mentioning where he was going—"Probably going to see his mistress," Rianna speculated under her breath.

Miggins and Horvath headed off in search of a ship's chandlery to find the materials they needed for their proposed modification of the hammership's sea sail. Julia climbed into the tender.

That left Rianna and Teldin alone on the dock. "Did your business go well?" she asked.

"As well as can be expected, I suppose," he replied. He glanced at the sun, which was hardly a finger-span above the horizon. "Coming into town for evenfeast?"

She shrugged. "What are your plans?" she asked. "Are you set on going back to the ship?"

He grinned at her. "Unless you've got a better idea."

"Maybe I do." She turned to Julia. "You head on back," she suggested. "I'll keep an eye on Aldyn."

Julia scowled at Rianna, an expression for which her face seemed little suited. She gave no answer, just told the ferryman, "The *Probe*."

Rianna watched with raised eyebrow as the tender pulled away from the dock. "Friendly sort," she remarked. "So, any preferences as to what you want to do?"

Teldin shrugged. "You know this city, I don't," he pointed out. He smiled. "I *do* remember an offer to show me around."

"Evening isn't the best time for sightseeing," she said with a grin, "but let's see what we can see."

They started up the hill into the city proper. As they walked, it seemed natural to Teldin to slip his arm around

Rianna's waist, his hand resting on her right hip. Without saying a word, she rested her right hand on top of his. Their fingers intertwined, and he pulled her closer.

The street Rianna had selected was wide and well paved. Most of the two-story buildings that flanked it seemed to be shops of some variety, closed for the day. In the deepening evening, the ground floors were dark, but lights showed in many of the upstairs windows—presumably these were the shopkeepers' homes. The couple saw no carriages on the street, and the few pedestrians seemed to be sailors.

"This is called the Processional," Rianna told him. "If you follow it all the way, it'll take you to Duke Admantor's castle. Last time I was here, some visiting dignitary's ship was in the harbor and this road was decked out in flags and banners, flowers and torches, like you wouldn't believe. I wish you'd seen it."

The road began to climb a little more steeply. Teldin felt under-used muscles complain in his calves. He tried to match Rianna's easy, swinging stride. Even though she was a little shorter than he, her legs—and hence her strides—were almost the same length as his. As they walked, Rianna was looking around as if searching for familiar landmarks. "Where are we headed?" he asked.

"There's a tavern around here, I think," she answered. "*If* I can just remember the side street, and *if* it hasn't closed since I was last here."

"We passed some inns back down by the water," Teldin pointed out.

Rianna shook her head. "Harborside taverns," she said dismissively, "catering to sailors, broken-down whores, and up-town failures. They're great if you're looking for a nice, diverting brawl, but I'm not in the mood. What I'm looking for—there it is," she interrupted herself. She put her arm around Teldin's waist and led him to the right down a narrow crossroad.

There were fewer lighted windows here, but fifty feet away Teldin saw ruddy firelight washing out into the street from an open doorway. A wooden sign hung above the door, but he couldn't make it out.

" 'The Pig and Whistle,' " Rianna announced, leading him

toward the door. She gave his waist a squeeze. "Buy a girl a drink, sailor?"

Teldin stopped in his tracks. He hadn't even thought of it before. "I don't have any money," he admitted. That wasn't quite true; he did have some coins, but they were steel Krynn currency. Odds were that it wouldn't be accepted here, and—worse—someone might recognize its origin.

She fixed him with an amused glance. "Don't they use money on Waypoint?" she asked ingenuously, then chuckled at his uncomfortable reaction. "Don't you worry, I've money enough. This time the girl can buy the sailor a drink." She led him through the open doorway.

Teldin had visited inns in a few of the larger towns he'd visited and thought he knew what a "big city" tavern would look like. The Pig and Whistle came as a complete surprise. It was a small room with pillars and crossbeams of dark wood supporting the low ceiling. The whitewashed walls were decorated with horse-brasses, bridles, and other pieces of tack. The floor was wooden planking dusted with a thin layer of sawdust to soak up spilled drinks. A fire burned in the small hearth opposite the bar itself. Teldin sniffed the air; he would have sworn it was a peat fire. By the bar was a narrow staircase that presumably led upstairs to the tavern's one or two guest rooms.

This was his first trip to Rauthaven, but Teldin *knew* this little pub. It was virtually identical to any number of village taverns around the Kalaman region where he'd grown up. Everything—the smoke-discolored ceiling, the feel of sawdust underfoot, the smell of peat smoke mixed with ale—was exactly as it should be. An overwhelming sense of homesickness, of loss, washed over him.

Rianna smiled broadly. "Well?" she asked. "What do you think?" When Teldin hesitated, her face fell. "I'm sorry," she said, "I thought you'd like it. I thought it'd remind you of home."

"It does," he explained.

"But too much." She squeezed his waist again. "I understand. Come on, we'll go somewhere else."

She tried to turn back to the door, but Teldin stopped her. "Oh, no," he said, "I *do* like this place. Anyway, you promised me a drink, and you're not getting out of it that easily."

Her smile returned. "And I thought I was off the hook," she said jokingly. "All right. Why don't you find a seat while I get the drinks?" With a final squeeze, she headed for the bar.

Teldin looked around the room. Most of the tables were occupied, but there *was* one—in the back corner—that was empty. Carefully he threaded his way over to it.

The table had no chairs around it—presumably they'd been "requisitioned" by the occupants of other tables—but there was a wooden bench with cloth-covered seat bolted to the wall. It's small, but there's just enough room for two, he thought as he sat down, as long as we don't mind sitting close. Teldin thought he could handle that.

Rianna was at the bar, watching the publican draw two pints of ale. As he waited, Teldin let his gaze drift idly around the tavern. There *was* a difference between the Pig and Whistle and the pubs of Kalaman, Teldin realized, but the difference wasn't in the institution itself. It was the *people* who were different. In a village pub at home, there was no way he could have made his way from the door to a back table without someone offering him a friendly greeting, trying to strike up a conversation, or challenging him to a friendly game of knucklebone. A village pub was more like a social center than a drinking establishment, particularly for the more aged.

The Pig and Whistle's patrons were city folk, however, and city folk always kept to themselves—or so Teldin had decided long ago. They'd never offer a greeting, for fear that it would be taken as an invitation to exploit the speaker somehow, or as a challenge. They'd respond to a greeting with either grave surprise—and often a close scrutiny, on the assumption that the speaker was either someone they should know or mentally deranged—or with surliness. As city people held their tongues, so did they control their glances. In Kalaman, a newcomer to a bar would immediately be inspected from crown to toe by the regulars, but there would be no hostility or challenge in the curious stares. In cities or large towns, Teldin had seen, people kept their eyes down and only shot someone a surtive glance if they didn't think they'd be caught at it. So things were in the Pig and Whistle.

There was movement in the doorway. He saw the flash of a profile, then the figure withdrew into the night. Why did that profile look so familiar? He racked his brain for a moment, then the answer came to him. It was Tregimesticus, one of the crewmen that the *Probe* had acquired from the neogi vessel. What was he doing here? Tregimesticus was one of those who'd adapted least well to freedom. Teldin couldn't imagine the ex-slave showing the initiative to ask for passage to shore, and then to track down a tavern for a drink. He could be wrong, of course . . . but then why did the man look around the place and leave?

Rianna's return disrupted his train of thought. She sat beside him, pressing the warmth of her hip against his. He immediately discarded thoughts of Tregimesticus for much more interesting considerations.

"Cozy," Rianna remarked. She set two tankards of ale on the table. "Barleycorn's Best Bitter," she announced, "The Resort's finest ale, in my opinion, and that's saying a lot."

He raised an eyebrow skeptically. "We'll see about that." He lifted the heavy pewter tankard and took a pull. Served at room temperature, the thick ale had a rich, nutty taste, with an underpinning of smoky sharpness. He let it linger on his tongue, giving the flavor time to develop, then he swallowed. He breathed out through his nose, enjoying the lush aroma. It was similar to the Krynnish ales he was familiar with, but just different enough to make it seem somehow exotic. And, he had to admit, it was excellent. Easily on a par with, if not marginally better than, the local bitters of Kalaman. "Not bad," he said noncommittally, trying to suppress a smile.

Dissembling didn't work with Rianna, though. A warm smile spread across her face. "Admit it," she said, digging him playfully in the ribs with an elbow. "It's excellent. Better than the best on Waypoint, isn't it?"

He looked away from her uncomfortably. I'm lying to her, he told himself. She's befriended me—maybe more—and I'm lying to her. He felt miserable.

She seemed to sense his discomfort and smoothly changed the topic. "I asked the bartender if he knew of any arcane in town," she told him. "You said you needed to meet one. For that kind of information, barkeepers are about the best sources around."

"And?"

She shrugged. "He said he didn't know but promised he'd ask around. We can check back here tomorrow and see if anything's come up."

Teldin nodded and took another full swallow of his ale. Again he savored the mouthful, but this time to give himself time to think. There was another subject he had to broach, but he wasn't sure of the best way to do it. Rianna seemed to sense his thoughts. She drank her ale as well, silently watching him and waiting.

"Well, we're in Rauthaven," he said finally, trying to keep his voice light and casual. "What are your plans now? Passage to—where was it?—the Tears of Selune? Another ship and back to work?"

It was Rianna's turn to hesitate for a moment. Her lips moved silently, as though she were rehearsing words that she was uncomfortable about speaking aloud. Her hands twisted in her lap. "I suppose so," she said at last, not looking at him. "That's what I should do." She raised her eyes. Her gaze was intense. "But not yet," she went on, "not for a while. I think . . . If it's all right with you, I think I'd like to spend some time with you, Aldyn Brewer." She smiled—tentatively, like a child asking for a gift but not expecting it to be given.

He met her gaze and felt for a moment as though he were drowning in the deep green ocean of her eyes. Something seemed to click in Teldin's mind. In an instant, all doubt and indecision vanished, and he knew exactly what he had to do. He stood. "Come on," he told her, taking her arm.

She resisted for a moment. "What's the matter?" she asked quietly. "If I said something wrong, I'm sorry. . . ."

He cut her off with a shake of his head. "*You've* said nothing wrong," he told her firmly. "It's me that's said something wrong, and I have to correct that. Come on." He drew her to her feet and led her out of the tavern.

Outside the Pig and Whistle, the street was dark, seemingly deserted. Teldin still had a grip on Rianna's arm, and he led her on, away from the main street, the Processional, away from the light spilling from inside the tavern. She didn't resist, but he could feel her confusion, her trepidation. When they were a good dagger cast from the door, sheltered by the darkness, he stopped. He put both hands on her shoulders and turned her to face him. "Tell me again what you just said," he told her.

Her gaze was steady on his face. "I think I want to spend some time with you, Aldyn Brewer," she repeated softly. There was no tremor in her voice, no trace of doubt. She said it as if she'd been stating some invariant fact of nature.

He shook his head slowly. "You're wrong," he said quietly. "You want to spend time with Aldyn Brewer. You might not want to spend time with *me*." Her eyes were uncomprehending, so he pressed on. "I'm not Aldyn Brewer. My name is Teldin Moore. I'm not from Waypoint. I'm from Krynn. And . . ." Here he came to a halt. How could he do what had to follow? How could he show her proof of the ultimate dishonesty? He knew he had to do it—if only because he'd come this far. He took his hands from her shoulders. She must be able to run away if she wants to, he thought. "And," he started again, forcing firmness into his voice, "there's more." He closed his eyes and allowed the false face to fade away. He heard Rianna's sharply indrawn breath and opened his eyes.

Rianna still stood before him. She hadn't backed away, but her eyes were wide and both her hands were at her mouth. He could hear her rapid breathing.

He stood before her, arms at his side, waiting. He wasn't sure exactly what reaction he'd expected: fear, maybe, or more likely anger, but Rianna surprised him.

Tentatively, she reached out a hand toward his face. Her fingers touched his cheek, the line of his jaw. "This is . . . you?" she asked, a catch in her voice. He nodded. Rianna smiled, a strained, wan smile. "Much more handsome," she murmured, almost too low for Teldin to hear.

"I'm sorry, Rianna," he said softly. "As the gods are my witnesses, I'm sorry."

She shook her head. Her strained smile was still in place. "I knew some of it," she said. "I knew you'd taken a false name. I knew you didn't come from Waypoint, but . . . *this!*"

"I'm sorry," he repeated miserably. He knew he should say something else, but he couldn't figure out what.

Rianna shook her head again. She closed her eyes and took a deep, cleansing breath. When she opened her eyes again, they were clear. She smiled, and this time it was the strong, warm smile that Teldin knew. "No," she said, her voice steady, too. "No, *I'm* sorry. You just . . . shocked me, that was all. I knew you wouldn't have taken a false identity without a good reason." She chuckled.

"In my business, I deal with more false identities than real ones, and I've gotten to the point that I can usually pick out even the best." She prodded him in the ribs with a forefinger. "Yours was far from the best, little chum, but I wasn't going to queer your pitch. If it was necessary for you to be Aldyn Brewer, then I'd spend time with Aldyn Brewer. Did you really think it was your *name* I enjoyed spending time with? Your shaky stories about coming from Waypoint? Even your face? Were those the only things I was interested in? Rather superficial, wouldn't you say?" Teldin nodded in dumb amazement. "*You're* none of those things," she went on, "and it's *you*—what's underneath all the make-believe—that I'm interested in. Do you understand what I'm saying?"

"I understand," he muttered.

She reached up and grasped his shoulders. For an instant, her smile faltered. "By the gods, you even *feel* different."

"Sorry," he started to say, but she hushed him peremptorily to silence.

Her grip on his shoulders was firm. "Remember what I told you aboard ship?" she asked. Her voice was low, but it almost crackled with intensity. "About how your secrets are your most valuable, most personal, possessions?"

"I remember."

She released one shoulder and reached down to take his hand. "I thank you for the valuable gift you've given me, Teldin Moore," she said softly. She kissed his palm.

Teldin stepped forward and wrapped her in his arms. Her body was warm and strong—steel under velvet—against him. He tilted his head, and her mouth was soft and welcoming. When she flung her own arms around him, the grip was almost fierce enough to squeeze the air from his body.

When the kiss finally ended—minutes or maybe centuries later—Teldin's body felt alive, as if he'd slept for twelve hours, doused himself in frigid rainwater, then swallowed two quick shots of ice-cold sagecoarse on an empty stomach. Rianna nestled close against his chest.

"They won't miss us if we don't go back to the ship tonight, will they?" she whispered.

Teldin smiled. "They won't miss us."

As one, they turned back toward the welcoming door of the Pig and Whistle.

* * * * *

Teldin felt wonderful. For perhaps the first time since he'd left his farmhouse on that fateful day—how long ago was it now?—he felt relaxed and full of energy. The gods are in their heavens and all's right with the world, he told himself. The salt smell of the sea was sharp in his nostrils, and the morning breeze was brisk and bracing in his—rather, Aldyn's—and Rianna's faces. The rocking of the small tender as it breasted through the low waves, taking them back to the *Probe*, just added to his pleasure. He felt like singing.

He looked at Rianna, sitting on the thwart next to him. The wind had brought even more color to her tanned cheeks. The soft skin around the bottomless sea of her eyes crinkled as she smiled at him.

The tender bumped gently against the hammership's hull, and Teldin veritably bounded up the rope ladder, over the gunwale rail, and onto the deck. Aelfred and "Bale Estriss" were on the forecastle. The big warrior was grinning broadly. If he smiles any wider, he'll swallow his ears, Teldin thought. He snapped a jaunty salute. Aelfred's response was to give an even broader, knowing grin, and to shake his head in feigned despair. Estriss, on the other hand, beckoned to him to come up onto the forecastle.

Teldin leaned over the rail to give Rianna a hand up. "Pay a toll to come aboard," he told her as she swung a long leg over the rail. She chuckled deep in her throat as he bent down to collect a kiss.

"I'm going below for a while," she told him, then slipped an arm around his waist and gave him a quick squeeze. "I'll see you later, . . . Aldyn."

He watched her until she disappeared belowdecks, then he crossed to the port ladder and climbed to the forecastle, where Aelfred was waiting for him.

"You look like the canary that ate the cat," the big warrior joked. He glanced over the rail to where Rianna had disappeared. "And I can't say as I blame you."

We were concerned about you. The illithid's mental voice was as sharp as Teldin had ever heard it.

". . . Until I told him the company you were keeping," Aelfred elaborated. He leaned forward to speak in a stage whisper: "I seem to recall a certain conversation in the officers' saloon. Estriss might not try to steal your girl, but he might not understand why you want to spend a night ashore with her either. A serious disadvantage to being sexless, eh?"

Teldin smiled but said nothing. Even though he knew Aelfred intended no harm, he didn't feel comfortable joking about someone who he'd suddenly realized meant a lot to him. "Any word from Barrab?" he asked.

Aelfred's expression sobered. "Not yet," he replied, "but I hear tell that our fat friend spent *his* night away from home, too. Meeting with his boss, I'll wager."

"Is there anything we can do to hurry things along?"

The warrior shook his head firmly. "Nothing. We wait."

As it turned out, they didn't have to wait long at all. Teldin had been back on board for perhaps an hour, which he'd spent in the officers' saloon, gazing out at the busy harbor, when a knock sounded and Aelfred entered. The big man was grinning like a bandit. "Message for milord Brewer," he announced, "just delivered by tender." He waited, obviously enjoying himself.

"It worked?"

"It worked," Aelfred confirmed. "You and two assistants are invited aboard the *Nebulon*—that's the arcane's ship."

Teldin grinned. He was almost there. "Did he say where the ship was?" he asked. "Are we taking the *Probe* up?"

"He *didn't* say where the ship was," Aelfred told him, "but it doesn't matter. Barrab's arranged a boat to take you up. Security, I suppose." The first mate grew serious. "The invitation says you may bring two people with you if you want," he said quietly. "And I suggest you do it, Teldin. I don't know why an arcane might want to set a trap for you, but if he planned to, this would be an excellent opportunity."

Teldin nodded slowly. As Aelfred had passed on the message, similar thoughts had been running through his mind. "I agree," he said. "Aelfred, do you want to come?"

The warrior smiled. "Just try to keep me away." He paused, then went on, "Estriss was there when I got the message and wants to come, too. I'd rather have one of my people come—Bubbo, maybe, as an intimidation factor—but . . ."

Teldin paused in thought. Aelfred was leaving the decision up to him. That was probably as it should be, but he wasn't comfortable with it. He considered. He'd feel a lot happier with the reassuring bulk of Bubbo at his back, but Estriss knew more about the arcane than either he or Aelfred—probably more than anyone else aboard. That knowledge could be vital. In a flash of recall, he saw an attacker staggering back under the illithid's mental attack. There was no doubt that Estriss could take care of himself.

For a moment Teldin considered Rianna—her company and moral support would be more than welcome—but he quickly rejected the thought. He still hadn't told her everything about the cloak—specifically, the defensive powers it had shown in battle with the neogi, and the fact that he couldn't remove it—even though the lie of omission made him feel uncomfortable, and that's what the conversation on the *Nebulon* would be about. On balance, he decided it would be better to limit the participants to people who already knew the whole story.

"I'll take Estriss," he said finally.

Aelfred nodded his acceptance. "I'll pass the word." He turned to go.

"Where's the boat?" Teldin asked. "Alongside?"

Aelfred grinned. "You'll see," he said cryptically.

Chapter Twelve

• • •

When Aelfred had used the word "boat," Teldin had pictured something like the *Unquenchable*'s longboat, or maybe a smaller version of the hammership. It turned out to be something entirely different. He and his "assistants," Aelfred Silverhorn and "Bale Estriss," took the tender in to shore, then walked through the town and out the main gate. The "boat" was waiting for them on the wide paved road, surrounded by a flock of curious onlookers.

It was a dragonfly, Aelfred told him. Resting on its spindly legs, it looked like a larger version of Rianna's mosquito. Like the smaller ship, it was long and slender, tapering to a sharp point astern. *Un*like the mosquito, it had two sets of wings: one arcing up and back over the afterdeck, the other sweeping below and almost brushing the ground. "Minimum crew of two," Aelfred explained, "a good ship's boat."

With Aelfred in the lead, they pushed through the throng of spectators—who, Teldin noticed, were standing a respectful distance from the strange craft—and approached the dragonfly. "Aldyn Brewer and party," the warrior called up to the deck. "Permission to come aboard?"

"Permission granted," a voice responded from above. A rope ladder was lowered from the main deck.

As they'd agreed beforehand, Aelfred was first up the ladder. Teldin watched the practiced ease with which the big man climbed the swaying ladder. The warrior swung himself over the rail and vanished from sight. After a few moments, he reappeared, beckoning the others to join him. "Come ahead, milord Brewer," he shouted. It had been agreed upon ahead of time that Aelfred would go aboard first. If the dragonfly was safe, he'd call down for "milord Brewer" to join him. If it was a trap—and somebody had a dagger at Aelfred's back—he'd shout down for "milord *Aldyn*," warning Teldin and Estriss to get away fast.

Teldin flipped the cloak—which he'd expanded—back over his shoulders to clear his arms. He grasped the swaying ladder and began to climb. It wasn't as bad as he'd expected. He was quickly on the small boat's deck, and, equally quickly, Estriss joined him. Aelfred was forward, talking with one of the dragonfly's two crewmen. The other hauled up the rope ladder. Almost immediately the small craft was underway, lifting silently into the cloudless sky.

Teldin wanted to lean over the rail and watch the city dropping away beneath them, but he'd decided that this wasn't appropriate for the role he was playing. "Milord Aldyn Brewer" would be used to such things. Oh, certainly, he knew he'd have to drop the pretense when he actually spoke with the arcane, but that meeting would be private if he had anything to say about it. In the meantime, he guessed that the crewmen had probably been hired by Barrab, and dropping his role in their sight would be a good way of alienating someone he might have to use again later.

To take his mind off the view he was missing, and to prevent himself from rubbernecking like the tourist he was, he looked around for somewhere to sit. He found a small bench abaft of the small ship's single mast and seated himself.

He tried to relax, but it was futile. Conflicting emotions warred within him. There was excitement—of course! If Estriss was right about the arcane, then in just a few hours he might be free of his burden. What then? A new life on Toril? Or on the Tears of Selune? Or maybe elsewhere in space? He forced those thoughts from his mind. There would be time for them later.

There was also fear. Mainly, it was the fear of disappointment, of failure. What if he somehow found out that the arcane *weren't* the creators of the cloak? If he found himself, now, as far—perhaps farther—from the end of his quest? He had no other clues to follow, unless you counted Estriss's theories. How could creatures who'd vanished from this corner of the universe several millennia ago free him from the cloak?

The conclusion was inescapable. He'd have to continue searching for the real creators. How long would that take? Years? Decades? His entire life? Maybe he'd *never* be free of the burden, free to live his own life as he wanted to live it. Maybe he'd always be controlled by the "gift" of the dead traveler, with little more real freedom than a prisoner in chains.

That was what he feared: disappointment, yes, but so much more. He toyed with the idea of yelling to the crew to return him to the city—after all, if he didn't face the arcane, he'd never hear bad news—but knew that was just fear talking. He forced his doubts, too, and anticipation, from the front of his mind.

He looked up into the sky over the swiftly rising dragonfly. From the ground, the sky had been the delicate blue of a robin's egg. Now it had darkened to a rich royal blue. He squinted and shielded his eyes from the sun. Directly overhead was a faint speck of white, barely visible in the bright sky. Was that a star? he wondered. Yes, it must be.

It took him a moment to notice it, but the sky was darkening as he watched. Slowly, almost imperceptibly, it shaded from royal blue to a darker, navy blue, then to a rich midnight purple. As the sky darkened, the single star above grew brighter. Clearer—and somehow *harder*—it looked now, like a cold chip of diamond mounted in the inverted bowl of the sky. It seemed somehow nearer than any other star he'd ever seen, and it didn't seem to twinkle at all.

He glanced at his companions. Aelfred Silverhorn had finished his conversation with the dragonfly's crew member and was leaning against the gunwale rail with Estriss. The first mate caught his glance and walked over to him. "Nice, isn't it?" the big warrior remarked. "I think this is my favorite part of spelljamming. Just wait for the stars."

Teldin looked up again. "There's already one there," he pointed out.

Aelfred looked up in some surprise, then he smiled.

"That's no star," he told Teldin. "That'll be the *Nebulon*." As if the warrior's words had been some mystical cue, the sky faded to black and the stars came out.

Even though he'd been on Toril for only a couple of days, Teldin was awestruck once again by the stars of space. From the ground, on a clear night, he could see what seemed like millions of stars, and they seemed crisp, bright, and immediate. But the star field from space . . .

The difference was almost unbelievable. In the cool vacuum of the void, he could see myriads more stars than on the crispest night planetside. Every star seemed sharp, cold, clear . . . almost solid, as if he could reach out and touch one, pluck it from the heavens, and have it set in a gold ring, as you could any other gem of great value.

Teldin's eyes were filled with light. Even against that brilliant star field, he could pick out the one dot of light that Aelfred had told him was the arcane's ship. Not only was it brighter than any other, but it felt closer. It was bigger, too. All the other stars were dimensionless points. The "star" that was the *Nebulon* was starting to show a disk.

Aelfred settled on the bench next to Teldin—at a respectful distance, as a "business assistant" should. The big man nodded deferentially to his "employer." "Have you figured out what you're going to say?" he asked quietly.

"I think so," Teldin replied.

"You know exactly what it is you want out of this meeting?" Aelfred pressed.

Teldin was silent. That's the big question, isn't it? The simple answer to "what do I want?" was straightforward: "To get rid of this damned cloak." But that wasn't the whole of it, by any means. Even if the arcane could open the clasp—and no matter how much he wanted his freedom—Teldin knew he had to confirm that the cloak was of arcane manufacture before he could hand it over to T'k'Pek. Just how was he going to do that?

At home, Teldin had always prided himself on his ability to "read" others, to pick out when they were telling the truth and when they weren't. He didn't know how he did it; it wasn't anything certain, more like a combination of factors, and it was felt rather than reasoned. He'd been burned a few times, but more often than not he'd proved to his own satisfaction that he could tell when someone was lying about something important. On the walk through the city, he'd decided that he'd have to depend on that ability now. He didn't know enough about the cloak to ask the arcane cunning questions, trying to trip him up. He'd just have to get T'k'Pek talking, then trust his instincts—"trust his gut," as his grandfather used to say.

Aelfred was still waiting for an answer to his question. Teldin patted his large friend on the shoulder. "I know what I want," he confirmed.

The dragonfly had maneuvered so that the *Nebulon* was now directly ahead, and close. Teldin examined the ship, fascinated. So far, every spelljamming ship he'd seen *looked* like some kind of vessel. The gnomish dreadnought, the *Unquenchable*, looked like some nightmarish rendering of a sidewheeler; the hammership *Probe* had the hull, decks, and rigging of a seagoing ship. Even the "insect ships"—the wasps, mosquito, dragonfly, and deathspider—looked as if they were built to sail or fly . . . at least to travel from one place to another. The *Nebulon*, however, bore absolutely no resemblance to anything that could ever float or set down on land. The arcane's ship was a cylinder about as high as it was wide—like a milking pail, Teldin thought. It was light gray, almost white, ribbed by black bands. From the way the white material shone in the harsh sunlight of space, Teldin was certain it wasn't wood, metal, or even stone. *Ivory*, he mused, *it reminds me of ivory, but they couldn't build a whole ship out of ivory, could they?* The arcane's ship tumbled slowly through space, recalling images of Rianna's tiny mosquito and the efforts of Vallus Leafbower and the crew to bring it under control.

There was no such problem here, however. The dragonfly deftly maneuvered to match the motions of the cylinder. As the ships moved relative to each other, Teldin felt an uncomfortable shifting of balance in his inner ear. Remembering his conversations with Horvath and other spelljamming "veterans," he assumed this meant the two ships were aligning their gravity planes so that the "local down" for each vessel was the same. Soon the *Nebulon* appeared to be stationary—

in relation to the dragonfly, at least—while the stars wheeled slowly about the two vessels. Teldin's sense of balance finally settled as well.

As the dragonfly drew closer, Teldin realized the scale of the ship he was seeing. From a distance he'd guessed the cylindrical ship to be about fifty or sixty feet in diameter. Now, as the dragonfly hovered over one circular end, he saw the *Nebulon* must be almost five times that size: its diameter was about equal to the full keel length of the *Probe*. The black bands he'd seen were rows of great windows. What a view they must give, he thought with wonder.

The dragonfly made a final course correction and settled to the large, circular deck. There was a slight jolt as the small ship landed and a barely heard creak as its legs absorbed the strain. This was followed by another, almost subliminal *thump*. One of the dragonfly's crew came aft and nodded respectfully to Teldin. "Welcome aboard the *Nebulon*, milord," he said. He gestured to the ship's rail. "You may disembark now."

Teldin nodded with what he judged to be the right mixture of politeness and indifference. He stood and waited for the crewman to throw down the rope ladder . . . but there apparently was no need for the ladder. One of the crewmen just swung his leg over the dragonfly's rail and vanished. Teldin walked over to the gunwale.

There was a narrow, steep staircase butted up against the dragonfly's hull, its top step almost exactly level with the small ship's deck. The staircase was made of the same featureless white material as the rest of the arcane's ship. Teldin leaned over the rail. The stairway wasn't resting on the deck, as he'd expected. In fact, there was no visible division between the staircase and the deck. It was almost as though the stairway had grown out of the deck itself.

One dragonfly crewman was standing at the bottom of the stairs. The other was at Teldin's elbow, ready to give him a hand as he climbed over the rail. Teldin glanced behind him. Yes, his "assistants" were flanking him. Aelfred shot him a meaningful glance—obviously the big warrior thought he should go first, in case of a trap—but Teldin shook his head almost imperceptibly. If this was a trap, they were certainly dead men no matter who went down those mysterious stairs first. And, unaccountably, Teldin found himself unwilling to let somebody else take the lead this time. Both Aelfred and Estriss—and the others aboard the *Probe*—had already put their lives on the line for him, to help him discharge an obligation that wasn't theirs, that really had nothing to do with them whatsoever. They'd done it of their own will, he knew, but that just made it worse. No matter how much Aelfred wanted to lead—and, to be honest, no matter how much Teldin would like to have the big warrior ahead of him—it was about time Teldin did what was right. Ignoring the crewman's proffered help, he swung his legs over the rail and started down the stairway.

For the first time he could see the cylinder's circular "deck" clearly. There was nothing—other than the stairway itself and the low rail around the circumference—to break up the featureless expanse: no forecastle, no mast or rigging . . . and no visible way of getting down inside the cylindrical ship. Well, he thought, we'll just have to leave that up to the arcane, or this will be a short and useless meeting.

The stairway had a rail, but it was only on one side and was higher than was comfortable for Teldin. The risers, too, were higher than normal and were uncomfortable for human legs. Of course, he thought, the *Nebulon* isn't a human ship. He wished he'd asked Aelfred or Estriss more about what the arcane looked like. From the construction of this staircase, he could guess they were considerably taller than humans, but what other surprises were in store? With an effort he pushed on.

There was one positive thing: the descent down the staircase gave him an opportunity to examine the white material that seemed to make up the entire ship. The rail under his hand didn't feel cold like metal or stone would. It was more a neutral temperature. The texture wasn't quite like ivory, but he realized his original guess was probably fairly close to the truth. The white substance felt very much like bone. A ship of bone? That was an uncomfortable image.

The crewman nodded respectfully as Teldin reached the deck. They waited while Aelfred, Estriss, and the other crewman joined them, then led the party to the center of the circular deck. The first crewman muttered a short phrase under his breath, and the deck opened up.

The solid material of the deck shifted, and a round opening appeared. To Teldin, it looked like a gigantic eye, . . . or a mouth, opening. He fought the urge to step back.

The circular opening expanded until it was about ten feet in diameter. Cautiously, Teldin looked down into the hole. There was warm yellow light like a summer afternoon down there, and he could see a spiral staircase leading into the ship's depths. The first crewman bowed to Teldin again. "T'k'Pek awaits you below," he said.

Teldin nodded. He stepped forward and probed the edge of the opening with his toe. The white material, which seconds ago had shifted like soft flesh, was as hard as any other part of the deck. He glanced back at Aelfred and Estriss. The warrior was looking a little uncomfortable, but the disguised illithid appeared totally unconcerned. He's probably seen this kind of thing before, Teldin thought. He stepped onto the first stair— also as firm as rock—and started to descend. His "assistants" followed him.

The spiral staircase, with its too-high steps, took four turns, then reached another deck. Teldin guessed he'd descended about fifty feet. He was in a small, circular room, not much larger than the span of the staircase itself. There was a single door ahead: almost as high as the ceiling, but otherwise normal in design. As he waited for the others to join him, he looked around for the source of the light. There were no lanterns or torches; the light seemed to come from everywhere. He glanced at his feet and saw no shadow.

This one staircase, just to get to one door? he asked himself, then immediately answered his own question. Just like the circular hatch, he thought. Other doors open when they're needed.

Aelfred and Estriss were quickly beside him. With a deep breath, Teldin reached out for the doorknob.

His hand was still inches away from it when the door swung silently inward. Teldin hesitated, then stepped forward.

On the other side of the door was a long, straight corridor. Walls, floor, and fifteen-foot-high ceiling all were constructed of the now-familiar white material. The corridor shone with sourceless light. Dead straight, it had to be a hundred feet long, maybe more. The walls were featureless—no doors, no embellishments or decorations, nothing to break the unrelieved whiteness. Again, he presumed that doors along the corridor would open as the arcane willed and required. At the far end of the corridor, though, he thought he could see a normal door, similar to the one he'd just passed through.

He counted his steps. Thirty-five strides, and Teldin knew that each of his strides was a little less than three feet long. His estimate of the corridor's length had been fairly accurate. Now he stood in front of another door. As he'd guessed, it was a twin to the door from the stairwell. He waited until the others had joined him, then reached out to open it, and again it swung open as if triggered by the proximity of his hand.

The view beyond the doorway literally took his breath away. The room—if you could call it that—was wide, perhaps fifty or sixty feet across. The doorway he stood in was almost exactly in the center of the long wall. Twenty or thirty feet in front of him was a wall of shiny silver—the first break in the otherwise-ubiquitous ivory material. Set into it were great windows, their curving lines evoking images of flames, of flower petals, or of leaves. Widest at about waist level, these windows narrowed to delicate tips some fifteen feet above the floor.

Teldin stood, transfixed. Before him, the distant stars wheeled slowly. That's right, he thought, the *Nebulon* is tumbling. The stars swung, silently, in a kind of stately procession, then something else moved into his field of view: something huge, blue-white . . .

He was looking down on the planet Toril. *Down*. He clenched his teeth, struggling to hold back a whimper of fear. His brain conjured a vivid image: his body plummeting down toward that blue-white sphere, bursting through the glass of those windows, and falling free—surrounded by glittering fragments—to the ground below. Logic told him that was impossible. He was in the grip of the *Nebulon*'s own gravity, but how could logic stand up against the emotional impact of a view like that?

He heard a gasp from behind him. It was almost impossible to tear his eyes away from the spectacle before him, but somehow he turned. Aelfred was behind him, eyes wide in surprise. Almost instantly, however, he shook off the effect, and his expression returned to normal. He grasped Teldin's shoulder with his calloused hand and squeezed reassuringly.

As if his friend's touch were a healing spell, Teldin felt his terror melt away. He stepped farther into the gallery room. Now that his mind was free of the view's hypnotic spell, he saw other details of the room. There were two other doors in the wall, he noted, one on each side of the portal by which he'd entered.

Infinitely more important, he saw he wasn't alone in the great gallery. Toward the left-hand end of the room was a massive chair of purple crystal, almost like a throne. The *Nebulon*'s helm? he asked himself. It was facing outward toward the void.

And the great chair was occupied. A blue-skinned giant sat motionless, gazing out at the wonders of the universe. For several heartbeats, Teldin didn't move, waiting for the giant to acknowledge his presence. He was about to clear his throat when the crystal throne turned silently as if on a well-oiled pivot. For the first time, Teldin could see the creature in the chair properly.

He was a tall, lanky humanoid with bluish-gray skin. His thin, almost spindly legs were crossed, and he leaned back in the chair in a posture that looked almost indecently relaxed and comfortable. Teldin regarded him with interest. Standing, he figured the creature would be about twelve feet tall, but much of that height would come from his long legs. His shoulders were narrow, and his chest appeared almost sunken in comparison with his height. He looks like a weakling, Teldin thought, then dismissed the idea. Don't underestimate him, he told himself, in any way.

Apart from the creature's blue skin, his narrow head could possibly be mistaken for a human's . . . in a thick fog at midnight. The arcane's bald skull showed a strange, double-domed structure that bulged slightly forward above his brow. His eyes were dark and very human-looking, but were sunk deep into his head and protected by protruding rings of bone. His cheeks were hollow, focusing attention on his small, almost pursed, mouth. The creature wore a flowing, shawllike robe of shimmering green—a perfect contrast with the dusty blue of his skin, Teldin had to admit. The arcane's hands were clasped comfortably in his lap and seemed to Teldin to have too many fingers.

"You will pardon my caution," the arcane spoke without preamble. His voice was quiet, a reedlike piping much too high-pitched for a creature of his size. While he had no discernible accent, he seemed to exaggerate the sound of consonants, so that fricatives became sharp clicks, almost like bone on bone. Teldin assumed that might tell an expert something about the anatomy of his vocal apparatus, but it meant nothing to him.

The arcane fixed Teldin with a sharp gaze. "You implied to my representative that we have met." His voice was totally devoid of emotion. "We have not."

Teldin stepped forward and inclined his head, a shallow bow of respect. "I apologize," he said. "I needed to speak to you, but Barrab wasn't going to allow it."

"He was doing his job," T'k'Pek pointed out flatly.

"I realize that, but I *had* to speak with you, so I tricked him."

"You played on his fear," the arcane stated. His voice remained emotionless. "Barrab has much fear." The creature was silent for a moment, then went on, "I assume from your actions that you wish to see me on other than a normal business matter. I also assume that your companions are thus more than business assistants." The blue-skinned giant's gaze flicked to Aelfred and Estriss.

"I didn't mean to be rude," Teldin said. "These are my friends, Aelfred Silverhorn and . . . Bale Estriss. I am . . ."

The arcane cut him off. "In many cultures it is an insult to appear at a meeting in a false guise." Even though the words themselves were sharp, the creature's tone was still utterly indifferent. "Is it your intention to insult me?"

"Of course not," Teldin said quickly. He took a deep breath, calming himself in preparation for dropping the face of "Aldyn Brewer," but then he hesitated. The arcane's gaze wasn't on him; it was fixed unwaveringly on Estriss.

The disguised illithid hesitated for a moment, then hissed a word under his breath. His features shifted like water, quickly resolving themselves into the mind flayer's familiar tentacled face. With a red-tinged hand, Estriss removed a small felt hat from his head. His featureless eyes were on the arcane.

"Interesting," T'k'Pek remarked, though his flat tone belied the word. "An illithid in the company of humans." He turned his dark eyes to Teldin. "We may proceed."

Teldin was silent for a moment. There was something not right about this. He wanted to look back at Estriss, to ask the illithid for guidance, but knew that was impossible. He debated for a moment whether to drop his own magical disguise—which T'k'Pek hadn't seen through! he stressed to himself—then decided against it. "Yes," he said, "we may."

"What is the business for which you must see me?" the arcane asked.

As the dragonfly had made its final maneuvers to land on the *Nebulon*, Teldin had taken the time to prepare his answer to this question. He spoke now without hesitation. "There's a particular item—you might call it an artifact—that's come into my possession," he said smoothly. "I need you to tell me the background, the origin of that item."

T'k'Pek's deep-set eyes opened a touch wider at the word "artifact," but his voice reflected none of his apparent attention. "Interesting," he said again. "Why would you think I might know this?"

"Two reasons," Teldin answered. "First, it's well known that the arcane are the premiere dealers of powerful magic in the universe. A good salesperson must be able to evaluate potential sales goods, isn't that so?" Teldin had gambled that even a creature such as the arcane would have a streak of vanity and that it couldn't hurt to play on it. When the blue giant hooded his eyes complacently, Teldin knew he'd guessed right.

"That is correct," T'k'Pek confirmed. "And second?"

"Second, I have reason to believe that the item is of arcane manufacture."

"Oh?" Despite the creature's even tone, there was definitely the spark of serious interest in his eyes. "You have the item with you, I trust?"

"I do."

"Well?" the arcane prompted.

Teldin walked over to the arcane, sprawled in his throne. He looked up into the blue-skinned giant's eyes. "The cloak," he said simply.

T'k'Pek held out a hand—*five* fingers and a thumb, Teldin noticed—waiting for Teldin to hand over the cloak. When Teldin didn't, the arcane made no comment, just leaned down and took the cloth between his fingers. He examined the weave, turned the cloth over to view the lining, then released the cloak and resumed his relaxed, almost bored, posture.

"Yes," T'k'Pek said, "the cloak was created by my race."

Teldin realized he'd been holding his breath. He emptied his lungs with an audible sigh. He'd found the creators. . . .

So why, then, was he feeling uncomfortable? He couldn't isolate the feeling, couldn't examine it, but it was there and it was strong. There's something very wrong here, he told himself. He needed time to think. And, he realized, he needed to keep the arcane talking. "How do you know that?" he temporized.

"Do you see the pattern in the weave of the lining?" T'k'Pek asked. "The three-petaled flower? That flower is a symbol widely used by, and widely associated with, my race. See?" The arcane extended his left hand. Around one of its long, multijointed fingers was a heavy ring of gold. The top of the ring was flat, like a signet ring, and bore a design. The pattern was complex, but at its center was, unmistakably, the trilaterally symmetrical flower woven into the cloak's lining.

"That flower is unique to the arcane?" Teldin asked—more to give himself time to think than because he wanted to hear the creature's answer.

"That is so," T'k'Pek told him. "That representation of the flower is used only by my race."

T'k'Pek's lying! The thought was so strong that, for a moment, Teldin imagined he was "hearing" Estriss's mental voice. He quickly realized, though, that the thought was his own. His eyes locked with those of the blue giant. Why do I think you're lying to me? he asked silently. No, the real question is, *Why are you lying?* If T'k'Pek were human, Teldin might have seen some reaction in his eyes. But the eyes that looked back were steady, cold, and very alien. He suddenly recalled a comment his grandfather had once made about a man that they both knew and disliked: "If the eyes are windows to the soul, he's learned how to close the shutters."

Teldin heard someone shifting behind him: Aelfred, it had to be. He could sense his large friend's puzzlement. He wants to know why I don't ask the arcane to remove the cloak, Teldin reflected, but I can't, not yet. The next thought was like a cold wind blowing through his soul: Maybe the arcane could do it.

T'k'Pek was still watching him silently. If the arcane sensed his deliberation, he gave no sign.

"So the cloak is an arcane magical device," Teldin said slowly. "Tell me about its powers. What can it do?"

"There are many such cloaks," the arcane said easily. "Most are made for specific purposes, so their powers vary. This only makes sense."

"Give me some examples," Teldin pressed.

The giant's eyes shifted; for the first time he seemed uncomfortable. "The powers vary," he said again. "None are greatly significant: protection against cold, perhaps, or immunity to fire." His eyes were now fixed unblinkingly on Teldin's. Watching for a reaction? Teldin wondered, like a fake fortune-teller watching for a clue to better tailor the story? "Some may allow their wearers to fly, or maybe to breathe in the void. The cloak's power will probably be something minor along those lines."

"Power," Teldin mused. "Each cloak will only have one power?"

"Not necessarily," T'k'Pek replied quickly. "Again, the cloaks will vary. As I say, my people create them for different purposes."

Teldin nodded. He suddenly felt very tired, very old. He knew what he was going to do, and that knowledge was like a heavy burden on his shoulders. Once more, his gaze met the arcane's. "I understand," he said quietly. "Thank you for your time. I appreciate your help."

The arcane's eyes opened wide in surprise, a ludicrous contrast to the creature's uninflected voice. "You want nothing more?" he asked.

"No," Teldin told him honestly. "I apologize for the inconvenience. Again, thank you." He turned away. Neither Aelfred nor Estriss said anything, but their looks were questioning. Teldin shook his head.

"Wait." For the first time, there was a trace of intensity in the arcane's voice. Teldin turned back. "The cloak was created by my race," T'k'Pek said. "I would like it returned. I wish to purchase the cloak from you."

"I'm sorry." Teldin shook his head. "It's not for sale."

T'k'Pek was shifting uncomfortably in his chair. The arcane looked almost desperate. "I offer you a price of fifty thousand gold pieces," the creature said.

Teldin wasn't familiar with Toril's currency, so the offer made no sense to him, but from Aelfred's startled reaction, he realized that it must be a huge sum. "I'm sorry," he said, turning away.

"One hundred thousand gold pieces."

Teldin didn't even turn back. Estriss was watching him closely. Aelfred leaned closer and whispered, "One hundred thousand! You could buy the *Probe* and have enough left over to buy your girlfriend a new mosquito." Teldin shook his head. The other two followed—a little unwillingly, in Aelfred's case—as he headed for the door.

"Name your price." The arcane's voice had taken on a sharp edge of desperation.

"Thank you for your time, T'k'Pek," Teldin said. "I'll be in touch."

Neither Aelfred nor Estriss spoke to him on the return flight to Rauthaven or the trip back to the *Probe*. Teldin was glad for the silence. He had a lot to think about. On returning to the hammership, he left the others and went below to the officers' saloon. Rianna had headed into the city on a shopping trip, he'd been told. It was just as well, he figured. While he'd have welcomed seeing her, he knew she'd have asked him questions that he couldn't even answer for himself yet. He pulled a chair to his normal place near the circular port and settled himself comfortably. The ship's gentle rocking relaxed him, cleared his mind.

What in the Abyss am I doing? he berated himself. The arcane made the cloak; the pattern's the same as the one on T'k'Pek's ring. Why didn't I ask the giant to remove it?

Partly because T'k'Pek lied, he answered himself. That flower *isn't* exclusively an arcane symbol. T'k'Pek couldn't answer my questions. He just tried to tell me what he thought I wanted to hear. He didn't even guess that I needed the cloak removed.

Or that I was disguised! he finished. That was the most telling point, Teldin thought. The arcane had sensed somehow that Estriss had shapechanged, but not him. Why not? Particularly if the cloak—and its powers—were created by T'k'Pek's own people? Shouldn't the creature be more attuned to the powers of his own race's artifacts?

He sighed and fingered the cloak's hem. The material was thin, almost weightless, but now the garment seemed to weigh down on him like a millstone around his neck. I should be free of this, he told himself.

At least his decision wasn't irrevocable. That was his one consolation. If he'd had the arcane remove the cloak—provided he *could* remove it—and handed it over, then found he'd been wrong, there would be nothing he could do. This way, he still had a chance to change his mind. He could always contact T'k'Pek—the arcane's eagerness to pay a king's ransom reassured him that he'd have little trouble setting up another meeting—and ask for the creature's help with the cloak. The blue-skinned giant wouldn't be leaving Rauthaven until after the auction the next morning.

Teldin forced himself to relax. He still had time.

Chapter Thirteen

• • •

Teldin spent the night aboard the *Probe*. The three gnomes were ashore—presumably still tracking down material for their invention—so he had the cabin to himself. At around midnight, Rianna returned from town, as excited as a child at her purchases. Mostly she'd bought clothes for herself, ranging from demure to downright naughty, and she hinted at how much she was looking forward to sufficient privacy to model them for Teldin properly. She'd also picked up a gift for him: a short sword with an elaborately gold-chased hilt, which she slipped into his scabbard. When he remarked that it looked too expensive, she feigned anger. "It's my money I'm spending, Teldin Moore," she told him, hands on her hips, "and if I think you're worthy of what that gift cost, then you're worthy of it. Anyway—" her frown broke into a jesting smile "—who's to say I didn't steal it from the hip of some sellsword who tried to win my favors?"

They spent the rest of the night in each other's arms. Although he could tell from her manner that she wanted to know how his meeting with the arcane had gone, she apparently sensed his confusion and didn't raise the issue. Teldin appreciated this, another indication of the woman's sensitivity—as if he needed anything more after her reaction to learning his true identity. As they finally drifted into sleep, he found himself wondering how he'd ever considered himself happy before he'd met her.

The next day dawned bright and sunny, but with a brisk wind that caused the hammership to roll at its anchor. When Teldin awoke, Rianna was already up and gone. He dressed slowly, enjoying the warm feeling of relaxation spreading throughout his body. In the back of his mind was the knowledge that he still had a decision to make—or, at least, to hold to—but he wouldn't let himself dwell on it. He'd have plenty of time to worry about that later. At the moment, he was feeling good and wanted to make the most of the experience. He made his way up on deck.

The sun was beating down, but the breeze was sharp and cold on his cheeks. He filled his lungs with air, enjoying the feeling of muscles stretching. In the bright sunlight, the white-and-red city shone. *Beautiful*, he thought, *I'll be sad if I have to leave here.*

Aelfred and Estriss—the latter once again magically disguised—were on the forecastle deck. Rianna was with them. She waved down to him. "Aldyn," she called happily, "get your lazy body up here."

He smiled. One thing he'd always prided himself on was his ability to enjoy life. He had to admit, though, in contrast to Rianna he seemed dull and repressed. He swung up the ladder and joined his friends on the forecastle.

"Good morning," he said, grinning happily. "Nice day."

"After a nice night, too, I warrant," Aelfred put in innocently. Rianna dug an elbow none too gently into his ribs, and the big warrior added in the same ingenuous tone, "The weather, I meant."

Teldin chuckled. Initially he'd felt a little uncomfortable about the first mate's somewhat . . . indelicate . . . humor, but now he was secure enough to accept it in the manner intended: as one friend ribbing another, with no harm or insult meant.

Estriss was watching the byplay with little comprehension. *He can travel with humans,* Teldin thought. *He can even take the face of a human, but he'll never really understand us.* He took pity on his alien friend. "The auction's today, isn't it, Estriss?" he asked.

The disguised illithid seemed happy to get back to a topic he could grasp. *Yes,* he replied, *in an hour or so. The tender has already been summoned to take us to shore.* He paused. *Would you like to join us?* he asked, a little diffidently. *You would be most welcome.*

"I want to go," Rianna said brightly. "It'll be fun, and maybe I'll learn something. I've never learned that much about history before." She turned to Estriss. "You'll tell us what's happening, won't you?"

Teldin smiled, a little indulgently. Rianna's enthusiasm was really running high this morning. He enjoyed seeing her like this, untroubled, unburdened by decisions. And why not? She was right: the auction would be interesting, and maybe he'd learn something of importance. In any case, even if he didn't, it might be the perfect opportunity to get his mind off the issue of what to do about the cloak. His grandfather had often told him that sometimes the best way to make a decision was to force yourself to forget it, to occupy your mind with something else. That way you freed up your subconscious, and quite often, when you went back to the problem, you'd find you had an answer plus all the reasons to back it up. It wouldn't hurt to try it out.

"Sounds like an experience," he told his friends. "I'd love to come along."

* * * * *

The Merchants' Rotunda was a large building just off a wide street similar to the Processional, near the docks. When he'd first heard the name, Teldin had pictured a building like a warehouse, filled with sacks of grain, and baskets and crates of other goods. Rianna had explained that it wasn't like that at all. All trading was done in *contracts* for goods. Representatives for the various guilds, the trading coasters, and the carriers would meet in the hallways or in the central hall. Deals would be offered, terms would be agreed to, and contracts— only contracts—would change hands. Ownership of hundreds of tons of goods and thousands of coins would shift, but no party would even have to *see* the goods involved if they didn't want to. As Teldin finally grasped the concept, he shook his head in amazement. Compared to this place, his farming community on Krynn was indeed backward, still depending largely on the farmers' markets to conduct business. Market day meant hours of backbreaking labor, loading and unloading goods, and the twilight ride home with a pouch jingling with coins. How much easier it would be to ride out and back with nothing but pieces of parchment.

The auction itself was taking place in the rotunda's central hall. This was a huge, circular room, a hundred feet or so in diameter. At its center, the hall was more than three stories tall. Ground level—the trading floor—was an expanse of polished marble, now covered with scores of wooden chairs moved in from who knew where. The floor above sported an open gallery, supported by fluted pillars, giving spectators a perfect view down onto the trading floor. Above that was a great domed roof, decorated with great murals that Rianna said depicted the growth of Rauthaven from a tiny village to a major metropolis. Light came from large windows set around the base of the dome and through a circular crystal skylight in the center of roof.

Matters were already underway when the disguised Estriss and his entourage arrived. Three quarters of the seats were filled by participants and spectators. More spectators craned over the railing of the second-floor gallery. As they found seats near the back, Teldin surveyed the attendees with interest. It was generally easy to pick out the real participants from the interested onlookers. The latter were dressed like anyone on the streets of Rauthaven. The former, however, wore clothes that immediately set them apart. Silk robes were trimmed with fur or cloth-of-gold, and ears and fingers flashed with gold and gems. It was easy to tell that these people had money and were willing to spend it.

A wooden stage had been constructed near one side of the rotunda, and it was here that the items were being auctioned off. Three young, burly men, similar in build to Aelfred, were available to hold and display items . . . and, presumably, to offer some kind of security. The auctioneer himself was a scrawny old man with a face that reminded Teldin of a dyspeptic buzzard, but with a rich voice that effortlessly filled the rotunda.

As Teldin took his seat, he saw that the item up for bid was a portrait. He stifled a grin. If he ever felt as sickly as the old gentleman in the painting, he'd certainly not choose that time to have a portrait done. The face in the painting was slightly asymmetrical, as though one side of its head were swollen, and its skin had a decidedly green tinge. Not the kind of thing you'd hang in your dining room, Teldin thought, or your bedroom.

"Final bid," the auctioneer was saying. "Final bid? . . . *Sold*." He rapped on his podium with a brass gavel. "Sold for ten thousand gold pieces." One of the young men carried the painting off, while another produced a heavy oaken chest. "This next item . . ."

Teldin didn't listen to the auctioneer's description of the chest. Ten thousand gold pieces? he repeated to himself. Aelfred had told him one hundred thousand gold pieces would buy him a hammership plus a mosquito. That meant the price that miserable painting fetched would be an excellent down payment on a major spelljamming vessel. This just confirmed something he'd always suspected: he knew absolutely nothing about art.

The next few items didn't fetch prices anywhere near that of the painting. After the novelty—and his amazement over the sum of money involved—had worn off, Teldin found his interest waning. He turned to his right, tried to get Estriss's attention, to ask how long until the significant items would be open for bid, but the illithid's eyes and attention were fixed unshakably forward. Rianna, sitting directly to his right, felt Teldin's restlessness and laid a calming hand on his arm. "Not much longer," she whispered to him, "then it'll get interesting, I promise."

He nodded, a little glumly. This was nowhere near as exciting as he'd expected. Instead of taking his mind off his decision, the auction was giving him too much time to think. And he thought better when he was free to pace. Well, Rianna was probably right. He'd give it a little longer. To relieve the tedium, he looked up at the ring of faces above him—the spectators encircling the second-floor gallery and staring down into the hall.

His gaze drifted idly around the ring. Suddenly, his peripheral vision caught a face that looked familiar. He focused on the spot, but the face was gone. There was movement there, though; apparently someone had moved away from the gallery rail.

Even though he'd seen it for only an instant, he was sure he knew that face: Tregimesticus, the ex-slave, the same person he thought he'd seen at the tavern.

Teldin leaned over to Aelfred. "Where's Tregimesticus?" he whispered.

Aelfred blinked in surprise. "Aboard the *Probe*," he answered. "Where else?"

"I thought I saw him in the gallery."

The warrior smiled. "That's doubtful," he pointed out. "Tregimesticus still has the slave mentality real bad. If he wanted to come ashore, he'd have to ask for permission to catch the tender. And before that, he'd have to decide he wanted to. Can you see Tregimesticus doing either of those things?"

Teldin remembered the exchange with Garay, how the ex-slave didn't even have the initiative to pick up the marlin spike that had fallen at his feet. Teldin grinned back. "Not really. I guess I just saw his twin."

"You mean there's someone who looks like Tregimesticus?" Aelfred asked in mock alarm. "Poor bugger."

Teldin chuckled as he settled back into his seat.

The auctioneer's drone suddenly stopped in mid-bid. There was silence for a moment, then the rush of whispered conversation. Throughout the rotunda, heads turned.

Teldin looked behind him. Another figure—obviously a participant—was entering the rotunda. The new arrival certainly stood apart from the others. Twelve feet tall, bald head brushing the underside of the gallery, T'k'Pek, the arcane, made his entrance. Standing, with his long robe hanging in unbroken swaths to the floor, the creature looked little like the gangly figure Teldin had seen aboard the *Nebulon*. Now he moved regally, imperially ignoring the consternation his arrival was causing. There was an empty chair in the back row. T'k'Pek seemed to consider it, then discard the idea. He would have looked ludicrous trying to squat on a human chair much too small for him, Teldin realized. The arcane turned his dark eyes on the staring auctioneer. "Pray continue," the giant said in his thin, high-pitched voice.

The auctioneer didn't respond for a moment, then swallowed visibly. "Of course," he muttered, "of course. The bid is—" for the first time, he had to consult the notes he was continuously taking "—three hundred fifty gold pieces. Do I hear four hundred?"

The auction quickly returned to normal. The participants refocused their attention on the stage, and even the spectators in the gallery eventually stopped whispering and muttering about the alien figure standing at the back of the crowd. "Bale Estriss" kept his head turned to the rear, his eyes fixed on the arcane.

Why? Teldin wondered. The illithid *knew* T'k'Pek was interested in the same items as he was. Why the surprised stare?

Maybe it was because the illithid had expected T'k'Pek to send his human representative, Barrab. That could explain it, Teldin decided. And it was a good point. Why would the arcane draw so much attention to himself—attention that could very well disrupt the auction—unless that was the giant's whole intention. . . .

"The next item," the auctioneer was saying, "is a long knife of unique design and unknown provenance." Estriss's face snapped to the front, his gaze unwavering. Teldin could almost feel the illithid's excitement. On the stage, one of the young men was holding a long knife—a short sword, really—of unusual design.

Unusual, but also familiar. Teldin had seen that smoothly curved blade before, that same long hilt, built up into a complex pattern of ridges and channels. It was a twin to the weapon Estriss had shown him aboard the *Probe*, soon after Teldin's scrap with the scavver. The knife that Estriss believed had been forged—no, *grown*—by the Juna.

The disguised illithid was almost quivering with tension. He was leaning over toward Aelfred, their heads almost in contact.

"Bidding is open," the auctioneer announced. "Do I hear five hundred gold pieces?"

There was a murmur from the crowd. Even though Teldin hadn't been paying close attention to the auction, he realized this was a high starting price for something so apparently mundane. Obviously somebody apart from the illithid suspected the significance of the knife. He glanced over toward Estriss. Maybe that would work to the illithid's advantage, however, he mused. It would certainly discourage anyone with only casual interest from pushing the price up.

Aelfred's strong voice cut through the background muttering. "Five hundred gold pieces."

So that's how they're playing it, Teldin thought. The big warrior would actually be placing the bids, under Estriss's silent instructions. A good system.

"I have five hundred gold pieces," the auctioneer echoed. "Do I hear six?"

Teldin glanced over his shoulder at the arcane. T'k'Pek stood motionless and silent at the back of the crowd. The giant's expression seemed a little bemused.

If Teldin was expecting the next bid to come from the arcane, he was surprised. An affluent-looking merchant in the front row gestured negligently. "Five hundred and fifty," he announced.

Aelfred responded immediately. "Six hundred gold pieces."

The murmurs started again. Six hundred gold pieces was already much too high a price to pay for a sword, particularly one of an impractical design. All around Teldin, people were speculating on why this particular weapon was worth so much . . . and whether that puzzle was related to the blue-skinned giant's presence.

"Six hundred gold pieces," said the auctioneer. "Do I hear seven . . . ?"

"Seven thousand gold pieces." The arcane's reedlike voice echoed through the suddenly silent rotunda.

The auctioneer swallowed again, his Adam's apple bobbing up and down his scrawny throat. "Milord," he began uncertainly, "the bidding is at seven *hundred* . . ."

"Seven thousand gold pieces," T'k'Pek said again. The creature's voice was as emotionless as the wind.

The marble-floored room rang with startled conversation. Seven *thousand* gold pieces? When seven *hundred* was already a ridiculous price to pay for such an item?

The auctioneer was finding this heavy going. He used his brass gavel to rap for silence. It took several tries before he could still the uproar. "The bid," he said, "is seven . . . *thousand* . . . gold pieces. Do I hear seven thousand five hundred?"

Estriss and Aelfred were in consultation. Naturally, Teldin could hear only Aelfred's voice. After a few moments, the big warrior nodded agreement. "Seven and five," he said clearly.

"Ten thousand gold pieces."

Once more, heads turned, almost quickly enough to dislocate vertebrae, and the noise level reached new heights. If the arcane was even aware of the stupefaction he had caused, he gave no sign. His face was expressionless, and his gaze was fixed unwaveringly on the sword displayed on the stage.

The man sitting on Teldin's left snorted in disgust. His plump cheeks were suffused with color; in fact, he looked almost apoplectic. " . . . just doesn't understand the concept of an auction," he was gurgling in outrage.

Teldin looked back toward Aelfred and Estriss. There was no conversation now. The first mate was looking at his captain, waiting for his next instruction. Estriss was gazing unseeingly forward. Even magically disguised, the creature's face showed the distress it must be feeling.

"The bid is ten thousand gold pieces," said the auctioneer. "Do I hear another bid? I have ten thousand. Final bid?" He looked directly at Aelfred. "Milord?"

Aelfred glanced once more at Estriss . . . then shook his head firmly.

"Final bid, ten thousand gold pieces," the auctioneer repeated. "And *sold*." He brought down his gavel with a conclusive crack. "Sold to the, er . . . the gentleman, er . . ."

Participants and spectators roared their consternation once more. Serenely, totally untouched by the tumult surrounding him, the arcane glided to the stage, where he handed over a small square of parchment to one of the attendants. Another attendant handed over the bizarre sword, which the giant concealed within the folds of his flowing garment. Then he turned his back on the auction and made a silent department.

Teldin glanced to his right. Estriss was halfway to his feet, apparently intending to pursue the arcane, for whatever reason. Only Aelfred's hand on the creature's arm restrained him. Teldin could imagine what the illithid must be feeling, and he had to grin. He knew what one of Aelfred's "gentle, restraining grips" felt like. The mind flayer wouldn't be going anywhere. Estriss recognized the reality of that, too. Grudgingly, he sat down again.

Rianna was looking at Teldin, her eyebrow raised in question. "Poor Estriss," he told her. "That sword was the major reason for coming here."

"Why's it so important?" she whispered back. "Ten *thousand* gold pieces?"

"Something to do with his life work," Teldin explained. "I'll tell you about it later."

With the arcane's departure, the auction returned to at least a semblance of normalcy. The next item—another old portrait—was displayed and bidding commenced in an orderly manner. With the blue-skinned giant gone, it was obvious that nobody really expected any further fireworks. In fact, in the minutes after T'k'Pek's departure, more than a few spectators and participants quietly left the hall. Probably, in contrast to the short but very sharp bidding war, the rest of the auction was seeming intolerably dull.

Estriss had settled down a little. The loss of the weapon had hit him hard, that was obvious, but he was still confident that other pieces of interest would come up for bid before the auction ended.

Bidding on the portrait quickly settled into a contest between two affluent gentlemen in the front row . . . who obviously hated each other. Already, pride and a refusal to let the other "win" had forced the price up into the low hundreds of gold pieces, and there was no indication the contest would slow soon. Even though the outcome was irrelevant to him— or maybe *because* of that fact—Teldin was enjoying the acrimonious struggle.

Without warning, he felt a light touch on his shoulder. He turned quickly.

Barrab, the arcane's human representative, was standing behind him. The large man's cherubic smile was back in place. "Milord Brewer," Barrab whispered. "My employer, T'k'Pek, would like to meet with you again. Now, if that's convenient."

Both Rianna and Aelfred had heard Barrab. The big warrior shook his head subtly.

Teldin hesitated. He knew that Aelfred didn't trust Barrab—and, to tell the truth, he didn't trust the man himself—but maybe the arcane had some new information, something to help him make the decision that still weighed on his mind. He couldn't dismiss that possibility.

"It's very important, milord Brewer," Barrab whispered. "My employer says to tell you specifically that something new has come to light, something you should know immediately. Will you meet with T'k'Pek?"

Aelfred and Rianna were still listening, and even Estriss was paying attention. Teldin glanced at his friends. "Give me a moment," he whispered to Barrab. "I have to talk with my . . . assistants."

Barrab nodded and withdrew, but not far. At least he was out of earshot if Teldin kept his voice down.

"Don't do it," Aelfred whispered sharply as soon as Barrab had stepped away. "If you want to talk to the arcane again, set up an official meeting."

"You don't trust Barrab," Teldin said.

"Less than I trust T'k'Pek, and that's saying something." Aelfred was silent for a moment. "I don't like this," he whispered finally. There was urgency in his eyes.

He was right, Teldin thought. But . . . "It could be important," Teldin answered. "I think I have to go."

Aelfred cursed under his breath. "All right, if you have to." He started to stand. "I'll come with you."

No. For the first time, Estriss joined the conversation. The creature's mental "voice" was sharp. *No,* he said again. *Aelfred, you must stay, to bid for me on the items I want.*

The first mate hesitated. Teldin could see the conflict on his face. Even though it was Aelfred who really commanded the *Probe*, Estriss was still his superior officer. The illithid hadn't given an order, but Teldin knew that was next. Then the warrior would have to decide whether it was an order he could obey.

"Aelfred . . ." Teldin began.

"I'll go with him," Rianna put in quickly. She grinned as Aelfred looked at her with surprise. "I'm used to taking care of myself. I can take care of him, too. I've got a good reason: I'm not done with my little playmate yet."

Aelfred hesitated, then he smiled as well. "Thanks," he said, and he meant it.

Barrab was shifting from foot to foot in nervousness—a rather amusing sight in someone so large and usually so controlled. As Teldin and Rianna left their seats, he smiled with relief. "Thank you," he said. "I was worried—"

"Where are we going?" she asked, cutting him off.

"Not far," the representative replied. "My employer wishes to avoid the crowds when he talks to milord Brewer."

That wasn't an answer, Teldin realized, as Barrab led them from the rotunda. From the first, he'd felt apprehension about this meeting, even though he knew he couldn't refuse. Now the anxiety had doubled. He looked at Rianna.

The woman's face was grim. She was taking this seriously, Teldin could see. Her right hand hovered near the hilt of her belt knife. He'd never seen Rianna under pressure or in danger, Teldin realized, but there was something about her manner that reassured him. He was glad to have her along.

Barrab led them toward a door to the outside—not the main lobby through which Teldin and friends had entered the Merchants' Rotunda, but a smaller portal at the rear of the building. "T'k'Pek has a carriage in the alley," Barrab answered Teldin's unspoken question. "We thought it would be more private." The representative led the way out through the door. Teldin followed, Rianna on his heels.

He stopped suddenly. There was no carriage, and Barrab had turned to face him. The large man's smile was predatory rather than cherubic now, and cold steel glittered in his right hand. Flanking him were three men that Teldin didn't know. He did recognize them by their wiry strength and the easy manner in which they held their unsheathed swords. These were hired bravos—"city wolves," his grandfather had called them. He and Rianna had been led—neatly and efficiently—into a trap.

Chapter Fourteen

• • •

Teldin glanced over his shoulder at Rianna. She had her blade drawn and stood in the same knife-fighter's crouch as the bravos. He saw her eyes flick from enemy to enemy and could almost sense her thoughts. Four on two: lousy odds. Or four on *one*, since she'd have no reason to believe Teldin could defend himself. But they were only a few paces from the door, and none of the hired blades was close enough to stop them from bolting back inside the Merchants' Rotunda.

As if on cue, the door opened behind Rianna. Another figure slipped into the alley; another blade glittered in the sunlight. Rianna spun, trying to keep everyone in her field of vision, but it was impossible. She and Teldin were surrounded.

Barrab chuckled, grinning hugely. He was thoroughly enjoying this, Teldin realized. "Sorry," Barrab said, "no easy escapes. Where would be the fun in that?" His expression sobered a little. "I suggest you drop your weapon, milady," he said quietly, "and that neither of you try anything untoward. Some of my . . . colleagues would be as happy to rip you as look at you."

Teldin looked from face to face. His attention was fixed immediately by the bravo nearest him. The man was as thin as a whip. His eyes made Teldin think of a rabid ferret and he smelled of violence, of death. While Barrab might warn him and Rianna not to try anything, this one was hoping they would. Then he'd be justified in cutting them down. Teldin's hand had strayed near the hilt of his short sword. Now he moved it, very obviously, away from the weapon.

Teldin spoke for the first time. "This isn't necessary," he said, struggling to keep his voice even, his tone reasonable. "I'm willing to meet with T'k'Pek. . . ." His voice trailed off.

Barrab's harsh laughter confirmed what he'd just realized. "I'm not working for the blue-skin anymore," the fat man amplified. "The head-eaters from Falx pay much better."

Rianna gasped. Barrab's words obviously meant more to her than they did to Teldin. "You treacherous bastard," she spat. "I hope you get your throat ripped out."

Barrab chuckled again. "Doubtful," he remarked casually. "The money this'll net me will take me a long way from here."

The bravos—even the rabid-looking killer—listened to this exchange with some interest, and even amusement. Their stares were on their employer and the woman, not on Teldin. He edged slowly to his left, where there was a slight opening. If he moved fast enough, maybe slashing the nearby bravo with his sword as he went past . . . That should distract them enough for Rianna to get free as well. He knew it was a desperate idea, but he had little choice. He tensed, ready to bolt.

The bravos' attention might have been distracted, but not Barrab's. At Teldin's first subtle move, he responded. "Oh, no," he snapped. The bravos' eyes were instantly back on Teldin, colder and crueller than before. The rabid one smiled, and his eyes looked like death.

Teldin froze. Again he slowly and obviously moved his hand away from his sword hilt. The other bravos relaxed a little. The rabid one, however, was still tense, ready to attack. Teldin's throat felt like a cylinder of solid ice. He's insane, he told himself.

"Relax, Spak," Barrab snapped at the feral bravo. "Relax, I said."

The rabid one seemed to quiver with internal conflict. I can't believe how much he wants to kill me, Teldin thought. Spak shot Barrab a speculative look, as though the killer were considering slaughtering him as well, then, with a visible effort, Spak lowered his sword and left his poised half-crouch. Teldin started to breathe again.

Barrab looked hardly less relieved, he noticed. The fa

man's authority over the bravo had held—*just*—but he might not win another battle of wills like that.

The arcane's representative spoke to the other bravos. "Enough of this. Take them," he ordered, pointing at Teldin, "but don't harm *him*." He grinned nastily. "I'm not concerned about her welfare."

Smiling like wolves, the bravos stepped forward.

"*No!*" Rianna shouted in outrage. She flung her knife at the nearest bravo—an underhand cast, neither accurate nor powerful, but the hired swordsman had to block it. That gave Rianna an instant of freedom.

Her hands swept through a complex gesture, and she barked a harsh syllable. Fire bloomed, a gout of flame that burst into existence right in front of Barrab and spread with a dull roar. "*Run, Teldin!*" Rianna screamed.

Teldin threw himself back from the fire, shielding his eyes with his cloaked arm. Even so, heat washed over his face and he felt his skin tighten with it. His eyes stung with tears and with smoke, and the air was heavy with the smell of burning cloth and flesh.

The roaring fire was gone as quickly as it had sprung into being. Barrab was reeling, screaming and slapping at small flames that still burned on his clothing. Much of his hair was gone, and his exposed skin was an angry red. One of the bravos was down, blackened and unmoving. The other sellswords were wiping streaming eyes or covering blistered faces.

Rianna was simply *gone*. No, there she was, sprinting down the alley, heading for the corner and safety. She'd almost made it when Spak, the feral bravo, opened his scorched eyes and saw her. With an animal snarl, he snatched a dagger from his boot and flung it with frightening force. The dagger caught the sunlight as it turned end for end—once, twice—and tore into the fleeing woman's shoulder. Teldin heard her scream in agony, but she kept running, and an instant later was around the corner. The bravos might still pursue, but she'd gained a good head start.

The sellswords hadn't looked Teldin's way yet. He had a moment or two to react.

He took the opportunity that Rianna had given him at such cost. He turned and ran down a narrow alley to the left.

Never had he felt quite so terrified. There was something almost paralyzing about turning his back on people who'd willingly kill him. As he ran, he braced himself to hear the pounding of pursuing footsteps or feel the bite of Spak's next thrown dagger in his back. The urge to look around, to at least face his death, was almost overpowering.

The narrow alleyway forked, then forked again. Both times, he took the left-hand path. Then he crossed another, wider alley. He flung himself around the corner to the right. Still he ran, and still he expected death to strike him in the next instant.

He didn't know how far he'd run. His lungs were on fire, and the blood was pounding so loudly in his ears that he wouldn't be able to hear pursuit even if it were right on his heels. He was lost now. He turned another corner, deeper into a twisted warren of narrow streets and alleys. His foot caught on something, and he fell forward. His knee hit the ground with a sickening crack and he howled with the pain. He jammed a fist into his mouth and gnawed on the knuckle to silence himself. For a time there was nothing he could do but lie there, huddled in on himself, engulfed in the waves of agony from his knee. If Barrab and his sellswords found him now, Teldin knew, he'd be helpless whether they wanted to drag him away or slit his throat where he lay.

It felt like years later, but eventually the tide of torment ebbed. When his vision finally cleared, he saw he was huddled in a garbage-strewn alley so narrow he'd be unable to lie full-length across it.

It took him a moment, but he eventually realized that one of the piles of garbage was watching him with rheumy and none-too-steady eyes. What he'd taken for a discarded cloak or a pile of cast-off rags was actually a wizened old man, squatting with his back to the alley wall. The figure was enveloped in a huge traveling cloak—or, more correctly, what once had been a traveling cloak—supplemented by other tattered rags. The only bare skin exposed to the elements was the man's lined face, and even that was partially shrouded by the cloak's hood and a scarf made from some other nondescript cloth. Beside the man was a small earthenware jug. Teldin sniffed. The alley reeked of urine and garbage, but mostly of soured wine

He nodded in comprehension.

Teldin started to climb to his feet, then hesitated. Might as well cover my tracks while I've got the chance, he thought. He closed his eyes and took a calming breath. He let the image of the feral sellsword, Spak, take shape in his mind, then he superimposed that face over his. . . .

It took only a moment. When he raised a hand to his face, he felt a sharp nose, thin lips. He looked up and stared steadily at the wizened heap against the alley wall. The old man quailed visibly. Teldin could understand that: he'd been on the receiving end of Spak's killing glares himself.

Teldin held the stare for several heartbeats, plenty long enough for the old man to remember the face. Then he extracted a coin from his belt pouch—a Krynnish coin, but the derelict probably would neither know nor care. He flipped it to the old man, who picked it out of the air with surprising dexterity. Rheumy eyes struggled to focus on the glitter of metal—polished steel, though the derelict probably assumed it was silver—then opened wide with shocked recognition. Frantically, before his feral-faced benefactor could change his mind, the tramp stuffed the coin into the folds of his cloak and struggled to his feet. He snatched up his earthenware jug, tucked it under one arm, and hurried away down the alley—no doubt heading for the nearest wine shop for a refill, Teldin reflected. The whole exchange had cost him one coin, probably valueless here, and no more than a minute—which was time well spent to allow his knee to settle down. What had it gained him? If his pursuers questioned the derelict—the only possible witness to Teldin's flight—he'd probably get a story about an evil-eyed man who gave him money . . . and nothing that Barrab could reasonably associate with Teldin. It might not help that much, but it certainly couldn't hurt.

Teldin took a few moments to change his magical disguise once more. If he ended up running into the sellswords, he definitely didn't want to be wearing Spak's face. He visualized the plump, florid-faced man who'd sat next to him at the auction and had complained so vociferously about T'k'Pek's bidding tactics. This time, he gave special attention to the body. Both Teldin and "Aldyn" were slender; if he made sure that his new body was fat, the chances of recognition would be that much lower.

It was a strange feeling as his clothes—normally comfortably loose—seemed to tighten around his belly and thighs. He had no mirror to check his appearance but guessed from feeling alone that he'd changed his build sufficiently. He climbed to his feet. . . .

And almost cried out from the flash of agony through his knee. The joint felt swollen, not so much outside as inside. It felt as if there were a small sac or balloon behind his kneecap that was inflated with hot liquid. He couldn't straighten the leg fully or bend it past a right angle. Any attempt to do so put pressure on the "balloon" and sent lightning bolts of torment through his leg.

Using the alley wall for support, he steadied himself and slowly put weight on the injured leg. As long as he kept the knee partially bent and applied pressure slowly, the pain was manageable, but if he transferred his weight too fast, or if he turned quickly and applied even the gentlest twisting force to the knee, the blast of agony was enough to blur his vision and wrench a whimper from his throat.

No running, he realized with a cold chill, not even a fast walk. He'd have to depend on his disguise and on luck.

He started down the alley in the direction the old derelict had run. It took him a dozen steps and several painful experiments to strike the right balance between a conspicuous hobble and blinding agony. Finally, though, he found a gait that wouldn't attract too much attention and that he thought he could keep up long enough to . . .

He stopped so suddenly that his knee erupted with pain. Long enough to *what*? Where in the Abyss was he going? Back to the harbor and the *Probe*? He was totally lost. In his blind flight through the alleyways, he'd lost track of direction and distance. He had no idea of which way led to the harbor. Certainly, it lay generally downhill—Rauthaven was built on the inner slopes of the hills that surrounded the bay—but in this maze of narrow streets and alleys he had no feel for the slope at all. The only way to regain his sense of direction would be to find a major street, something like the Processional, that was wide and long enough to let him see the lay of the land. Of course, if Barrab had any sense at all, that's where he would have positioned his sellswords.

Even if he did find his way, his enemies knew where he was going. Barrab knew that Teldin Moore—or Aldyn Brewer, if the difference still mattered—was staying aboard the hammership *Probe*. He cursed himself for a fool. He'd been so proud of his plan to manipulate Barrab. Now he realized that his cleverness might well kill him. Barrab would make sure that the harbor was watched, and anyone trying to reach the *Probe* would be detained.

With an effort, Teldin calmed the panicked flow of his thoughts. *Barrab's only got four bravos. Three. Rianna's magical fire killed one, didn't it? How close a watch can he keep with three men?* he thought.

His relief lasted no more than a heartbeat before logic crushed it. Barrab's got money, he realized, lots of money, if he was staying at the Edgewood. How much would it cost to hire three sellswords, or another score, if that's what he needs? No, Teldin understood, the cordon at the harbor would be as tight as Barrab wanted it to be, plenty tight enough to check every tender that was ferrying people to ships at anchor. If he was caught in that cordon, on his way to the *Probe*, he'd be detained, possibly killed, whether or not he was disguised.

Then there was the problem that Estriss had put into words when they'd discussed the cloak's powers. There might well be magical means for tracking the cloak. If that were true, then capture *certainly* spelled disaster, because he definitely couldn't get rid of the cloak.

What could he do? He had to get out of the city somehow. Or he could go to ground, but how would that help in the long run? His only chance of survival was to get the cloak to "the creators" and have them remove it from his shoulders. Hiding out in Rauthaven—assuming that he could find sanctuary—wouldn't get him any closer to that goal.

He settled back against one wall of the alley and slid down into a sitting position. He stretched his leg out as far as he could—not too far—and rubbed the damaged knee gently. The pain was still there, and the sense of internal swelling, but at least both were becoming more manageable. Most importantly at the moment, they didn't interfere with his thinking.

All right. The goal, then, was to get the cloak to "the creators." From what Estriss had told him, it seemed most likely that the cloak had been created by the arcane. T'k'pek had claimed the same thing and had shown at least some proof in the form of the tripartite flower on his ring. At the time, Teldin's gut reaction had been not to trust the blue-skinned giant, but now, with the current turn of events, how much faith could he put in as unsubstantiated a feeling as that? Wasn't this just like not buying a horse because you don't like the color of the trader's eyes? Logically, he had no reason to doubt T'k'Pek's words. Everything the creature had told him made sense and was internally consistent. Why should he expect the arcane to instantly and instinctively know every power and attribute of any particular item created by his race?

Teldin felt familiar doubts churning in his stomach, but ruthlessly forced them down. I've got no proof against T'k'Pek's story, he told himself, and some *for* it. I'm not going to get myself killed over a feeling. That was it, then. The cloak had to go to the arcane.

But how? The momentary relief he'd felt from that decision vanished. He still had the major problem: how to avoid Barrab and his bravos while reaching T'k'Pek. The arcane had left the auction as soon as he had acquired the sword he had come for. He probably would have returned immediately to the *Nebulon*.

How could Teldin reach the ship? There was the ship's boat, the dragonfly, but presumably the first trip up had been arranged through Barrab. Teldin had no way of summoning the craft, of forcing the crew to take him to the *Nebulon*, or of flying the ship without them.

That left the *Probe*. The question had come full circle. How could he get to the hammership?

Swim? Maybe, as a last resort. The hammership was anchored a good distance offshore, and Teldin wasn't a particularly strong swimmer. . . . No, trying to swim would more than likely prove just an uncomfortable method of suicide.

On balance, the only reasonable option was to head for the harbor and hope that he spotted one of the *Probe*'s crew— Aelfred Silverhorn, by choice—before Barrab's men spotted him. Aelfred and Estriss probably still thought that he'd gone to a meeting with T'k'Pek, but wouldn't they wait for him on the seawall? Or at least leave some crewmen to wait for him?

There was Rianna—assuming she was still alive, he thought grimly. Would she be looking for him, or would she have gone to ground to save her own life? She loved him, he was sure of that, so he assumed the former, but even if he could make contact with her, could she help him? Thinking logically, if she knew she was helpless, she wouldn't try to make contact until she figured there was some value in the meeting.

Since he was already making so many assumptions, Teldin assumed that Barrab and crew couldn't detect the cloak. If he was wrong on that score, he was dead no matter what he did. A better disguise was in order. He looked down at his clothes. The cloak was already reduced to its smallest dimensions, making it difficult to notice for one who didn't know exactly what to look for. Barrab knew what the rest of his outfit looked like, though, so that had to change.

With a sigh, he struggled back to his feet. Clothes, then, were the first order of business, then the harbor. He looked at the sky. The sun was near the zenith, giving him precious little sense of direction. He shrugged and continued down the alley the same way the derelict had gone. One direction was as good as another, and if he just kept going straight, he'd eventually have to strike a major street.

It wasn't easy to keep straight through the rat's nest of streets and alleys, Teldin quickly found. Gazing down on Rauthaven from the descending *Probe*, he'd thought that the orderly-looking city must have been laid out by a geometer. If that's the case, he must have done *this* section on the morning after a major wine binge, Teldin grumbled to himself, or left it to his assistant, who happened to be insane. There seemed to be no rhyme or reason to the arrangement. Mazy streets started with no apparent purpose and ended for no readily discernible reason. There were doors in the low buildings, but no windows.

There was virtually no one around. Those few people who Teldin spotted looked little better off than the derelict to whom he'd tossed his coin. They all watched him with interest and undisguised hostility—or was that just his paranoia talking?

Whether he was overreacting or not, he decided against asking for directions. What better way to draw attention to myself, he thought with wry amusement, than go up to somebody and ask, "Excuse me, but how do I get to that big piece of water where they keep all the boats?"

At least his immediate problem solved itself quickly. Laundry habits in this part of town included hanging wet clothes on the sills of windows to dry in the sun. It was a matter of minutes only to snatch a new jerkin from here, a pair of leggings from there, and duck into a noisome alley long enough to put them on.

Eventually, as he knew it would, the winding street he was following disgorged into a major road—not the Processional, but something very much like it. The wide thoroughfare led very noticeably downhill, and he could even see the reflection of sunlight off water in the distance.

For the first time, Teldin was almost thankful for his injured knee. Without it, the temptation to burst from the alley and sprint down to the harbor probably would have proven irresistible. Instead, though, he stayed within the mouth of the alley, looking cautiously left and right. It was near noon, and the street was crowded. That was good. He'd have a much better chance of not being spotted if he could lose himself in a crowd. But, of course, the crowd also made it more difficult for him to spot anyone who was looking for him.

The first step out of the alley's relative safety was the hardest. It took him a minute to get up the nerve, his heartbeat sounding like a drum's tattoo in his ears. He felt drained of energy. Before, in the alleyways, his fear had driven his flight, but now it seemed to sap his will. He took one final deep, calming breath and walked out into the street.

The crowd engulfed him. Hemmed in on all sides with bodies, he felt paranoia and claustrophobia surge within him, but he drove the fears down into the depths of his mind. For a moment he wished for the crystal clarity of thought—and the lack of emotion—that the cloak had bestowed in the past, but it didn't come. He forced himself to walk downhill toward the harbor.

He concentrated on his gait, trying to minimize the limp. His knee burned. In fact, he found that walking downhill, even on this gentle slope, put additional stress on the joint and increased the pain. Paradoxically, he found that the pain helped keep his mind clear. He walked on.

A hundred yards or so downhill, the road widened into a square. Stalls were everywhere around the marketplace and spreading into the central space. Buyers milled around them, and the cries of hawkers filled the air. It was so much like market day at home that his throat tightened with sudden homesickness. He forced himself to keep walking.

The fringe of the marketplace seemed less crowded than the center. He stayed to the left, keeping to the less-packed areas. Many of the stalls were selling cooked goods and sweetmeats. The smell of unfamiliar spices assaulted his nostrils.

As he walked, his eyes flicked back and forth, looking for familiar faces—friends *or* foes. He kept his head forward, however; obvious rubbernecking might attract attention.

He almost yelled out as a firm hand fell on his shoulder. He spun away, expecting to be faced by Barrab, or maybe Spak. . . .

It was Vallus Leafbower, the *Probe*'s Helmsman. The elf was standing in the mouth of a small alley between two stalls, both selling smoked sausages. Teldin stepped back in fear. How in the Abyss had the elf recognized him? *How?* There was something very wrong here. He should have been thinking of the elf as an ally, a savior. Instead, he found he was terrified of the aloof figure. How did he know?

The elf didn't say a word, just beckoned to him. Teldin hesitated, then realized that he was attracting attention just standing there. He moved his right hand to the hilt of his sword—not actually touching the grip, but near. Vallus beckoned again and stepped farther into the shelter of the narrow alley. Cautiously, Teldin stepped toward him.

As soon as he saw that Teldin was following, Vallus turned away and walked deeper into the alley. *He turned his back on my sword,* Teldin noted. *A sign of trust, or of unshakable confidence?* He followed slowly, tensed and ready for anything.

When they were a dozen paces from the alley's mouth, Vallus turned back to face him. The elf's hands were empty, held palms-up at waist level. Maybe it was supposed to reassure Teldin. Teldin kept his own hand near his weapon.

The elf spoke quietly. "Those who search for you are waiting at the north entrance to the marketplace," he said tersely. "You must take another route. Down this alley, then turn right on the next road. It, too, leads to the harbor, though not directly, and I think nobody watches it yet."

Teldin's thoughts were in chaos; questions tumbled over questions. The elf stood silently, waiting for him to respond. Finally he forced his mouth to work. "*How?*"

The elf shook his head. "No time to talk," he said. "You must go now. Don't trust to your disguise. I sense it for what it is. Others can, too."

"The cloak . . ."

"The cloak is of elven creation," Vallus cut him off. "You must protect it. That is paramount. Take it to the elves of Evermeet. The imperial fleet can be your only safety." He must have seen Teldin's confusion, because he amplified, "The island of Evermeet, some seven hundred leagues north of here, the home of Toril's elves. You must take the cloak there. Now, go." He pointed deeper down the alley. "*Go.*" With no sound or warning, the elf blinked out of existence. Apart from Teldin, the alleyway was empty.

Teldin searched for some trace of the vanished elf, but with no success. He gave up and took a few moments to think matters through. He had no reason to trust Vallus—By the Abyss, he thought, I've got no reason to trust *anybody* anymore—but the elf's words made sense. Barrab and crew must have realized Teldin would have to follow a major road to the harbor, and the downhill end of the sloping marketplace would be one of the natural "choke points" to guard. Then he wondered why the elf was trying to help him. He obviously knew about the cloak, and just as obviously wanted it for his own people. Why didn't he just take it himself? Did he doubt his own ability to do so, even with his considerable magical abilities? Or was he just channeling Teldin toward an ambush where he and some comrades could take the cloak more easily, at less risk? If so, following the elf's directions would be fatal.

He shook his head in disgust. That way lies paranoia, he thought, echoing the words of Aelfred after the neogi attack against the *Probe*. The choice was basically simple: stick to the crowded thoroughfare, even though his own logic told him the way would be guarded, or trust the elf. Put that way, the choice was easier. He set off deeper into the alley.

As Vallus had said, the alleyway soon joined a narrow road, much less traveled than the major thoroughfare. The few people that passed were all intent on their own business and didn't even spare him a glance. That was good. Even better, this road, too, led downhill. He turned right, as instructed.

This route was much less direct than the main road through the marketplace. It wound back and forth and intersected other roads, but the continuous throbbing pain in Teldin's knee told him it was always heading downhill. His level of paranoia was still high, and he kept a sharp lookout for anything that might be the elf's ambush, but he saw nothing to cause him any alarm. After a dozen minutes, he reached the harbor area.

He stopped in the mouth of a narrow street, staying as much in the shadows as possible while still keeping a reasonable field of view. He was looking out at what Aelfred had facetiously called the "Widow's Walk." This was the wide seawall that ran around the harbor, traditionally the place where sailors' wives—"sea widows," as Aelfred called them—watched for their husbands' return. By day, it was a hive of activity: longshoremen loading and unloading cargo, hawkers selling their wares from barrows, ships' crews seeking taverns or other diversions, and those whose livelihood came from offering those diversions. At night the traffic thinned out somewhat, though the wandering sailors and the women who beckoned to them never seemed to leave. From his position of shelter, Teldin tried to get his bearings.

It took a few moments, then the landmarks that he saw matched his mental map of the area. He was on the western arc of the harbor. A couple hundred yards to his left he could see one of the breakwaters that sheltered the anchorage. That meant the harbormaster's building was to his right, as was the dock where people boarded the tender to take them out to their ships.

That also meant that Barrab and his bravos were somewhere to his right, waiting for him to try to reach that tender. How was he going to get past them?

Or did he have to get past them at all? He'd been thinking exclusively in terms of the tender—naturally, since that was the way he'd always traveled back and forth to the hammership, but this was a working harbor. There were small boats everywhere, weaving through the larger ships that swung at anchor. Most seemed to be ships' boats, ferrying cargo and crew to and from major vessels, but there were also small skiffs that looked like fishing boats. Wouldn't a port city such as Rauthaven have an active fishing fleet? Most would probably be outside the breakwater, returning before nightfall and readying for departure the next day at dawn. Surely there would be some that weren't at sea, however—in for repair, or to give their crews a day of rest. There would be no way that Barrab's watchers could guard the entire length of the Widow's Walk.

His first instinct had been to turn to the right, to head toward the tender dock. Now he looked to the left. Luck was with him. The docks a score or two of yards to his left seemed to be those devoted to fishing craft. The people who congregated there were hard-bitten types, many of them older and showing the leathery, weather-beaten faces that he associated with fishermen. A few yards farther on were a handful of younger men who were mending a large net. That looked promising. If the net was being repaired, wouldn't that mean the boat wasn't at sea? Teldin quickly checked his belt pouch. He had perhaps a dozen gold coins that Rianna had jokingly given him as an "allowance" that night at the tavern. Maybe he could hire one of the fishermen to take him out to the *Probe*.

He'd been standing in the mouth of the narrow street for too long; his indecision was too evident. On a nearby bench, an ancient scrimshander with a wooden leg had looked up from the piece of ivory he was working, and was watching Teldin with suspicion. He had to move.

He stepped out into the traffic along the Widow's Walk.

His nerves felt like taut wires. If his foes could detect the cloak's magic, if discovery was going to come, now was the time. He'd hear the shouts, the grasp of a strong hand, or maybe the bite of Spak's dagger. He struggled to keep his step steady and his expression free of the fear that threatened to dominate him.

He was concentrating so hard on spotting foes that it took him a few moments to realize that he could see a friend. Up ahead, in the mouth of an alley, was an unmistakable figure. Rianna's hair shone like spun gold in the sunlight. Her face was pale and drawn with pain, but her gaze was steady as she scanned the crowds. Flanking her were two large, brutal-looking men, cut from the same cloth as Barrab's sellswords.

His heart leaped, and it was all he could do not to break into a run. Forcing himself to keep to the same slow stride, he made his way through the passers-by toward her. With every step, he thanked whatever gods there happened to be that she'd survived.

He was no more than ten paces from her when her gaze passed over him and continued on. A moment later, he saw her eyes flick back to him and focus on the hilt of the sword at his hip—the sword she'd given him. He saw relief in her green eyes, but she had the self-control to keep her expression indifferent. As if bored with her vigil, she turned and walked deeper into the alley. Her bodyguards flanked her.

When he saw no one watching, he followed into the mouth of the alley. He glanced one last time over his shoulder, and his heart almost stopped. There were two more bravos behind him. They were twenty or thirty feet away, partially screened by other pedestrians on the Widow's Walk, but there was no way he could fail to recognize them. Compared to the people around them, they stood out like night wolves among a pack of lap dogs. They carried no visible weapons, but judging by their size, they'd rarely need any. Fear tightened in his throat.

The two bravos stopped right in the mouth of the alley, engaged in apparently casual conversation, blocking the narrow entrance almost as effectively as a portcullis would have. With a wash of relief, Teldin realized they, too, were on Rianna's payroll.

He turned. Rianna stood a dozen paces deeper in the alley. He rushed to her, heedless now of caution. He made to throw his arms around her, to hug her to him in a grip he never wanted to break, but stopped himself at the last minute, mindful of her injury. Instead he gently grasped her shoulders and just stared into her beautiful face, trying to pour out through his eyes the emotions he could never put into words. She smiled at him, a tired, sweet smile, and he felt that his heart would melt. At this distance, her pain and exhaustion were even more apparent. He could see there was a rudimentary dressing—originally white, but now stained dark—on her shoulder.

"Are you all right?" he asked at last. "How is your shoulder?"

"Messy," she admitted, "and painful, but not dangerous." She grasped his wrists. "And you, how did *you* fare? Oh, gods, Teldin—" there was a catch in her voice "—I hated to run like that, but I guessed that those wolves would sooner pursue the dog that had bitten them than pay attention to you. I see it worked."

"It worked," Teldin agreed, "but you're hurt for it."

She shrugged that off. "I'll heal." Her smile faded. "You're in deep trouble," she told him quietly. "I'm not sure you know how deep. Now, I don't know all the details about this cloak of yours—" she raised a hand to cut off his incipient comment "—and I don't *want* to know all the details, but I've figured some of it out. There are various groups involved, and they're all after the cloak. Isn't that right?"

Teldin nodded reluctantly. "I'm sorry I didn't tell you everything earlier."

"You told me what it made sense to tell me at the time," she said. "If I were in your place, I wouldn't have told so much." A brief smile lit up her face. "But I thank you for your trust. In any case," she went on, serious again, "one of the groups is a contingent from Falx. Do you know what that means?"

He shrugged. "Barrab said it," he remembered. "Who's Falx?"

"Not 'who,' but 'where,' " Rianna explained. "Falx is a planet." She looked him squarely in the eyes. "A planet ruled by mind flayers. Do you understand what that means?"

Teldin stared at her. "Oh gods," he muttered. "Estriss."

"Perhaps," she stressed. "Estriss might be an independent, or he might just be an innocent, like you," she added with a smile, "who got caught up in events."

"I can't trust Estriss."

She shook her head wordlessly.

Teldin had thought he'd become so hardened that further shocks couldn't affect him. He was wrong. His entire body felt cold, and his chest was so tight that he could hardly draw a breath. He stared at Rianna, wishing he could disbelieve her, but he couldn't afford to. Too many other pieces of the puzzle now fit together. How did the *Probe* come to rescue me? he asked himself. Coincidence? I don't believe in coincidences anymore. He closed his eyes for a moment in despair. Was there nobody he could trust other than Rianna? Not even Aelfred . . . ?

No, he corrected himself quickly. The *Probe* must have been in Krynnspace on Estriss's orders. *Not* Aelfred's. That, at least, was something to cling to. He looked back into Rianna's eyes. "What are we going to do?" he asked.

She smiled grimly. "I was hoping *you* might have an idea, little chum."

Behind Teldin, steel clashed and a scream ripped the air. Teldin spun to face the alley's opening. One of Rianna's two bravos, her rear guard, was down clutching his stomach and writhing in pain. The other, short sword drawn, was facing three other hard-faced men with naked steel. As Teldin watched, one of the attackers aimed a whistling cut, which Rianna's sellsword parried at the last moment. Rianna's man riposted, but his opponent had danced back out of range, and the bravo had to parry again, desperately, to block a cut from another attacker. The guardian had to give ground, and the attackers were advancing cautiously.

"Hold them," Rianna ordered from behind him. The two bravos who'd been flanking her rushed past Teldin and hurled themselves into the melee. Swords sang their song of death as Teldin stood transfixed, watching helplessly. The attackers had to be Barrab's men, he told himself.

Rianna grabbed his arm. Her face was drawn, even paler than before—blood loss, overlaid with fear. "Come on," she yelled, dragging him deeper into the alley.

He briefly looked back to see that Rianna's three sellswords were still standing, but now were facing six attackers. Apart from the first casualty, who was no longer moving, none seemed wounded. The woman's bravos were still being forced to give ground, and it was obvious to Teldin that they eventually would be overwhelmed.

"Come *on*," Rianna screamed again. She was already half a dozen paces down the alley but had turned and was waiting for him impatiently. There was nothing Teldin could do but follow her.

* * * * *

Teldin's knee was pure agony. He thought the pain couldn't be any more intense if he stuck his leg into molten lead, but still he forced himself on. At first, Rianna had left him behind, but then she'd realized that he, too, was injured and slowed her pace to match his.

They'd bolted down the alleyway, then taken the first turn to the right. It was that running turn that had inflamed Teldin's knee so badly. He cried out at the pain of it, and the world went dark and hazy around him. Somehow he managed to cling to consciousness. He'd felt Rianna's hand on his arm, dragging him farther on, and he followed blindly.

He had no idea how far they'd run, but finally the mad flight ended. Rianna was leaning against a wall, her full chest heaving with exertion. Teldin himself sank to the ground, clenching his teeth in a vain attempt to hold back a whimper of agony. He looked up at Rianna through blurring tears. "How did Barrab find us?" he asked weakly.

"Find *me*, you mean," she corrected between gasps. "They probably didn't know it was you back there. Unfortunately, I've got little choice but to wear my own face." She was silent for a moment, her expression that of someone chewing on a bitter truth. Finally she looked steadily at Teldin and told him, "We have to separate."

"*Why?*" he demanded, even though he thought he understood her reasoning.

"Because I'll get you killed. If they catch me, they catch you. I'll give you the names of some contacts. Maybe they can help you out—"

He cut her off the simplest way he knew how, grabbing her

by the shoulders, pulling her body to him, and stopping her lips with his. When they parted, her somber expression had softened. "Forget it," he told her firmly. "We're going to make it through this together."

Chapter Fifteen

• • •

Rianna gave him a tired smile. "All right," she said, "together. So where do we go from here?"

Teldin didn't answer immediately. The pain in his knee had diminished from the almost unbearable to the merely abominable. Slowly he worked the joint, testing its range of motion. Rianna watched him silently. Finally he looked up. "It's got to be the arcane," he told her.

"Why?"

Quickly he summarized his logic for her. "I've got no reason to doubt T'k'Pek," he concluded. "Once he has the cloak, he should be able to protect us."

"From the neogi?" Rianna asked. "They've been after you from the start, haven't they?"

He shot her a sharp look. "I never told you that."

She chuckled deep in her throat. "You talk in your sleep, little chum." Then she grew serious again. "How do you feel about the arcane possessing the cloak?" she asked quietly.

He shrugged. "I don't know," he told her honestly, "but I'd feel worse about the neogi getting it." He paused. "Why in the hells do they all want the cloak anyway?" he asked. "Why is it so important?"

"I haven't got a clue," she replied. "but there's no doubt it *is* important. The neogi want it, the arcane, and the Falx illithids. . . ."

"*And* the elves," he added. "But *why?*"

"Neogi aren't interested in much except power," Rianna pondered. "And they want the cloak. What does that tell you?"

"It's powerful," he answered. "More powerful than I really want to think about."

"So it's the arcane?"

"I don't have any other choices," he replied candidly. Wincing with pain, he forced himself to his feet. *The problem hasn't changed,* he reflected. *It's how to get to the* Nebulon. He turned back to Rianna. "Can you get us a ship?" he asked. "Something the two of us can fly?"

The woman thought for a moment, then shook her head. "I don't have any personal contacts here," she said slowly. "There are places where you can rent ships, but Barrab will have them watched."

Teldin had figured as much, but he'd had to ask. "It's the *Probe*, then," he told her. "Can you get us aboard?"

"Yes," she said simply.

Teldin looked at her speculatively. *No questions?* he wondered. *No doubts? Does she have such faith in me?*

He glanced up at the sky. It was midafternoon, by the sun. "How long will it take?" he asked.

"Not long."

* * * * *

How many contacts does Rianna have? Teldin found himself wondering. *And how many sellswords are trying to make a living in Rauthaven?* Rianna had made only one stop, at a disreputable wine shop off a back alley that smelled of ordure. Teldin had waited in the doorway, his eyes watering from the fumes of stale wine, while she spoke with the hard-bitten sailors within. She'd then beckoned him in, to join her at a corner table from which she could keep an eye on the door. They hadn't spoken as they'd waited; it seemed that both had more than enough on their minds to keep them occupied.

The proprietor—a big man with a face like a scarred fist— had belligerently demanded that they order if they were going to stay. The two of them sat, each with a cup of wine on the table in front of them now. Out of curiosity, Teldin took a sip of his drink . . . and almost spat it back on the table. What is it? he asked himself. Vinegar and acid, with some lamp oil added for flavor? With an effort, he swallowed the foul stuff. "Gah," he whispered to Rianna, "my mouth tastes like a latrine."

She whispered back, "That's the house's best." She turned her eyes back to the door. As she watched it, he watched her. Even exhausted and wounded, she was beautiful.

To Teldin it felt as though they'd sat in the wine shop for hours, but according to the smoky time-candle burning on the bar, it had hardly been half an hour when a large figure appeared in the doorway. Rianna's face showed relief as she recognized the man and rose to join him. They spoke for a few moments in voices too quiet for Teldin to hear, then returned to the table.

"We can go," she told him quietly. "I've hired some people to back us—people I can trust—and a boat to take us out to the hammership."

"From where?" Teldin asked. "Aren't Barrab's men watching the docks?"

"From the western breakwater," she replied. "And, yes, Barrab did have a man watching the area, but not anymore." She grinned impishly. "Willik here slipped him a few coins to take the afternoon off. It's amazing how loud money talks."

He grinned back, glad of her competence and seemingly unflagging confidence. "Shall we go?" he suggested.

The small boat was an open fishing vessel very like the one Teldin had considered hiring, but there were no fishermen aboard. Teldin and Rianna sat in the stern—he wearing a new face and form, she with the hood of a tattered cloak pulled forward to shield her face. The oars were manned by twelve steel-hard men. As they'd boarded the boat at the western breakwater, Teldin had seen that each one was virtually a walking armory beneath his concealing cloak. A substantial boarding party, he thought. Let's hope that won't be necessary.

How could it *not* be necessary? he wondered. Am I going to walk up to Estriss and say, "Take me to the *Nebulon*," and he'll say, "Of course"? Doubtful. If Estriss were connected with the illithids from Falx, impossible. Aelfred alone might agree, but it wasn't his ship. Maybe if Estriss was still ashore when they arrived . . . but how likely was that? No, it seemed inevitable that there would be some kind of confrontation. He looked at the twelve bravos, facing aft toward him, throwing their weight on the oars. While none was as obviously unstable as Spak, he knew full well that they were men used to solving problems with violence. Unless he handled matters just right, things could easily get out of hand. One thing, he swore to himself, *no killing*.

He shifted on the aft thwart, trying to find a more comfortable position. Rianna was distracted, tense. She's as positive as I am there's going to be a confrontation, he realized. Otherwise, why bring the bravos?

Another uncomfortable thought struck him. "You can find the *Nebulon*, can't you?"

Rianna smiled, a little tightly. "If Willik's information is right, and we've got to assume it is."

Teldin nodded. More assumptions.

Teldin had hardly noticed—after all, he'd had more important things on his mind—but clouds had been gathering, filling the sky. For a while, the sun had been shining down through a break in the cloud cover, in parallel beams that had seemed to spotlight the harbor like a bull's-eye lantern. The sun finally had slipped behind a cloud, and the sky had darkened. A cold and miserable drizzle began to fall. Fitting, Teldin found himself thinking.

He half-stood, careful of the boat's balance. The *Probe* was directly ahead, now less than a bow shot away. He could see movement on deck and thought he recognized a large figure on the forecastle as Aelfred Silverhorn. Wouldn't Aelfred still be ashore, looking for him? Teldin wondered. Or does he have reason not to look for me? He shook his head. That was paranoia again. He had to trust Aelfred, otherwise there was no hope left at all. The fishing boat drew closer.

Rianna touched his arm. "How are we going to do this?" she asked.

Teldin had been struggling with the same question. He looked again at the *Probe*. Yes, it was Aelfred on the foredeck. "I'll go up alone," he told her. "I'm going to talk to Aelfred."

Her eyes were troubled. "Do you trust him?"

"I've got to," he said.

She nodded, accepting that. "I'll come with you."

"No," he told her. "Stay in the boat. I think it'll go better if I speak to him alone."

She nodded again, a little unwillingly. "If things start to go bad, just yell," she said. She smiled grimly. "You'll be surprised how fast I'll be there to help you."

He squeezed her hand in silent thanks.

"Ahoy, fishing boat!" A familiar voice echoed across the water. Aelfred leaned against the main deck rail, hands cupped around his mouth. "State your business."

Teldin closed his eyes for a moment—no longer than a blink—and let his false face fall away, then he threw the hood of his cloak back from his head and rose to his feet. The boat rocked alarmingly, but Rianna held his arm to steady him. "Teldin Moore," he called back. "Permission to come alongside?"

"Permission granted." He could hear the relief in Aelfred's voice. "Just where in the Nine Hells have you been?"

The sellswords obviously had some experience working with boats. The small fishing vessel drew smoothly alongside the hammership. The port side oarsmen shipped their oars, and the boat bumped gently against the *Probe*'s hull. Immediately, a rope ladder rattled into the longboat's scuppers. Aelfred was leaning over the hammership rail, ready to give Teldin a hand up.

Teldin gave Rianna a last, reassuring smile, then clambered up the ladder. As he neared the top, Aelfred's big fist grasped his wrist, and the burly warrior hauled him up over the gunwale rail as if he'd weighed no more than a child. Aelfred's face was split in a broad, lopsided grin. He wrapped his arms around Teldin in a hug strong enough to force the air from the smaller man's lungs with a loud *huff*.

"By the gods, it's good to see you alive," the first mate said gruffly as he released Teldin. "I wasn't sure I would set eyes on you again."

Teldin smiled at his friend. The big man's sincerity was undeniable. How could he ever have doubted him? The relief that washed over him was enough to bring tears to his eyes.

Aelfred stepped back. No, *limped* back. For the first time, Teldin noticed that there was a bulky field dressing on the warrior's right thigh. The first mate saw the direction of his gaze and smiled wryly. "Aye," he growled, "I had a little mishap."

"What happened?"

"What *didn't* happen?" Aelfred grumbled. "When you didn't come back to the auction, I finally persuaded Estriss to go looking for you. Estriss had bought a couple of pots and boxes and insisted on dragging them along with us." Teldin mirrored Aelfred's grin. He could easily picture the disguised illithid weighed down with his precious items. "I knew which way you'd left," Aelfred went on, "so we followed. We stepped out into the alley and a couple of men jumped us, just like that."

"Describe them," Teldin cut in sharply.

Aelfred gave him a questioning look, but obeyed. "I only really saw one," he answered, "the bastard who put two feet of steel into my thigh. Real nasty type: face like a rat, and fought like a cornered rat, too." He shot Teldin a speculative look. "You know him?"

That could only have been Spak. "I know him," he said quietly. "Did you kill them?"

"Aye," Aelfred replied, a little uncomfortably. "They didn't give us any choice. All-out attack, no chance for parlay." He shook his head. "Anyway, no matter what you farm boys think, that kind of thing doesn't normally happen in cities. It had to mean that you were in deep trouble. I wanted to go looking for you, but my leg was bleeding pretty badly. Estriss ordered me back to the ship." He grinned ruefully. "I'm afraid I was a little insubordinate. He nearly had to drag me back. Good thing he did; I passed out on the way."

"Are you all right now?"

Aelfred slapped his wounded thigh—but not too hard, Teldin noticed. "Mending nicely. They poured a potion or two down me. I won't be doing the hornpipe for the next couple of days, but at least it'll hold my weight now."

"What happened then?"

"Estriss was worried about you," Aelfred continued, "almost as worried as I was. He sent most of the crew ashore to find out what happened to you, your friends the gnomes in the lead." He paused. "What *did* happen to you?"

Teldin shook his head. "I'll tell you when I've got time." He looked around the ship. There weren't many crewmen visible. "Have you got enough crew to set sail?"

"Sail, no," the mate replied. "Fly, yes. Why?"

Teldin took a deep breath. This is it, he told himself. "I need to get to the *Nebulon*," he said quietly. "I need to go now."

"Well." Aelfred was silent for a moment. "I'll call Estriss from below." He started to turn away, but Teldin grabbed his shoulder.

"Aelfred." The big warrior turned back. "Aelfred," he repeated, "wait. I . . . I learned something. I think Estriss may be . . ." He took another deep, calming breath. "I think Estriss is involved with the people who are after the cloak."

The first mate stiffened. "What?"

"There's a group of mind flayers who are after the cloak," Teldin explained. He struggled to keep his voice steady, unemotional. "I think Estriss is in with them. Or, at least," he added, feeling it was vital that he tell as much of the truth as he knew, "he might be. I'm afraid he is." Aelfred was silent. "We talked about coincidences," Teldin went on earnestly. "Remember? What are the odds of meeting another ship in wildspace? Next to zero, you said. Remember?"

Aelfred nodded, a little unwillingly. "Aye," he said.

"What was the *Probe* doing in Krynnspace, Aelfred? Why did Estriss want to go there?"

The burly warrior was silent for a dozen heartbeats. "I don't know," he said finally. "He never told me."

"Did you put down on a planet?" Teldin pressed.

"Yes, one of the moons of Zivilyn."

"Why?"

Aelfred shrugged. "There was another ship there," he said, "somebody that Estriss had arranged to meet on business. I don't know who, or what kind of business."

"Why did you sail to Krynn, then?" Teldin asked urgently. He struggled to recall the conversations he'd had with the gnomes about the makeup of the Krynnish system. "It's a long way from Zivilyn, isn't it?"

"Aye," Aelfred answered quietly, "about six days."

"And did you land on Krynn?"

"No."

Teldin nodded. The further he went into this, the more doubt turned to certainty. Estriss *had* to be playing a deeper game, following his own agenda. Once again Teldin felt the icy knot of fear in his stomach. "Why did Estriss say it was necessary to approach Krynn?" he asked.

"He didn't say."

"You just sailed near Krynn, saw the longboat being attacked by pirates, and you saved me, then you left Krynnspace again. Isn't that so?"

"That's so," Aelfred said slowly.

"As if, in finding me, Estriss had got what he wanted?" Teldin pressed.

"That's so," Aelfred repeated, quieter.

Teldin returned to his original point. "I need to get to the *Nebulon*."

"You'll have to talk to Estriss." Aelfred's voice was firm, but his eyes showed doubt.

An image flashed into Teldin's mind—an image of an attacker collapsing under the lash of the illithid's mental attack. "I can't," he said. "Can you take the *Probe* up without Estriss? Without his say-so?"

Aelfred's eyes went cold and steady, like a blade in the hand of a master swordsman. "It sounds like you're counseling me to make a mutiny, old son," he said softly.

Teldin paused. There was real danger now. He could hear it in Aelfred's voice. He's my friend, he told himself, but friendship can go only so far. "I need passage," he said carefully, "and I can't go back into town or I'll be killed. Why would I lie about this?"

The first mate hesitated, obviously torn between friendship and duty. "You'll have to talk to Estriss," he said again. This time there was indecision in his voice as well as in his eyes.

"I can't, Aelfred. You've got to help me."

Aelfred pointed to the fishing boat that was still hard against the hammership's hull. The dozen sellswords were undoubtedly just what they were: hired bravos. Nobody could ever have mistaken them for fishermen. "If I don't help you, are *they* here to make me?" The big warrior's voice was casual, but all the more dangerous for that. "Could it be that you plan to take the *Probe*, Teldin? Take it at sword-point?"

"*No*," Teldin shot back forcefully. "You're my friend. You've been my friend through everything. I can no more turn against you than I can fly this ship myself." He spread his hands in an open, disarming gesture. "All I can do is depend on that friendship. *Help* me, Aelfred. Save my life again. You're the only hope I've got left."

That took the big man aback, Teldin could see. They stood silently for several score heartbeats. Teldin watched the play of emotions over his friend's face—painful emotions, many of them. It was hard to keep silent, hard not to press the point, hard not to plead, but Teldin understood enough about Aelfred Silverhorn to know that this would be the worst thing he could do. He had to respect the man, had to give him time to make the difficult decision on his own.

"Aelfred!" The call from a crewman on the forecastle was enough to make Teldin jump with shock.

The first mate turned away, obviously glad to be spared from his dilemma, if only for a few moments. "What?" he barked.

The crewman was pointing toward town. "Message from the harbormaster, sir," he called down. With a muttered curse, Aelfred looked to where the man was indicating.

There was a string of flags running up one of the flagpoles atop the harbormaster's building. Like the ones telling us where to dock, Teldin remembered. A premonition of danger tingled through his nerve endings. He wished he could read the message. As he watched, another string of flags ran up the second flagpole.

"What in the name of all the fiends . . ." Aelfred stared at the flags in open stupefaction, then he turned to Teldin, an expression of enforced calm on his face. "Just what have you been doing ashore?" he asked.

"Running for my life," Teldin answered truthfully. He indicated the flags. "What do they say?"

"The *Probe* is impounded," the mate said disbelievingly. "We're ordered to remain in place. There'll be a vessel coming out to secure the ship, and to arrest a fugitive from justice, one Aldyn Brewer." He fixed Teldin with a flint-edged stare. "What have you done?"

"Nothing," Teldin replied, his voice little more than a whisper. Nausea rippled in the pit of his stomach. He was horrified; the corruption, the involvement, goes high enough to involve the harbormaster? Virtually the whole city could be turned against him.

No, he realized, it needn't be quite that bad. Somebody had reported that "Aldyn Brewer" had committed a crime. Maybe it was Spak's murder, or maybe the whole thing was fabricated from nothing. No, it wasn't as bad as he'd originally thought, but it definitely was bad enough.

"I didn't do anything," he repeated to Aelfred. "They're trying to get the cloak. They'll do anything they can to get it, including impound the ship and kill anyone who gets in the way."

"And who's 'they'?"

"I don't know," Teldin answered. "Everyone." The enormity of his danger almost overwhelmed him again. "Everyone," he replied, struggling for control. "Illithids, the elves . . ." He squared his shoulders, fought to keep his desperation out of his voice. "Please, Aelfred. Take me up there. It's my responsibility. We'll say I threatened you. When it's over, when I've seen the arcane, I'll surrender and you'll be off the hook."

"Hardly," Aelfred said derisively. His cool gaze searched Teldin's face, then the big man's steel-hard expression softened into a wry smile. "I believe you," he said. He chuckled, a little grimly—or was it sadly? Teldin asked himself. "Well, I was getting tired of shipboard life anyway. Do you think anybody around here needs a mercenary?"

Teldin remembered the seemingly endless supply of sellswords and smiled. "I don't think that'll be a problem."

The decision made, Aelfred was his familiar, efficient self. "The ship they're going to send is going to be a military vessel. We're on skeleton crew. There's no way we can repel it. Get your crew on board," he snapped to Teldin. "If you're afraid of Estriss—and I don't blame you, honestly, from what you've told me—send an 'honor guard' to escort him." He turned away and started barking orders at the few crewmen remaining aboard.

The bravos had been waiting impatiently. The moment Teldin beckoned to them, they swarmed over the gunwale rails, eschewing the rope ladder. On deck, they stood waiting for their orders. Rianna, because of her wounded shoulder, was slower coming aboard. As she climbed over the rail, Teldin saw Aelfred's smile of welcome. With his two best friends beside him, Teldin was starting to feel he might have a chance of making it through.

He turned to the sellswords. "You five," he said, pointing, "I want you to bring the illithid on deck." He described the location of Estriss's cabin.

He noticed that the bravos glanced at Rianna for approval before nodding, which was only right, he accepted. It was she who'd hired them, not him.

"I don't want any violence," he stressed as they started below. "He's captain of this ship, and you're his honor guard. Please treat him that way."

Aelfred had watched the exchange with some interest and visible approval. He snapped Teldin a perfect salute. "We'll be underway in a couple of minutes, Captain," he barked.

Teldin shook his head. "Don't call me that," he told the mate quietly. He paused, then asked, "You said we can't sail."

"That's right," the warrior replied, "but I also said we can fly. I've got Thorn on the helm. We're taking off from right here. Hideously illegal, of course, but I don't honestly give a damn." He grinned hugely.

He's enjoying this, Teldin realized. Mutiny, and he's having a good time. He shook his head.

Silently, Teldin watched the crew readying the hammership for space. There weren't many of them—Teldin counted only about twenty—but they were working fast enough for twice that number. Curiously, he looked around for the ex-slave Tregimesticus, but didn't spot him. Was that significant? He shook his head to clear it. There was no reason to worry about that now.

He gazed out toward the city. Rauthaven was no longer beautiful, under the gray-black clouds; it was threatening, rather than enticing. Or was that only a reflection of his own mood? He could see no sign of the ship that was supposed to be coming to secure the *Probe*, but that would just be a matter of time. His enemies wouldn't have made an empty bluff.

Teldin, Aelfred. The cool words formed in his mind. He looked around. Surrounded by the "honor guard," Estriss had emerged from belowdecks. For whatever reason, the creature was no longer disguised. His facial tentacles moved in agitation. *What is the meaning of this mutiny?*

Teldin drew a breath to answer, but Aelfred beat him to it. "No mutiny, Estriss," he said calmly. "Teldin needs passage to the *Nebulon*. I agreed to take him, on my own authority. I'll return the ship to you when that's done."

It is mutiny. The mental "volume" of the illithid's words didn't increase, but the crew immediately stopped their work and turned their eyes on their erstwhile captain. Teldin knew the mind flayer was broadcasting his thoughts for all to pick up. *I order you to belay your work,* Estriss continued. *I reverse all orders that Aelfred Silverhorn might have given, and I relieve him of his authority.*

Several of the crew set down the lines they'd been hauling on, or stepped away from the rigging, but most didn't move. All eyes were on Aelfred.

The warrior stood, solid and commanding. Only his eyes moved, flicking over his crewmen. After a score of heartbeats, he spoke. His voice sounded quiet, but somehow it carried to the farthest reaches of the hammership's deck. "You know me," he said calmly. "You've served under me, some of you for years. Do you think I would do this for no reason? Do you think I'd make mutiny on my captain if I had any other choice?" His voice dropped further. Teldin saw crewmen move closer to him to avoid missing his words. "This is a mission of mercy," the mate continued. "You know me. You trust me. Will you follow me?" He put his balled fists on his hips and bellowed, "*Will you follow me?*"

There was no movement aboard the *Probe*. Teldin stared at the frozen tableau, afraid to speak, afraid to shatter the spell that seemed to have fallen over them all. Then, one by one, the crewmen returned to their tasks.

With an audible sigh, Teldin let out the breath that he'd been holding. He looked at Estriss. The illithid still seemed frozen; even his facial tentacles were motionless. His featureless eyes were fixed on Aelfred Silverhorn, but Teldin could read no expression in them. The bravos flanking the illithid were almost vibrating with tension, hands hovering near weapon hilts.

I will return to my cabin, Estriss said at length. *Aelfred Silverhorn, you have made your choice. The responsibility is yours.* He turned away and returned belowdecks, his "honor guard" following a little belatedly.

Aelfred didn't even watch the mind flayer go. If Estriss's words had made any impact on him, he didn't show it. Julia appeared on the forecastle. Teldin was surprised by the rush of pleasure he felt, knowing she was on board. That emotion was followed by a sense of sadness. He numbered her as one of his friends aboard the *Probe*. And now, due to him, she was in the same serious trouble as Aelfred. If you want a long, trouble-free life, *don't* get involved with me, he thought grimly.

"Helm's ready," Julia called.

Aelfred nodded. "Take us up," he ordered. "Fast."

The officer nodded and disappeared below. Aelfred turned to Teldin, showing a sharklike grin. "Here we go," he said. "Want to see how many laws of the spaceways we can break?"

The deck surged beneath Teldin's feet as the hammership lifted clear of the water. A rushing filled his ears as water poured off the wooden hull. The ship's sail filled, and the ship heeled slightly. The harbor dropped away quickly.

"Ready hand weapons," Aelfred called out to the crew. "Anything that comes near—sea gulls, *anything*—put an arrow into it." He turned to Teldin and lowered his voice. "Who knows? It could be a wizard sent to stop us."

* * * * *

Despite Aelfred's misgivings, nothing—not even an unfortunate sea gull—tried to interfere with the *Probe*'s departure. The vessel quickly picked up speed, climbing straight upward. Teldin's last view of Rauthaven showed a slate-gray harbor surrounded by a lighter-gray city—no longer the almost-magical place he'd seen on the approach. Then the hammership plunged into the lowering clouds and the land below was lost from view.

It was cold and wet in the cloud deck. Teldin expanded the cloak to full size and pulled it tighter around him, glad for the warmth it gave him. The clouds were so thick that he couldn't see from his position near the forecastle even as far back as the stern turret. Wisps of cloud-stuff were chill and clammy against his skin. He ran his fingers through his hair, then shook off the droplets of moisture that had collected on his hands.

Under Aelfred's orders, the crew deployed the four triangular fins that added so much to the hammership's sharklike appearance. Others trimmed the sail, while one unfortunate was detailed to clamber up the mast to take station in the crow's nest.

Teldin felt a presence by his shoulder. It was Aelfred. "I think we're clear," he told Teldin.

As if the big warrior's words were the necessary incantation, the *Probe* burst out of the clouds and into open air. Teldin was facing west, and the brilliance of the evening sun dazzled him. He turned away, wiping streaming eyes.

The cloud deck was spread out below them like the landscape of another planet. The dark gray of slate below, it was a lighter gray, almost white, from above. It formed rolling hills and plains, deep chasms and towering mountains. It looked as solid as the land that surrounded Rauthaven, easily solid enough to bear the weight of a man, or even of something larger. He stared at the cloud topography. It was easy to imagine creatures living up here: humans—or maybe more exotic beings—driving herds of cloud-sheep to graze on the cloud-hills. The cloud-people would have cloud-cities, he imagined, and would climb the heights of the cloud-peaks for enjoyment.

He forced himself to look away and shook his head to clear it. He was exhausted, he knew. The buzzing he felt in his head—and, more, his fantasies about cloud-creatures—told him that he had to sleep. Fatigue poisons were coursing through his body, numbing his nerves and twisting his thoughts as if he'd drunk too much of Aelfred's sagecoarse. When had he last slept? He remembered with difficulty: it was only last night that he'd lain in his cabin aboard the *Probe*, with Rianna in his arms. No more than twelve hours, then, but it felt like twelve years. He reviewed the events of the past day: the auction, the ambush, the flight. . . .

He shook his head again. Now was no time to think of such

things. No matter how much the stress he'd been under made his body cry out for sleep, he couldn't indulge himself. He'd be meeting with T'k'Pek soon. He had to be sharp when he spoke to the arcane. There was still much that he had to do . . . not the least of which was confirm that his own life would be safe after he was free of the cloak. He turned away from the cloud-landscape and climbed the ladder to the forecastle to join Aelfred.

Rianna was below with the hammership's navigator, Sylvie. Teldin was relieved to realize that Willik's information about the *Nebulon* was correct. Already the vessel hung like an oversized star against the darkening sky.

The hammership approached the arcane's vessel quickly, much quicker than had the dragonfly. Soon Teldin could make out the vessel's cylindrical shape, then the dark bands that were the great windows encircling the massive vehicle. The *Probe* slowed, coming to a halt above one end of the arcane's ship. There was no sign of the ivory stairway that had given them access to the *Nebulon*'s deck. Of course not, he told himself, that would only be for invited guests. For a moment he wondered if the great cylinder were defended. What weapons might the arcane possess to drive off *un*invited guests?

Nothing had attacked them as they'd approached, and why would defenders strike now, when wreckage from the *Probe* would crash onto their own vessel? There was another issue, even more important, though. . . .

How would they get aboard the *Nebulon*? There was no way the hammership could land on the circular deck. Not only was the *Probe* too large, but he knew full well that it was built for water landings only.

Luckily, Aelfred had that one figured out. "Helm," he called below, "hold us in position." Then he turned to the crewmen on the main deck. "Warin, Kell, put out ladders," he ordered. "Go down and tie us off to the rails." The crew went quickly about their tasks.

Teldin watched nervously as the two crewmen worked on the deck below. They were vulnerable down there, open to any kind of attack. While he couldn't picture T'k'Pek himself leading an assault, Teldin knew from personal experience how easy it was for virtually anybody to hire people to do their dirty work.

Aelfred seemed to have had the same thought. While Warin and Kell worked, the first mate detailed other crew members to stand ready with missile weapons, "covering" their fellows.

Despite both men's fears, nothing interfered with the crewmen's work. Soon the hammership was secured to the rails surrounding the *Nebulon*'s circular deck. It hung two dozen feet above the bone-white deck, held in position by four thick ropes. Aelfred glanced at Teldin. "Easy," he muttered. Teldin had no difficulty reading the big warrior's true meaning: *too easy*. He nodded uncomfortably. It was time for him to board the arcane's ship, time for what should be the last step in the quest that had been driving him since Krynn. Everything about the approach to the *Nebulon* was triggering alarms in his brain.

What could he do, though? Turn back now? He had to see this through to its conclusion. He looked around. "Rianna," he said, "I want to take the men with me."

"I'm coming, too," she told him.

"It's too dangerous," he argued, "you're wounded. . . ."

She cut him off sharply. "There's not a chance in Gehenna that I'm letting you go in there alone. I'm not much of a mage, but I'm better than nothing."

"It's too dangerous," he repeated.

She reached out and took his hand in a firm grip, her eyes locked on his. "You're not my keeper, Teldin," she told him quietly. "I have the right to make my own decisions, and my decision is that I'm coming with you. Will you accept that?"

He hesitated for a moment, then squeezed her hand. "I accept that," he said. He turned to the expectant Aelfred and spoke quietly. "I know what you're going to say," Teldin told him, "but I need you aboard the *Probe*. I don't feel comfortable about any of this—" he smiled "—but I'll feel a lot better if you stay here and make sure the *Probe* doesn't go anywhere." Aelfred's expression told him all he needed to know about the warrior's doubts. He grasped his large friend's arm. "I need you to do this," he said earnestly.

Aelfred was silent for a moment, then he nodded. "I agree," he said. "I don't like it, but I agree. At least let me send someone with you."

"I'll go."

Teldin turned. It was Julia who'd spoken. She'd just climbed to the forecastle from the bridge. Her straight hair, cut in page-boy style, shone like burnished copper in the harsh sunlight of space. Her expression was deadly serious, though, and her hand was on the hilt of her short sword.

Teldin felt something hard press against his hand. Instinctively, he grasped it. It was a dagger, handed to him by Aelfred. While everyone was looking at Julia, the warrior must have retrieved one of his concealed daggers. Why? Teldin asked himself, then shrugged. There was nothing wrong with packing an extra weapon. He slipped the small blade into his jerkin, under his wide belt. The steel was cold against his skin.

"Will you accept that?" Aelfred asked, echoing Rianna's words.

Teldin had to smile. "I accept that," he replied. "Then, if we're ready . . ."

A mental voice cut him off. *I demand to come.*

Estriss—still dogged by the "honor guard"—had re-emerged from belowdecks. Teldin noticed that Estriss wore a dagger of his own on his belt. Probably, the strange knife the illithid associated with the Juna was still concealed within the creature's clothing. Estriss is dressed for trouble, Teldin realized. "Why?" he asked the mind flayer.

For my own reasons, Estriss replied flatly. When Teldin didn't respond, the illithid continued, *There is something wrong here. The arcane protect their privacy. If something has happened to T'k'Pek, perhaps I can save the item he purchased at the auction.* Again Teldin didn't respond. *You have taken my ship*, Estriss concluded, and there was a sharp—almost peevish—note to his mental voice. *I demand to come. You owe me at least that much.*

Slowly Teldin nodded. He was fairly certain that the illithid and the arcane weren't working together. If they were, he was as good as dead anyway. Assuming, then, that Estriss was playing his own game, where could he cause the most trouble? Put that way, the answer was straightforward: the illithid would be more of a danger if Teldin left him aboard the hammership. Even though the crew had agreed to follow Aelfred, that might change—particularly if it came to open conflict. The crew might agree to ignore their erstwhile captain's orders; they almost certainly wouldn't agree to physical violence against him, should that become necessary. No, Teldin realized, it was much more dangerous to leave a potential enemy behind him. The illithid would have to come along, escorted and guarded by a retinue of bravos.

"You can come," Teldin said at last, "if you agree to an escort." He gestured at the bravos.

Hardly the escorts I would have chosen, Estriss said sourly, *but I agree.*

Teldin turned to the others, ready to speak, but Rianna touched his arm. "I suggest we take only six of the men," she said quietly.

"Why?"

"To help guard the ship," she answered. "If we take any more than six, we'll be getting in our own way belowdecks. And if we run into more trouble than six men can handle, we shouldn't be here in the first place. We just get the hell out of here and write the whole thing off as a bad idea." She smiled grimly. "That way, we'll have a better chance of having a ship to get the hell out of here *on.*"

Teldin didn't respond immediately. Rianna's reasoning was much the same as his concerning Aelfred, but something just didn't sound right. What was it? He shrugged, then nodded to Rianna. "Six it is."

They went down the ladders to the *Nebulon*'s deck. Julia took the lead, followed by two bravos, and they spread out across the great expanse of deck, searching for hidden dangers. It wasn't long before they beckoned to the others to come down; apart from them, the circular deck was empty.

Teldin was next over the rail. The rope ladder swayed uncomfortably under his weight, even more so than usual. It had to be because of relative motion between the two ships, he realized. Even though the *Probe* was tied down, it could still move slightly in relation to the *Nebulon*. He was glad when his feet were on the ivorylike deck.

The group reformed quickly, with Estriss in the middle surrounded by the "escorts." Teldin led the way to the center of the deck. The circular hatch—the one that had opened like a mouth—was already gaping wide. An invitation or a trap? Come into my parlor, said the spider to the fly, Teldin thought. As one, the group drew swords.

The spiral staircase was wide enough for two, so Teldin and Rianna led the way. Julia took up the rear. The stairway was lit by the same sourceless yellow light that Teldin remembered from his first visit. Thank the gods for small favors, he thought. Just the idea of exploring this strange ship in the dark was enough to unnerve him.

They reached the landing. As before, there was only one door. Teldin reached out, expecting the door to swing wide before he touched it. This time, though, he had to push the door open. He glanced back at Estriss, but the illithid's gaze was noncommittal. He probably doesn't understand any more than I do about all this, Teldin thought. But, then, he's probably angry enough that he wouldn't tell me even if he did. Teldin stepped into the doorway.

The long hallway was just as it had been when he'd first visited the *Nebulon*. No, not quite; the lighting seemed dimmer, more yellow. For a moment, Teldin was overcome by the desire to turn and leave. Things weren't the way he'd expected them to be. Things were *wrong*, and that scared him.

Almost immediately, the fear turned to a burning anger—at the arcane, at this great ship, and at his own reaction. The whole situation was some kind of test—whether intended that way or not—and it was a test he was determined to pass. To turn away now, from a potential danger that could very well be an artifact of his own doubts, was ridiculous.

From childhood, Teldin had always tried to suppress anger in himself. Although nobody had ever told him so, he'd decided that anger was an unworthy emotion, and anyone who let himself feel it was also somehow unworthy. Now, though, he let the emotion build within him, felt its fire spread throughout his body. He felt the compass, the boundaries, of his anger. As he strode down the corridor, it was as much his anger as his will that drove his steps. He glanced over his shoulder. The others were behind him. Julia was still taking up the rear, looking over her shoulder regularly to watch for anyone—or anything—that might be following them.

He reached out toward the door that led to the great windowed room. Again it didn't open in response to his proximity. What does that mean? he asked himself. He pushed on the door, and it swung open smoothly.

Everything was exactly like his first visit to the *Nebulon*. The "throne" of purple crystal was facing one of the great windows, and Teldin could see the blue-skinned giant staring out into space.

"T'k'Pek," Teldin said. The arcane didn't move, gave no sign that he was even aware of Teldin's presence. "T'k'Pek," he repeated louder. He walked closer and froze in horror.

The arcane wore the same green, shawllike robe as in their first meeting, but now the front of that robe was drenched with a pale, pinkish fluid that still flowed sluggishly from a great wound across the creature's throat. T'k'Pek gazed out at the universe with eyes that would never again appreciate its wonders.

Chapter Sixteen

• • •

The arcane was dead.

The burning anger that had sustained Teldin was doused like a candle in a hurricane. He was cold, empty, as though there were a hole in the core of his being.

A sharp cry—a female cry—rang out behind him. He spun.

The cry had been Julia's. One of the bravos had the fingers of one hand entwined in her red hair, while the other hand held the edge of his sword against her throat. Another bravo reached down and removed Julia's sword from unresisting fingers. The woman's eyes were wide with mingled fear and anger. The other bravos hemmed Estriss in with a fence of steel. There was no way the illithid could kill or incapacitate them all before one managed to end the creature's life with a sword thrust. One pulled the mind flayer's dagger from his belt sheath and stashed it in his own boot.

Rianna had stepped away from the others, closer to Teldin. She held her sword casually, but her other hand held an item too small for Teldin to make out—material components for a spell, he guessed. She was grinning broadly, wolfishly, at him.

Understanding came like a physical impact. For a moment, the world seemed to dim around him. His throat tightened, almost enough to cut off his breathing, and it felt like there was ice in the pit of his stomach. His gaze was locked on Rianna's face.

"Don't look so tragic," she told him. That familiar, subtle

throb of amusement was in her voice, and it was enough to make him ache. "It could have worked out a lot worse. The neogi could have caught you themselves."

One too many shocks. Teldin felt numb. When he spoke, it was with a voice devoid of emotion. "You're working for the neogi," he said. She just grinned. "Tell me why, Rianna. I think you owe me that."

She shrugged. "There's no reason not to tell you. Most of what I told you about myself was true," she began. Her voice was as unemotional as his, as if they were discussing nothing more significant than the weather. "I'm a message-runner. That's all I've ever wanted to be—alone in a ship, alone with the stars. You remember the talk we had about the stars?" Teldin's only answer was a curt nod. He didn't want to think about their talks. "I left home young," she continued, "and from then on I was always in business of one kind or another. It took me years, but I saved enough money to buy my ship, the *Ghost*. And that's when I finally got the life I wanted. Since then, I've done whatever it's taken to guarantee that I'll always have that."

"The neogi," he prompted.

"It happened much the way I told you. I was inward bound from Garden, and I met a neogi deathspider. I turned back to Garden and tried to lose them among the rocks, but they hit the *Ghost* a couple of times, and my helm went down. When they boarded me, I expected to be killed. I was ready to fight, ready to sell my life as dearly as I could. . . ."

"But you didn't have to," he finished for her.

"I didn't have to. They offered me a deal. They'd set me adrift in space right across the course your ship would be following." She smiled. "They understand humans very well. They knew you'd rescue me. They offered me enough to buy myself a much bigger ship."

"And you trusted them?" he asked with scorn. "*Neogi?*"

She shrugged. "Business is business. I've dealt with humans who are worse than neogi. At least they kept it on a very professional level, just the way I like it. Plus—" there was real satisfaction behind her smile "—they may understand humans in the abstract, but they don't understand *me*. I don't want a bigger ship. I want something I can crew myself. The advance payment was more than enough for the ship I'd buy. So if they didn't come through with the rest of the money, I'd still be ahead."

"They have no hold over you, then," Teldin pointed out.

"When I cut a deal, I stick to it," she said sharply.

They'd drifted off the important topic. "So we rescued you," he said. "Then what?"

"Then I was to stay with you and relay information back to them through some other spies they've got on Toril."

Teldin was shocked. "How did they know I was coming to Toril at all?"

"They didn't say and I didn't ask," she answered simply. "They knew you'd be coming to Rauthaven and guessed you'd try to contact the arcane. Barrab was one of their people. So was the bartender in the Pig and Whistle. I got further instructions through those two: to lead you somewhere where we could get the cloak with the least amount of fuss."

"But Barrab betrayed you, didn't he?"

"That *pig*!" Rianna spat. "He turned. He cut a deal with the mind flayers. I hope it gets him killed."

Teldin stared at Rianna as though seeing her for the first time. In a way, he was. The woman before him wasn't the same person he'd fallen for. "What about us, Rianna?" he asked quietly. "That was a setup, too, wasn't it?"

She laughed. "Of course it was. Didn't you ever think our romance was happening too fast? Are you usually that quick to give your heart and your trust to a stranger? I *charmed* you, Teldin, that night in the tavern. Such a simple little bit of magic, but, oh, so effective."

New emotions twisted within Teldin's breast. Anger was there, anger over being used, but overpowering the anger was a deep sense of humiliation. His cheeks burned with it. He'd been used—used in a way he hadn't imagined possible. His will had not been his own; he'd been nothing more than a puppet, and Rianna had pulled the strings.

With a vast effort, he forced the emotion into the background. "Why are we here?" he asked.

"Why not?" Rianna replied simply. "Why not arrange things so you go—of your own free will—where my employers wanted you?"

Teldin remained silent. After all, what more was there to say?

Rianna studied him, and her smile faded a little. Teldin could read her doubts in her expression: Why is he taking this so calmly? she must be wondering. What does he know that I don't know? Then her face cleared and she laughed. "You're expecting good old Aelfred to help you, aren't you?" she asked in feigned wonder. Her face and tone hardened. "Forget it," she told him. "He's dead. As soon as we left the ship, my men were to kill him, stab him in the back. The *Probe*'s secure, and there's nobody left to make that daring last-moment rescue. How sad." She raised her blade to point at his chest. "Now, your sword, if you don't mind."

Teldin didn't respond. Another friend dead, he thought: Aelfred, of the lopsided grin and hearty laugh, soon to be followed by Julia, of the copper hair, then by himself. Such a long road he'd followed, to end up here. The effort, the pain, the loss—all had been for nothing. All had led—simply and inevitably—to this, the final loss. He looked into Rianna's cold eyes. Why? Was he looking for mercy, for compassion? There was none of that to be found. Her sword glittered in the starlight. The blade was steady. There was no way she'd hesitate to kill him.

"Drop it," she snapped.

He felt dull surprise as he realized he still held his sword—the sword she'd given him. He looked down at the weapon in his hand, then up at Rianna's face. Why not? The thought came unbidden. Why not attack her now? He'd lose, he knew that, but he was going to die anyway. Why not try to inflict at least some faint echo of his pain on her? If I'm to die, why not with the song of steel in my ears? He remembered Gomja, the giff, and the gnome, Dana. They'd both died the way they'd wanted. How did Teldin want to die? Trying to kill the woman who'd betrayed him? *Why not?*

Rianna had been watching his eyes. Now hers widened and she took a step back from what she'd seen in his gaze. He felt his lips draw back from his teeth in a feral grin.

Do not do this. The words formed, cool and precise, in his mind. It took all of his effort to keep himself from looking over at Estriss. Rianna hadn't reacted: the words hadn't been directed at her.

His mind raced. Perhaps Rianna didn't know that the illithid could communicate privately. Was there some way he could turn that to his advantage? No, there was nothing he could think of, not unless he could talk to Estriss without the others knowing. He gripped his sword tighter.

Do not do this, the mind flayer repeated. *A life thrown away is opportunity lost.*

Teldin hesitated. The illithid's words sounded somehow like a proverb of some kind, then the meaning hit home. When he'd been growing up, one of his grandfather's favorite aphorisms had been "While there's life, there's hope." To tell the truth, he'd always thought it one of the only really fatuous things his grandfather had ever said. But now, for the first time, he saw the truth in it. No matter how dearly he sold his life, his only payment would be death and the knowledge that the cloak would fall to the neogi. If he waited, there was always the chance—no matter how small—that he could do *something* to better the odds, even to overcome them. After all, he could make that final, all-out attack at virtually any time. He twisted his body slightly and felt Aelfred's dagger against the skin of his stomach, held in place by his belt. However the big man had guessed, he'd guessed right. Teldin let his feral smile fade and loosened his grip. The short sword's blade rang as it fell to the ivory deck. Showing empty hands, he stepped back from the weapon.

Cautiously, never taking her eyes from his, Rianna pocketed her spell components—if that's what they were—and bent to pick up the dropped sword. She straightened and slipped the sword into her own scabbard. Her smile was broad, much more confident now. "Good choice," she cooed, then her voice hardened again. "Now," she said, reaching out toward him, "the cloak, please. . . ."

She didn't realize he couldn't remove the cloak! Teldin realized with a shock. Of course not: he'd never mentioned it. Was there any way he could turn that to his advantage?

"No," a harsh voice spat from behind Teldin. "Own prize I will take."

Teldin knew that voice. He'd heard it, or one very much like it, on Krynn once before, and he knew the creature that produced it. He turned slowly.

The neogi had emerged from the door nearest the left end of the room. It advanced slowly toward him, the claws tipping its eight insectlike limbs clicking on the bonelike deck. Its bare, fleshy neck moved restlessly, like a snake's. Its mouth was open in a grin that showed needle-sharp teeth. The creature's pelt virtually blazed with a profusion of colors—the colors of a chaotic rainbow, or of the flow.

"Prissith Nerro Master," Rianna said, with a bow.

"Yes," the neogi hissed. Its small red eyes flicked back and forth between Rianna and Teldin. "Yes," it repeated, "*master*. You, woman: my prize you brought, but touch it you will not. Too great the temptation to betray."

"Betray." Rianna picked up on the word. "Master, the one known as Barrab has betrayed you. He's sold his services to the illithids. He . . ."

Prissith Nerro cut her off with a gale of harsh neogi laughter. "Master not learn this, you think? Lesser races meat are, only, no more." The creature fixed her with an evil smile. "Ambition of Barrab greater than wisdom, always. To me meat returned, for higher price meat asked." The neogi laughed again. "Higher price meat *paid*." The eellike head turned, and the creature barked a short phrase in an ugly tongue.

Another creature appeared in the doorway from which the neogi had emerged. Again, Teldin had seen its kind before, during the battles at Mount Nevermind and aboard the *Probe*. Eight feet tall it stood, bulging with great muscles beneath its black, armored hide. The umber hulk bore a bundle in its great, taloned arms, a bundle the color of burgundy. It threw its burden down to land with a soggy thump at its small lord's feet.

Teldin had expected to see Barrab again, one way or another—but not like this. The man lay crumpled, blood already pooling beneath him. His whole body seemed to be raw flesh, with hardly a scrap of skin remaining intact. Only his face was untouched. Another death, Teldin thought, another death over this cloak.

Barrab's eyes opened, rolling wildly. The eyes were glazed with agony beyond description, but still, deep within them was a spark of awareness—and of horror greater than any living creature should have to face. The neogi's head flashed down, and the spark was extinguished forever. Prissith Nerro smiled at Rianna. Its thin black tongue licked red gobbets from its teeth. "Thus to all traitors," it hissed. It took another clicking step toward Teldin. "Now, *prey*," the creature spat. "The cloak."

Teldin backed away—one step, two. He bumped into something. Rianna. She was shaken—he could see that in her face—almost as shaken as he was, but he saw, too, that she was in control of herself. She forced a shaky smile onto her face. The point of her sword pricked into his back. She stepped back from him—farther from the neogi and Barrab's remains—until her sword was at arm's length, its point still against Teldin's flesh. "Sorry, lover," she said quietly. "I told you: a deal's a deal." He saw that her left hand again held spell components: a scrap of fur and something that looked like a tiny rod of amber.

Prissith Nerro clicked forward. Teldin felt as though a scream were bubbling in his throat, fighting for release. He looked around wildly—for escape, for help . . . for *anything* that could deliver him from this ultimate horror. The bravos still encircled Estriss. They'd stepped back, instinctively, away from the neogi, away from the monstrous slave and its burden. Their eyes certainly weren't on the illithid, but their swords were steady, ready to end his life if he so much as moved.

Julia? No, the sellsword still held her tightly, his blade poised to slice her throat open. There was no help anywhere.

"The cloak," Prissith Nerro repeated.

The cloak. The words echoed in Teldin's brain. *The cloak.* Memories clashed in his brain, so powerful, so intense that the remembering was a physical pain. He closed his eyes in an uncontrollable flinch. The *Probe*'s foredeck—he could *see* it around him: The swordsman stepping forward, blade swinging to take his life; the flare of power—behind him, around him, *within* him; skin tingled, bones burned, the feeling of sunlight, of blue-white radiance.

The overwhelming force of the memories diminished, but the thrilling within his bones remained. He opened his eyes.

The lighting was different—brighter, harsher—and every eye in the room was fixed on him. The pricking of Rianna's sword was gone from his back.

It took him a moment to realize that the cloak around his shoulders was glowing with a hard, brittle light.

The neogi reared back, hissing in horror, its tiny eyes half-lidded against the glare. "Control it, meat does," it spat. "*Wield* it, meat does." Then Teldin saw realization dawn on its face. "No," the creature murmured. "Control it meat does *not*. Reflex it is. Nothing more." The neogi smiled thinly and moved forward again. "For giving me fear meat will pay."

As the light bloomed around him, Teldin had expected the same crystal clarity and focus of thought he'd experienced before, but there was no trace of calm within him. Fear still possessed him. He looked around wildly, instinctively. The sellswords had backed away farther; in the knot of figures, only Estriss had held his ground. The bravo holding Julia had lowered his blade a fraction.

Claws clicked. The neogi was so close that Teldin could feel its warm breath on his face, could smell the reek of corruption it exuded. "*Prey*," it spat once more. Its sinuous neck reached forward and its jaws opened to tear the cloak from around Teldin's shoulders.

No! The mental voice blasted into Teldin's brain with such power that he screamed with the pain of it and clutched his skull with both hands, as if to stop it from exploding. He spun.

Estriss lunged forward. One bravo was reeling backward, mouth open in a silent scream, clawing at his head in unendurable agony. The bizarre, Juna-made knife was in the illithid's red-tinged hand. The curved blade lashed out, and another bravo collapsed, his head almost cleaved from his body. One of the sellswords was quicker to react than his fellows. He lunged, opening a gash in the mind flayer's side, but Estriss was free of the circle. The illithid flung himself forward, at the neogi, at Teldin. His empty hand reached out, an attempt to grab the neogi's throat . . . or to snatch the cloak for himself. Teldin couldn't be sure which. Prissith Nerro responded instantly. Its head lashed out and its teeth sank into the illithid's neck beneath the writhing tentacles. The two creatures, locked together, staggered toward Teldin. He stepped back, raising his hands to protect himself. . . .

And the power blossomed within him. Fire coursed through his veins, flashed along every nerve. He felt that his skull would rupture, that his eyes would burst from his head. Agony mixed with ecstacy. He *howled*.

Light burst from his extended hands, a blinding curtain of energy. The air in front of him sizzled.

Illithid and neogi reeled away from the coruscating wall of light. Together they slammed into one of the huge windows. The crystal cracked, then shattered, and glittering fragments were blown outward into the void. Still the creatures were locked together; the neogi's teeth were still sunk into Estriss's flesh, while the mind flayer's facial tentacles were wrapped around Prissith Nerro's skull. The illithid dropped his blade, dug his fingers into the neogi's fleshy throat—more for support, Teldin thought, than from any attempt to further harm the creature. They teetered for a moment on the lip of the shattered window, silhouetted against star-speckled blackness. Then, silently, they plunged from sight.

As suddenly as it had arisen, the power that had flooded through Teldin's body vanished. In its wake was weakness and biting cold. His legs buckled, and he collapsed to his hands and knees on the hard deck. Gray fog clouded his vision. It was all he could do to cling to consciousness. Sounds of chaos surrounded him: the skirl of steel on steel, a man's shout of agony, the umber hulk's frenzied barking and roaring. He simply couldn't bring himself to care. There seemed to be no energy left in his body or mind.

Rianna's voice cut through his exhaustion. "Get back," she shouted. "*Back!*"

His head might have weighed half a ton for the effort it took to raise it. He moaned with the pain, but at least the exertion seemed to clear the mist from before his eyes.

The umber hulk was waving its arms and clashing its mandibles in obvious rage as it advanced on Rianna . . . and on Teldin. "Get back," the woman yelled to him. "It'll kill us all."

It was the hardest thing he'd ever done in his life, but he managed to force himself to his feet. He shambled back, away from the advancing creature.

Rianna stood her ground. She'd dropped her sword, keeping only the spell components. She held the scrap of fur in one hand, the amber rod in the other. Quickly she rubbed them together, muttering phrases of power under her breath, then she thrust a finger out toward the approaching hulk.

Blue-white lightning leaped from her fingertip, smashed into the creature's bulging chest, and burst out through its back, leaving a blackened, smoking hole. The creature screeched, flailing its arms in paroxysms of agony. It stumbled back, but it didn't fall. The gaze from its four eyes, blood red with hatred, was fixed on Rianna.

Teldin backed farther away. His foot caught on something, almost sending him sprawling. He looked down. It was Estriss's Juna knife. Quickly he scooped it up. Even that little exertion dimmed his vision again, but through pure willpower he fought back the darkness.

The umber hulk was advancing again—slower now, but still advancing. Rianna took a measured step back, her hands weaving another spell. Another lightning bolt tore into the creature, this time striking it in the center of its misshapen head. The skull burst asunder. The headless body remained standing for an endless moment, then crashed to the deck.

Behind Teldin, a man screamed in terminal agony. Teldin spun around.

Julia had broken free of the bravo who'd held her. He lay on his back behind her, the hilt of a dagger protruding from his throat. Another sellsword writhed on the deck, bright blood seeping from a horrible wound in his stomach, while a third lay motionless beside him. The final bravo—the one who'd screamed—was slowly crumpling to the deck. Julia's sword was buried to the quillions in his chest. As Teldin watched, Julia pulled the blade free and stepped back. The small woman's face was grim, and her eyes were hard. Her jerkin was soaked with blood—hers and others'. Her left arm was gashed across the biceps and hung uselessly at her side, and there was another deep wound in her right shoulder. *She must be in agony,* Teldin realized, *but her control is colossal.* Her bloody blade was steady in her hand as she stepped over her last victim's body and advanced toward Rianna. She shot Teldin a quick, tight-lipped smile, then turned her flint-cold eyes on Rianna. "Get away from him, you whore from hell," she grated.

Rianna stepped back from the murder in Julia's eyes, then she smiled—a feral, killing smile. She hissed a phrase through clenched teeth. Three tiny projectiles, like burning embers, burst from the fingertips of her left hand.

"*No!*" Teldin cried, but it was much too late. The missiles screamed through the air, striking Julia full in the chest. The impact flung the small woman backward, to land crumpled and boneless like a rag doll.

"Why?" Teldin wheeled on Rianna. "*Why*, damn you?" he demanded again. "You've discharged your *duty*—" he spat the word "—and you're free of your bargain. *Why?*"

Rianna turned her fierce smile on him. "The cloak," she told him, "why else? You're right, I'm free of my bargain. That means I can take the prize for myself."

"Why do you want it?" he asked, really wanting to know her answer. "They'll all be after *you*."

She laughed, a harsh sound. "You handled it wrong," she told him flatly. "I don't intend to make the same mistakes. No quest to find your mythical 'creators.' Just auction it off to the highest bidder. I'm sure the bids will be very high." Her smile faded. "Now hand it over."

Teldin looked into her sea-green eyes. There was no trace in them of the person that he thought he'd loved. There would be no mercy from Rianna Wyvernsbane.

He looked deeper. There was no mercy, but there *was* a trace of fear. Maybe he could play on that. "Take it," he told her softly, "if you think you can."

That made her pause, then her smile returned. "I think the neogi was right," she said slowly. "I don't believe you can control the cloak at all. It's just reflex, random reflex."

She's trying to convince herself, he realized. The bluff might just work. "If you really believe that," he said evenly, "then take it."

Rianna was silent for a moment, indecision mirrored in her eyes, then her expression hardened. The bluff had failed. "I will," she said. Smoothly, she drew her second sword—Teldin's sword—from her scabbard. The polished blade was steady, its point on a level with his throat, as she stepped forward.

The Juna knife, the weapon that Estriss had dropped, was still in Teldin's hand. He snapped it up into an *en garde* position. The grip, with its alien network of ridges and furrows, felt strange in his hand, but it felt somehow comforting, too. My fate's in my own hands, he told himself, just the way I've always wanted. "I'd like to see you try," he said.

Rianna backed off a half-step, her eyes on the wickedly curved blade, then she chuckled. Her eyes half closed, and she started to mutter under her breath. She raised her left hand, and the fingers began to weave a complex pattern.

Another spell! If he let her complete it, he'd be dead—like Julia, like Estriss, like Dana. . . . With a scream of rage, he flung himself forward. In that instant, he remembered Aelfred's training, the big man's voice: "Get that left hand back. You're just asking to have it cut off." He flicked the blade out toward Rianna's empty left hand.

The long, curved knife bit home, cleaving flesh and bone. Rianna shrieked, her spellcasting forgotten in the sudden pain.

Teldin recovered from the cut, poised himself on the balls of his feet for an instant, and aimed a vicious thrust at the woman's chest. With a normal short sword, it might well have connected, but the curved blade's balance was different, and the hilt simply wasn't designed for human hands. The thrust was fractionally too slow, giving Rianna just enough time to parry. The tip of the blade tore the cloth of her jerkin, ripped the soft skin of her side, instead of piercing her spine. She riposted, the point of her blade flashing toward Teldin's throat, and he barely managed to position the unfamiliar weapon in time to deflect the lightning-fast thrust.

Rianna backed away, obviously trying to give herself time to prepare another spell. Teldin moved forward, pressing her. Steel rang against something that wasn't steel as she parried another thrust.

"*Forget* it," she spat, punctuating the phrase with another snake-quick thrust that Teldin barely managed to counter. "You'll never best me. Drop your sword, and I'll let you live."

"You're a liar," he hissed. Another thrust, another parry.

"You're right," she chuckled. Thrust, parry, riposte. She danced back out of range of his counter. "Drop your sword, and I'll kill you painlessly. Otherwise, I'll make it last."

Teldin followed her retreat. Keep pressing her, he told himself, keep pressing or you're dead. He took another step forward, and his foot slipped in Barrab's blood, not much, but enough to slow him for an instant.

Rianna reacted with the speed of thought. She lunged low, under his guard. He snapped his right arm down, the pommel of his strange weapon slamming into her blade, deflecting it a little but not enough.

The woman's blade ripped through his flesh and along his ribs on the right side. Instantly his entire body was aflame with pain. He gritted his teeth against it, fought to smother the cry that erupted from his throat. Rianna stepped back again, in plenty of time to avoid his slow riposte.

"I'll make it last," she said again.

He cursed one of the blistering mercenary oaths he'd heard Aelfred use. With his left hand, he clutched at the ragged tear in his right side, feeling hot blood on his fingers. He gripped tight, trying to staunch the bleeding, almost making himself faint with the agony. His left forearm was pressed against something hard on his stomach. For the moment, he couldn't remember what it was. *"Damn you!"* he screamed. "You killed them *all!*" In the churning delirium of his suffering, he wasn't talking to Rianna. He didn't really know *whom* he was referring to. The cloak, perhaps . . . or maybe himself. *"Damn you to the Abyss!"* He lurched forward.

Aelfred's lessons, the words of the soldiers he'd talked to, everything he'd ever learned about swordwork—all were gone from his mind. All that was left was rage and pain and the desire to kill. He swung the Juna knife in a hissing arc, directly at Rianna's head.

She hardly managed to raise her own weapon in time. The nonmetal weapon bit into her blade, notching the tempered steel. For several heartbeats, they were frozen in that position: her blade parallel with the floor, holding up his weapon, preventing it from cleaving down into her skull. Their bodies were close together. He could hear her labored breathing.

Rianna grunted with the effort of it, then her mangled left hand lashed out toward Teldin's face, her remaining fingers like claws reaching for his eyes. He ducked beneath the grasp ing hand and lurched backward. The movement sent bolts of agony radiating outward from his ripped side. Something sharp pricked the skin of his abdomen.

It was Aelfred's dagger. With his left hand he pulled the weapon from beneath his belt, slashed it upward at Rianna's sword arm. The razor-sharp blade sliced into the soft flesh of her forearm, grating sickeningly against bone.

For an instant, Rianna stood there howling, staring uncomprehendingly at the gouty gash that had laid bare tendon and bone. Then Teldin's Juna knife shot out, the full weight of his body behind the thrust as Aelfred had taught him. The curved blade bit into the flesh of her chest, sank quillion-deep.

Rianna gasped. Her eyes found Teldin's. The sea-green orbs were wide with pain and pleading, then they closed, and she sank to the deck, unmoving.

For an immeasurable time, the two of them remained thus, Teldin still grasping the hilt of the Juna knife. Then he released it, and stepped back. Seemingly of its own volition, his right hand wiped itself—again and again—on the blood-soaked cloth of his jerkin, as if trying to remove some stain or taint.

He gazed down at the body of the woman he'd loved. Her face, now in final repose, was untroubled and heartachingly lovely. He felt appreciation for her beauty, but there was no love anymore. The charm was broken. He turned away.

His stomach was suddenly wrenched by convulsions. He sank to his knees and was wretchedly, rackingly sick, each muscle spasm sending jolts of almost unendurable pain through his wounded side.

Finally the spasms ended, leaving him weak and drained. He wiped his mouth with his sleeve. Why don't I just stay here, he asked himself, with the other dead? It would be so much easier that way, simply to fade away into oblivion. All in all, he reasoned, oblivion would be the easiest, the most comfortable choice.

"Teldin." The voice was weak, barely more than a whisper. At first, Teldin wasn't sure that he'd heard it at all, wasn't sure that it wasn't some result of the pain-induced delirium that clouded his mind. "Teldin."

This time he looked up.

It was Julia. Somehow she'd forced herself to a sitting position. Her face gave him some indication of the effort—the overwhelming agony—the movement had cost her. "Teldin," she whispered again.

He sighed. No, he couldn't let himself drift into the silent darkness, not now. He had one final duty to perform. If he could save one life—Julia's—he'd at least have made one small effort at redemption, at making up for the many lives he'd already cost. He closed his eyes against the red flashes of pain and forced himself to his feet. He swayed there a moment and slipped Aelfred's dagger into his belt, then he trudged slowly and painfully to where Julia lay.

Calling to him had taken much of what little remained of her energy. She'd slumped back to the deck, but her eyes were still open. They looked up at him out of the young woman's chalk-white face. She smiled. "I'm glad you're still alive," she whispered.

He gazed down at her. Her petite body was twisted with pain, marred by multiple wounds. Her red hair was matted, redder here and there with spilled blood. She's lovely, he suddenly realized. Even like this, she's lovely. He felt a warmth in his chest, a warmth that expanded until he thought his heart would burst. He smiled. "I'm glad you're still alive," he echoed.

* * * * *

Teldin would never understand where he'd found the strength. Maybe it had come from the cloak, or maybe it had come from somewhere within him, some wellspring of his being that he'd never before been able to tap. Somehow he'd managed to lift Julia from the deck and sling her over his left shoulder. The effort had almost killed him, he knew. Darkness had filled his vision, narrowing his field of view down to a tunnel that looked as narrow as a gold coin held at arm's length, but somehow he'd managed it.

Every step had been torture; each shift of weight had sent lightning bolts of pain through his rent side. The white corridor, the one leading to the gallery—to the killing field—was only a hundred feet or so long, but on the return journey had seemed like ten times that distance. Several times he'd been sure that he couldn't continue, that he'd collapse and never be able to move again, but each time he'd found himself able to draw on some mysterious reserve of strength. He'd carried his burden up the spiral staircase that seemed as tall as a mountain peak. Now he finally emerged onto the huge circular deck. The great hammership loomed overhead, still secured by its docking tethers. The rope ladders still hung in place.

Teldin stopped. He set Julia down, as gently as he could, on the ivory deck. Her eyes were closed, but he could still see her breathing—shallow, but steady. Tenderly he brushed the blood-matted hair back from her face.

He'd come as far as he could. Now he had to depend on others. Aelfred was dead—Rianna had said as much, and on this he had no reason to doubt her. The bravos she'd hired were in command of the *Probe*. Their mistress was dead, though. Would they still have any reason to kill Teldin Moore? He wondered how much they knew of Rianna's real motivation. Had she told them about the cloak, so they might want it for themselves? He doubted it, but he might be wrong. He'd been wrong before, more times than he cared to count. If he *was* wrong now, what was left? Nothing but the final option he'd turned away from on the arcane's great gallery: to sell his life as dearly as he could. He took a deep breath, readying to call out to the ship above. . . .

"Teldin."

It was a voice from a nightmare—harsh, at once familiar and alien, with a horrible undertone of bubbling agony. He turned.

It was Rianna. Slowly, agonizingly, she dragged herself out of the *Nebulon*'s circular hatch. As she moved, she left a trail of red on the white deck. Her eyes spoke of overwhelming, crushing pain—but also of hatred. In her right hand she held a small amber rod; in her mangled left, a scrap of fur. Teldin knew those items for what they were: components of the lightning spell that had felled the umber hulk.

"Teldin," she hissed again. She took a deep breath—her eyes told him the pain it cost her—then she started to mutter an incantation.

Without thinking, he pulled Aelfred's dagger from his belt, drew his hand back, and *threw*. The motion sent agony shooting through his side. He watched the blade flash in the starlight as it turned end over end, once, twice—as it missed its target and skittered across the deck.

Rianna drew back bloody lips from red teeth in a feral smile. Her incantation neared its conclusion.

Something hissed down from the sky. Magically, a spear sprouted from between Rianna's shoulder blades like some strange, bare tree. Rianna Wyvernsbane convulsed once, then lay still.

Teldin raised his eyes. A figure was looking down at him over the rail of the *Probe*: a familiar figure, its face split in a lopsided grin.

"You're dead," Teldin cried.

"*She's* dead," Aelfred Silverhorn corrected him. The burly warrior touched a blood-soaked bandage that encircled his brow. "I'm just a little the worse for wear. Sylvie will need some time to recover, but she wasn't hurt too badly."

Teldin shook his head. The delirium of pain hummed in his ears. "How?" he managed to ask.

"Only *six* sellswords?" Aelfred laughed. "I should be insulted." He turned away from the rail and shouted, "Bial, Valin, go down and get them."

As the figures appeared, swarming down the rope ladders, Teldin did the only thing he could. He fainted.

Epilogue

• • •

The distended star that was the *Nebulon* was falling away astern when Teldin returned to consciousness. He was still exhausted, drained, but the agony that had racked his body had been replaced by blissful numbness. He felt something tight around his ribs, a dressing over his torn side, it had to be. For a moment he luxuriated in the simple pleasure of being alive, of feeling his breathing, of being whole—well, almost. Then memory flooded back. He looked around him.

He was in Aelfred's cabin. The first mate was sitting on a stool watching him. The relief in the big man's eyes was obvious.

"Julia?" Teldin asked. His voice was a croak.

"She'll make it," Aelfred answered. "While they were patching her up, she told me what you did, Teldin. She sends her thanks." He smiled. "While you're at it, accept mine as well. That was one hell of an effort."

Teldin nodded. Yes, he thought, it had been. *I didn't know I had it in me.*

"What happened to Estriss?" Aelfred asked.

"He fell," Teldin replied quietly. Briefly he described the neogi's advance, the illithid's headlong rush, the flare of power from the cloak. "Maybe Estriss was trying to save me," Teldin finished. "Maybe he was after the cloak for himself. I don't know." He was silent for a moment, then a disturbing thought struck him. "The gravity plane," he croaked. "The gravity plane would have caught them."

"For a while," Aelfred amended. "Things caught in a gravity plane drift slowly outward, away from a ship, then they fall free. There's no way we could have gotten to them in time, Teldin. Estriss is gone."

Teldin nodded again. He imagined the long, terrifying plunge to the planet below and shuddered. "Where are we going?" he asked finally. "Back to Toril?"

The big man grinned broadly. "Not a chance." He paused, then continued, "When I signed on with Estriss as first mate, he gave me a sealed document to be opened only when I was convinced he was dead or not coming back. I opened it a while ago."

"What did it say?"

"The *Probe*'s mine," Aelfred stated. "I have title to the ship, and I'm her captain."

Teldin smiled at his friend's obvious satisfaction. "I thought you said you were getting tired of shipboard life," he pointed out.

"That was as first mate. As captain?" He shook his head.

"So," Teldin asked again, "where are you going?"

"I don't know yet," Aelfred said. "Out there somewhere. I haven't decided." The big man's expression sobered. "What about you?"

Teldin paused. What *about* me? he wondered. Where should I go now? He still had the cloak, but where should he take it? *Who* were "the creators?" Estriss had given him one answer; T'k'Pek, the arcane, had given him another. Both were dead now, and Teldin couldn't honestly say which one he believed, or whether he believed either one. The one thing he knew was that everybody—with the possible exception of the gnomes—was after the cloak.

He sighed. He was virtually back at the beginning. Everything he knew about the cloak—everything he *thought* he knew about it—had come from Estriss. And how far did he trust Estriss's words now?

He remembered the words of Vallus Leafbower, when they'd met for the last time in the alleyways of Rauthaven. "The cloak is of elven creation," Vallus had said. "Take it to the elves of Evermeet. The imperial fleet can be your only safety." Mere weeks ago, Teldin probably would have believed those words. Trust had always been his nature. But now? No, blind trust was just a way toward death.

Teldin wasn't sure he trusted Vallus Leafbower any more than the others, but maybe he could learn more of the elves' imperial fleet. If he eventually did go to Evermeet, perhaps he'd see the aloof Vallus again and be able to ask him his part in the whole affair. Maybe he'd meet up with Horvath, Miggins, and Saliman again, he added. That would be pleasant.

Aelfred was still waiting for an answer to his question. "I'm coming with you," Teldin said quietly. "Away from here."

The first mate—No, Teldin corrected himself, the captain— smiled. "In that case, I have a proposition for you," he said. "I need a first mate, someone I can have confidence in during a scrap. That describes you, old son. Are you interested?"

Teldin sighed. "Why is it that everyone wants to put responsibilities on my shoulders?" he asked.

"Because they know you're capable of handling them," his friend said simply. Aelfred rose. "No need for you to decide now. I should see to my ship. I'll be back to check on you later." He left the cabin, shutting the door quietly behind him.

Teldin closed his eyes. There were too many questions, he told himself, too many unknowns. He'd have to deal with them eventually, but not now. For the moment, all he wanted to do was rest.

As he settled back onto the cot, the hammership cruised silently away from Toril, into the darkness of space.

Into the void.

SPELLJAMMER™ BOOKS

● The Cloakmaster Cycle ●

Follow one unlucky farmer as he enters fantasy space and gets caught up in a race for his life, from the DRAGONLANCE® setting to the FORGOTTEN REALMS® world . . . and beyond.

Book One
Beyond the Moons
David Cook

Little did Teldin Moore know there was life beyond Krynn's moons until a spelljamming ship crashed into his home and changed his life. Teldin suddenly discovers himself the target of killers and cutthroats. Armed with a dying alien's magical cloak and cryptic words, he races off to Astinus of Palanthas and the gnomes of Mt. Nevermind to try to discover why . . . before the monstrous neogi can find him. On sale no

DRAGONLANCE and FORGOTTEN REALMS are registered trademarks owned by TSR, In SPELLJAMMER is a trademark owned by TSR, Inc. ©1991 TSR, Inc. All Rights Reserved

Prism Pentad
BOOK ONE
The Verdant Passage
Troy Denning

KALAK: AN IMMORTAL SORCERER-KING WHOSE EVIL MAGIC HAS REDUCED THE MAJESTIC CITY OF TYR TO A DESOLATE PLACE OF BLOOD AND FEAR. HIS THOUSAND-YEAR REIGN OF DEATH IS ABOUT TO END.

BANDING TOGETHER TO SPARK A REVOLUTION ARE A MAVERICK STATESMAN, A WINSOME HALF-ELF SLAVE GIRL, AND A MAN-DWARF GLADIATOR BRED FOR THE ARENAS. BUT IF THE PEOPLE ARE TO BE FREE, THE MISMATCHED TRIO OF STEADFAST REBELS MUST LOOK INTO THE FACE OF TERROR, AND CHOOSE BETWEEN LOVE AND LIFE.

DARK SUN is a trademark owned by TSR, Inc. ©1991 TSR, Inc. All Rights Reserved.

FORGOTTEN REALMS
FANTASY ADVENTURE

▪ THE HARPERS ▪

A Force for Good in the Realms!

This open-ended series of stand-alone novels chronicles the Harpers' heroic battles against forces of evil, all for the peace of the Realms.

The Parched Sea
Troy Denning

The Zhentarim have sent an army to enslave the fierce nomads of the Great Desert. Only one woman, the outcast witch Ruha, sees the true danger—and only the Harpers can counter the evil plot.

Elfshadow
Elaine Cunningham

Harpers are being murdered, and the trail leads to Arilyn Moonblade. Is she guilty or is she the next target? Arilyn must uncover the ancient secret of her sword's power in order to find and face the assassin.
Available October 1991.

Red Magic
Jean Rabe

One of the powerful and evil Red Wizards wants to control more than his share of Thay. While the mage builds a net of treachery, the Harpers put their own agents into action to foil his plans for conquest.
Available November 1991.

FORGOTTEN REALMS is a registered trademark owned by TSR, Inc.
©1991 TSR, Inc. All Rights Reserved.